TOM
CLANCY

SSN

Tom Clancy SSN

Since the phenomenal worldwide success of his first novel, *The Hunt for Red October*, Tom Clancy has become the world's fastest-selling author. Three of his novels have now been made into highly successful films: *The Hunt for Red October*, *Patriot Games* and *Clear and Present Danger*. He is also the author of the non-fiction books *Submarine*, *Armoured Warfare*, *Fighter Wing* and *Marine*, and the co-creator of the bestselling *Op-Centre* series. He lives in Maryland, USA.

Tom Clancy's recent novels include *Debt of Honour* and its acclaimed sequel, *Executive Orders*, which have both been record-breaking *Sunday Times* and *New York Times* #1 bestsellers.

Praise for Tom Clancy:

'Clancy is the supreme exponent of the technothriller.'
Sunday Times

'With the grip of a born storyteller, Clancy casts a potent spell.'
Guardian

'The best in the business . . . he remains #1.'
Los Angeles Times

'He constantly taps the current world situation for its imminent dangers and spins them into an engrossing tale.'
New York Times

TOM CLANCY

SSN

Strategies of Submarine Warfare

HarperCollins*Publishers*

Tom Clancy SSN is based upon Tom Clancy *SSN*,
an interactive submarine combat thriller
available on CD-Rom

HarperCollins*Publishers*
77–85 Fulham Palace Road,
Hammersmith, London W6 8JB

www.**fire**and**water**.com

This paperback edition 1997

First published in Great Britain by
HarperCollins*Publishers* 1997

First published in the USA by
Berkley Books 1996

Cover illustration by James Wang

The Author has asserted the moral right to
be identified as the Author of this Work

ISBN 978-0-00-779638-0

Set in Meridien by
Rowland Phototypesetting Ltd, Bury St Edmonds, Suffolk

Printed and bound in Great Britain by
Clays Ltd, St Ives plc

CONTENTS

ACKNOWLEDGMENTS

I'd like to thank my friend and colleague Captain Doug Littlejohns, Royal Navy (Ret.), for his invaluable contributions to the interactive game upon which this book is based. I would also like to thank Commander Craig Etka, US Navy (Ret.), Eric Wertheim, and Mike Harris for their contributions to the creation of the manuscript and for their relentless fact-checking. I would like to acknowledge the assistance of James Adams, Martin H. Greenberg, Larry Segriff, Robert Youdelman, Esq., Tom Mallon, Esq., and the fine folks at The Putnam Berkley Group, including Phyllis Grann, David Shanks, and David Highfill. In addition, this book would not have been possible without the efforts of Elizabeth Mackey, Ken Gordon, and Keith Halper of Simon & Schuster Interactive, Paul Wirth of the Virtus Corporation, Bill Howe of Photri, Inc., and Steve Fahrbach of Magellan Geographix. And as always I would like to thank Robert Gottlieb of the William Morris Agency, my agent and friend, without whom this book and the interactive game would never have been done.

And thanks to you, my readers, who have come to love submarines and the men who man them as much as I do.

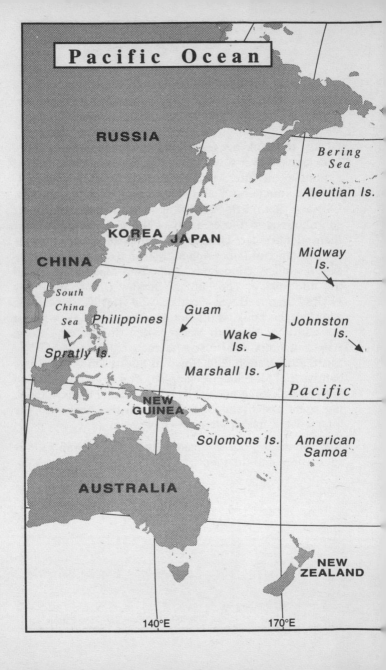

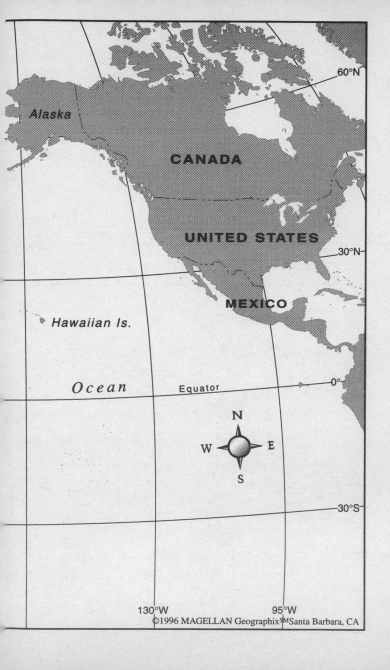

Alaska

CANADA

UNITED STATES

MEXICO

Hawaiian Is.

Ocean   Equator   0°

60°N

30°N

30°S

N

W   E

S

130°W   95°W
©1996 MAGELLAN Geographix℠Santa Barbara, CA

Note to the Reader

This book is based upon the CD-ROM game Tom Clancy *SSN*, co-published by Simon & Schuster Interactive, a division of Simon & Schuster, C.I. Entertainment, Inc., and Virtus Corporation. Developed by Tom Clancy with Captain Doug Littlejohns, CBE, British Royal Navy (Ret.), *SSN* is a groundbreaking, action-packed submarine combat game and a full-screen, live-action cinematic thriller.

This book, however, is intended to serve as more than a faithful adaptation. While based on the game, this book is intended to serve as a strategy guide to submarine warfare, and as such it contains some minor variations from the CD-ROM game: an additional class of enemy submarines, a wider range of weaponry, and a broader spectrum of available tactics and strategies.

Both the game and this book share a common goal: to put you, the reader, in charge of a United States nuclear attack submarine at war. If you come away with a taste of what life in the silent service is like, with a better understanding and appreciation of the efforts of those brave sailors who serve aboard boomers and attack submarines everywhere, and with an idea of the dangers these sailors face every day, then this book and the game upon which it is based have done their jobs.

Life aboard a submarine is filled with hard work, close quarters, and the constant threat of silent enemies and the deep, dark pressure of the ocean. Slip into your naval uniform – the one with the golden dolphins on the collar – and step aboard one of the finest submarines in the United States Navy – the USS *Cheyenne*. But don't forget your seat belt. There's a war on, and it's going to be a bumpy ride.

Prelude to War

Though the name may sound obscure, the Spratly Islands have been a cause of conflict in East Asia for quite some time. Sovereignty over all or part of this potentially resource-rich archipelago in the South China Sea is presently contested by Vietnam, China, Brunei, Malaysia, the Philippines, and Taiwan. Although the Manila Declaration by the Association of Southeast Asian Nations in 1992 promised to resolve this dispute peacefully, the nations involved have yet to arrive at a consensus about the future of this territory. In the past few months, tensions have mounted between the East Asian nations, and the need to have the United Nations serve as a mediating force has been suggested. At this point in time, many of the countries have stationed troops on the islands and some have begun to build their own infrastructures, causing further disagreements.

'The dispute over the Spratly Islands has served as a further impediment to healing many of the rifts existing within East Asia. This issue needs to be addressed on an international level before it escalates into higher forms of conflict. The Special Political and Decolonization Committee will attempt to consolidate the interests of all parties involved and hopefully diminish a source of growing regional conflict in the world.'—*The New American*

'China's aggressive search for oil near the Spratly Islands off Vietnam's coast has become the most serious threat of war along China's frontier.'—Jim Landers, *The Dallas Morning News*

Chinese leader dies, power struggle anticipated

July 19, 1997
Web posted at: 12:00 P.M. EST (1700 GMT)

From Beijing bureau chief Julie Meyer
BEIJING (TCN) – Chinese leader Deng Xiaoping died today at the age of ninety-two. Having suffered multiple strokes in the previous two years, Deng had reportedly been living in a military hospital for the past eighteen months and was said to have been barely able to speak for much of that time.

Deng's successor, President Jiang Zemin, was chosen by Deng himself over a year ago, yet could not assert full leadership rights until Deng, as 'paramount leader,' had died. Now that Deng is dead, many experts feel that Jiang's position will be challenged by his peers among the Chinese government, and that a power struggle will ensue.

Among the suspected challengers to Jiang is Premier Li Peng, a Marxist conservative who played a major role in the quashing of the 1989 Tiananmen Square demonstrations. Li is said to be intent on scaling back China's economic growth, which he feels to be unstable, should he take control.

Another possible contender is Zhu Rongji, senior vice premier and the liberal economist responsible for much of China's economic growth under Deng. However, Zhu has alienated much of the Chinese bureaucracy with his infamous temper and acidic comments, and experts believe that he does not enjoy the support necessary to win the leadership battle.

When asked for an opinion regarding the power shift in China, prominent Tufts University international relations professor and Asian affairs expert Adrian Mann stated that great 'political instability' lay ahead and that 'there is a very good chance that the power struggle may lead to a Soviet-style breakup of China,' a view shared by many senior White House political advisers.

The President, who is currently vacationing at Camp David, issued a statement earlier today saying that 'the United States offers her sincere condolences to the people of China on the loss of their esteemed leader' and that 'we have every confidence that the new Chinese leadership will assume office with the minimum of disturbance.' When asked the President's position on the possible power struggle within the Chinese government, a White House aide said: 'the President is watching with great interest.'

United Fuels Corp. discovers oil, stock soars

July 21, 1997
Web posted at: 2:00 P.M. EST (1900 GMT)

From New York financial correspondent Bill Mossette
NEW YORK (TCNfn) – A spokesman for United Fuels Corporation stated today that the company had recently located a large and, until now, undiscovered oil deposit six miles from Mischief Reef, one of the Spratly Islands chain located in the South China Sea.

The deposit is thought to be the largest of its type yet discovered, with a conservative estimated yield of close to one trillion barrels. This information caused a massive surge in United Fuels stock, which peaked today at eighty-nine dollars a share, up nearly 200 percent. Experts predict that the stock will continue to skyrocket if the find is fully substantiated.

However, many financial advisers are wary of investing in United on the basis of this new find, due to the political instability surrounding the area in which the oil lies. The Spratly Islands have long been contested, with China, Vietnam, Taiwan and other neighboring countries all claiming sovereignty. Wall Street experts say that the oil find will be contested by the governments of the aforementioned countries, among others, and that it may be years before such disagreements may be resolved. During this time, of course, United Fuels Corporation will be unable to drill in the area.

Nevertheless, United has already started to build a drilling platform at the site, staging construction from the prospecting ship that located the enormous oil deposit, *Benthic Adventure*.

Coup in China, Li takes control

July 23, 1997
Web posted at: 3:00 P.M. EST (2000 GMT)

From Washington chief correspondent Michael Flasetti
WASHINGTON (TCN) – In a stunning development, Premier Li Peng has staged a coup d'état and gained control of the Chinese government in the early hours of this morning. Aided in the coup by General Yu Quili, leader of the so-called Petroleum Faction, Li has apparently ordered the arrest of Jiang Zemin, president and successor to the late Deng Xiaoping, and Zhu Rongji, senior vice premier. Both political rivals in the struggle for political control, Jiang and Zhu, have yet to be located, and are presumed in hiding.

Li, a conservative with broad support from both the Chinese Communist Party and the Chinese military, issued a statement to the effect that Deng's liberal economic policies were causing ruin within China, destroying the socialist ideals that the Communist Party has been striving to maintain. He also stated that rampant capitalism and greater economic ties to the West threaten to undermine the 'national focus of China' and that 'it was time that the people of China stood together in a common cause.' Precisely what that cause is remains to be seen.

However, Taiwan has requested aid from the United Nations, fearing that Li may attempt an invasion of the country, which China has regarded as a renegade province since 1949. If such an invasion was to take place, it would probably be masterminded by General Yu Quili, the one-armed army veteran who led the Petroleum Faction, a group of engineers that developed the rich Daqing oil field in Manchuria with the aid of then Chairman Mao Ze-dong.

The Petroleum Faction wielded enormous power over China's economic policy until Deng consolidated his own power base within the government in the early 1980s. Now, with Li and other allies, including Wang Tao, chairman of the China National Petroleum Corporation, General Yu seems poised to take a place among the executive elite of China.

East Asia political expert Adrian Mann commented today on the current radical shift of government power. 'Energy production seems to have become the engine for a neoconservative upheaval in China. Politically, those who control the means of energy production can control the country. It's a very strong position.' Doubly strong, Dr Mann went on to argue, in a country with a well-documented shortage of raw power.

The White House has so far been unresponsive to the developments in China, as the President wishes to confer with UN chiefs before making any official statement, which is expected later today. Sources report that the President will need full support from the UN before action, if any, is to be taken, in light of America's historically rocky relationship with China.

President reacts to Chinese coup, UN sanctions expected

July 23, 1997
Web posted at: 12:00 P.M. EST (1700 GMT)

From Washington chief correspondent Michael Flasetti
WASHINGTON (TCN) – After conferring with other permanent members of the UN Security Council for most of

the day, the President made a statement condemning the Chinese coup, led by Li Peng. In addition, both the US and UN have officially refused to acknowledge the new Chinese government, demanding instead that Jiang Zemin, chosen by ex-paramount leader Deng to be his successor, be restored as China's new leader. However, many believe Jiang to be dead, killed by troops under Peng during the coup. Senior vice premier Zhu Rongji is also missing.

Li Peng responded to the demands by stating that both Jiang and Zhu were wanted for 'crimes against the state' and that he would not give up his new position, which is supported by the leaders of China's industrial-military complex. He went on to decry the UN mandates as yet more 'interferist Western meddling in China's interior affairs' and said that China would not submit to any of the UN's requests.

Deadlocked, the UN is convening immediately to analyze the situation and discuss the possibility of sanctions against China.

China invades Spratly Islands, oil ship seized

July 26, 1997
Web posted at: 12:00 P.M. EST (1700 GMT)

From Beijing bureau chief Julie Meyer
BEIJING (TCN) – In a show of military might, China has occupied the long-contested Spratly Islands. Both Vietnamese and Philippine forces, which had established a presence on the islands, were quickly overrun by the Chinese navy in the course of the two-day campaign. Leading the ten-ship attack fleet, the Chinese destroyer *Haribing* quickly and utterly eliminated all threats in the area, and the islands now look to be completely under the control of the Chinese.

The rationale for such an overtly aggressive act, at a time when the current Chinese leader, Li Peng, faces opposition to his leadership by the United Nations, is made clearer in light of the discovery of a massive oil field last week by the United Fuels Corporation prospecting ship *Benthic Adventure*. The ship, which has been seized by the Chinese, is moored six miles from Mischief Reef, the island nearest the position where the oil deposit is suspected to be situated. This is seen as a very serious act, say military experts, especially in light of the fact that *Benthic Adventure* is a US-flagged ship, and was seized in international waters. 'The President would be 100 percent justified calling the seizure of *Benthic Adventure* an act of war,' said one top aide today, apparently echoing the thoughts of many chiefs within the Pentagon.

In addition to the massive resource boost the Spratly Islands may provide China, many analysts feel that the invasion has significant tactical motivations, as well as economic. 'Control over the Spratly Islands provides a staging ground for the South China Sea,' a senior Pentagon aide commented today. 'China understands the true value of these islands.'

The Spratly Islands may also be utilized to mount an invasion of Taiwan, which China has never recognized as a sovereign nation. Experts say that although China has considered reclaiming the country since 1949, up-to-date military plans for such an action were drawn up last year. The Chinese Foreign Ministry calls such plans 'completely groundless,' reiterating their comments to similar accusations leveled last year. Nonetheless, the Taiwanese president Lee Teng-hui has appealed to the United States for military support, echoing requests made in 1996.

The President has made no statement on the situation, preferring once again to confer with the UN Security Council before passing comment. Sources say that the proceedings continue with much tension on all sides.

President announces military response to China

July 27, 1997
Web posted at: 3:00 P.M. EST (2000 GMT)

From Washington chief correspondent Michael Flasetti
WASHINGTON (TCN) – The President, after a round-the-clock session with UN chiefs, made a statement announcing America's military commitment to opposing China's claim to the Spratly Islands. Having received no concessions from Beijing, the President feels that conflict is inevitable unless the Chinese withdraw.

The secretary-general of the United Nations has also pledged the support of the world organization in ousting Chinese presence from the disputed islands. She stated that the Chinese have clearly violated the Manila Declaration of 1992, a treaty signed by the Association of Southeast Asian Nations, of which China is a member, that resolved to settle the Spratly Islands dispute in a diplomatic manner. In response to this violation of international law, the US Navy will begin mobilization immediately, with the aircraft carriers *Nimitz* and *Independence* entering the area within the week.

Chinese reaction to today's announcement was one of diplomatic indignation. 'We have every right to the Nan-Sha Islands,' said the Chinese ambassador, referring to the Spratlys by their Chinese name, 'and we will defend them as we would any other part of our homeland.'

Russia selling arms to China, US Navy concerned

July 30, 1997
Web posted at: 12:00 P.M. EST (1700 GMT)

From Washington chief correspondent Michael Flasetti
WASHINGTON (TCN) – As tensions mount in the South China Sea, a confrontation between the Chinese and UN military, led by the US Navy, seems inevitable. Adding to the danger of the situation is the news, reportedly obtained

by the CIA, that Russia has been arming China with advanced weapons, among them nuclear attack submarines that may be deployed into the waters surrounding the Spratly Islands.

The news that Russia has been selling arms to the Chinese is not new. Over the past two years, China has taken delivery of four Russian Kilo-class diesel submarines, which are considerably less advanced than Russia's nuclear submarines. However, the possibility that Russia has sold more advanced submarines to the Chinese is of great concern to White House military advisers.

A source close to the Joint Chiefs of Staff has disclosed that the Russians have even collaborated with the Chinese on a prototype nuclear attack submarine, and that the submarine may see action in the Spratly conflict. If true, this presents a possible shift in the balance of naval power in the region, and a great concern to the recently downsized US Navy.

Russian president Gennadi Zyuganov, himself a conservative Communist like Chinese leader Li Peng, refused to comment on the possibility of advanced weapons sales to China, yet did say that Russia enjoys a balanced trade agreement with China on the sales of certain weapons, including Kilo class submarines. Russia, cash-poor since the breakup of the Soviet Union, clearly depends on submarine sales to China to help fund social and economic projects, as well as the upgrading of its own navy.

Chinese submarine sunk, war expected soon

August 2, 1997
Web posted at: 1:00 P.M. EST (1800 GMT)

From Beijing bureau chief Julie Meyer
BEIJING (TCN) – Fighting began today in the South China Sea between the UN-backed United States Navy and the Chinese navy in and around the Spratly Islands. The first skirmish occurred when the aircraft carrier USS *Nimitz* was

attacked by a Chinese submarine, suspected to be an aging Han class attack submarine. While the submarine came within striking distance of the *Nimitz*, it was sunk by an American Los Angeles class submarine that was escorting the carrier. All hands are reported lost.

In response to today's conflict, the Chinese navy appears to have adopted a more aggressive posture in the area and more conflict lies ahead. In fact, China is officially expected to declare war against the United States of America within the week.

'This isn't going to be over as quickly as the Falkland Islands conflict fifteen years ago,' says international relations professor and China policy specialist Dr Adrian Mann. 'China is much stronger than Argentina, and they hold considerable tactical advantages over the US Navy forces in the area.' Other experts are telling a similar story. However, in the face of lengthy combat, the use of nuclear weapons is a great concern to many, including Dr Mann. 'I doubt that the Chinese will consider the possibility, and I think it likely that all sides will agree to keep the fighting localized to the South China Sea.' Indeed, the President and the secretary-general of the UN are said to be drafting an offer to Chinese leader Li Peng proposing just that.

In the meantime, US and UN sanctions against China continue, with the General Assembly of the UN signing a broad package of economic restrictions of trade with China. The effects of these sanctions should be felt immediately, as they ban the import of all goods into China, with the exception of food and medical supplies. In addition to economic sanctions, the President said today that he is fully committed to expelling China from the Spratly Islands and aiding in the restoration of Jiang Zemin to power.

ONE

First Blood

The USS *Cheyenne*, a Los Angeles class nuclear attack submarine, cast off the tugboat's lines at precisely 0100 on 12 August 1997, and moved under its own power into the dark waters of San Diego Bay. Astern of *Cheyenne*, the lone tugboat hauled in the lines and headed back to its berth at the San Diego Naval Base, headquarters of the Third Fleet.

The atmosphere aboard *Cheyenne* was taut with pre-mission tension. Her crew had performed admirably during her abbreviated shakedown cruise, but now she was on high alert and headed into almost certain conflict.

A few years earlier, as a result of the post-Cold War defense drawdown, the Third Fleet had relocated from Pearl Harbor to San Diego Naval Base. With the Chinese moving on the Spratly Islands, *Cheyenne* had been ordered to ready for deployment. She was now on her way from her berth at the Ballast Point Naval Submarine Base to the Pearl Harbor Naval Submarine Base to complete her outfitting. From there she would take up station in the South China Sea.

Cheyenne was the newest attack submarine in the US Navy. She was also the last of an era. Given the hull number SSN-773, *Cheyenne* was the last of sixty-two Los Angeles class nuclear attack submarines to be funded by Congress. Built by Newport News Shipbuilding in the Virginia town of the same name, *Cheyenne* was 360 feet long and displaced 6,900 tons. She was equipped with the latest advanced weapons and sensor systems.

Cheyenne's pressurized-water, S6G General Electric

reactor had been critical for some time and the OOD (officer of the deck) had earlier passed the word, 'Rig Ship for Dive.' When she was farther away from land, reaching the water west of Point Loma, where it was deep enough for the submarine to dive, sailors on board *Cheyenne* completed readying the submarine for submergence. From the sonar room to the torpedo compartments, sailors hurriedly confirmed that all was well in their compartments. The final message came back to the OOD, '*Cheyenne* is now rigged for dive.'

Captain Bartholomew 'Mack' Mackey was pleased with both his ship and his crew. A big man, Mack had been engineering officer of an earlier 688, and executive officer and plank owner (new construction crew) of an improved 688-like *Cheyenne* – the 688I USS *Greenville* (SSN 772), *Cheyenne*'s predecessor at Newport News. Mack was a rising star, two years deep selected for O-5 (Commander) and two years deep selected for O-6 (captain). Mack was a real captain, not just in terms of the Navy tradition of referring to a commanding officer as 'captain,' but in pay grade as well.

Mack knew his crew had heard the rumors of a possible war with China. The recent Chinese actions concerning the US-flagged *Benthic Adventure*, a United Fuels Corporation prospecting ship sailing in international waters off the Spratly Islands, had been considered by many in the United States to be an act of war. Even more blatant was the Chinese invasion of the long-contested Spratlys.

But Mack knew the rumors were true. As of 2 August, a virtual state of war had existed between the United States and China. On that date a Chinese Han class nuclear attack submarine came within striking distance of the US aircraft carrier *Nimitz* with what appeared to be hostile intentions. In defense of *Nimitz*, an American escort submarine sank the Han, killing all aboard the Chinese vessel.

The story had saturated the news. There had been no

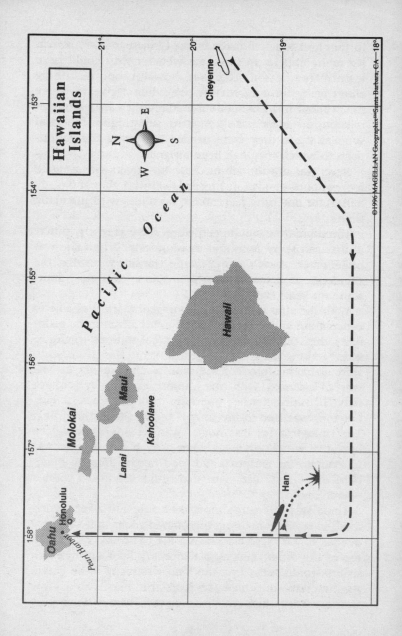

©1996 MAGELLAN Geographix℠Santa Barbara, CA—18°

Hawaiian
Islands

Pacific Ocean

N
W E
S

153°
154°
155°
156°
157°
158°

21°
20°
19°

Cheyenne

Hawaii

Maui

Molokai

Lanai

Kahoolawe

Han

Oahu

Honolulu

Pearl Harbor

further hostile action taken by the Chinese military, which led many experts to speculate whether they could have learned their lesson. That was, however, one nice thing about being on a submarine. One didn't have to worry much about news. Attack submarines often stayed out on missions for as long as six months, surfacing for food and supplies when they were needed or visiting the various ports to which they had been assigned.

News was not the job of *Cheyenne* – theirs was a much more important mission: proceed to Pearl Harbor and ready herself for potentially imminent hostilities with mainland China.

The submarine submerged when she was ready, slowly at first and then more and more quickly. When she was underwater, the OOD began the transit by turning the submarine in a southwesterly direction – the most direct route for Pearl Harbor.

With the ship underway submerged, Mack was able to concentrate on the main obstacle to his mission, the possibility that Chinese nuclear attack submarines might be lurking along his path. His orders were clear: If *Cheyenne* were to come into contact with a Chinese vessel, she was to proceed with the utmost caution and attack only in self-defense. In other words, Mack knew, *Cheyenne* was free to fire only if she was fired upon first. The United States was not at war yet – 'yet' being the operative word. When *Cheyenne* arrived at Pearl she was to load up on weapons and food needed for the possibility of a long cruise – one that could turn into a combat operation.

There was not much room on a submarine for storing food, so crates containing the canned goods that the crew needed to eat were loaded into the passageways, one on top of the other, making a temporary floor upon which sailors would walk until the food was ready to be eaten. As the crew consumed the food, the floor would grow shorter. Until then, the passageways would be a very

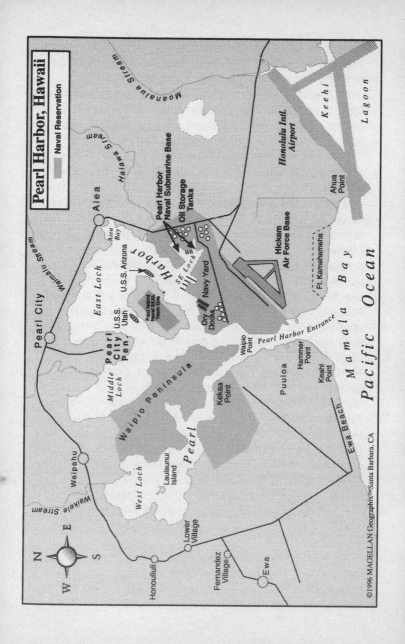

dangerous place for taller members of the submarine crew. They would have to walk with their heads hunched down to avoid hitting overhead pipes and wireways.

As Captain Mackey walked toward the tiny wardroom he'd be using as the briefing room, he grinned at the thought that everything from canned tomato sauce to string beans was stored beneath his feet.

Cheyenne was two hours from San Diego Bay. Travelling at twenty-six knots, this put her fifty-two nautical miles from home.

Entering the wardroom, Mack motioned to his officers to sit. 'As you are all aware,' he said, 'we are currently in a highly tense environment due to the recent hostile actions taken by the Chinese military.' He was careful to point out that these aggressive actions were by the military – not, as the media often claimed, by the people or the politicians. 'I would just like to inform all of you that we received a message that a Canadian P-3 Orion operating on a training mission out of San Diego thinks that they may have picked up a submarine 237 miles southwest of our current position. They even got positive MAD (magnetic anomaly detection) contact, but they lost contact after tracking the submarine for about twenty minutes. The P-3 crew is pretty confident that what they found was an SSN. Naval Intelligence thinks it may even be one of the Chinese Han class of nuclear attack submarines, but up to this point they haven't been able to confirm anything. We have been instructed to keep our ears open for this possible contact while at the same time proceeding as fast as we can to Pearl so that we can arrive safely on station in the South China Sea. We are to avoid taking any actions against the submarine – unless, of course, he tries to kill us.'

The officers took this news in stride, and while the meeting was not as rousing as the captain had hoped, it had gotten his point across. Word would soon be buzzing throughout *Cheyenne* that they would be on the lookout for a nuclear attack submarine, possibly Chinese, lingering far too close to United States waters for comfort – even if being in international waters was within the legal realm of international law.

For her transit to Pearl Harbor, *Cheyenne* was given a small loadout of torpedoes. The full capability of her torpedo room was twenty-six weapons, including four in the torpedo tubes, consisting of a combination of Mk 48 torpedoes, Tomahawk cruise missiles (land-attack and antiship varieties), Harpoon antiship missiles, and sometimes, though rarely, Mk 67 submarine-launched mobile mines. However, for this transit, *Cheyenne* was given only 12 Mk 48 ADCAP torpedoes. With a top speed of over fifty knots while running deep, and a range in excess of 30,000 yards, the Mk 48 ADCAP was arguably the best heavy torpedo in existence. Its only real competition came from the British Spearfish, which was carried by the submarines of the Royal Navy.

The Mk 48 ADCAP, which stood for Advanced Capability, was a heavy wire-guided torpedo weighing over 3,000 pounds. Nearly 20 percent of its weight, or 650 pounds, consisted of PBXN-103 high explosive. One of the advantages of the Mk 48 was that it could be used against both submarine and surface targets, which made it much easier on logistics. It also pleased many submarine captains who still preferred the thrill of launching a torpedo over the newer vertical launch Tomahawks or encapsulated Harpoon missiles.

Each Mk 48 was wire guided so that targeting data during the initial stages of the torpedo launch could be transmitted back and forth from the Mk 48 to the BSY-1 fire-control system onboard the attack submarine. During the terminal stages of the attack, the Mk 48 would use its powerful active seeker to detect, home in on, and then destroy its target. As long as the wire was intact, information from the torpedo was constantly relayed to *Cheyenne* until detonation.

After the meeting, Mack returned to the control room. Knowing that there might be a nuclear attack submarine in the area, he ordered that instead of running at twenty-six knots for much of the way to Pearl Harbor, as he had originally planned, *Cheyenne* would now slow more frequently in order to listen to her surroundings. This 'sprint and drift' technique was one of the best methods of arriving at a destination quickly while also allowing the submarine's passive sonar to search for any possible sonar contacts.

Cheyenne was now at an ordered depth of four hundred feet. At this depth, she was in her own element, that of the depths of the ocean. If necessary, she could still be reached by the relatively new, albeit slow, ELF, or extremely low frequency, band of communications. If there were a dire emergency, or a change in her orders, *Cheyenne* would be instructed by a short coded ELF message to come to communications depth in order to receive important message traffic.

Running at twenty-six knots was not always quiet. The screw, known to those outside the Navy as a propeller, was working feverishly to propel the submarine at this speed. If too shallow, this created tiny air bubbles, which made a popping noise when they collapsed. This noise was known as cavitation and could give away a submarine's presence in the area. At this moment, Mack did not care as much about his stealth capability as he did about two other concerns: locating the submarine that was lurking dangerously near the West Coast, and arriving at the Pearl Harbor Naval Submarine Base with *Cheyenne* intact.

All aboard *Cheyenne* were aware that they were making slight cavitation noise and that anyone who was close enough and quiet enough could determine their location. The frequent slowing and so-called clearing of the baffles, the normally 'sonar blind' area astern of submarines, evened the score somewhat.

At 1100 on 12 August, just ten hours after leaving San Diego, the OOD ordered *Cheyenne* to slow to one-third. Exactly eleven minutes later the sonar room came alive as *Cheyenne* slowed and her course was changed toward the north.

'Tonal contact, center bearing 187 on the end-fire beam,' called one of the young sonar operators. The consoles, which looked like computer screens with green lines running through them, were often the sonar operator's most important ally.

An instant later the sonar supervisor, who had been paying close attention to the goings-on in this important center of the submarine, called to the captain, 'Conn, sonar, we have a possible submarine contact bearing 187. We're only receiving blade rate information so far.'

Mack entered the sonar room, joining the five other men already there – including the sonar supervisor and the sonar officer. Everyone in the room knew that there was the possibility of encountering a Chinese submarine, but also knew it was highly unlikely. Chinese naval vessels rarely ventured this far away from home waters. This was especially true of the Chinese submarine fleet, which consisted largely of older-model diesel boats with just a few very noisy nuclear-powered attack submarines of the Han class.

If there was a Chinese submarine patrolling off the West Coast of the United States, however, Mack was fairly sure that it would have to be a Han class. Naval intelligence reports had repeatedly explained that only one type of submarine was capable of travelling this far from Chinese home waters and operating – without surfacing – for an extended period of time. That type was a nuclear submarine, and the only Chinese SSN currently in service was the Han class.

Captain Mackey was, as were all experienced submariners, at least slightly familiar with the Han class of submarine. In addition, when word was passed of a possible war with China, the intelligence officer assigned to SubRon 11 from SubGroup 5 had quickly prepared a brief report of what was known of the Han class in the US intelligence community. According to that report, construction of the Han class had stopped after only five submarines due to extremely high internal radiation levels, and all of those were currently in service with the Chinese navy. They carried the pennant numbers 401, 402, 403, 404, and 405 painted on their sail. One of the class had, of course, been destroyed earlier that month by a US SSN. Naval intelligence was still unsure which number it was, but they reported that it was probably number 402, the second of the class. They were assuming this because it had been tracked since leaving Ningbo Naval Base in China's East Sea Fleet four days prior to the actions involving *Nimitz*.

The torpedo complement fitted to the Han class was reported to be a mix of the older straight-running types as well as some of the newer Russian homing varieties. According to the reports, numbers 401 and 402 carried only torpedoes, but the last three submarines of the class, numbers 403 to 405, carried the Ying Ji. Also known as the Eagle Strike, this antishipping missile was a sea skimmer and caused great concern in the eyes of naval commanders. The most recent intelligence reports stated that while these missiles could be a significant threat to warships, the submarine needed to surface in order to launch them. And submarine commanders knew all too well that a surfaced submarine was an easy target.

Unlike the USS *Seawolf*, *Cheyenne* did not have a wide aperture array, or WAA, so she would have to triangulate the position of her passive sonar contacts in order to determine their exact bearing, speed, and range. The ship maneuvers to accomplish this would have to be done very quietly, especially if the contact, now designated Master 1, was a direct-path contact. But it was a painfully slow process.

'Captain,' the sonar supervisor said, 'it's possible the submarine was tracking us but lost us when we slowed. With these convergence zones out here in deep water, it could be in excess of 75,000 yards away. My guess is that he thinks we passed him, and based on its blade rate, is running full speed in an attempt to catch up with us and regain contact.'

That was a good guess, Mack thought, but it was still just a guess. He wanted something more than that. Proceeding to the conn, he ordered the OOD to station the Section fire-control tracking party so the BSY-1 computers could be used to determine the solution on the target. The OOD would maneuver the submarine in order to change the bearings received by the towed arrays.

Mack also ordered the OOD to house the TB-16 towed array and deploy the TB-23 towed-array. Unlike the 240 feet of TB-16 hydrophones, the TB-23 towed-array sonar measured over 900 feet in length, mounted nearly 100 hydrophones, and was towed at the end of a 2,600-foot cable. Then he returned to the sonar room.

'Captain, blade rate indicates Master 1's speed is steady at eighteen knots,' reported the sonar supervisor. 'We're getting more tonals now, including one from the conformal array. She's definitely not American. The tonals compare to those listed in the sonar intelligence manuals as unique to Chinese Han class, number 402.'

That stopped Mack. 'I thought 402 was sunk by the submarine escorting *Nimitz*,' he said.

'So did naval intelligence,' the sonar supervisor replied. 'I guess they got their numbers mixed up. Wouldn't be the first time.'

The captain called to the OOD, 'Begin retrieving the TB-23. I don't want to get tangled up in case we have a fight on our hands.' The towed-array sonar was valuable

21

for quietly listening to passive sonar contacts, but Mack, like many submarine captains, preferred to retrieve it before engaging in close combat with an enemy submarine.

Mack left the sonar room and went back to the conn to see how the fire-control solution was coming.

'Conn, sonar, our contact, Master 1, just stopped his shaft.'

Seven more minutes passed, Cheyenne's sonar operators carefully monitoring the tonals from the Chinese submarine's reactor coolant pumps. These had to be run constantly in order to avoid destroying the reactor, one of the few drawbacks of a nuclear-powered submarine. A conventional, or non-nuclear, submarine could stop dead in the water, running entirely on her battery power, and be completely silent. A nuclear submarine, however, such as Cheyenne or Han number 402, had to constantly pump reactor coolant in order to keep the reactor critical and prevent its overheating. That difference meant that it sometimes could be easier to hunt an SSN than a regular diesel boat – especially when the SSN was an old, 1970s-vintage Han with reactor plant problems.

The silence ended when the sonar supervisor called, 'Conn, sonar, single active pulse from Master 1.' Moments later there was a second sonar pulse.

Mack ordered the chief of the watch to 'Man battle stations torpedo,' then took the conn from the officer of the deck.

With battle stations manned, the executive officer, in his role as the fire control coordinator, reported to the captain, 'Master 1 is now bearing 169, BSY-1 range is 22,000 yards. He was not in a convergence zone.'

Aboard Han 402, the Chinese commander felt as if he had little choice but to give his position away. His sonar had acquired only intermittent contact on the American submarine maneuvering in this area, and he needed to locate it in order to accomplish his mission: sink the submarine and then continue on against American merchant ships. He knew an American submarine was out there, but didn't know where, and didn't know it was *Cheyenne*. Unfortunately for him and his crew, however, he had thought that he was much closer to the Americans than his active sonar told him he was. 22,000 yards was out of torpedo range for his submarine, but not for *Cheyenne*'s Mk 48s.

Those two active 'pings' were a calculated risk on the Chinese captain's part. He knew his submarine was as noisy as a bull in a china shop and he suspected the Americans had been tracking him. Once he'd figured out that the American submarine had passed him he knew they could not be far off. If he waited too long, he would miss his chance to attack.

Aboard *Cheyenne*, Mack was trying to outguess the Chinese captain. He knew that Chinese submarines were notorious for having very poor sonar outfits, but he didn't think they were bad enough that the captain of number 402 would have no choice but to use his active sonar, giving away his own exact location. *No*, Mack thought. *This does make sense. If the Chinese captain knew we were tracking him, he probably had figured that we knew his location, so all he was really doing was leveling the playing field – giving away information we already had in order to learn our location as well.*

What this amounted to was that the Chinese submarine had gone active on the American submarine and both submarines now had an accurate firing solution. Mack didn't expect the Chinese captain to let this opportunity slip away. The Han was currently outside its own torpedo range, but that could change rapidly.

'Conn, sonar, the Han just started up again. It's making turns for twenty-five knots, sounds like she's really straining. They are closing quickly.'

Captain Mackey reversed course to minimize the range

23

closure while he ordered tubes one and two made ready in all respects.

'Torpedo room, fire control, make tubes one and two ready in all respects and open the outer doors.'

When the outer doors were open, Mack turned back toward the Han and increased speed to full. Both submarines were headed straight for one another in an underwater game of chicken that could potentially ignite a third world war.

'Conn, sonar, we have a torpedo in the water! Type SET-53, bearing 163. It's active, Captain.'

'Range to Master 1 is 21,000 yards,' reported the fire control coordinator.

Mack looked around his control room. There was a look of horror in the eyes of the young sailors who had not yet been in the Navy for six months.

'All stop,' he ordered.

'All stop, aye, sir,' the helmsman repeated. Seconds later he added, 'Maneuvering answers all stop.'

The normal procedure for countering a torpedo was turn and run, flank speed, in the opposite direction. This was not, however, a normal situation.

The US intelligence community had managed to secretly buy three of the Chinese type SET-53 homing torpedoes from the Russians in a not-so-friendly transfer of technology. From their various tests, they had determined that the maximum range of the SET-53 was five nautical miles, or 10,000 yards. Even building in a large margin of error by doubling that range to ten nautical miles, or about 20,000 yards, Mack knew that there was simply no way that the Chinese torpedo could hit *Cheyenne*.

It did, however, make Captain Mackey furious, and not just because this was an act of war against the United States by a Chinese submarine. More than that, this was an aggressive action against him, his submarine, and his crew.

Cheyenne was not in any immediate danger – not yet, at least. Just in case, however, the captain calmly ordered, 'Rig ship for depth charge.'

The Chinese captain had put his submarine in a very bad position. The Chinese leaders, wanting to demonstrate their power to the Americans, had given Han 402 orders to attack American submarines and surface ships operating in the area. The 402's captain was following his orders faithfully . . . but he didn't believe those orders included suicide. And he knew all too well that attacking a Los Angeles class submarine was tantamount to suicide. If he could manage to get in close enough to attack *Cheyenne*, he would do so. If not, he would follow his orders and launch at whatever range he felt he could without getting himself killed, and then he would dive deep and hunt for American merchant ships.

When the active 'pings' revealed *Cheyenne*'s location, the Chinese captain realized that he had given away their location much too far away to effectively attack the Americans. With their own location revealed, closing with *Cheyenne* would put the Han at serious risk, which meant that his only real choice was either to simply turn and run or to first shoot at the Americans and then turn and run. The first option appealed to him the most, but the second option was what his orders demanded.

The Han captain gave the command to release a single torpedo and then began turning to his right. His only plan was to make a turn to the east and get away from the now-angry American submarine.

Mack thought about that torpedo in the water and what it meant. The Han had fired upon him without provocation, which meant that China had decided to escalate. They would be starting hostilities at any moment, and all submarines would by now have been tasked by the Chinese navy to sink any American warships, merchant ships, or submarines as they exited their home ports.

All around the world, wherever Chinese vessels came in contact with American ships, there would be bloodshed. Some of them would get lucky. Some would win, and some would lose. But this particular Chinese captain had gotten unlucky when he decided to attack *Cheyenne* rather than a defenseless merchant vessel.

And it was too late to change his mind.

Mack immediately saw what the Han was doing. It was turning and running – in the direction of San Diego, which could only mean one thing. China was at war with the United States.

'Conn, sonar, the Chinese torpedo just settled dead in the water,' the sonar supervisor reported. 'Based on run time, it didn't even make it 6,000 yards.'

Mack nodded. The Chinese had had their turn. Now it was *Cheyenne*'s.

The Los Angeles class attack submarine began to pick up speed rapidly, rushing to get behind the Han. The Chinese submarine was running from them in an attempt to escape the American submarine and return to a safe haven, hiding somewhere off the West Coast, but *Cheyenne* wasn't about to allow that.

The Han's top speed was twenty-five knots; *Cheyenne* was doing thirty-one knots, and the range to Master 1 closed rapidly. Both commanding officers knew it would only be a matter of time before the Americans were within firing range.

Aboard the Han, the Chinese captain's options were limited once again. He could continue to run, prolonging things for a short while longer, or he could turn and fight.

His orders were clear, and so was his choice. At his command, his submarine came around in another slow turn and bore down on *Cheyenne*.

It was a noble gesture, but a futile one. The Han captain was racing to get within torpedo range, knowing that the effective range of the American Mk 48 ADCAP was more than double that of his Chinese SET-53.

'Conn, sonar, two torpedoes in the water, more SET-53s, bearing 165.'

The fire control coordinator reported the range to Master 1 as 18,000 yards.

Mack wasn't worried. Clearly, the Chinese had done this out of desperation. They wanted to go down fighting, and their only hope was to get lucky – and a torpedo in the water was a chance to get lucky; a torpedo unlaunched was nothing.

Cheyenne had closed to within striking range, but Mack didn't give the orders to shoot yet. There were still two chances for the Chinese to get lucky, if those SET-53s really had a range of 20,000 yards. Captain Mackey once again gave the orders to prepare for a possible torpedo hit, and also to take evasive action by launching two ADC (Acoustic Device Countermeasure) Mk 2 decoys.

The decoys, which were launched out of what were in effect mini-torpedo tubes, accomplished exactly what they were intended to do and decoyed the torpedoes in a direction other than that of *Cheyenne*. The Chinese torpedoes ran out the length of their course without hitting anything solid. Their momentum spent, they settled to the ocean floor, taking Han 402's hopes with them.

Though Mack had trained nearly his entire career for firing on an enemy submarine, he had never really expected it to happen. But Mack, like the others aboard *Cheyenne*, was a professional. He was calm as he gave the command, 'Firing point procedures, Master 1, tubes one and two.'

A BSY-1 operator reported the relevant target data to the captain.

'Match sonar bearings and shoot, tubes one and two,' Mack said, his voice cool and steady.

'Match sonar bearings and shoot, tubes one and two, aye,' the fire control coordinator repeated the command.

The Mk 48s were launched from the weapons control console and were ejected from their tubes. Their Otto fuel engines came to life, powering their powerful pump jets.

'Tubes one and two fired electrically,' said the combat systems officer at the weapons control console.

As soon as the torpedoes entered the water, the Chinese submarine began to turn. Mack guessed that they were going to try a ninety-degree turn away from the Mk 48s, but the seeker heads on the ADCAPs were doing what they had been designed to do: hunt down an enemy submarine. They stayed with the Han as it twisted and turned.

'Both torpedoes have acquired Master 1,' reported the combat systems officer. Both Mk 48s had found the enemy submarine with their own sonars and no longer needed to be guided by *Cheyenne*'s fire-control system via their guidance wires.

'Cut the wires, shut the outer doors, and reload tubes one and two,' ordered Captain Mackey.

'Conn, sonar, two explosions, bearing 162.'

A cheer erupted in the control room, but Captain Bartholomew Mackey did not join in. The sailors were celebrating the fact that *Cheyenne* had just achieved her first blood, but Mack knew that more than that had just happened.

War with mainland China was now a fact of life.

A short time later, Mack secured from battle stations and ordered *Cheyenne* to proceed to periscope depth. Using SSIXS (Submarine Satellite Information Exchange System), Mack communicated their actions to the higher-ups in the Department of Defense and the Navy. As Mack had suspected, message traffic indicated that their encounter had not been an isolated incident and *Cheyenne* soon learned that what seemed like an all-out war had been started by China in an attempt to assert its position in the new world order.

Cheyenne's orders were again confirmed and she was to remain on course, sprinting and drifting until arriving at Pearl Harbor so that she could resupply and join other

American units in the South China Sea. There was one important change in her orders, however: she was now allowed to attack any Chinese naval vessel she encountered so long as her trip to Pearl would not be overly delayed.

● ● ●

The remainder of the trip to Pearl was a tense one. Every moment that passed increased the likelihood that they would once again face combat. Running at four hundred feet toward the submarine safety lanes southwest of the Big Island of Hawaii, the OOD brought the submarine shallow to copy over the floating wire any news that might have occurred since their last venture toward the surface. The news was not good.

Two Spruance class destroyers, the USS *Fletcher* (DD 992) and the USS *John Young* (DD 973), were operating in conjunction with the Coast Guard cutter *Midgett* (WHEC 726). One of the SH-60 Seahawks from *Fletcher* had dropped a line of sonobuoys about 150 miles south of Honolulu and detected a possible sonar contact. All vessels had been told of the friendly submarine traffic in the area, but the contact the *Fletcher*'s Seahawk detected did not match any of the sonar profiles of the submarines expected to be operating nearby.

Another Seahawk from *John Young* was en route to the area. Its orders were to assist in determining what type of contact the sonobuoys were tracking.

Cheyenne went to periscope depth. Word came to them over the periscope communications antenna, on the 'Navy Red' encrypted circuit from one of the helicopters, that there was a possible enemy submarine operating in the area, which turned out to be forty-two nautical miles north of *Cheyenne*'s current location. The message also indicated that *Cheyenne*'s assistance would be greatly appreciated. Mack acknowledged the pilot's request, and then ordered

Cheyenne to return to operational depth and proceed toward the reported datum.

Forty-seven minutes later *Cheyenne*'s towed-array sonar detected the sonar contact. They were still out of range and could not tell much about the contact. They knew only that it might be a submarine, and that, if it was a submarine, it was attempting to be as quiet as possible. The sonar supervisor designated this new contact as *Cheyenne*'s Master 2.

On the surface, the two US destroyers and the Coast Guard cutter were hunting the sonar contact. The surface ships were attempting to keep their distance from the contact, wary of a possible torpedo attack. The Seahawks did not have to worry about that, and at 1340, moments after the surface ships had confirmed that the contact was indeed another Chinese nuclear submarine, *Cheyenne* heard the sounds of two Mk 50 torpedoes entering the water.

'Conn, sonar, torpedoes in the water . . . Mk 50s, bearing 017. The Seahawks just dropped weapons on the submarine contact, Master 2.'

A short time later the small helicopter torpedoes went active. *Cheyenne* heard two noisemaker decoys being launched, followed by the loud cavitation of the Chinese submarine as it attempted to outrun the Mk 50s – to no avail.

'Conn, sonar, two explosions, bearing 023.'

'Radio, Captain,' Mack said. 'Send congrats to the helo pilots over Navy Red; they just sank themselves an enemy submarine!'

Cheyenne's crew was justifiably jubilant at having witnessed the destruction of a second Chinese submarine. Perhaps it had not been as exciting as their initial taste of combat, but it had boosted their confidence in their naval brethren hundreds of feet above them.

More than that, though, they were buoyed by the fact that every aspect of their first mission had gone off without a hitch. Mack ordered *Cheyenne* to proceed to Pearl. Once there, they would complete their mini-refit, and prepare *Cheyenne* for her next operation: her transit to the home waters off China – the South China Sea.

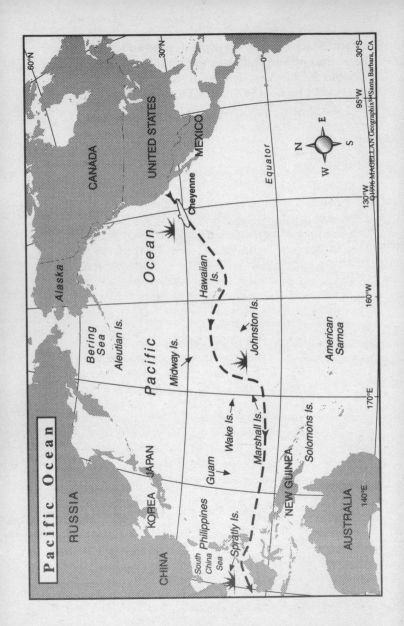

TWO

South China Sea Station

Captain Mackey looked around the small wardroom, meeting the gaze of each of the officers assembled before him. 'The price of success,' he said. 'The Navy was so pleased with our operations while en route to Pearl that they decided to send us directly into harm's way. *Cheyenne* has been ordered to rendezvous with the USS *Independence* (CV-62), which will be heading in the direction of the recently occupied Spratly Islands. *Independence* is currently steaming in the Indian Ocean. We are to meet up with her one hundred miles northwest of Natuna Island. Upon crossing the Pacific Ocean we will chop (change operational commander) to the Seventh Fleet.'

Mack kept his voice and his gaze steady. Such transfers were common between fleets, but this one carried the connotation of an increase in risk. The Third Fleet was remaining on station closer to home; the Seventh was on the front lines of this new war.

'Naval intelligence reports that there are large numbers of enemy warships operating in the area,' Mack went on. 'We will, without a doubt, come into contact with many of these. Our first priority, however, remains meeting up with *Independence*. We will take this dangerous mission one step at a time. Remember, they have the home-court advantage.'

He looked around the wardroom one last time. 'We'll depart as soon as our refit is complete.'

If only that were true, Mack thought. But the truth was, they would be leaving *before* they were completely outfitted. As was always the case during peacetime, materiel was never ordered in large enough quantities to satisfy the demands of wartime operations. There were too many ships steaming into Pearl for supplies, and not enough weapons and ammunition to go around.

More was on order, of course, and it wouldn't be long before Pearl was fully stockpiled, but by then *Cheyenne* would be halfway to the South China Sea.

Cheyenne's loadout included sixteen Mk 48 ADCAPs, six Tomahawk land-attack cruise missiles, and four Harpoon antiship missiles for medium-range attacks on surface ships. The loading was a long process. The Mk 48s had to be slowly and carefully lowered into the loading hatch one at a time, and the Tomahawks in their loading canisters were loaded directly into *Cheyenne*'s vertical launch tubes.

If Mack had had his way, though, the loading process would have taken even longer. He'd take *Cheyenne* out as soon as she was ready, of course, but he would have been happier if she'd had a full complement of weapons.

The transit to the rendezvous with *Independence* would take *Cheyenne* in a southwesterly direction through the Pacific Ocean and past the Marshall and Solomon Islands, both sites of grisly combat operations over fifty years ago. She would then pass by the Caroline Islands and cut through the Celebes Sea before entering the Sulu Sea and, finally, the South China Sea.

Naval intelligence had confirmed that *Cheyenne* had sunk the second of the Chinese Han class of nuclear attack submarines, number 402, and that she had been witness to the destruction of what turned out to be Han number 404 south of Honolulu. These two confirmed kills, along with the Han destroyed earlier by the submarine escorting *Nimitz*, meant that the Chinese navy had only two remaining nuclear powered submarines. Or at least, Mack reminded himself, only two that the United States knew about.

Addressing that lack of intelligence was a part of *Cheyenne*'s mission. Once in China's home waters, *Cheyenne*'s

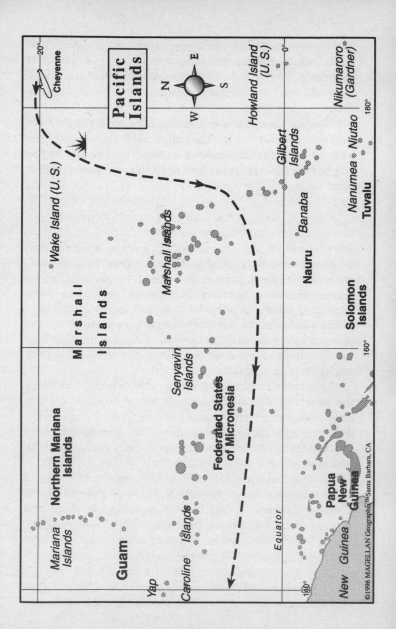

orders were to gather intelligence on Chinese naval operations while making her way south in the direction of Indonesia. There, 100 miles northwest of Natuna Island, their old friend USS *Independence* would be waiting for them.

Thinking about their mission and the tools they'd have available to complete it, Mack adjourned the meeting. The loadout would be complete in less than two hours, and he wanted his officers and sailors ready for imminent combat operations.

●　●　●

Somewhere in the central Pacific, a Chinese Luda class destroyer sat quietly, dead in the water. One hundred meters below it lay its partner in crime, a Romeo class diesel attack submarine. Their mission was simple: sink as many American vessels as possible. They had heard the news of China's losses in the Pacific Ocean, so they were pleased to detect a merchant ship, *The Southwest Passage*, an American merchant vessel two days out from Japan, en route to one of the Hawaiian Islands.

The merchantman was not a big ship, but she was flying the American flag, and that made her a target. As soon as *The Southwest Passage* came within eighty miles, the destroyer captain launched one of his two Harbin Z-9A helicopters in order to confirm the identity and nationality of the ship.

The merchantman did not, at first, realize the danger she was in, and her captain kept her on course. When the Chinese helicopter finally buzzed the bridge, however, he radioed their observations in to the US Navy and received orders to alter their course to avoid, as the Navy radioman described it, 'a possibly life-threatening situation.'

Unfortunately for the merchant ship and her crew, it was already too late. Without warning, three Chinese HY-2 missiles, variants of the Silkworm surface-to-surface missile family, came streaking across the sky, directly into the hull of *The Southwest Passage*. All three impacts came within seconds of one another, two in the aft section of her hull, the third closer to the bow.

The Southwest Passage went down like a rock, not even pausing to break up. All hands were lost, most of them dying in the explosions.

Aboard the Chinese destroyer, the captain was well pleased with the results. They had struck back successfully at the Americans. Even better, he had used only his destroyer in the attack. With luck he would be able to keep his submarine a secret, saving it as a surprise for a bigger fish, perhaps even a US warship.

Having just passed Midway Island, *Cheyenne* was about to begin turning southward when she received word of the attack on *The Southwest Passage*. Since getting underway submerged from Pearl, Mack had maintained the floating wire communications antenna streamed to get any information that the Navy might wish to pass along to them. He had expected intelligence updates, and information on the latest developments, but he hadn't been expecting news like that.

According to the message, the attack had occurred due south of *Cheyenne*'s current position. The coordinates were located approximately one day's travel at full speed – or about a day and a half at their current rate of twenty knots. Mack didn't hesitate. His orders allowed him some latitude, and he was prepared to take full advantage of that.

Reading the message a second time, he gave the order to turn *Cheyenne* and head full speed toward the destroyer's reported position. In the absence of a formal declaration of war, the Chinese government would undoubtedly brand the destroyer a renegade. Which was fine with Mack. He intended to bring them to justice . . . American style.

Twenty-six hours later *Cheyenne* received her second surprise. They had picked up a target, but it wasn't the

37

destroyer. Instead, there was another signal masking the one they'd expected.

Sonar quickly identified it as a diesel submarine, Romeo class. The Chinese submarine must have been having a problem with her snorkeling system because she was recharging her batteries on the surface – and making a tremendous amount of diesel noise in the process. It was another two hours before they picked up the Luda destroyer running at about thirteen knots.

Mack ordered battle stations manned. 'Quite a day for going hunting, don't you think?' he said to the diving officer.

'Sure is, Captain. It's not often you find an enemy submarine on the surface with its pants down like this one.'

For targets such as these, the Harpoon surface-to-surface missile – or, in this case, submarine-to-surface missile – was without a doubt the weapon of choice, especially since both the Chinese submarine and the destroyer were operating so noisily. *Cheyenne* was able to determine their positions precisely and easily, something that was highly uncommon at this distance.

'Conn, sonar. Master 11 is bearing 013. Master 12 is bearing 002.' Master 11 was the Romeo-class submarine; Master 12 was the destroyer. Neither of them had any idea what was about to be sent their way.

Over the next ten minutes, the BSY-1 computers were able to determine rough ranges of forty-three nautical miles to Master 11, and forty-two nautical miles to Master 12. *Cheyenne* didn't need the actual range. As long as the targets were within reach of the Harpoons, it was the accurate bearings that counted.

Mack was pleased with the target acquisitions. 'Torpedo room,' he called from the conn. 'Remove the torpedoes and reload tubes two, three, and four with Harpoons. Leave an ADCAP in tube one.'

The response was immediate. 'Remove the torpedoes

and reload tubes two, three, and four with Harpoons, leave an ADCAP in tube one, aye, sir.'

Mack would have loved to shoot off all four of his Harpoon missiles, but that was cowboy tactics. The two known targets were making so much noise that he had to keep in mind the possibility that there was a third – and much more quiet – enemy in the area. He needed to keep one torpedo ready to shoot in case he ran into one of the remaining Han class attack submarines they knew about – or, worse, an enemy they didn't know about and weren't prepared for.

The Luda destroyer was the bigger target, and it was more mobile than the surfaced Romeo class submarine. Mack decided to target two Harpoons to the Luda and only one to the submarine. At his command, *Cheyenne* decreased speed and began to creep silently through the water.

'Tubes two, three, and four are loaded with Harpoons,' reported the combat system officer. *Cheyenne* was now ready to fire her missiles.

The UGM-84, the submarine-launched variant of the Harpoon, came 'wrapped' inside a buoyant capsule that was shaped to fit inside a torpedo tube. Upon firing, the UGM-84 would rise to the surface and, after ejecting the nose to the capsule, would ignite its rocket booster. Then, after dropping its booster, the Harpoon's turbojet engine would light off and the missile would accelerate on course toward its target. As the UGM-84 neared its target, the radar seeker head would switch on and the Harpoon would commence its final approach.

For this mission, Mack ordered each Harpoon programmed to make a 'pop-up' maneuver before attacking its target. This would confuse any antimissile systems the enemy destroyer might have onboard. *Cheyenne* was only going to have one easy launch window at these two Chinese vessels. Mack wanted to make sure that his shots counted.

'Firing point procedures,' Mack ordered, 'tube two, Master 11; tubes three and four, Master 12.'

He gave the order to fire the Harpoons two minutes later. They were launched to the surface by the weapons control console and the sonar man heard the rocket boosters ignite. 'Reload tubes two, three, and four with Mk 48s,' Mack commanded.

Flying at just under the speed of sound, the missiles found their marks in less than five minutes. This time it was the Chinese who never had a chance.

Three large explosions marked the success of *Cheyenne's* attack. The Romeo was hit first. The Harpoon came from its cruising altitude, performed its pop-up maneuver, and slammed into the top of the Romeo's afterdeck while the submarine was recharging on the surface. The Chinese navy had tried to save money by not repairing the damaged snorkel system. That decision cost them their submarine.

The missile's 510-pound high-explosive warhead detonated on impact, tearing a large hole in the hull and sending the force of its explosion down into the belly of the submarine. The thin steel hull burst apart, splitting the submarine into two pieces. Both halves quickly filled with water and sank, opposite ends first, into the sea.

Twelve seconds later, it was the destroyer's turn. The first missile hit its front end, directly under the 130mm gun. There was a horrific explosion and the entire fore section of the destroyer was bent in a downward direction, bringing a large amount of water into the ship. The second Harpoon hit the ship's bridge, killing the captain and all in its command center.

The 3,400-ton destroyer did not sink right away. It didn't break up quickly enough for that. It would be three long hours before it sank into the depths of the Pacific. Instead, it sat, dead in the water, a spreading pool of oil and diesel fuel marking what would become its watery grave.

Aboard *Cheyenne*, the captain and crew knew only that they should have hit their targets, but they had no way of determining how well the missiles had done their job. As soon as the Harpoons were launched, *Cheyenne* descended to 375 feet and immediately departed the area. If there were any other enemy vessels nearby, they would undoubtedly be looking for her at this very moment. Mack waited for nearly an hour before he secured from battle stations.

Cheyenne had done her job extremely well, Captain Mackey thought. Mack's grandfather had served in the 'Silent Service' of World War II, and Mack thought the old man would be very proud of their accomplishments, if only he were still alive.

Cheyenne was the newest operational attack submarine in the entire US submarine force. She had been on active duty for only a short while. But already she had been directly responsible for two kills of enemy submarines and one kill of an enemy destroyer. Mack didn't know it, but *Cheyenne* was well on her way to becoming one of the most decorated submarines of the entire Pacific Fleet.

• • •

Life aboard a submarine was often a lonely existence, in which sailors had little personal space and almost zero privacy. The newest sailors were often required to 'hot bunk' – sharing bunks on a rotating sleep schedule. As soon as one sailor rolled out of bed, another crewman would take his place in the same bunk. The uncomfortable feeling of climbing into an already warm bed gave rise to the term 'hot bunking.'

After their most recent encounter, however, life aboard *Cheyenne* was anything but lonely. Every sonar contact seemed to signal an enemy, every noise from their reactor or propulsion plant threatened to expose them to the Chinese, and every incoming communication held the promise of action. Running at twenty-six knots in the same 'sprint and drift' mode they had employed in their transit to Pearl, Mack wanted to reach *Independence* as quickly as was practically possible.

As time passed, however, with no further encounters, the tension levels on board gradually returned to normal, and before the crew realized it they were approaching the Celebes Sea. Once through this, they would have only the Sulu Sea between them and their rendezvous in the South China Sea.

Cheyenne had received word that *Independence* was on station and awaiting her arrival. Mack and his crew were currently a little over 1,200 miles from *Independence*'s location. At flank speed, *Cheyenne* could be there in a little over two days, but travelling that fast could prove to be too noisy. At the slower but safer twenty-six knots, running in sprint-and-drift mode, *Cheyenne* would still make her rendezvous in less than four days.

Midway through the Celebes Sea, Mack received an update. *Cheyenne* was instructed to use extreme caution once she passed through the Celebes and Sulu seas and into the South China Sea. Naval intelligence was reporting that mines might have been laid there, and they could pose a danger to *Cheyenne*.

That was news. China typically deployed coastal and moored contact minefields – technology that certainly wasn't obsolete, but which would not seriously threaten *Cheyenne*. Recent intelligence reports, however, indicated that the cash-strapped Russian military had sold the Chinese an unconfirmed number of 'Cluster Bay' and 'Cluster Gulf' antisubmarine mines, the latter of which could be used in 2,000 meters of seawater. That meant that *Cheyenne* would have to be on guard against the older, less advanced mines, and they would also have to watch out for the very real possibility that they might 'come into contact' with these deep-water mines as well.

Mack was not pleased with this news, and he liked the next bit of intelligence even less. An extremely large Chinese surface and submarine fleet was currently forming, and naval intelligence expected them to leave Guang-zhou Naval Base sometime within the next thirty-six hours. Naval intelligence assumed – and Mack agreed – that the Chinese force's mission most probably consisted of two parts: hunting for any US naval vessels in the area and, more specifically and more immediately, attempting to sink the US Carrier *Independence*.

Once they reached the eastern entrance to the Sulu Sea, Mack cut *Cheyenne*'s speed to ten knots. She would travel through the Sulu Sea slowly and quietly until she reached the Balabac Strait, south of the relatively tiny island of Palawan. That would be her last opportunity to listen care-fully before entering hostile waters.

As planned, *Cheyenne* stayed slow and listened for any danger signs before entering the South China Sea to her southwest. The recently invaded Spratly Islands lay several hundred nautical miles away in the center of the South China Sea. These were reportedly heavily guarded by a large Chinese contingent intended to prevent another invasion of the islands.

After *Cheyenne* passed silently into the South China Sea, Mack ordered, 'Deploy the TB-23,' calling for his crew to stream their passive 'thin-line' towed-array.

Designed to detect very low-frequency noise at long dis-tances, the TB-23 was one of the newest additions to the improved Los Angeles class submarines. *Cheyenne* was also one of the first submarines to receive this new system.

The TB-23, which was reeled into the submarine's main ballast tank instead of being housed internally and running down the side of the pressure hull like the TB-16, was so long that even with *Cheyenne* running at twenty knots, she would still be able to detect distant sonar contacts.

The towed-array worked beautifully, and its dozens of hydrophones detected more sounds than the submarine's computers often knew what to do with. Everything from large fish to fishing trawlers had been detected on their submarine's TB-23 since their abbreviated shakedown cruise and they were now very confident in its operation.

Almost immediately, the TB-23 detected a large number of contacts. Distance was hard to gauge with the TB-23; the signals it picked up could be coming through a convergence zone, and without the sea room to maneuver very much, precision bearings and ranges were very difficult.

From the initial detections, Mack guessed that these contacts were from surface contacts very far away – over 100 miles. If he was lucky, these tonals would turn out to be from the Chinese task group sent to attack the *Independence* Carrier Battle Group that had entered the South China Sea south of Borneo.

Creeping along at five knots in a westerly direction, Mack took *Cheyenne* farther into the South China Sea.

The TB-23's detections were correct, and so was Mack's guess. The contacts *were* the Chinese task group, and it was very large indeed. It consisted of seven fast attack craft, four Jianghu class frigates, three Ming class attack submarines, and two Romeo submarines. The Chinese task group had two primary missions to accomplish: mine the South China Sea and sink *Independence*.

American carriers had been a thorn in the Chinese government's side since the very beginning of this conflict. They had lost their first Han class submarine to a US submarine accompanying *Nimitz*, but *Nimitz* herself was not currently a target. She waited outside the South China Sea, just south of Taiwan, ready to enter if the need arose. The danger of mines in the South China Sea was a serious one and was one of the major reasons that *Nimitz* waited out of harm's way, at least for the time being. But the aircraft carrier *Independence* (CV-62) had now been in the South China Sea for over one month, and for the Chinese she was a big, attractive, and highly desirable target. After laying their mines, the Chinese task group headed directly toward *Independence*.

With the aid of overhead imagery, US naval intelligence quickly guessed the Chinese task group's mission, but they had no immediate way to inform *Cheyenne*. Since ELF coverage in the South China Sea was sporadic, the submarine was essentially out of contact until she came shallow enough for the floating wire to be able to copy traffic.

At 1000 hours on the day after entering the South China Sea, *Cheyenne*'s floating wire antenna reached close to the surface and stayed there just long enough to copy recent traffic. An S-3 from *Independence* relayed the latest intelligence on this rather large Chinese surface and submarine group. The message relayed through the ASWC (anti-submarine warfare commander) to CTF 74 – Commander Task Force 74, also known as Commander Submarine Group 7, located in Yokosuka, Japan, also included *Cheyenne*'s new orders.

Cheyenne was instructed to pass silently near the Chinese task group and find out exactly how many submarines were operating in cooperation with this group.

Most Chinese surface vessels had only a limited ASW (anti-submarine warfare) capability, and so the main threat to *Cheyenne* would come in the form of attack submarines and maritime patrol aircraft such as the Chinese versions of the Russian Il-28 Beagle known as the Harbin H-5. These aircraft carried bombs and torpedoes, and could pose a serious threat to *Cheyenne*. Captain Mackey was counting on *Independence*'s F-14s to handle at least some of these aircraft.

In addition, there was also a shorter-range threat from Chinese helicopters that many of their surface combatants carried on board. Similar in concept to the American LAMPS program, the Chinese had dozens of Chinese models of the French Dauphin helicopter equipped for ASW operations. Once *Cheyenne* got close to the surface fleet, she would have to be extremely cautious.

Cheyenne picked up speed in order reach her objective. The Chinese fleet could only move as fast as their slowest vessels, and their overall speed was less than ten knots. They were currently positioned a little over six hundred miles away from the American Carrier Battle Group, just at the edge of the *Independence*'s aircraft range, but outside of normal CAP (Combat Air Patrol) search sectors. *Cheyenne* was seventy-five miles east of the Chinese task group.

After a brief run at 12 knots, *Cheyenne* cut this distance to less than fifty miles. Then the fleet of enemy warships slowed even further. At first glance, it appeared that one of their destroyers was having trouble with its power plant and, wanting to keep the fleet together, they had all stopped. But Mack wasn't fooled. What the Chinese were doing was laying mines.

Their intent, as Mack saw it, was to lay a minefield in case one of the nations that claimed the Spratlys attempted to invade them. In fact, Mack was willing to bet that all available Chinese naval vessels were now tasked with laying mines at every access to the South China Sea.

Mack figured that after seeing the disastrous loss the Iraqis suffered in the 1991 Persian Gulf War, the Chinese had realized that the only way to defeat the American Navy was by the use of naval mines. This was the American weakness, and the South China Sea – China's home waters – would be where they would exploit it.

Within an hour, the Chinese task group had come to a complete halt, but that didn't bother Mack at all. The stoppage of the Chinese fleet allowed *Cheyenne* to close the remaining distance quickly.

Half an hour later, with battle stations manned, Mack was within range to attack the closest vessel in the fleet, a lone Romeo class submarine that had wandered to the east, away from the group, in an attempt to detect possible enemy operations. As *Cheyenne* crept closer to the group, at a cautious speed of four-and-a-half knots, it was clear that the Romeo was not aware of her silent presence.

'Conn, sonar, we now have five submarine contacts, all diesels on the surface, operating with this group,' the sonar supervisor advised the captain. 'It looks as if they have three Mings and two Romeos. I think the submarines are patrolling the area while the surface vessels lay their mines.'

Mack acknowledged the report and ordered the Mings designated Masters 15, 16, and 17, and the Romeos designated Masters 18 and 19. His assessment of the situation matched that of the sonar supervisor.

As *Cheyenne* closed on the Chinese task group, Mack was faced with the difficult decision of whether or not he should attack any units in this enemy force. His orders had been to find out how many submarines were operating with this group. He had done that. His obligation now was to convey that information to *Independence*, but with that first Romeo, Master 18, sitting solidly on his track, Mack's instinct was to blow that Chinese submarine out of the water.

Mack shook his head and let the Romeo slip away. He had something better in mind. What *Cheyenne* would do, he decided, was to wait until she had passed outside the range of the Romeo. Then she would use her Mk 48s to attack one of the Jianghu frigates and one of the Ming submarines, since the Ming was the better of the two submarine classes. *Cheyenne* would then race away and silently head for *Independence*.

That was Mack's plan. No battle plan, however, he reminded himself, survives first contact with the enemy.

He got his chance to test that maxim exactly ninety-three minutes later. *Cheyenne* had reached the outer ring of the rest of the submarines, and the only danger to her now was the ASW helicopters that might be patrolling the area.

The submarine and frigate Mack had targeted were operating within three thousand yards of each other. This would be a perfect Mk 48 shot. He had decided to target the Ming submarine, Master 15, first, and the Jianghu frigate, Master 20, second, because the Ming posed a more serious threat to *Cheyenne*.

Mack announced firing point procedures for an attack on the Ming, Master 15. 'Make tubes one and two ready in all respects, including opening the outer doors!'

Confirmation of his command was almost immediate. Tubes one and two were ready, with their outer doors open.

'Match bearings and shoot, tubes one and two, Master 15.'

Again, confirmation was almost immediate. The first torpedoes were away.

'Cut the wires, shut the outer doors, and reload tubes one and two,' Mack ordered, his voice brisk and efficient.

With their wires cut, the Mk 48s would have to find their target without the help of their guidance wires, but they were close enough to their target that they were virtually certain of acquiring.

Mack put the first two torpedoes out of his mind. They were gone and on their own, and would fail or succeed without his help. Now he had to worry about their next target.

'Make tubes three and four ready in all respects, including opening the outer doors,' he said, beginning the procedure once again. Within moments, the second pair of Mk 48s was headed straight for Master 20, the 1,500-ton frigate.

Aboard the Ming submarine there was little time for reaction. The Chinese captain ordered flank speed in the opposite direction of the torpedoes, but the two Mk 48s continued to close the gap.

The Ming reached its maximum speed quickly, but it simply did not have the ability to outrun the speeding ADCAP torpedoes, cutting through the water at over fifty knots.

The frigate was encountering a similar type of panic. Its first reaction was to begin dropping ASW mortars into the water in an attempt to throw the torpedoes off course.

These mortars, which carried the designation RBU 1200,

were unguided but still dangerous. They essentially threw small bombs out to a range of slightly more than 1,200 yards. Since each mortar 'shell' carried seventy-five pounds of explosive, their effects were spread out over a large area. There was always the danger that the explosion might damage *Cheyenne*, even though she was out of their direct range and path.

'Rig ship for depth charge,' Mack ordered.

The mortars were a bad idea. Their explosions did not reach *Cheyenne* – in fact, they posed a greater risk to the Ming patrolling closer to the frigate. What's more, rather than harming *Cheyenne*, they actually helped her. With the loud explosions masking all other sounds – including preventing *Cheyenne* from learning whether her torpedoes had found their marks – Mack ordered flank speed as he turned to run from the Chinese task group.

Two hours later, with *Cheyenne* clear of the area and out of danger, her floating wire confirmed that her presence in the area was no longer a secret – but she had announced herself in fine fashion. Three of her four torpedoes had hit their targets, costing the Chinese a frigate and a Ming class submarine.

Along with this information came *Cheyenne*'s previous orders: continue with the rendezvous with *Independence*, still some six hundred miles from *Cheyenne*'s current position.

Mack was pleased with both the intelligence and the orders, but he knew that they'd have to be even more cautious from now on. *Cheyenne* was no longer a secret, and she was wearing the enemy's blood. Every available Chinese ASW asset would be hunting for *Cheyenne* and attempting to kill her.

But they'd have to find her first, and then they'd have to catch her. And *Cheyenne* ran fast. Her mission was now to reach *Independence* – which, at her current speed of twenty-five knots, and allowing for the sprint-and-drift technique, would take about fifteen hours.

Mack secured from battle stations and the rig for depth charge, and then settled in for the transit to *Independence*.

With *Cheyenne* running at twenty-five knots four hundred feet beneath the surface of the South China Sea, Mack had time to wonder about his decision to attack the Chinese frigate and submarine. Had he been too aggressive? The captain suddenly felt both guilt and vulnerability for attacking the task group. There had been other, more stealthy alternatives, and perhaps he should have taken them.

This was one of the dangers of post-action letdown. Too many people used that time to play the 'what if?' game and to second-guess their own decisions. *What if* Cheyenne *had been damaged?* he thought to himself. After all, his main objective was to reach *Independence* safely, not attack enemy warships. *Independence* could easily have handled that task group herself.

In addition to the risk of the encounter, Mack knew that he had cost *Cheyenne* the element of surprise. She was known, now, and being hunted. Perhaps it would have been a better idea to silently drift alongside the Chinese task group, obtain the required intelligence, and then head for the carrier.

These questions troubled him as he prepared to proceed to periscope depth to get information concerning *Independence*.

'Conn, sonar,' the sonar supervisor reported, 'the towed-array picked up a helicopter overhead. We can tell it's a helo because of the high turbine rpm.'

Hearing this, Mack ordered an immediate excursion to 325 feet. He soon heard the ping of the helicopter's active dipping sonar through *Cheyenne*'s hull, and the sound sent chills up his spine. He began to worry, once again, about the wisdom of his earlier decision to attack the Chinese task group.

'Conn, sonar, we just detected a submarine on the surface. It's beginning to submerge!'

Mack remanned battle stations. The atmosphere in the sonar room grew very tense as everyone waited for the next contact evaluation. It wasn't long in coming, and it wasn't good news.

'Conn, sonar, we've got another contact,' reported the sonar supervisor. 'This one sounds like a Romeo. It must have been waiting for us, playing dead in the water, because we didn't hear it before the active sonar from that helo.'

Sonar designated the helo as sonar contact Sierra 179. Mack designated the Romeo as Master 21.

Antisubmarine helicopters were always a danger. They were hard for submarines to detect, and their dipping sonars and sonobuoys could provide enemy forces with valuable data on the location of *Cheyenne*. And that was exactly what this one seemed to be doing.

And if the helicopter was within its torpedo range, Mack realized, they could also drop a torpedo in the water. *That would definitely ruin our day*, he thought.

'Range to the Romeo, Master 21, is seventeen thousand yards, bearing 025,' the fire-control coordinator reported.

'Sonar, conn, what's the classification on the one that just submerged?' Mack asked.

'Conn, sonar, it sounds like another Romeo. It sounds closer, bearing 027, sir. Designate Master 22?'

The BSY-1 operators quickly determined that two enemy submarines were five thousand yards from one another. *Cheyenne*, it turned out, was on a bearing directly between them, the reciprocal bearing 206 if they detected her.

At that moment, the helicopter's dipping sonar was active again, and this time it was directly overhead.

Mack smiled. That helo pilot had just done them a favor. The two Chinese submarines may have already acquired *Cheyenne* – which meant that the latest 'ping' didn't help them at all. But the sound energy reflecting off their hulls into *Cheyenne*'s waiting sonars and the BSY-1 computers gave her accurate firing solutions for both Romeo class submarines.

'Make tubes one and two ready in all respects,' Mack ordered. 'Open the outer doors. Firing point procedures, tube one, Master 21, and tube two, Master 22.' Mack wanted the first torpedo going after the closer submarine and the second torpedo aimed at the other.

His orders were confirmed quickly and efficiently.

'Match sonar bearings and shoot, tube one, Master 21 and tube two, Master 22,' he ordered.

'Match bearings and shoot, tube one, Master 21, and tube two, Master 22, aye, Captain.'

Both torpedoes quickly acquired.

Mack acknowledged the reports. 'Now, let's get the hell out of here before we get attacked by that helo. Cut the wires, shut the outer doors, and reload tubes one and two. Ahead flank, right full rudder, make your depth 800 feet, steady on course 180.' Mack was calm as the directed commands were repeated by the persons intended for them. *Cheyenne* had become a fine-tuned fighting machine. Each man knew what was expected of him.

Above them, high in the sky, a lone F-14 flying from the aircraft carrier *Independence* saw the target blip on its radar long before the Chinese helicopter had any idea what was about to happen. With permission of the flag watch officer aboard *Independence*, the 000–045 sector F-14 pilot was allowed to advance his sector since he had radar contact on the Chinese helo that was harassing *Cheyenne*. After he cut in his afterburners and approached the target at supersonic speed, permission to fire was passed from the TAO (tactical action officer). With a thumb push on the pickle, the pilot reported 'Phoenix 1 away.'

Behind him, in the backseat, his RIO (radar intercept officer), who had done all the targeting work, said, 'Phoenix is locked on. That submarine captain sure owes us one.'

Aboard *Cheyenne*, the sonar supervisor couldn't explain his latest detections to Mack. 'Conn, sonar,' he said, 'the helicopter, the one above our position . . . I think she just crashed! Something fell in the water and the TB-23 is not picking up any helo turbine noise anymore.'

'I guess we just broke Murphy's law,' Mack replied, his voice as calm and efficient as ever.

Mack had decided not to designate the helo with a Master number. He would leave that to the aviators. However, the helo would find itself in the history of submarine warfare, in Mack's patrol report, by virtue of *Cheyenne*'s 'Sierra' designation assigned to the helo as one of *Cheyenne*'s many sonar contacts.

The remainder of their transit into the southern end of the South China Sea proved, to the delight of both the captain and the crew, to be entirely uneventful. Mack had not realized how enjoyable an uneventful stretch of time could be when the alternative was someone shooting at his submarine.

When they met up with *Independence* northwest of Natuna Island, Mack and his crew learned that both Mk 48s had found their marks and the Chinese were now down another two submarines. Mack had also discovered the true story behind the 'crash' of their Chinese helo.

Mack sent a message to the SEC (submarine element coordinator) on board *Independence*, requesting a special 'thank-you' for the F-14 pilot – a thank-you that, whenever they got a chance to get ashore to buy one, would include a very nice bottle of wine.

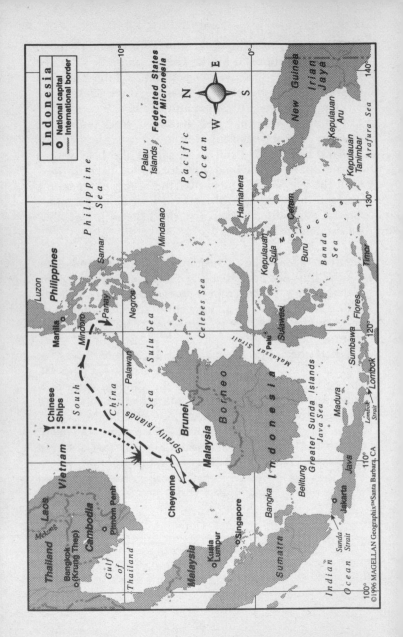

THREE

Four if by Sea, Six if by Land

'Come to periscope depth,' Mack said. 'I want to have a quick look around before proceeding.'

Cheyenne moved slowly from her current depth of three hundred feet beneath the surface of the South China Sea, pausing at one hundred thirty feet to clear baffles. When the sonar supervisor reported no contacts to the OOD, *Cheyenne* completed her excursion to fifty-nine feet. Before arriving, the OOD, Mack, and the crew members who were trying to eat could feel the effects of the sea state.

Mack had raised the Type 18 periscope while the OOD rode the leaner, less detectable, Type 2 attack periscope. Two sets of eyes were better than one, especially since the sea state could easily mask quiet surface contacts. Once they were near ordered depth, the tops of both periscopes were intermittently awash in the four-foot swells, which were frequently topped with significantly higher waves.

In order not to broach, *Cheyenne* had to take the swells, caused by a distant storm, no more than forty-five degrees forward of the beam. Otherwise, she would have a tendency to pitch with a ten-second period due to the ninety-foot wavelength of sea state four. Pitching up or down with *Cheyenne*'s forward momentum could result in an uncontrollable angle, causing either the sail to be exposed during an up angle or the stern to be exposed during a down angle. Exposing the stern was more dangerous because the seven blades of *Cheyenne*'s screw would pass through the air-water interface, causing unwanted high-torque jolting of the shaft as each exposed blade once again encountered the water. The weather on the surface was terrible, with violent thunderstorms breaking over the entire region. The power and majesty of the storms were breathtaking, but Mack found himself thinking more about how much they might be affecting flight operations on board *Independence*. He knew how much bad weather could degrade surface ship operations. That was just one of the many reasons he loved working far beneath the turbulent surface. Unlike their surface counterparts – and especially pilots and land-based soldiers – submariners were rarely affected by the weather, except when they needed to go to periscope depth.

On behalf of the crew, Mack decided to keep the time at periscope depth to a minimum. After copying the SSIXS broadcast and verifying that there were no surface contacts in the vicinity, Mack ordered the OOD to proceed deep beneath the storm, which unfortunately had eroded the first thermal layer, causing an isotherm (constant temperature) from the surface to over six hundred feet.

Six hours earlier, *Cheyenne* had arrived safely at her rendezvous point with the carrier *Independence* one hundred miles northwest of Natuna Island. The entire *Independence* Battle Group was now heading in the direction of the Spratly Islands. *Cheyenne*'s current assignment was to patrol the nearby waters in search of any enemy submarines that might try to sneak up on the Battle Group.

In a way, *Cheyenne* was operating like a fighter pilot assigned to air cover. She was *Independence*'s first line of ASW defense, 130 miles ahead where the noise of the Battle Group's ships would not degrade *Cheyenne*'s sonars, and where the F-14s from *Independence* could, in better weather, provide about a ten-hour heads-up to *Cheyenne* on approaching surface targets.

Mack was looking forward to the escort duty, a chance

to be the SSN(DS) (direct support) for which the Los Angeles class was originally built. Not only would it be a nice change of pace but, more important, it meant he could have assistance from the carrier if and when he needed it.

The only problem was that *Cheyenne* was alone. Instead of sharing the 180 sector forward of the Battle Group with two other SSNs, Mack had it all. That was fine for the prevention of mutual interference, especially in a shooting war, but it was an impossibly large area of responsibility for a single SSN.

Independence was the last active member of the Forrestal class of aircraft carriers. These vessels, the first real 'super-carriers,' were built during the 1950s. By 1997 they all had been decommissioned except *Independence*. At one point, there had been plans to turn 'Indy's' sister ship, *Forrestal*, into a training carrier, but those plans had been scrapped due to budget cuts. *Independence* herself had been scheduled for decommissioning in October of this year, but Mack suspected that this war might change things.

All aircraft carriers' strength lay with their aircraft, and CV-62 was no exception. *Independence*'s aircraft were as good or better than any combat aircraft in the world. Her current complement of aircraft included twenty F-14 Tomcats for long range interceptor missions. With their new precision strike capability, the F-14s were sometimes referred to as the 'bomb cat.' *Independence* also carried F/A-18 Hornets, which were perhaps the best dual-capable (fighter/attack) aircraft in the world. The *Independence* air wing commander, now an aviator O-6 major command billet, could use them to defend the carrier or to attack far-off targets on land or at sea. Also on board were four E-2C Hawkeyes and four EA-6B Prowlers. The Hawkeyes were early warning planes and each one carried the APS-145 radar in a large disk connected to the top of its fuselage. The Prowlers specialized in radar jamming and other forms of electronic warfare.

Perhaps her most valuable aircraft, at least as far as Mack was concerned, were the S-3B Vikings, the submariner's favorite. This was one of the world's great aircraft designs, combining an extremely long range and an excellent ability to hunt 'enemy' submarines. During several exercise encounters with S-3s, Mack had learned to respect them greatly, and he was glad that they were on his side.

The only aircraft that could possibly compete with the Viking was the SH-60 Seahawk helicopter. It lacked the range of the S-3, but *Cheyenne* had seen for herself just how effective the Seahawks could be. This was the aircraft that had earlier destroyed the Chinese Han submarine while *Cheyenne* tracked their actions by sonar, and *Independence* carried six of them. Because of her immediate locality to the war zone and the risk from Chinese submarines, *Independence* had been designated as the test ship for the new SH-60Rs – the newest type of Seahawk. This was the first to carry both the new airborne low-frequency dipping sonar, usually referred to as ALFS, and sonobuoys. It also had two torpedoes on board – either the powerful Mk 50 or the older Mk 46. These factors combined to make the SH-60R the most dangerous short-range ASW platform hovering over the seas.

Even with all this firepower on board, the carrier still had her serious vulnerabilities. She needed to be escorted by surface vessels, and her entire group was vulnerable to modern enemy submarines. And that was where *Cheyenne* came into play. She would act as an advance party for *Independence*, proceeding well ahead of the Battle Group and either clearing a safe path or warning them of possible dangers that the F-14 radars couldn't detect. This combination of surface ships, aircraft, and submarines resulted in what Mack referred to as 'synergism,' where the end result of operating together would be far more devastating to the Chinese than if each warfare community operated alone.

Unmindful of the weather, the *Independence* Battle Group

got under way, steaming northward in the direction of the Spratlys. Travelling at flank speed, *Cheyenne* executed a quick sprint to regain her station in front of the Battle Group. If Mack fell behind the trailing edge of his moving search sector, *Cheyenne* would be free game, the so-called friendly fire problem that was a sad reality of warfare. When she was near the leading edge of her moving haven slightly over an hour later, *Cheyenne* slowed and waited.

After slowing, Mack ordered the OOD to deploy the TB-23 towed array for its long-range tonal-detection capability. The report came back exactly as he'd hoped – no contacts on the towed array. The sonar room watch standers watched their consoles and waited for Mack's next orders.

'Officer of the deck, prepare to come to periscope depth,' Captain Mackey ordered. Mack wanted to relay information about the safety of their route back to the *Independence* Battle Group.

'Prepare to come to periscope depth, aye, sir,' the OOD replied.

But Mack didn't get the chance to report to *Independence*. Before *Cheyenne* came shallow enough to transmit, she began to receive message traffic over the floating wire.

'Sir,' the communicator reported, 'it looks like we just got new orders!'

Mack went to the radio room, grabbed the sheet of printer paper, and quickly read the message.

'Looks like a strike mission to me,' the communicator said, with a note of eagerness and brashness. 'What do you think, sir?'

That annoyed Mack. It was a breach of protocol, and not smart. He looked at the communicator and shook his head. 'Call a meeting in the wardroom in ten minutes,' he said, putting an edge in his tone. 'I want the executive officer, the combat systems officer, the operations officer, and yourself there.'

The communicator knew he'd screwed up. 'Ten minutes, in the wardroom, aye, sir,' he said. The cocky note was gone from his voice.

Cheyenne returned to a patrol depth of 247 feet since the first thermal layer was gone, and within eight minutes all requested officers were waiting for Captain Mackey to arrive in *Cheyenne*'s wardroom. Mack came in five minutes late. He carried a plain manila folder in his hand.

'Gentlemen,' he said. 'I have called this meeting in order to pass on our new orders. From our present position in the South China Sea, we are to proceed to the north of the Chinese-held Spratly Islands. Once there, three hundred miles north, we will launch six Tomahawk land-attack missiles at the Chinese submarine base which has recently been set up near Cuarteron Reef, one of the islands in the Spratly chain.'

He paused to see how the others would react. He was pleased to see that, while there was some tension, it was mostly excitement, with only a touch of healthy caution. He was also pleased that the communicator kept his mouth shut.

'As you all know,' Mack continued, 'naval intelligence has reported large numbers of Chinese submarines operating in this area. We've confirmed this with our own detections. Our new orders are to do something about that.' He paused again, making sure that everyone was paying full attention. 'We are going to enter the belly of the beast,' he said. 'We will launch our Tomahawks as ordered, and then we will meet up with the submarine tender USS *McKee* in order to rearm.' He grinned and added, 'Maybe we'll even get a quick glimpse of life on the surface.'

His lighthearted joke helped to ease the tension slightly. The assembled officers had a few questions. They discussed their options, and then Mack dismissed them to return to their duties. When he had returned to the conn, he used the 1MC to inform the crew of their new mission. From there on out, *Cheyenne* would use sound-powered phones instead of general announcing systems.

Forty-five minutes later *Cheyenne* once again went to periscope depth. The seas had abated somewhat, but copying SSIXS required the use of the long, multipurpose communications mast to preclude the loss of synch caused by waves slapping over the Type 18 periscope communications antenna.

Mack stayed at that depth just long enough to receive preliminary Tomahawk targeting data. This information, which they would confirm when they got closer to their launch position, would be fed to their cruise missiles prior to launching the Tomahawks. Mack hoped the weather would be better north of the Spratlys.

When the data transfer was complete, *Cheyenne* detached from the *Independence* Battle Group without report and proceeded on her own. Mack had enjoyed having the carrier nearby for backup and air defense, but now *Cheyenne* was going back to doing what she did best: operating on her own, sneaking up on the enemy, and blowing them to hell.

Three hundred fifty miles southwest of Cuarteron Reef, running at four hundred twenty-five feet, *Cheyenne* picked up her first contact. Mack was in the sonar room.

'Captain,' the sonar supervisor reported, 'we have a sonar contact bearing 020 on the spherical array. The contact's intermittent, so I think we're receiving the sound source via a convergence zone. We pick her up loud and clear, then we lose her and don't hear anything for a while.'

While normal sound traveled through water in waves that gave at least some predictability, there were some areas in which sound waves were turned up toward the surface and then often bounced back into the sea. These were called convergence zones, and they could allow sonar to detect these sound waves at far greater ranges than would otherwise be possible. If the water was deep enough and the sound velocity excess was present at depth, these zones commonly occurred about every thirty miles. In a way, the ray paths of the acoustic energy were much like AM radio transmissions, which could travel in a straight line, then bounce off the ground and up into the atmosphere, and then come back to earth. This allowed AM frequencies to broadcast much farther than FM, though beyond their immediate range they could be picked up only in pockets and were more affected by weather.

'My guess,' the sonar supervisor added, 'is that it's in the second convergence zone from us.' That would put the signal's source at a range of more than sixty nautical miles, or 120,000 yards.

'Keep an eye on that contact,' Mack said. If the sonar supervisor was right and *Cheyenne*'s operators had indeed heard their sonar contact through a convergence zone, then the signal's source was far out of *Cheyenne*'s weapons range. It also meant that the thermal gradients in the deeper waters of the South China Sea had not been eroded by the storms. But if the sonar supervisor was wrong, *Cheyenne* could be in for some very dangerous close combat.

Sixty-three miles away, 200 feet below the surface of the South China Sea, crept one of the newest additions to the Chinese fleet, and one of China's best submarine captains. The Chinese Kilo submarine had been in service for less than two years and had made its crew very proud.

The first Chinese Kilo submarines had been bought from Russia in 1993 and delivered in February 1995. The Chinese had planned to buy up to fifteen of these powerful diesel submarines and had hoped that they would be able to build five more themselves, under license from Russia.

This particular submarine had excellent equipment, with the exception of her passive sonar outfit. That was the problem with all Russian submarines, as its captain knew. The Russians could not make a decent passive submarine sonar – at least not one that his country would be allowed to buy.

And that was a problem. At any given moment, there might be an American Los Angeles class submarine sneaking up on his position, and he would never know it until it was too late.

The captain of the Chinese submarine wasn't too worried about it, though. His was the lead ship of three. Below the waves, his Kilo was working in tandem with an older Romeo class diesel submarine. Above them, *Jinan*, a Luda class destroyer, patrolled the surface. Their mission was to hunt down and destroy any American ships and submarines. In addition, there was another Kilo well off to the side – not part of his task force, but it could provide assistance if he needed it.

The captain of the Kilo welcomed *Jinan* more than he did the Romeo. For one thing, the destroyer's two turbines were loud, which would hopefully distract any enemy's sonar from any noises his Kilo might make. Even more important, however, *Jinan*, like all Luda type II destroyers, carried two French ASW helicopters. Those would be very useful if the Kilo needed help while engaging an American submarine.

As pleased as the Kilo's captain was with the surface ship, he was equally displeased with the Romeo. It was an old attack submarine that had been reactivated from the naval reserve, and, in his opinion, it was more of a threat to his own submarine than it was to the enemy. It was too noisy, for one thing. That could be desirable when the noise came from the surface, but down below it would only serve to alert the Americans to the presence of one or more Chinese submarines in the area.

Worse, the farther he tried to get from the Romeo, the more it tried to stay close to him. The Romeo captain was no fool. He knew he stood a better chance under the protection of the Kilo than he did on his own.

Assuming, that is, that the Kilo captain didn't sink the Romeo himself.

Back on board *Cheyenne*, sonar was trying to reacquire contact. Mack had gone back to 247 feet to continue the search, while at the same time maintaining copy over the floating wire.

In the control room, Mack was looking at the BSY-1 fire-control console, which he liked to keep online for himself. 'Sonar, conn, have you regained contact on Master 24?'

'Conn, sonar, we're working on a possible contact,' the sonar supervisor said, 'but I'm not sure it's the same convergence zone one. This one may be a surface ship. Master 24 was tentatively classified as a submerged submarine.'

Several minutes later, the sonar supervisor reported that he had not one contact, but two, one Romeo submarine and one Luda destroyer, both bearing 020. They were both given new Master Numbers, designated Masters 25 and 26 respectively, since the sonar supervisor was not sure if either one was Master 24. Reconstruction would have to sort it out later. Without hesitating, the OOD ordered his section fire-control tracking party manned. Mack went to the sonar room.

'Good job,' Mack said, unaware that they had failed to detect the Kilo that was in the area of Masters 25 and 26. 'Anything else out there?'

'Not that we can tell yet, Captain,' the sonar supervisor said, 'but those two contacts are loud. We can hear them aurally, so there could be more ships operating in the area.'

Mack left the sonar room and went back to the control room. The BSY-1 operators had a rough solution on range, about 30,000 yards.

At *Cheyenne*'s current speed of ten knots, Mack would soon be within range to launch his Mk 48 ADCAPs at the Chinese contacts. When he got closer, he would slow. No need as yet for long-range shots. *Cheyenne* was currently running with the TB-23 towed-array fully deployed and, with the OOD's maneuvers, the section fire-control tracking party at the BSY-1 computers was getting better and better solutions on the Chinese destroyer and submarine.

'Conn, sonar, the TB-23 just picked up a helicopter overhead,' the sonar supervisor announced. 'Probably flying from the Chinese destroyer.'

'Take her down fast, to five hundred feet!' Mack ordered the OOD. This was another helo 'Sierra' addition to his patrol report.

Throughout *Cheyenne*, sailors grabbed for whatever they could as the submarine headed down at standard speed with a twenty-degree down angle. The diving officer, helmsman, and planesman had all buckled their seat belts as soon as they heard 'take her down fast.'

Above them, the Chinese Z-9A helo hovered and began to lower its powerful French HS-12 dipping sonar via the hydraulic winch. The winch was touted to be 'high speed,' but it didn't seem fast enough for the helo pilot as it slowly lowered the HS-12 toward the water.

'Conn, sonar, we just received a sonar pulse from the helicopter's dipping sonar. It's a French type, HS-12 – the same kind they sold to China. The transmission came from the opposite direction of the Romeo. I don't think they could have detected us, sir. Signal level of the pulse was low.' Which probably meant the helo was quite a ways off or else it hadn't dipped its sonar beneath the layer.

Mack acknowledged for the OOD. 'Very well, sonar, we have it out here on the WLR-9 as well,' he said. 'Were we able to pick up any other information from the transmission?'

'Sonar, conn, negative,' the sonar supervisor answered. 'It wasn't a very strong pulse. Let's hope she ran out of batteries.'

Mack smiled at the joke. Unlike the communicator's earlier gaffe, this comment was well timed, and helped to ease the tension slightly.

One hour and fifteen minutes later *Cheyenne* had closed to within 20,000 yards of her targets, Masters 25 and 26. Mack ordered battle stations manned.

A few minutes later the helo was active again. The WLR-9's acoustic intercept receiver at the conn picked that one up also, even though it was near the baffles.

'Conn, sonar, that was a loud one, sir,' the sonar supervisor said.

Mack smiled. 'She must have recharged,' he said, in a deadpan voice. 'Designate the helo Master 27.'

'Conn, sonar, she got us on that one, sir – but that's not all she painted! Captain, we've got another submarine out there, a Kilo class, one six-bladed screw, making turns for ten knots. It's bearing 025, near the same bearing as the Romeo. It's been hiding from us all this time.'

All humor was gone from the conn. Considering their situation, Mack was pleased with how well his officers and crew were handling the sudden tension. Not aware they had regained old Master 24, the Kilo was designated Master 28.

Cheyenne had just been pinged on by a directly overhead Chinese ASW helicopter, which had undoubtedly received an exact fix on their present location five hundred feet below the surface. The helo would now probably be making an MAD (magnetic anomaly detection) pass to confirm *Cheyenne*'s position. Mack was concerned that they would follow that up by dropping a torpedo directly on top of *Cheyenne*.

'Conn, sonar, the Kilo, Master 28, just picked up speed. It's heading directly at us, making turns for seventeen knots. It must suspect that the helo gave their position away.'

'What's the range to the Kilo?' Mack asked the fire-control coordinator.

'Twenty-four thousand yards, Captain. We're within ADCAP range for the Kilo – it's making lots of noise at seventeen knots. Recommend making tubes one and two ready.'

Mack nodded and initiated firing point procedures on Master 28. 'Torpedo room, fire control, make tubes one and two ready in all respects. Open the outer doors.'

The order was acknowledged. One minute later it was confirmed. 'Tubes one and two are ready in all respects, sir. Outer doors have been opened.'

'Sonar, conn, stand by.'

'Conn, sonar, standing by.'

'Match sonar bearings and shoot tube one, Master 28.'

'Match sonar bearings and shoot tube one, Master 28, aye, sir.'

Mack then came right to clear the datum.

'Tube one fired electrically,' the combat system officer reported. That was as far as he got. Before he could report on the torpedo's status, the sonar supervisor spoke up.

'Conn, sonar, torpedo in the water bearing 180! It's a Chinese Mk 46 copy, Mod 2.' Mack had been correct in assigning the helo a Master number, which were usually reserved for potential threats to *Cheyenne* herself, or to targets of significant intelligence value.

'Cut the wire and shut the outer door,' ordered the captain. 'Reload tube one.' Mack was throwing away his torpedo, and he knew it. The Kilo was too far away and maneuvering. The Mk 48 would probably not be able to acquire on its own, but right now Mack had a different torpedo to worry about.

'Left full rudder, all ahead flank, steady course 305,'

Mack ordered. 'Cavitate. Make your depth 750 feet.' He waited for acknowledgment and then added, 'Rig ship for depth charge.'

Cheyenne's power plant was now running at peak capacity in an attempt to get away from the deadly torpedo racing their way.

'Conn, sonar, another torpedo in the water. Master 27 just dropped a second Mk 46 on us, bearing 245.'

'Release a noisemaker,' Mack ordered.

Confirmation was quick. 'Noisemaker away.'

Cheyenne's top speed was nearly forty knots. The two torpedoes chasing her were knifing through the water at forty knots, but Mack wasn't worried. Not yet, anyway. Sonar reported the Chinese torpedoes bearing 268 and bearing 187. If Mack maintained his course and speed, the torpedoes would both run out of fuel before they closed the distance.

The problem was that, at flank speed, *Cheyenne* was making more noise. She was announcing her exact location to every nearby sonar device. On top of that, she was making enough noise that she could barely hear anything around her.

Mack knew that in order to outrun the torpedoes, they would need to keep running at this speed, blind to anything but the noisy torpedoes, for at least another five thousand yards.

That was when *Cheyenne* caught her first break. 'Conn, sonar,' the sonar supervisor reported, 'the first torpedo just fell for the noisemaker. It's off our tail.'

'Sonar, conn, what about torpedo number two?' Mack asked.

'Conn, sonar, it's at the edge of our port baffle.' There was a brief pause and then the sonar supervisor added, 'It just went active, Captain.'

'Release another noisemaker.'

'Releasing noisemaker, aye, sir.'

The tension level slowly mounted.

'Conn, sonar,' the sonar supervisor announced, 'the Mk 46 just latched on to the noisemaker decoy . . . lost the torpedo in our baffles!'

Mack nodded. The Mk 46s were fast, but they were easily fooled.

'I guess those noisemakers really do work,' one of the sonar operators said to the operator sitting beside him.

'Ahead one third,' Mack ordered. He wanted to run slower until he knew what was going on around him.

It took several moments for *Cheyenne* to slow down enough to start listening once more. Mack slowly turned to the northeast to clear his baffles.

'Sonar, conn, report all contacts,' Mack said, once they had slowed enough. He wanted to know who was out there and exactly where they were.

'Conn, sonar, report all contacts, aye, sir,' the sonar supervisor acknowledged.

Less than five minutes had passed since the first Chinese Mk 46 had been fired at them, but to the officers and crew on board *Cheyenne* it seemed like only five seconds. It was ironic, Mack thought. The minutes it took for their own torpedoes to acquire and complete their runs seemed to stretch into hours, but when hostile torpedoes were coming toward *Cheyenne*, time passed much faster.

'Conn, sonar, we've got three contacts, Captain,' said the sonar supervisor. 'One Kilo class submarine bearing 278, making turns for fifteen knots. One Romeo class submarine bearing 020, making turns for about six and a half knots. The third contact is a Chinese Luda class destroyer, which is probably where that helo came from, bearing 350. The destroyer is also heading in our direction. The TB-23 doesn't hold the helicopter above us, which may be because we're too deep, but my guess is that it's rearming on board the destroyer.' Mack would be sure to mention his battle stations sonar supervisor in his patrol report.

The BSY-1 operators confirmed the sonar supervisor's expert calls. The Romeo was previous Master 25 and the Luda was previously Master 26. However, the Kilo's bearing was too far to the left for it to be the previous Master 28, which *Cheyenne* shot at earlier. Master 28 was added to the kill list and the new Kilo was designated Master 29.

'We'll take out the Kilo, Master 29, first,' Mack said. It was the closest target, and potentially the quietest, and Mack wanted it out of the picture. He gave the orders to prepare tube two in all respects, including opening the outer door. As soon as his orders were acknowledged and confirmed, he gave the command to match sonar bearings and shoot tube two, Master 29.

Seconds later, the combat systems officer reported, 'Tube two fired electrically, sir.'

'Conn, sonar, unit from tube two running hot, straight, and normal.'

The Kilo knew the moment the torpedo entered the water. It tried to turn and to run in the opposite direction, but the Chinese submarine had little chance. The Kilo had been closing on *Cheyenne* at top speed, and with a torpedo heading its way, it didn't have much room to maneuver.

The Kilo zigged and zagged, tossing its crew about as the Chinese captain tried to confuse the torpedo at the same time that he tried to reverse his heading. The Chinese submarine released a noisemaker decoy to buy time, but Mack, listening to the reports from sonar, didn't think it would work this time.

He was right.

'Conn, sonar, the Mk 48 passed right by their noisemaker. It's still on course, bearing 275.'

Several minutes later sonar reported hearing the explosion. The 650-pound explosive warhead literally peeled open the Kilo's back end, beginning with its screw. The Chinese Kilo roamed the sea no more.

'Reload tube two with a Harpoon,' Mack ordered. There was no time to relish the victory. He wanted the destroyer, Master 26, next. With luck, the helo would still be on board. 'Diving officer, make your depth one hundred feet.' Mack needed to get closer to the surface so that they could launch the missile.

'Reload tube two with a Harpoon,' acknowledged the fire-control coordinator.

'Make my depth one hundred feet, aye, sir,' the helmsman finished the round of repeat backs, acknowledging the diving officer's order.

The Luda II class destroyer was a fairly large target, so Mack was going to fire two weapons at it. He would have preferred to make them both Harpoons, but *Cheyenne* had already fired three of her four anti-shipping missiles in previous actions. He would have to attack the Luda with only one Harpoon and one Mk 48. The torpedo had a bigger warhead, but it also had a much shorter range.

'What's the current range to the destroyer?'

'Range to Master 26 is 30,500 yards, bearing 354,' the fire-control coordinator answered.

'And what's the range on the Romeo?'

'BSY-1 computes 28,000 yards, sir. Master 25 is not moving. I think they figure that if they move, we'll hear them and kill them.'

Mack ran through the situation in his mind and quickly made his decision. 'Make tubes one and two ready in all respects, including opening the outer doors,' he said. 'Firing point procedures, tube two, Master 26; tube one, Master 25.'

He waited for those orders to be acknowledged and executed and then said, 'Match sonar bearings and shoot tube two, Master 26 and tube one, Master 25.'

Torpedo tube two, containing *Cheyenne*'s last remaining

71

UGM-84 Harpoon, fired first. Tube one was fired as soon as the ejection pump ram had returned to battery.

'Conn, sonar, the Harpoon's on her way, sir, and the Mk 48 from tube one is running hot, straight and' – there was a brief pause, and then the sonar supervisor said – 'normal!'

The Romeo wasn't as quick as the Kilo. It took them two minutes to realize there was an enemy torpedo coming through the water at them, and several minutes longer to increase their speed. And by then, it was simply too late.

'The Mk 48 has acquired the Romeo, Master 25, Captain.'

'Cut the wire, shut the outer doors on both tubes, and reload tubes one and two with Mk 48s.'

It would be several minutes before the torpedo reached the Romeo, but its fate was sealed. The Romeo had nothing onboard that would fool the Mk 48 once it had acquired.

The Luda, however, was a different matter. The Harpoon was very fast, covering the seventeen miles to the Chinese destroyer in less than three minutes.

The Chinese sailors launched a cloud of chaff to try and decoy the missile away from the ship. When that failed, and the Harpoon began its final descent, *Jinan* fired its twin 25mm guns into the air, putting up a 'wall of steel' in front of the UGM-84.

Years earlier, Saddam Hussein had tried that unsuccessfully around Baghdad against US Tomahawk land-attack missiles. It didn't work any better for the Chinese sailors. The Harpoon slammed into the vessel directly underneath its antiship missile launchers, impacting downward and tearing a large hole in the hull.

'Conn, sonar, we just heard an explosion on the surface. We hit the destroyer bad, sir. I'm hearing breaking-up noises already.'

'What about the Mk 48?'

'Impact in four minutes, Captain, but it's a lock. That Romeo's not doing much to get out of the way.'

The combat systems officer knew his weapons well. A Romeo-class submarine could do thirteen knots at top speed – but only if it was in good condition. This one did not seem able to get above nine knots.

Mack was pleased, but he wasn't satisfied. He ordered tubes three and four readied, and then initiated firing point procedures against the damaged destroyer. When that had been done, he ordered, 'Match sonar bearings and shoot tube three, Master 26.'

'Match bearings and shoot tube three, Master 26,' acknowledged the fire-control coordinator.

Tube three was fired electrically, but sonar didn't have the chance to report on the torpedo's status before the Romeo was hit. The old, antiquated reserve submarine had tried to evade, tried to flee, but *Cheyenne* had it outgunned and outmaneuvered.

'Conn, sonar, we have the sounds of a submarine filling with water. Master 25 is sinking, sir.'

Mack acknowledged the report and asked, 'What's the status on the second Mk 48?'

'Conn, sonar, it's running hot, straight, and normal, sir.'

The combat systems officer announced acquisition.

When the Mk 48 acquired its target Mack ordered the wire in tube three cut, tube four secured, and tube three reloaded with an Mk 48. When that had been done, he gave the command to take *Cheyenne* deep once more. Moments later a loud explosion marked the death of the already damaged Chinese Luda II destroyer.

Now Mack was satisfied. The Harpoon might have been enough to sink it. Now, however, the destroyer went down with all hands and both helicopters onboard. Mack gave the order to secure from battle stations.

*   *   *

Ten hours later *Cheyenne* was approaching her launch point north of the Spratlys.

'How long until we arrive at the launch point?' Mack asked.

'We should be at our launch point within seven minutes,' the navigation officer replied. With *Cheyenne* currently 2.5 nautical miles south of her launch point and running at twenty knots, Mack manned 'battle stations missile.'

Mack ordered *Cheyenne* brought to periscope depth to confirm her location by GPS and receive any new orders. This also gave them a chance to verify the targeting information they'd downloaded earlier.

With everything confirmed, *Cheyenne* proceeded to her launch point and prepared to launch six land-attack missiles at the Cuarteron Reef Submarine Base. Two of the Tomahawk missiles were the UGM-109D varieties, each of which carried 166 BLU-97/B combined-effects munitions. These would be able to take out soft targets and destroy electronic sensors and early-warning systems protecting the base. The remaining four were fitted with a 1,000 pound 'bull-pup' warhead that was designed to take out the base headquarters and the piers where the submarines were being rearmed and refueled.

One by one, *Cheyenne* launched her missiles, and then slipped deeper into the sea. She would now have to wait on word from naval intelligence to determine if her mission was a success.

'Diving Officer, make your depth five hundred feet. Let's get out of here before they know what – and who – hit them.'

Mack was pleased. His crew had performed well, Cheyenne had carried out her mission, and now they were heading toward the Sulu Sea. *McKee* would be there waiting for her, and *Cheyenne* would get a mini-refit. Mack secured battle stations once more, hoping it would be the last time this trip.

Mack didn't know what his next orders would be, but he was sure *Cheyenne* was going to need all the weapons *McKee* could give her.

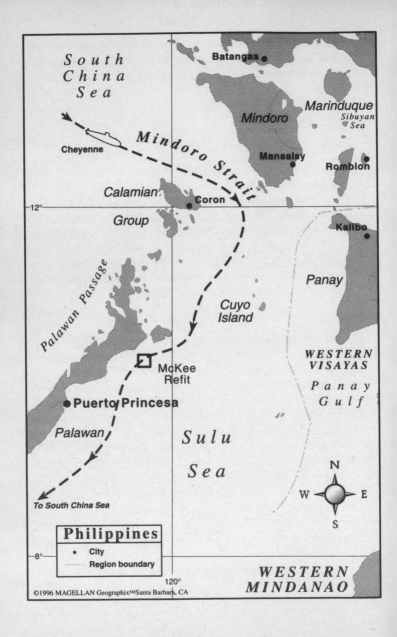

South
China
Sea

Batangas

Mindoro

Marinduque

*Sibuyan
Sea*

Cheyenne

Mindoro Strait

Mansalay

Romblon

Calamian

Coron

12°

Group

Kalibo

Palawan Passage

Cuyo
Island

Panay

McKee
Refit

WESTERN
VISAYAS

Puerto Princesa

*Panay
Gulf*

Palawan

Sulu
Sea

N

W   E

S

To South China Sea

Philippines
• City
⋯⋯ Region boundary

8°

120°

WESTERN
MINDANAO

FOUR

Dogfight

Mack walked through officer country on board the submarine tender *McKee*, accompanied by his combat systems and operations officers, his navigator and communicator, and his sonar officer. *Cheyenne* was just completing her mini-refit, and Mack and his officers were on their way to their final briefing. The refit had taken several days, and for each of those days the officers from *Cheyenne* had taken their meals in the vast wardroom onboard *McKee*. This day, the final day of their refit, Mack had elected to take his breakfast with his own officers rather than in *McKee*'s flag mess.

Mack was pleased that the refit had gone smoothly. On the first day, his executive officer and his chief yeoman, along with the communicator and officer-in-charge (OIC) of the naval security group (NSG) detachment on board *Cheyenne*, had been responsible for transferring numerous boxes from *Cheyenne* to *McKee*. Those crates and boxes had contained the myriad logs, data sheets, and sonar and radio and ESM tapes that *Cheyenne* had amassed during the period of time from when she departed Pearl Harbor until she arrived in the Sulu Sea alongside *McKee*.

Among this, carefully stored in box 1, was the three hundred-page 'Patrol Report of *Cheyenne*, Pearl Harbor to Sulu Sea,' which Mack had signed earlier. This was a running narrative of events and tactics employed, along with a written guide to the rest of the items in the boxes.

Mack always enjoyed looking back through this report. It was compiled four times a day by the off-going officer of the deck and his assistant, the junior officer of the deck.

As soon as it was compiled, the ship's yeomen typed it up on the high-speed PCs in the ship's office. The color printer and color scanner made the patrol report an interesting novel, complete with color pictures of the tactical encounters experienced.

This report, with all the details of *Cheyenne*'s first adventures, would remain on board *McKee* for some time. Eventually, couriers from *Independence* would transfer the materials from *McKee* to the carrier, and from there they would travel by C-2 aircraft to the Yokosuka Naval Base.

The pilots of these C-2 Greyhounds, called 'COD' for 'carrier onboard delivery,' were used to making 3,000-mile flights. They had already completed numerous deliveries to and from *Independence* and the island of Diego Garcia while *Independence* steamed south of the Arabian Sea.

Not that *Cheyenne*'s successes were being kept secret. Interim reports had been submitted as required, and as soon as she had surfaced inside Mindoro Strait, Mack had released a long message containing a condensed version of the patrol report and a tabulation of the contents of the boxes to be shipped. This message was already in the hands of *Cheyenne*'s superiors. Picked up and relayed by one of the numerous SSIXS satellites, this one perched high in its equatorial synchronous orbit over the Indian Ocean, the message had been printed out and copies had been distributed all the way to the Joint Chiefs of Staff in Washington, DC.

On that first day alongside *McKee*, while some of *Cheyenne*'s people dealt with the patrol report, the engineer officer's people had been busy with the details of taking on shore power. This was vital to *Cheyenne*'s taking steam out of the engineering spaces and shutting down the reactor for the duration of the refit.

They were also responsible for some of the more delicate procedures. The engineering laboratory technicians first had to transfer a quantity of nuclear waste materials generated during their periodic sampling of the reactor coolant to ensure its purity. Once this transfer was complete, they would assist in refilling the coolant charging system's pure water tanks with CPW. This 'controlled pure water' was generated onboard *McKee* by passing SSN discharged coolant from start-ups through the submarine tender's massive ion beds. The coolant was no longer radioactive, yet it was controlled because of its source. This way the water from the SSNs alongside was constantly recycled rather than discharged to the environment.

While all this was going on, with the executive officer supervising the transfer of the patrol report and the engineering officer overseeing the power plant, the combat systems officer and his people had their hands full. The combat systems officer was responsible for readying the vertical launch tubes for removal of the spent Tomahawk loading canisters so that the tubes could be reloaded. Others of his crew had to ready the three decks between the weapons-loading hatch and the torpedo room.

Mack smiled to himself, remembering how well it had all gone. Those activities had mainly been *Cheyenne*'s responsibility, and they had all occurred on their first day alongside *McKee*. After that, *Cheyenne*'s officers and crew had been able to rest while the refit crew took over the rest of the normal operations.

After the rigors of their contested ingress and transit of the South China Sea and the relatively simple TLAM-C and TLAM-D attack on the Chinese submarine base at Cuarteron Reef, the officers and men of *Cheyenne* appreciated this rest a great deal. Even more, they appreciated the assistance of *McKee*'s crew. In peacetime, a tender like *McKee* would not have been employed for such a short refit. But this was war now, and peacetime rules did not apply. Especially since it appeared that *Cheyenne* would be the only US submarine in the South China Sea for a good while.

Cheyenne's officers and crew understood this. 'No rest for the weary,' as the saying went. It was simply an extension of a policy established for returning war patrol crews in Pearl Harbor during World War II. The only difference was that this time there was no relinquishment either of command or of the individual officers' responsibilities. Refits like this one were merely opportunities for rest and recreation, unlike the twenty-four-hour refit/repair periods which so many submarine crews had experienced during peacetime.

All of which meant that the policy was logical and intelligent – but policy was generally not made by the people it most directly affected. *Cheyenne*'s officers and crew agreed with the policy, and they appreciated it – but they appreciated the hard work and extra effort put forth by the sailors and engineers from *McKee* even more.

McKee was good, with a seasoned crew, and the refit had gone well. *Cheyenne* was restocked and resupplied. The executive officer, engineer officer, the remaining junior officers, and their leading petty officers would attend to the final details of turnover from the refit crew. As soon as this briefing was over, Mack and his officers would be ready to return to active patrol.

Entering the war room, Mack immediately noticed that the eagles (captain's insignia) on the collar of the Commander Submarine Group Seven (CSG 7), also known as Commander Task Force Seventy-four (CTF 74), had been replaced with single stars. Mack had expected that. With war declared in his theater of operations, it was standard procedure for the commodore, as he was addressed during peacetime, to be frocked to rear admiral, lower half.

After exchanging greetings with the captain of *McKee* and CTF 74, Mack and his officers quietly took their seats in the front row as the briefing officer dimmed the lights for his presentation of the bomb damage assessment at Cuarteron Reef.

The satellite photography provided clear evidence that each TLAM-C and TLAM-D, which had been launched from *Cheyenne*'s vertical-launch tubes at a comfortable, uncontested datum north of the Spratly Island chain, had reached a mark. Not necessarily the intended mark, but at least damage enough to put the Chinese submarine base out of business for a while.

Mack had seen the smoke and fire from the explosions through the high-power, 16X magnification of the Type 18 periscope, but, because the Chinese submarine base was beyond the horizon of the periscope's height of eye, he hadn't been able to discern the actual targets that were hit. He listened carefully as the briefing officer said that the main repair facility and weapons stowage buildings had been hit as planned, with 1,000 pounds of explosives per Tomahawk.

The national command authority and the USCINCPAC target staff had done a nice rush job in providing both the terrain contour matching (TERCOM) data for the entire length of the Philippine Island of Palawan, and the final, more accurate, digital scene-matching area correlation (DSMAC) data, especially since Palawan was not previously a high-priority digital terrain-data-collection effort. With the Tomahawk Block III Global Positioning System (GPS) providing updates to the missiles, the three hundred-nautical-mile flight from the last DSMAC update on the southwest tip of Palawan had not degraded the targeting accuracy.

As the briefing officer went over this, Mack found himself thinking that the last-minute sighting of missiles arriving at Cuarteron Reef from the east must have been totally confusing to the Chinese. Moments later, the briefing officer confirmed that guess. If the Chinese had known *Cheyenne*'s position, they would have sent some of their assets after her. But that hadn't happened. Although the base infrastructure was essentially out of commission, satellite imagery showed that a number of Chinese submarines and a few surface ships remained in port, still moored to only slightly damaged piers.

Mack knew that the Chinese would be able to make

some guesses about *Cheyenne*'s position. Because the missiles had not arrived from the west, the Chinese remaining in port would assume that *Cheyenne* was lingering in the safety of deep water to the north of the Spratlys. And they'd be right . . . but only to a point.

Cheyenne had indeed launched from the north, but she was not lingering in the area, having entered the Sulu Sea from the north via the Mindoro Strait. Mack knew that the delay in the Chinese exodus from Cuarteron Reef should give *Cheyenne* the opportunity to reposition from her safe haven alongside *McKee* in the Sulu Sea. They should end up in their prime location west of Cuarteron Reef before the Chinese decided to deploy their submarines and surface ships to the safety of the sea. Attacks from *Cheyenne* off Cuarteron Reef also might make the Chinese believe they had more than *Cheyenne* with which to contend, a ploy which the submarine force had used in previous conflicts.

The briefing officer continued with the latest status of the location of the USS *Independence* Battle Group and background on the Battle Group transit into the South China Sea. Prior to Mack's rendezvous and reporting in as the SSN(DS), *Independence* had steamed to the southern coast of Borneo, having passed through the Lombok Strait with her AO (oiler) and AE (ammunition ship), while several of her surface ships, including the two Ticonderoga class cruisers *Gettysburg* and *Princeton*, had slipped through the Sunda Strait to the west under the cover of darkness the night before.

The CVBG admiral had wisely split his forces to ensure that all his eggs were not in the same basket should the Chinese have sympathizers, or even their own soldiers, on Java, Sumatra, or Bali. Both the Lombok and Sunda Straits were narrow enough that even small-arms fire from the cliffs overlooking the straits could inflict damage to personnel on deck.

At any rate, the no-longer-covert show of force from the

CVBG, which rendezvoused in the Java Sea near Belitung Island, was intended to flush the Chinese at Cuarteron Reef to sea for attacks on the Battle Group.

The briefing officer went on to explain that once *Independence* had recovered the S-3 aircraft, which had provided air cover of both straits, the Battle Group steamed north to a position northwest of Natuna Island. There they maintained position until *Cheyenne* had rendezvoused and notified the submarine element coordinator (SEC) and the anti-submarine warfare commander (ASWC), co-located on-board *Independence* with the SEC's submarine advisory team (SAT), that the time was right for the Battle Group to continue safely to the Spratly Islands without fear of Chinese submarine attacks.

The orders for *Cheyenne* at this stage of the naval war against China were clear and simple: unrestricted submarine warfare on Chinese submarines and surface warships, with the main targets expected to be those departing Cuarteron Reef.

Mack had known this, of course. Because there was a strong possibility of encountering Chinese warships, *Cheyenne* had taken on four UGM-84 Harpoon missiles instead of a full load of twenty-six Mk 48 ADCAP torpedoes. In addition, a mix of TLAM-C and TASM had been reloaded into the twelve vertical-launch tubes: TLAM-C in case another land attack would be authorized while *Cheyenne* was at sea, and TASM in case they needed their longer range against the Chinese surface ships. The TASM had an extra two hundred nautical miles of range over the Harpoon. Either way, for those long range shots, over-the-horizon targeting from Battle Group aircraft would be necessary unless the Chinese surface ships themselves provided enough radar targeting information to *Cheyenne*'s ESM antenna for bearing-only launches.

So far, there was no need for TLAM-N, which would be a waste on the relatively tiny islands. Besides, the digital terrain data of the Chinese mainland itself, which met the Tomahawk TERCOM and DSMAC data requirements, more fully supported TLAM-N. Unlike the Spratlys, data on the mainland had been accumulated and processed years earlier, in less of a rush, against the possibility of future US nuclear bomber attacks on China.

The briefing was professional and highly detailed. Mack came away with all his questions answered, and a clear sense of *Cheyenne*'s mission. But no briefing was ever absolutely complete. The briefing officer could not pass along information he didn't have, and on the last day of *Cheyenne*'s refit naval intelligence had not discovered – or, as sometimes happened, had somehow neglected to pass on – the fact that there was a new player in the area. The Chinese already had a large fleet of submarines purchased from the economically ailing Russians, and that fleet had just gotten bigger. The Chinese had recently acquired a Russian Alfa class SSN, and the Alfa was now on patrol in the South China Sea.

Mack didn't know about the Alfa yet, but he did know that his submarine and his crew were ready for anything the Chinese cared to throw at them, though with the sheer numbers of assets the Chinese had hunting them, *Cheyenne* would have to be cautious. The Chinese had the advantage of being used to dealing en masse; *Cheyenne* had the advantage that their enemy obviously had no coordination of surface and subsurface forces – something Mack had noted in his previous encounters.

After the briefing, Mack's officers went back to *Cheyenne* to get her ready for departure. Mack stayed behind for a little while longer.

Mack met with the *McKee* Captain and CTF 74 in the admiral's sea cabin. *Cheyenne* was facing the possibility of shallow water operations, and her crew needed to prepare for that. Shallow water operations were difficult and dangerous, and there had simply been no opportunity to practice before *Cheyenne* was ordered to ready herself for deployment.

In the admiral's sea cabin, Mack reported to the other two officers that after departure, *Cheyenne*'s crew would practice shallow water, high speed maneuvering, and shallow water towed-array operations first. That way, if the TB-16 array were to touch bottom before their proficiency had peaked, the soft bottom of the Sulu Sea would ensure that the array would be undamaged. Mack needed to ensure that his diving officers, helmsmen, and planesmen were ready so that they would not overreact during high speed, shallow water maneuvers, and either broach the ship or drag the propeller and lower rudder through the bottom. Mack knew that it didn't take much angle for a 360-foot submarine in 20 fathoms of water to subject itself to the dangers of the surface or the ocean bottom.

In addition, Mack requested and received permission to use the *McKee* captain's gig in their exercises. This would provide an adequate surface target for active sonar detection and tracking in the irregular contours and the varying wind driven thermal gradients. Mack would use the gig to practice active sonar tracking with the BSY-1 spherical array at low power and short pulse lengths and with the higher-frequency MIDAS under-ice and minehunting sonar as they approached the Balabac Strait south of Palawan.

Cheyenne would have to wait for the rocky bottom and shoals off Cuarteron Reef to once again be their proving grounds should the Chinese submarines decide not to venture forth into deep water. The captain hoped MIDAS would be able to distinguish between the coral reefs and the anechoic coatings of the Chinese submarines. But then, active sonar would be used only if *Cheyenne*'s presence were otherwise known.

There was one other point Mack had to bring up. He liked to assume that the Chinese had equivalent overhead satellite imagery capability, and he was concerned for *McKee*'s safety.

The admiral advised him not to worry, however, since

they intended to weigh anchor shortly after *Cheyenne*'s departure and would periodically relocate outside the Chinese intelligence satellites' footprints. The actual location of the next rendezvous would be provided to *Cheyenne* as soon as it was decided upon. It might even be in port in Brunei, or off that coast, where carrier air protection could be afforded both *McKee* and *Cheyenne* during their next reload period.

Mack was pleased to hear that – and doubly pleased to know that chances for another reload were good – but he also knew that it would only be true if he could keep the Chinese submarines away from the basically defenseless *McKee* before the *Independence* Battle Group arrived to relieve him of the burden of protecting the tender.

● ● ●

Shortly after getting under way from alongside *McKee*, *Cheyenne* quietly submerged. They weren't scheduled to come to the surface again for quite some time – and, depending on how much action they saw and how well they fared in *Cheyenne*'s next war patrol off Cuarteron Reef, it might be even longer before they saw *McKee* again.

As he had briefed his admiral, Mack made sure that they practiced the shallow water, high speed maneuvering en route. This maneuvering was not unlike flying an airplane – even some of the terminology was similar. In deep water, where the automatic depth-control system would frequently be used, the submarine's vertical position in the water column was referred to as 'depth.' During these maneuvers, however, the term was 'altitude,' with added emphasis on maintaining a comfortable safety margin or altitude in the water column above the ocean bottom. To help with this, the upward-looking beams of the under-ice sonar, MIDAS, continually displayed the distance to the surface, while the secure fathometer, with its narrow sonar beam, provided the altitude information.

As Mack had hoped, the *McKee* captain's gig turned out to be a useful target for active sonar tracking. In addition, it provided a source of sonar passive tonal information. In shallow water like this, the TB-16 towed array's entire 2,600-foot tow cable, with its 240 feet of hydrophones at the end, could not be totally deployed. Instead, it would be deployed at a 'short stay,' an optimum length for all hydrophones to be at some distance away from its own ship tonals, yet short enough to ensure that it remained off the bottom during maneuvers, its own 'towed-array altitude.'

The longer TB-23 thin-line array, with its 960 feet of hydrophones, would remain stowed for these war patrol shallow water operations, thus ensuring its availability for deep water tracking operations when – and if – the Chinese ventured into the deeper waters of the South China Sea. The depths northwest of the Spratly Islands, ranging to over 15,000 feet, were ideal for convergence zone tracking of the noisy Chinese submarines while they were running at high speeds.

Cheyenne had nearly completed her exercises when Mack heard over the speaker at the periscope stand, 'Captain, radio, incoming flash traffic!'

Proceeding quickly to the radio room, he arrived in time to see the printer spitting out new orders. *Cheyenne* was to proceed at best speed to a location west of Cuarteron Reef. Overhead imagery had shown that the Chinese were stirring, probably preparing to deploy under cover of darkness, which was only hours away.

Mack was ready. Before beginning the high speed, shallow water maneuvers, he had decided that *Cheyenne* should not dally inside the Sulu Sea. Instead, he had decided to continue west while conducting the proficiency training, and now he was doubly glad that he had made that decision.

Cheyenne had earlier released the captain's gig to return to *McKee*. Now, having already cleared Balabac Strait, deep water was nearby, so the captain used the radiomen's microphone to pass the order, 'Officer of the deck, Captain, shift main coolant pumps to fast speed and then proceed to flank speed. Make your depth four hundred feet.'

The OOD repeated the captain's order verbatim, then ordered maneuvering to shift the main coolant pumps to fast speed. The OOD could have accomplished the same thing by ordering flank on the engine order telegraph, a 'jump bell,' but that method, which was faster than ordering maneuvering to shift the coolant pumps, was saved for when speed was of the essence . . . as in torpedo evasion.

Cheyenne arrived northwest of West Reef shortly after nightfall, remaining outside the 100 fathom curve for the time being. Upon receiving the report from the officer of the deck that they were on station, Mack proceeded to the control room.

'Make preparations to come to periscope depth,' he said.

After acknowledging the captain's order, the OOD slowed to two thirds and brought *Cheyenne* up to 130 feet, above the layer, and cleared baffles. He then advised the captain that he had no sonar contacts and was ready to proceed to periscope depth.

'Very well,' Mack replied. 'Come to periscope depth.'

'Come to periscope depth, aye, sir. Sonar, radio, conn, proceeding to periscope depth.'

'Conn, sonar, aye. No contacts,' replied the sonar supervisor.

'Conn, radio, aye . . . manned and ready.' That acknowledgment came from the communicator.

'Diving officer, make your depth six zero feet smartly,' ordered the OOD as he raised the Type 18 periscope and started his underwater visual sweeps to make sure there were no dead-in-the-water underwater hulls for *Cheyenne* to run into during this last, most tenuous part of the trip to periscope depth.

'Make my depth six zero feet, smartly,' answered the

diving officer. 'Smartly' meant that the diving officer would maintain the two-thirds bell as he ordered the helmsman to fifteen rise on the bow planes and ordered the planesman to a fifteen degree up bubble. Using the stern planes to control *Cheyenne*'s angle, the bubble would be eased as *Cheyenne* was nearing eighty feet for the final glide to sixty feet.

'Seven zero, six five, six four, six three, six two,' the diving officer said, counting down their depths.

When the count hit six two, the OOD called out, 'Braking,' and quickly swung the periscope through a 360-degree arc. A moment later he said, 'No visual contacts, Captain.' There were a number of radar contacts chirping over the Type 18 ESM receiver, but the periscope wasn't picking up any visuals.

'Ahead one third,' Mack ordered quietly to the OOD, not wanting to be entered in the deck log as having assumed the conn.

'Conn, ESM, I have five ESM contacts, one a Chinese radar, and four Russian radars. HULTEC indicates a Han class, three Kilo class, and one Alfa class. The closest is the Han at signal strength three and increasing.'

Captain Mackey and the OOD looked at each other with surprise.

Mack turned to the microphone. 'ESM, Captain,' he said, 'are you sure about that Alfa?'

'Yes, sir, Captain,' answered the voice of the NSG OIC. 'It's an Alfa. We've seen him, this particular one, in the North Fleet numerous times. No mistaking it, sir. He's well registered in our computer database.'

'Executive officer,' spoke the captain calmly as he turned to the executive officer standing aft in the darkness of the rig for black. 'Are you back there?'

'Yes, Captain. Should I draft a message report on the Alfa?'

'Please do so. Release it when ready. We need to find out what gives.' The Alfa was designated Master 31, the

Han Master 32, and the three Kilos Masters 33, 34, and 35.

In less than half an hour, *Cheyenne*'s flash message report had been sent and answered by the communicators at CTF 74 headquarters in Yokosuka.

Mack read the CTF message and filled in his executive officer on what he'd learned. 'ESM is right. It seems the "friendly" Russians have sold a North Fleet Alfa to the Chinese,' he said, 'who then crewed it and overhauled it, apparently at Cuarteron Reef. How many more Alfas are being transferred to China is anybody's guess at this time. Naval intelligence is working on the problem. They're paying special attention to the recent lack of openness of the Russian submarine bases at Vladivostok and Petropavlosk.'

Mack chose this method of informing his executive officer, rather than filling him in during a private briefing, because he'd made a policy of ensuring that all his crewmen were knowledgeable about any enemy they were likely to encounter.

Because of this, the messenger of the watch – who had heard the initial ESM report but not the follow up – knew, or thought he knew, the implication of an Alfa, a Russian submarine, in the immediate area. The messenger of the watch quickly spread the word through the crew's mess as he stood there with his red goggles on, drawing coffee for the control room watch standers. The movie operator even shut down the movie and turned on the lights so they could all discuss the new information.

But for all Mack's openness, the crew was never as well informed as the officers. In this case, because the messenger of the watch had been sent for coffee before hearing Mack's final report, none of the crew on board *Cheyenne* knew that the Alfa was manned not by Russians but by Chinese sailors.

The captain called for an immediate meeting of all officers in the wardroom to share with them the new intelligence on the Alfa, manned by Chinese, and its current exodus with a Han and three Kilo SSKs. He expected the SSNs to wait for deep water before diving, but anticipated the Kilos would dive in twenty fathoms.

That was as far as Mack got before the OOD called him on the sound-powered phones, allowing the mess specialist to sneak out of the wardroom galley and pass the word on the Chinese crew to the already buzzing crew's mess.

'Captain, ESM reports the Kilo radars and the Han radar have shut down. They were drawing left while the Alfa radar is still drawing right.'

'Okay, men. We have our work cut out for us. The three Kilos and the Han have probably submerged. And the Alfa may be trying to do an end around to get behind us. It's time to man battle stations.'

Mack's reading of the situation was correct. Sonar had just finished reporting tonals from the Han SSN to the conn as the captain arrived and ordered the OOD to man battle stations torpedo. There was still nothing from the Kilos acoustically, but the Alfa had also shut down its radar – last bearing due south of *Cheyenne*.

As directed by the captain, who was now the conning officer, the executive officer, in his role as the fire control coordinator, passed the order to the torpedo room over the sound-powered phones, 'Torpedo room, fire control, make tubes one and two ready in all respects, including opening the outer doors.' He wanted to get the tubes ready as early as possible and as far from the enemy submarines as possible.

The order from the captain, carried by the open microphone at the periscope stand, alerted the sonar operators that noisy evolutions would be taking place near the BSY-1 spherical array so they could attenuate the sound level reaching their sensitive ears.

The torpedo room crew acknowledged the order. 'Make tubes one and two ready in all respects, including opening the outer doors, fire control, torpedo room, aye.'

Moments later, the torpedo room reported completing

the ordered evolution with the torpedo tubes. The executive officer relayed the information to Mack. 'Captain, tubes one and two are ready in all respects. Both outer doors are open.'

'Very well, fire control,' answered the captain.

The Han was drawing left and closing. It was not quiet by any means, and was easily tracked by the TB-16, spherical, and conformal arrays at the same time. The inputs to the three BSY-1 computers made the solution a snap for the fire-control party.

When the BSY-1 operator and the fire-control coordinator were satisfied with the TMA (target motion analysis) solution on Master 32, the Chinese Han class attack submarine, the captain ordered, 'Firing point procedures, Master 32.'

The combat systems officer reported the target course, speed, and range.

'Sonar, conn, stand by,' ordered the captain.

'Conn, sonar, standing by.'

'Match sonar bearings and shoot, tubes one and two, Master 32.'

'Match sonar bearings and shoot, tubes one and two, Master 32, aye.'

After the large piston of the torpedo-ejection pump ram drove home, the Mk 48 ADCAP torpedoes were ejected from their resting places at the same time that their Otto fuel engines were coming up to full speed. 'Tubes one and two fired electrically,' reported the combat systems officer.

'Conn, sonar, units from tubes one and two running hot, straight, and normal,' came the report from the sonar supervisor as the two torpedoes executed their wire clearance maneuvers and accelerated rapidly to fifty knots en route to convergence with the Chinese submarine.

'Very well, sonar,' Mack said. Then, a moment later, he asked, 'Time to acquisition?'

'Eight minutes, Captain,' answered the combat systems officer.

To Mack, it seemed like an eternity before he heard, 'Unit one has acquired . . . Unit two has acquired.'

'Cut the wires, shut the outer doors, and reload tubes one and two,' Mack ordered now that the Chinese submarine's fate was in the hands of the Mk 48s. There was no escaping their relentless attack. The subsequent reverberations and breaking up sounds were deafening.

'Conn, sonar, we have a torpedo in the water, SET-53, bearing 089!' The sonar supervisor's excited report came just as the ocean started to quiet. Apparently the Han CO had launched a snap shot at the bearing of the incoming torpedoes as part of a last-ditch effort prior to his certain death.

'Right full rudder, all ahead flank. Cavitate. Make your depth one thousand feet,' Mack said, followed rapidly by his calm, but forceful words over *Cheyenne*'s 1MC, 'Rig ship for depth charge.'

With the ship already at battle stations, the reports from *Cheyenne*'s various compartments came in quickly to the chief of the watch at the ballast control panel. The engineering officer of the watch (EOOW) had ordered main coolant pumps shifted to fast speed, and the throttle man answered the ordered bell as soon as the pumps were reported in fast speed by the reactor operator.

In fact, the throttle man was a little quicker than the EOOW had expected. With the precision of his training, he had acknowledged the engine order telegraph backup to the captain's orders and was already nearing 50 percent steam flow. Now he was just waiting for the chance to complete his spinning open the main engine throttles, which he couldn't do until the steam generator automatic level controls allowed him to. The safeguards were there to prevent excessive level swell, which might result in carry-over of water into the steam piping.

Within minutes, *Cheyenne* was at flank speed, on course 185, and at one thousand feet. The bearing rate presented to the Chinese torpedo made no difference as the SET-53 locked on to the knuckle created by *Cheyenne*'s powerful maneuver. That was a direct result of Mack's order to cavitate, and had formed over a thousand yards away from *Cheyenne*'s current position.

'Conn, sonar, two explosions, bearing 055, range 8,540 yards.' Knowing the depth of water and the sound velocity profile, sonar could determine the range by the difference in time between the direct path and the bottom bounce path of the incoming explosion noises.

Above the cheers in the control room, Captain Mackey ordered, 'Chief of the watch, over the 1MC, secure from rig ship for depth charge.'

When the word was passed, Mack picked up the 1MC microphone and spoke to the officers and men of *Cheyenne*. 'This is the captain. Gentlemen, *Cheyenne* has sent another enemy submarine to its fiery grave. Excellent work. You can be truly proud of your team-work, each and every one of you. *Cheyenne* is you. Carry on.'

Replacing the microphone, he added, 'Chief of the watch, secure from battle stations.' Mack knew that the stand-down from the tension could easily be short lived, especially if the Han had been accompanied by quieter Kilo class diesels running on their batteries.

The officers adjourned to the wardroom for the captain's standard critique of the attack. Mack also had every battle stations sonar man there. This review was very positive, but Mack added a note of caution about not allowing their guard down. This was war, he pointed out, and the Chinese shouldn't be expected to sit back and watch their submarine force be devastated. *Cheyenne* and her crew needed to proceed with caution back to an interdiction point so that they could detect and attack some of those Kilos.

Mack's plan was a good one, but it was circumvented by events. Even as he was critiquing their most recent battle, sonar reported regaining contact on the Alfa, Master 31. The Alfa was proceeding north toward the sounds of the Han's demise, and *Cheyenne*'s turn toward the south during the torpedo evasion nicely closed the range.

Mack's attack on the Alfa started out the same as the attack on the Han, except that this time Captain Mackey elected to exercise torpedo tubes three and four. But that was as far as the similarity went. The Alfa, with its forty-knot speed, was able to evade both torpedoes.

The Chinese had learned to drive the Alfa, Mack realized, but fortunately they still had things to learn about their submarine. If that had been a Russian crew onboard that submarine, *Cheyenne* might have had to contend with their torpedoes.

Mack wasn't ready to take on the Kilo SSKs, which were probably lurking in the shoals while communicating with the Alfa, so he decided to withdraw to the deep water to the northwest. From there he could report the Han and Alfa attacks to CTF 74. He didn't need to return to *McKee* yet since *Cheyenne* still had sixteen torpedoes. And he had to clear the area before *Independence* could steam north to the Spratlys.

His message was quickly acknowledged by CTF 74, who passed traffic from the SEC and ASWC on board *Independence*. *Cheyenne* turned to the southwest and prepared herself for shallow water operations.

* * *

'Conn, sonar, sonar contact bearing 195. Sounds like the Alfa, Master 31, coming back for more.'

The captain ordered the towed array to short stay as *Cheyenne* ventured inside the 100-fathom curve south of Fiery Cross Reef. He intended to confuse the Chinese by operating in the shallow water. The Alfa SSN, he knew, would remain outside the shoals, unable to hear *Cheyenne* until – if things went according to plan – it was too late. A shorter range attack would preclude the Alfa from responding and evading the torpedoes.

Battle stations were manned once again as the range to

the Alfa closed to inside 40,000 yards – and none too soon, as sonar reported transient noises bearing 125 and 135. Mack nodded. As he'd expected, the Alfa was out in deeper water, but the Chinese Kilos had remained in the shoal waters, massing for guerrilla operations against *Cheyenne*.

They could have been a problem, but *Cheyenne* was ready with two outer doors already open.

'Snap shots, tubes one and two, bearings 125 and 135 respectively,' Mack ordered. That order meant that the Mk 48s would have to do their own thing in detecting, tracking, and sinking two of the Kilos, but Mack didn't have the luxury of assisting them.

It worked. The two torpedoes quickly acquired the Kilos. The two SSKs tried to flee, increasing speed and cavitating heavily, but to no avail. Both torpedoes found their marks and destroyed the SSKs, but Mack wasn't satisfied. Where was the third Kilo? he wondered.

He didn't have long to wait before finding out.

'Conn, sonar, we have transients bearing 180 that sound like Christmas balls falling off a tree and breaking . . . like a tinkling sound. Seems that the third Kilo was spooked by our torpedoes and ran into a coral reef.'

Mack grinned. He was happy to take the kills any way he could. Only the Alfa remained, and *Cheyenne* had lost contact after the first explosion against the Kilos.

Sonar was not able to reacquire the Russian submarine, and Mack gave the orders to take *Cheyenne* out of the area. They'd have another chance at the Alfa, he hoped, before he had to submit the next patrol report.

The only question that was bothering him was how the Alfa had slipped away. He hadn't expected that from a Chinese crew on a Russian submarine.

Then *Cheyenne* moved into deeper waters. As she resumed her patrol, Mack found himself wondering whether the Alfa had acquired a Russian adviser, or, worse, a full Russian crew.

* * *

A few days later, *Cheyenne* had been ordered to head to the south to meet up with *McKee*, anchored near Brunei, for a quick reload and resupply. Then she was to rendezvous with the *Independence* Battle Group and await further orders from CTF 74. Mack didn't know it yet, but they would not have the chance for a briefing in *McKee*'s war room for some time to come.

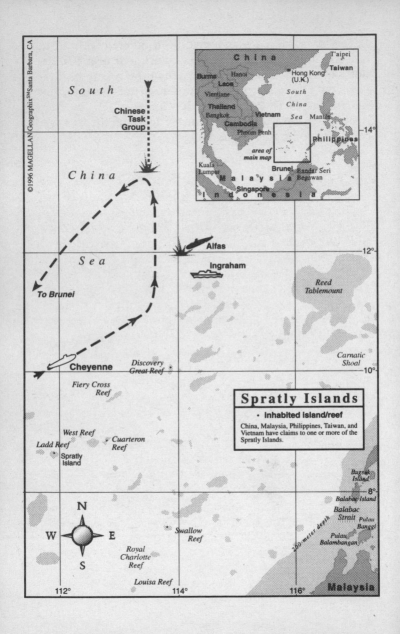

FIVE

Interdiction

The *Independence* Battle Group, to which *Cheyenne* was assigned as the sole SSN(DS), was operating south of the Spratly Islands. Having completed a quick reload and resupply, *Cheyenne* was with them, patrolling around their position, keeping the surface ships safe. Only this time, Mack's patrol area was not the forward 180 degrees, which he preferred. Instead, it was an area the shape of a donut: a full 360-degree annulus, centered on *Independence*, with an inner diameter of forty nautical miles and an outer diameter of eighty nautical miles. Mack didn't like being reined in like that.

'Radio, conn, stream the floating wire,' the OOD ordered.

'Conn, radio, stream the floating wire, aye, sir.'

Cheyenne's floating wire communications antenna was functionally similar to the communications buoys carried by Ohio class Trident ballistic missile submarines. *Cheyenne* could deploy this wire from depth, without having to raise a communications mast above the surface.

'Incoming message traffic,' the communicator said. He'd learned his lesson from their previous patrol and did not speculate on their new orders.

The OOD acknowledged and summoned both the captain and the executive officer to the conn.

Mack arrived in a few minutes along with the executive officer. Captain Mackey read the message, passed it to the executive officer, and then called a meeting in the wardroom. He requested that the communicator, the executive officer, the combat systems officer, and the engineer officer be present.

'We have our new orders,' Mack said as the briefing began. 'Naval intelligence has determined that a large Chinese surface task group has been sighted leaving Zhanjiang Naval Base, China. Satellite reconnaissance has confirmed this information. The task group is expected to form in the Mandarin Sea south of that base. All information indicates that they are headed in the direction of the Spratly Islands. Normally, they would be taken care of by aircraft and surface units. However, the Navy doesn't want to send the carrier too far north as yet, or to divert any of the carrier's defensive escorts away from their protective zone. They are worried about a Chinese air attack on the Battle Group.'

Mack looked around at his officers. They were a good group, and getting better with every mission. His last post-attack critique had reinstilled the need for redundancy, the formal repeat backs, during the attack phase. There was no room for error.

'Our orders,' he went on, 'are to detach from the Battle Group and proceed north of the Spratly Islands to attack the Chinese task group.'

Cheyenne was currently deployed south of the Spratly Islands chain. Her new orders would send her on a voyage of over 660 miles.

She had completed her mini-refit with *McKee* only a few days earlier, and the weapons she had taken onboard during the load-out should serve nicely in the upcoming battle. She had twenty Mk 48 torpedoes and six Harpoon missiles ready for loading in her torpedo tubes, and six Tomahawk antishipping missiles (TASM) in her VLS tubes.

This was the time when some submarine commanders delivered a pep talk to the officers and crew, but Mack didn't believe in that. His men were all professionals, and he wanted them to act that way. They didn't need to be pumped up to do their jobs. They simply needed to carry out their duties in a calm and proficient fashion.

Mack smiled to himself at that thought. He'd leave the rah-rah speeches for cheerleaders and football coaches, who dealt with million-dollar prima donnas. Mack much preferred being able to rely on the competence and professionalism of the sailors onboard *Cheyenne*.

• • •

Over a thousand miles away, the Chinese naval base at Zhanjiang was bustling with activity. The surface group had finally left port and was now headed in the direction of the Chinese Spratly Islands. They were going to position themselves between the American Carrier Battle Group and their islands in order to prevent the US Navy from taking any actions against the Spratlys.

This surface group was one of the most powerful surface-action groups ever to be assembled by the Chinese navy. Consisting of two of the new Luhu destroyers, three Luda I destroyers, and three Jianghu frigates, the group totaled eight ships in all, and they were all heavily armed.

The two new Luhu destroyers carried two French Z-9A helicopters apiece, and each surface ship carried a substantial quantity of surface-to-surface antiship missiles. Many of their vessels also were equipped with the French naval Crotale SAM system, which could take out any American helicopters that might stray too close to the Chinese force.

The fleet had been rushed to sea, and though they were well armed, their commander couldn't help wondering how well prepared they were. The Chinese People's Liberation Army (Navy) had made great strides in gaining new equipment and training since he had graduated from the Canton Surface Vessel Academy, yet there were great strides remaining.

The thing that bothered the Chinese commander the most was that, for all the strength and numbers of his surface group, he did not have the support of many submarines. The military, he knew, was strong in numbers, but much of their equipment was old and antiquated. Were the submarines in such a poor state of disrepair that they were unable to go to sea?

This bothered him in part because of its implications for the Chinese armed forces as a whole. More important, however, like most of the officers in the navy, he had heard rumors of American submarines wreaking havoc on the Chinese forces in this area. If those rumors were true, without many SSNs or SSKs of his own, his surface group was a large, heavily armed, sitting duck.

On board *Cheyenne*, Mack and his officers and crew were doing everything they could to substantiate those rumors – and maybe add a few new ones.

Four hundred feet below the surface, *Cheyenne* picked up her next sonar contact.

'Conn, sonar,' the sonar supervisor reported, 'we're getting a sonar contact, sounds like a Chinese merchant ship. It's heading toward Swallow Reef.'

Mack thought the situation over quickly and decided to ignore the merchant vessel. *Cheyenne* had a mission to perform, and he didn't want to be delayed by taking out a noncombatant. He also didn't want to alert the Chinese task group that *Cheyenne* was heading their way.

Mack went to the conn. 'Proceed at full speed, course 316,' he ordered the OOD. 'Let the merchant go.'

The OOD acknowledged his captain's order.

Slowly the Chinese merchant vessel steamed out of sonar range as *Cheyenne* continued on her way, not knowing that it had been a target and was saved by the graciousness of Captain Mack Mackey.

Eighty-five miles southwest of the Spratlys, *Cheyenne* turned and headed northwest to bypass the Chinese-occupied Spratlys. Naval intelligence had reported a high probability of mines in the area, and Mack had opted to avoid the risk.

The Chinese task group was still being tracked by the US satellites. In addition, the carriers *Independence* and *Nimitz* – which were currently sailing in the Pacific – were monitoring radio traffic and electronic signals for any indications of the Chinese fleet's plans.

Cheyenne continued the 'sprint-and-drift' technique during her long transit, but she also periodically went to periscope depth to communicate via SSIXS and to obtain better information on the position of the Chinese fleet. She also received a refinement of her orders – a refinement that Mack approved of, even though it carried an element of risk.

Cheyenne was scheduled to arrive on station a full day ahead of the Chinese task group. Within twelve hours, Chinese helicopters would come within range of *Cheyenne*'s position, dropping lines of sonobuoys all around them. *Cheyenne* would have to stay like this, deep and silent, until the task group came within fifty miles of her position. Depending upon Mack's assessment at the time, his SSN was then supposed to proceed to shallow depth and launch her Harpoon antiship missiles. If there were more targets than Harpoons, *Cheyenne* was instructed to attack the remaining ships with her Tomahawk antiship missiles (TASM).

The TASM was a longer range missile than the Harpoon, and it carried a warhead with nearly twice the explosive. The Harpoon, on the other hand, was smaller and about fifty knots faster and thus much harder to destroy. The alternative was for *Cheyenne* to use only her Tomahawks and attack the Chinese task group from more than 250 miles away. But that would require external targeting information from either a US aircraft or a satellite.

That would be safer for *Cheyenne*, at least initially, but with only six Tomahawks on board, *Cheyenne* had no chance to destroy the entire task group from such a distance. Mack would then have to decide between allowing at least two Chinese ships to get away, or waiting for those ships to close to within Harpoon range before he could attack them.

Mack didn't want to do that. In the long run, it put *Cheyenne* more at risk. Launching the Tomahawks would give away their general bearing, and every helicopter and surface ship in the area would be coming after *Cheyenne*.

No, Mack liked the other plan better. He'd wait until he could release a large number of missiles all at the same time. *Cheyenne* would then dive deep and head back to the Sulu Sea and the waiting submarine tender *McKee* in order to rearm and resupply for another mission.

Mack had the OOD slow and come shallow enough for the floating wire to copy.

'Conn, radio, we're receiving important traffic on the floating wire. It seems there may be some submarines operating at our planned launch point. The reports indicate that they might even be Alfas.'

'Maintain your present course and speed,' Mack said to the OOD.

'Maintain my present course and speed, aye, sir,' the OOD replied.

Cheyenne was making ten knots at 247 feet, close to the point of inception of cavitation. Mack made his best selection of speed versus depth for continuous broadcast copying.

●   ●   ●

The American frigate *Ingraham* (FFG-61) was nearly five hundred miles from *Independence*, and she was alone. She had been ordered to an area north of the Spratly Islands so that her two SH-60B Seahawk helicopters could help *Cheyenne*'s target missiles. Her captain was pleased with neither her mission nor the reasoning behind it.

Ingraham, an Oliver Hazard Perry class frigate, had been selected for this mission for two simple reasons: she could do the job and she was expendable. The 3,500-ton

Ingraham was cheap, inexpensive, and had about 150 fewer sailors on board than did the more powerful Ticonderoga class cruisers.

The captain had received word of this mission three days ago when his ship was dispatched from the *Nimitz* Carrier Battle Group into the South China Sea. He knew that *Nimitz* could have sent one of the more powerful Aegis cruisers or destroyers, but that would have left the carrier more vulnerable to attack.

Ingraham's captain didn't like being thought of as expendable – but he couldn't really argue with the logic. And it didn't matter anyway. He would carry out his orders to the best of his ability, whether he liked them or not.

He didn't know much about *Cheyenne*, the submarine he would be supporting. He knew that, like *Ingraham* herself, *Cheyenne* was the last of her class. He also knew that *Cheyenne*, though commissioned less than a year earlier, had already become one of the most successful submarines in American naval history. And he knew that her skipper, Captain Mackey, was a good man and a highly respected commanding officer. He hoped that this mission would put his own selection board jacket on the top of the pile when the O–6 selection board was next in session.

For this support mission, *Ingraham* was equipped with a full loadout of weapons, which had both pleased and surprised her captain. He guessed that the full loadout was his admiral's way of compensating for sending *Ingraham* on such a mission, without any support. *Ingraham*'s armament included thirty-six standard SM-1 surface-to-air missiles, four Harpoon missiles, and a full load of Mk 46 torpedoes for their Mk 32 torpedo tubes, plus lots of ammunition for both their Mk 75 gun and their 20mm Phalanx CIWS. The frigate also carried two SH-60B Seahawks, each of which was equipped with a powerful APS-124 surface-search radar under its nose. This radar would be invaluable in providing mid-course guidance to the antiship missiles launched from *Cheyenne*.

Ingraham's job was to support *Cheyenne*. If any of the submarine's missiles failed to hit their mark, *Ingraham* had permission to fire her Harpoon missiles at the Chinese task group. She was also permitted to fire on any enemy vessels or aircraft with which she came into contact, but the emphasis of her mission was to support *Cheyenne*.

On board *Cheyenne*, the communicator had an update for Mack. 'Captain,' he said, 'we just received word that *Ingraham* has arrived in position. She relayed a message for you, Captain. It reads, "all quiet on the northern front."'

Mack smiled at that. 'Funny,' he said. 'How long until we reach our launch point?'

The OOD conversed quickly with the QMOW (quartermaster of the watch) and determined that *Cheyenne* was currently ninety-two miles southwest of where she needed to be. 'If we increase speed to full, our ETA will be in four hours, Captain,' answered the OOD.

Mack acknowledged that. 'Come right to course 045, speed full, depth four hundred feet,' he ordered.

Two hours later the sonar room began buzzing with action.

'Conn, sonar, we have two convergence zone contacts on the spherical array, classified as probable Alfa class SSNs, bearing 010 and 014.'

As the sonar supervisor continued the basis of his classification, a picture emerged that Mack didn't like – and one that *Ingraham*'s captain was going to like even less.

The frigate was supposed to be on station forty-three miles north-east of *Cheyenne*. Mack didn't know it yet, but the two sonar contacts, Masters 37 and 38, were traveling next to each other forty miles northwest of *Ingraham*, which put them at the third point of an almost equilateral triangle, approximately forty-two miles from *Cheyenne*.

Making turns for 12 knots, the Alfas were running at a depth of fifty meters, not knowing that *Cheyenne* was approaching the area. They were heading toward

Ingraham, closing in for what they thought would be an easy kill.

'Come to periscope depth,' Mack ordered the OOD. 'I want to alert *Ingraham*.'

Within minutes, *Cheyenne* was at sixty feet and the 'flash' message was sent via satellite to the lone frigate. The message included *Cheyenne*'s estimated position and bearing to the two Chinese submarines and the fact that *Cheyenne* had tentatively classified them as Alfas.

'Conn, sonar, Masters 37 and 38 have increased speed. Blade rate indicates they're running at thirty-eight – make that forty knots, sir. It looks like they're making their move.'

Mack frowned. That wasn't what he'd wanted to hear. He'd wanted to remain silent until he launched his missiles, but that was no longer an option. Not with two Chinese Alfas racing to destroy *Ingraham*. There were few circumstances where Mack would have stood by and watched an American ship come under fire, and this wasn't one of them. He needed *Ingraham*. He needed it to guide *Cheyenne*'s missiles over the horizon. Without *Ingraham*, *Cheyenne*'s mission was likely to fail.

'Increase speed to flank,' he ordered. 'I want to intercept those Alfas. Come right to course 025.'

'Increase speed to flank and come right to course 025, aye, sir.'

Cheyenne's message, rapidly turned around at CTF 74 headquarters, galvanized *Ingraham*'s officers and crew. The SH-60 crew members ran toward their helicopters, strapping their gear to their flight vests as they ran.

'Launch both helos,' the *Ingraham* captain ordered.

In the operations center on the frigate the sonar room was silent, listening. They had detected the two Alfas, bearing 310 and 320 from them, as soon as the Chinese submarines increased their speed to flank.

'Captain, sonar, we just detected what must be *Cheyenne*, bearing 235. She's running at flank speed also. It looks like she's trying to put herself in between us and the Chinese submarines.'

'Way to go, Mack,' *Ingraham*'s captain said softly.

But the frigate wasn't out of the woods yet. The Chinese Alfas could accelerate up to forty-three knots submerged. On a good day, with a clean hull, *Cheyenne* maxed out at nearly forty knots which meant that the Alfas were going to arrive first.

Not if I can help it, the *Ingraham* captain thought to himself. 'Helm,' he ordered, 'come left to 235, all ahead flank.' He planned to head toward *Cheyenne* at his frigate's top speed. With luck and a strong tail wind, *Ingraham* just might have a chance.

Even running at flank speed, *Cheyenne*'s sonar was able to detect *Ingraham*'s maneuver. The bearing indicated to Mack that she was on station where she was supposed to be. It didn't take Mack long to figure out what her captain had in mind. On the 1MC, Mack himself ordered, 'Man battle stations.'

According to the BSY-1 computers, the range to the Alfas was closing fast. The Chinese submarines were heading southeast at forty-two knots, and *Cheyenne* was heading northeast at 38 knots. Mack would have liked to stay silent, but flank speed was *Cheyenne*'s only hope of heading off the Alfas. Besides, at forty-two knots, the Chinese submarines had no chance of hearing *Cheyenne*'s approach.

When the range to the closest Alfa, Master 37, reached 30,000 yards, Mack ordered tubes one and two made ready in all respects. He also ordered the outer doors opened. The range to the second Alfa, Master 38, was just under 33,000 yards.

'Sir,' the fire-control coordinator reported, 'we're in range of the first Alfa, Master 37. We'll be in range of Master 38 in three minutes.'

Mack nodded, but he did not give the command to shoot.

'I want to wait until they are within 28,000 yards,' he said. 'Tell me when Master 37 comes within that range. Firing point procedures, tube one, Master 37.'

Travelling at this speed, *Cheyenne* was relying on her BSY-1 computers to give her any information she required on the positions of the sonar contacts. Because of her speed, sonar was not able to hear much beyond the water rushing by the hull.

As *Cheyenne*'s BSY-1 computed range neared 28,000 yards, and the *Ingraham*'s CIC (combat information center) reported the range to the Chinese submarines as 25,000 yards, the SH-60 Seahawks from *Ingraham* came into play, laying down lines of sonobuoys one after the other in an effort to determine the exact location of the Alfas. Once they had that information in their onboard computers, they could drop their own torpedoes on the Alfas.

The fire-control coordinator informed Mack the moment the range had decreased to 28,000 yards. Without hesitating, Mack ordered, 'Back full. Match sonar bearings and shoot, tube one, Master 37.'

With *Cheyenne*'s headway quickly killed by the backing bell, Mack ordered, 'Ahead one third.'

'Conn, sonar, unit one running hot, straight, and normal.'

If the Alfa continued on its present course and speed, the torpedo would reach it in seven and a half minutes.

The crew of the lead Alfa was excited. They had been chasing their quarry for some time now and were finally closing in for their first kill – against an American warship, no less. For all their excitement, though, they had no idea that there was an American Mk 48 headed their way.

A hundred feet above the surface, one of *Ingraham*'s SH-60 LAMPS III helicopters detected *Cheyenne*'s first torpedo within moments of its launch. The helos each had a single Mk 50 on board, which were smaller than *Cheyenne*'s torpedoes. The Mk 50's hundred pound warhead was less than a sixth the weight of the explosive packed into Mack's Mk 48.

A quick communication flashed between the two helos, and moments later both pilots launched their Mk 50s – but not at the lead Alfa. *Cheyenne* wasn't likely to need their help with that one. Instead, they targeted the second Chinese submarine, Mack's Master 38.

Below the surface, *Cheyenne* was now comfortably within range of both submarines and was steering the Mk 48 into the lead Alfa, Master 37.

'Conn, sonar,' the sonar supervisor reported, '*Ingraham*'s SH-60s just dropped two torpedoes, sounds like Mk 50s, on the bearing to the second Alfa, Master 38.' There was a pause and then the fire-control coordinator added, 'It looks like they're going to hit, too, sir. BSY-1 shows they dropped them right on top of it.'

Neither of the Chinese submarines had any idea that they had been targeted by any American torpedoes. The lead Chinese Alfa never would.

The 650-pound warhead of *Cheyenne*'s Mk 48 detonated directly aft of the Alfa's single screw and blew off the stern of the submarine. Running at four hundred feet, the crew on board the lead Alfa never had a chance. Those that didn't drown immediately as water rushed into the engine room were crushed by the pressure of the deep sea.

The second Alfa, still running at top speed, was unable to hear either *Cheyenne* or the two Mk 50s heading toward it, but its crew heard the explosion from the Mk 48 on the bearing of their sister ship. The second Alfa's captain slowed immediately to assess the situation – which was the worst thing he could have done. By stopping directly in the path of the American Mk 50s, he had sealed his own fate.

'Conn, sonar, two explosions, sir,' the sonar supervisor said to Mack. 'The Mk 50s just hit their mark.' A moment later he added, 'But she's not breaking up, sir.'

That didn't surprise Mack. The Alfa class SSNs had

always been thought of as one of the hardest types of submarine to kill. Unlike most other submarines, the Alfa had a hull constructed not of steel, but entirely of titanium. This allowed it to dive extremely deep, probably 3,000 feet, and it also made her a very hard target to destroy. Alfas were almost as hard to sink as the double-hulled Typhoon.

The Alfa had gotten lucky, but she hadn't come away undamaged. The two American light weight torpedoes had hit the Alfa on its starboard side, damaging the starboard ballast tanks. To make matters worse, their reactor had automatically shut down when the control rods came unlatched as a result of the torpedo concussions. Without its reactor, the Alfa could not run away.

The officers and crew of the Alfa had just begun to get a grip on their problems when *Cheyenne* fired her second torpedo at Master 38, and things suddenly became much worse.

'Conn, sonar, unit 2 running hot straight and normal,' the sonar supervisor said.

There was nothing for the Chinese submarine to do except wait and die. If it tried to surface, it would list heavily to starboard. With their sonar barely working, the Alfa's sonarmen listened as Mack's torpedo came closer and closer to their submarine. One minute before impact, the Chinese captain did try launching a noisemaker, but the Mk 48 ignored it and continued to close on the helpless submarine.

The torpedo detonated on the same side as had the smaller Mk 50s, but it had more of an impact. The titanium hull had already been weakened by the earlier explosions. This one cracked it clean through, flooding the Alfa and killing all forty-seven men onboard. From the moment *Cheyenne*'s torpedo had acquired, they never had a chance.

That didn't bother Mack at all. This was war, and he knew the Chinese hadn't planned on giving *Ingraham* any chance, either.

The Alfas were gone, and now *Cheyenne* and her crew

had to focus on their mission once more. The Chinese task group was still headed her way, but there was little time left for *Cheyenne* and *Ingraham*'s helos to prepare for the quick but deadly upcoming attack. Mack allowed his crew a short respite from battle stations.

Nineteen hours later, *Cheyenne* came to periscope depth with battle stations remanned. She received word that one of *Ingraham*'s helicopters had detected the Chinese task group 150 miles to the north of *Cheyenne*'s position. *Ingraham* had relocated about fifty miles to the south of *Cheyenne*, but her Seahawks were flying as rotating radar pickets to detect the enemy fleet. As soon as the Chinese task group was discovered, the second Seahawk, freshly fueled and armed, was sent to relieve the first one and allow it to return to the frigate for refueling.

The Seahawk's powerful surface-search radar allowed the helicopter to stay out of Chinese SAM (surface-to-air missile) range while she painted the task group with radar waves. This data would be used to guide *Cheyenne*'s Harpoons into their targets.

Cheyenne proceeded back down to her normal patrol depth and increased her speed to twenty-five knots. Two hours later she was well within Harpoon missile range of the Chinese task group, with Harpoons in all four torpedo tubes and 'battle stations missile' manned.

Mack's orders were unchanged, and so was his plan. He intended to fire his six Harpoons in salvos and then launch his TASMs at the remaining targets. His biggest concern was the speed with which *Cheyenne* would have to operate – both for her own sake and because, if they took too long, the Seahawks risked entering SAM range and being engaged by Chinese missiles.

Cheyenne had trained for this kind of mission, and Mack had always felt that this type – striking at unsuspecting surface ships – was very much the same as that of a waiting sniper: get in position, wait for an opportunity, fire, and slip away.

Cheyenne came to one hundred feet and within minutes had launched all her Harpoons. Without missing a beat, Mack ordered VLS tubes five through ten fired. The Tomahawks were launched one by one as the hatches on each tube opened in sequence and the missiles were ejected skyward.

When the last TASM was away, Mack ordered *Cheyenne* back down to four hundred feet and headed toward the submarine tender *McKee*. They had fired off many of their weapons and needed to rearm in order to remain effective.

Battle stations were once again secured while the torpedo tubes were reloaded but, as was always the case when attacking distant targets, *Cheyenne*'s crew would have to wait to learn how well they had performed. They knew only that twenty-five minutes after the attack, sonar had reported twelve very large primary and secondary explosions. This was a good sign, especially considering that there were only eight vessels in the Chinese task group, but official confirmation of the kills would have to wait.

●   ●   ●

McKee, like all submarine tenders, was an auxiliary vessel with little weaponry and no sonar. Which meant that, ironically, though she had spent nearly all her life servicing submarines, she was virtually defenseless against them and had no way of knowing if one was sneaking up on her.

The *McKee*'s captain was not known for his sense of irony. He would not have been amused to know that, even as his ship was operating quietly off Brunei in wait for *Cheyenne*, a lone Ming class submarine was stalking her. He had weighed anchor after *Cheyenne* left the last time in order to conduct sea training for his crew.

●   ●   ●

Thirteen hours after launching her missiles, *Cheyenne* came to periscope depth to catch up on the latest intelligence and to inform *McKee* that they were en route and would arrive in about twenty-five hours. *Cheyenne* was at periscope depth for as short a time as possible. She was soon on her way to the southern portion of the South China Sea once more, unaware of the enemy submarine that was heading toward *McKee*.

●   ●   ●

The Chinese submarine captain had closed to within twenty-six miles of *McKee*. He would maintain his speed of five knots until the American tender came within range of his SAET-60 homing torpedoes with their 400-kilogram warheads. The maximum range for these torpedoes was 16,400 yards, or a little over eight nautical miles, so the Ming would have to move in close.

Three hours later, the Ming had closed the gap. *McKee* was at the extreme edge of the torpedo's range, and the Chinese captain began preparing his submarine for firing.

Mack was in the control room talking with his watch standers when the report came from sonar.

'Conn, sonar, we just picked up a sonar contact bearing 173; it's opening its torpedo tube doors. The bearing is to the west of *McKee*'s reported position.'

'Come to periscope depth,' Mack said. 'Radio, Captain, contact *McKee* and ask her if any friendly submarines are expected near her location.' Mack had to ask the question, but he would have been surprised if the answer was yes. That would have meant that CTF 74 was losing control of submarine mutual interference.

Battle stations were quickly manned as sonar reported Master 47 to be a probable Ming class SSK. Then the response from *McKee* came back.

'Conn, radio, that's a negative, sir, they're only expecting us. We are the only submarine that should be in the area.'

'Radio, conn, tell *McKee* to get under way at best speed, course 090.' That would take *McKee* directly away from the enemy submarine.

Cheyenne sent the message and then Mack headed deep. Moments later, the sonar supervisor reported contact on *McKee* and that *McKee* had started to move on course 090 and was picking up speed.

'Ahead flank, steer 173,' Mack ordered.

That would serve two purposes, he knew. First, and most important, it would get them within range to fire on the Chinese submarine. Second, and almost as vital, it would serve notice to the Ming, warning them that if they didn't back off from *McKee* they were going to be facing a big, angry American submarine.

The Ming heard *Cheyenne* cavitating, but it didn't alter course. Instead, it increased speed in the direction of *McKee* and fired two torpedoes. Only then did the Chinese submarine change course, but by then it was too late.

Mack had already slowed and, with the BSY-1 computer solutions, had fired two Mk 48s at the Ming. Minutes later, the torpedoes acquired their target and homed in on the enemy submarine. The sonar supervisor reported two explosions, followed by the sounds of the Ming filling with water. The Ming was dead.

'What about the Chinese torpedoes?' Mack asked. 'How's *McKee* doing?'

He didn't have to worry, though. *McKee* was running away from the SAET-60s as fast as she could. At twenty knots, she wasn't able to outrun the torpedoes, but she was able to stay ahead of them until they ran out of gas.

When sonar lost contact on the second Chinese torpedo, Mack ordered *Cheyenne* to periscope depth. 'Radio, conn, tell *McKee* we're coming in.'

He was going to be glad to reach the tender. *Cheyenne* needed to rearm and resupply. But he had the feeling that the captain and crew of *McKee* would be glad to see them, too.

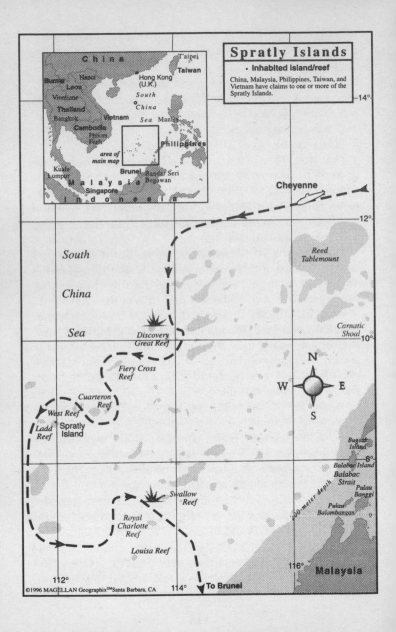

Spratly Islands

- Inhabited island/reef

China, Malaysia, Philippines, Taiwan, and Vietnam have claims to one or more of the Spratly Islands.

China
Burma
Hanoi
Laos
Vientiane
Thailand
Bangkok
Cambodia
Phnom Penh
Vietnam
T'aipei
Taiwan
Hong Kong (U.K.)
South China Sea
Manila
Philippines
area of main map
Brunei
Bandar Seri Begawan
Kuala Lumpur
Malaysia
Singapore
Indonesia

Cheyenne

South

China

Sea

Reed Tablemount

Discovery Great Reef

Fiery Cross Reef

Cuarteron Reef

West Reef

Ladd Reef

Spratly Island

Carnatic Shoal

N
W E
S

Bugsuk Island

Balabac Island

Balabac Strait

Pulau Banggi

200-meter depth

Pulau Balambangan

Swallow Reef

Royal Charlotte Reef

Louisa Reef

Malaysia

To Brunei

©1996 MAGELLAN Geographix℠ Santa Barbara, CA

SIX

Ambush

Cheyenne's crew was well rested after their relatively relaxing stay onboard the submarine tender *McKee*. *Cheyenne* had been rearmed and their food and supply stocks had been replenished. Captain Mackey was even looking forward to his next mission.

According to naval intelligence, that mission was going to be a 'breeze' compared to his last several – and Mack hoped they were right. By now, his officers and crew were combat-hardened veterans who had more than paid their debt to their country. If Mack had his way, he'd give each and every one of them a medal and a promotion for their service.

The captain called the executive officer into his small stateroom. This was one of the few places where the captain could have a quiet moment to himself. He had asked the executive officer to join him because he didn't always trust naval intelligence and he wanted a second opinion on the orders *Cheyenne* had received.

When the executive officer arrived, Mack handed him the message. He didn't say a word. He didn't have to.

The orders called for *Cheyenne* to enter into the Chinese claimed Spratly Islands and patrol several of the now-abandoned oil rigs in the area, including the partially built rig bordering on Swallow Reef.

The executive officer studied them for two minutes and then looked up. The look on his face made it clear that he wasn't any happier than Mack was. A week earlier, naval intelligence had proclaimed those waters too dangerous to enter. Now they were claiming that they'd been deloused and were clear of all enemy submarines.

Mack had gotten what he'd wanted – confirmation of his suspicions. *Cheyenne* had her orders, and she would carry them out, but she would be expecting trouble, no matter what those intel guys said.

'Gather the officers,' he said. 'I want them all in the wardroom in fifteen minutes.'

Ever since he first met the executive officer, Mack had liked him and trusted his opinion. During wartime, Mack knew, one could never be too reliant on intelligence reports from thousands of miles away. The executive officer had agreed with his feelings on their orders and that made Mack trust him even more.

Fifteen minutes later, the wardroom was quiet when Mack entered. He looked around at the assembled officers and decided to get right to the point.

'We've been ordered to enter the Spratly Islands chain and patrol several oil rigs in the area which are believed to be possible locations for submarine supply depots,' he said. 'Naval intelligence doubts this finding, but they have sent us to investigate nonetheless.'

Because the intelligence analysts didn't think that they would find anything in the area, CTF 74 had decided it would be cost efficient to load *Cheyenne* with only twenty Mk-48 torpedoes; no Tomahawks and no Harpoons. So even if Mack did find a remote Chinese operating location, he couldn't attack it with Tomahawks as he would have liked to. He was ordered to report back, and then the Navy would order an air strike.

He hated this kind of thinking.

The assembled officers were silent, waiting for him to continue. 'Naval intelligence reports that due to our successful actions during the past several weeks, as well as the actions of the rest of the Navy, the Chinese units in the area are running low on supplies and morale. They expect that, at the most, we will come into contact with only a handful of submarines in these waters.'

Mack looked around the room, assessing his officers. 'This mission is supposed to be an easy one,' he said, 'but you all know what that means. It just means we have to be extra careful and keep on our toes. I don't like being that close to Chinese occupied waters any more than you do. But we have our orders.'

After the usual number of questions, the wardroom was cleared and the captain went back to his stateroom, where he again examined his orders. He still didn't like what he was reading.

Mack looked at the chart he normally kept in the wardroom. It was one of the few good charts he'd ever seen of the Spratly Islands. The chain was oval, shaped roughly like a football, with four islands that *Cheyenne* needed to patrol.

As Mack examined the chart, he decided he would steam silently from the north into the waters surrounding Discovery Great Reef. From there, he would proceed in a counterclockwise direction, continuing west and south until he arrived near Cuarteron Reef, right in the center of the oval.

From there, *Cheyenne* would travel to Swallow Reef, near the southern border of the islands, and then sail northeast until she arrived at her last search area, Carnatic Reef. Assuming that Intel was right – an assumption Mack was not prepared to make – and the area was clean, *Cheyenne* would then continue on to the north to await further orders.

Cheyenne was now passing the island of Palawan to the east. Navigating the remaining 200 miles in the narrow but deep channel leading to Mindoro Strait would require a number of GPS fixes en route. The submarine tender *McKee*, from which he had just finished rearming, would remain on station in the Sulu Sea until ordered by CTF 74 to relocate.

After the recent submarine attack on *McKee*, the *Independence* and the *Nimitz* Battle Groups had each decided to part with one ASW helicopter, and the two LAMPS III helos were now being flown to *McKee*'s position.

The SH-60s would be operated from *McKee*'s landing pads in order to protect the tender from any possible future submarine threats. The SH-60Bs were also equipped to carry the Penguin antiship missile, which would offer *McKee* an antisurface defense as well. The Navy would not be taking any more chances by sending a defenseless tender into the line of fire.

One other good thing came out of that attack on *McKee* – at least from Mack's point of view. *McKee*'s Captain was very appreciative of *Cheyenne*'s timely rescue and had provided as much fresh fruit as *Cheyenne*'s storage spaces would allow. Fresh fruit was scarce on board a submarine and stocks often ran out quickly. This gesture on the part of *McKee*'s captain was greatly appreciated, and while the fruit would not last long, it would help ensure that the beginning of *Cheyenne*'s cruise would be enjoyable.

Having found a Ming SSK in the Sulu Sea, Mack could not afford the luxury of running on the surface until clear of Mindoro Strait. Still, the channel out to the Sulu Sea was narrow and treacherous, so Mack decided to supplement the GPS fixes with occasional active sonar. The threat of other Chinese submarines was real, but so was the threat of running into the side of the channel.

Once past the shallow waters of Mindoro Strait, *Cheyenne* accelerated to twenty knots, on course 300 toward the start of her counterclockwise search of the Spratly Islands. Upon arrival, Mack ordered the OOD to run at four knots until they determined that the area was clear before continuing on their way.

The TB-23 towed array was streamed to help in the search of the deep water in case there were Chinese SSNs trying to slip in from the north. After a careful sonar search,

Cheyenne increased speed to full and altered course for Discovery Great Reef.

The more Mack thought about this current mission, the less he liked it. He was all too aware of how easy it would be for a diesel submarine like a Kilo to hide in the island waters near the oil platforms. An enemy submarine could lie in wait near the bottom of the shallow water, hiding until *Cheyenne* came within torpedo range. They could even bottom without damage, since the Chinese diesel submarines didn't have a GRP (glass-reinforced plastic) sonar dome or seawater cooling for a steam propulsion plant to worry about. Captain Mackey didn't like that thought at all.

Mack decided that once he was within twenty-five miles of each search area, he would reduce *Cheyenne*'s speed to eight to ten knots and that once he was within ten miles he would slow to four to seven knots. He didn't want anyone sneaking up on them, and running slow was the best way to keep *Cheyenne* quiet.

When *Cheyenne* was twenty-five miles north-northeast of the Spratlys, Mack proceeded to the control room, looked at *Cheyenne*'s position on the quartermaster's chart, and then ordered the OOD, 'Slow to ten knots.'

'Slow to ten knots, aye, sir.'

The change in the speed of the submarine, while sudden, was not overly drastic for the crew. They had gotten used to the rough riding of a submarine in close combat.

Hours before, *Cheyenne* had shifted from the TB-23 to the TB-16 towed array. The sonar operators were listening quietly, but heard nothing on the towed array or the spherical and conformal sonars, and the sonar supervisor soon reported that there were no contacts. Mack was pleased with that report. He knew that if they were to encounter an enemy submarine, they would be in for a dangerous, shallow water fight.

Cheyenne was not at home in coastal waters like these.

The Los Angeles class submarines were designed for blue water operations. *Cheyenne* and her sister ships performed best in the open ocean. While they still performed well in areas like the South China Sea and, more specifically, the Spratly Islands, their superiority gap was narrowed markedly.

A Los Angeles class SSN was 360 feet in length – nearly 100 feet longer than an Alfa submarine, and the Chinese and Russian Kilo submarines were smaller still. The Kilo was a perfect weapon system for these dangerous waters. Measuring 229 feet, it could weave in and out of tight spots that *Cheyenne* would not even want to venture into.

As *Cheyenne* approached Discovery Great Reef, Mack decided to remain relatively shallow. That would allow *Cheyenne* to copy any radio traffic which might be broadcast to them. In addition, he didn't trust the water depths in this area. He figured he had a better chance of running aground than he did of being detected by the enemy.

When *Cheyenne* crossed the 100 fathom curve inbound for Discovery Great Reef, Mack ordered, 'Come to periscope depth.'

Cheyenne had already been running shallow at 200 feet. Now, however, Mack would use the periscope to check out the notorious 'oil platforms.'

'Conn, sonar,' the sonar supervisor called a short time later. 'I think we've got a contact on the towed array. It sounds faint, but it may be a submarine ... although the computers haven't been able to confirm a thing.'

The contact was currently too weak for *Cheyenne*'s sonar operators to do much with. Mack made a mental note to keep checking on it, though. He was sure that if this was a submarine they were picking up, *Cheyenne* would be going after it soon.

Mack was also sure that whatever they were picking up had not yet detected their own presence in these waters. *Cheyenne* was currently running at only three knots to minimize the periscope 'feather,' the wake caused by the periscope barrel as it moved through the air-water interface, and she was nearly as quiet as she could be.

'Captain, we are currently seventeen miles northeast of the first oil rig,' the navigator reported.

'Sonar, Captain, do you have any additional information to report on that contact?' Mack asked.

'Conn, sonar, we classify Master 48 as a probable submarine contact to the southwest. It appears that it's on the other end of the abandoned oil rig from our position. It's barely making a sound, though.'

Mack acknowledged the report and ordered battle stations manned and the towed array housed. He still didn't know for sure what that contact was, but he had the feeling that *Cheyenne* was about to go into battle once more.

• • •

Southwest of *Cheyenne*, at the other end of the abandoned oil rig, a Chinese Kilo submarine was getting into position near Discovery Great Reef. The Kilo was running silently, and its captain was confident that they could not be detected. But then, based on estimates from Chinese intelligence, he did not expect any American SSNs to be near his position for at least another day.

The Chinese intelligence machine was very different from its American counterpart. The Chinese focused their intelligence on the human aspect, or HUMINT, while the Americans focused their intelligence on ELINT – electronic signals interception and satellite photography.

These differences made sense in terms of the backgrounds of the two countries. China had a massive population, with citizens and former citizens scattered around the world. America, on the other hand, had massive quantities of money which they could use to invest in their defense industry.

These differences came into play off the Spratlys. *Cheyenne*, with her advanced technology and sophisticated sonar equipment, was able to pick up traces of the Kilo. The Chinese boat, however, was relying more heavily on human observers – but *Cheyenne*'s submerged transit of the Philippine Islands area had precluded any HUMINT by Chinese observers on the islands.

The captain of the Chinese Kilo finally arrived in his position slightly more than one nautical mile west of the oil platform. He planned to wait there in silence for passing American naval vessels, hoping for some to venture close enough for him to strike.

He didn't know it, but he was about to get his wish.

• • •

'Conn, sonar,' reported the sonar supervisor, 'we just lost contact on Master 48.'

'What was the last position of Master 48?' Mack asked the fire-control coordinator.

The executive officer, who was acting as fire-control coordinator for this watch, said, 'Captain, Master 48 was about nineteen thousand yards west of the Discovery Great Reef oil rig. Do you think she heard us?'

The question was a good one.

Could they have heard us? Mack wondered. The most probable reason that they would lose contact with a submarine was either that the enemy submarine's noise was being shielded from *Cheyenne*'s sonar, possibly by a thermal layer or the surf noise, or that the submarine had detected *Cheyenne*'s presence and had either stopped or was running silently. The silence indicated that if there was a submarine out there, it was probably a Chinese diesel boat, running on its batteries.

Slowly, *Cheyenne* approached the oil rig, which lay within one mile of Discovery Great Reef. The water was extremely shallow in this area and the huge rocks surrounding the now dilapidated oil rig served to shield the diesel's sounds.

Cheyenne's passive sonar suite was severely degraded in the shallow environment of the littorals. In this environment, active sonar would work almost as well as passive, if they used MIDAS to discriminate between rocks and a submarine's longer hull, but Mack didn't seriously consider the idea. He knew that using his active sonar would give away *Cheyenne*'s exact position. He'd rather have both submarines blind than give away his position to the enemy.

Through the periscope, Mack could see the Discovery Great Reef oil rig. At a glance, he could tell that it had been destroyed during the Chinese occupation of the island. But he needed to give it more than just a glance. He was supposed to get some accurate photographs of the rig for intelligence back in Washington. In addition, he needed to ensure that the rig was not being used as a Chinese submarine depot which could rearm or refuel Chinese SSKs.

He made another quick circle as he 'danced' the periscope around the surface. He could find no evidence that the rig was being used for anything – or that it was even in the process of being repaired – but still he was cautious. This was a very dangerous place for *Cheyenne* to be running at periscope depth.

Six nautical miles away, or about 12,000 yards from *Cheyenne*'s current position, the Chinese Kilo submarine was operating in its silent mode – running on its batteries. With no noise coming from their own ship, the Chinese sonar operators listened carefully to their low frequency sonar, searching the waters for the sound of any American vessels.

They heard nothing.

The Chinese had been loitering here, running silently on their batteries, for seventeen hours, keeping their depth shallow at 45 feet and their ears open. The captain was waiting for the Americans to walk into his trap.

After seventeen hours, however, the captain of the Kilo grew impatient. He'd had enough of this waiting. Slowly the Kilo pulled out of its hiding spot and began to pick up speed. Its captain had decided to make a run at six knots, slowly and quietly circling Discovery Great Reef, searching for any American naval vessels.

As soon as the Kilo moved, it lost its protection against American sonars, and *Cheyenne* heard it.

'Conn, sonar, we just reacquired Master 48. It's a Kilo, single six-bladed screw. It just increased speed to six knots and it's heading north.'

A short time later a BSY-1 operator reported the Kilo's range, and Mack knew *Cheyenne* was in trouble. The Chinese submarine was only 11,000 yards away, which meant that Mack had unknowingly brought *Cheyenne* well within weapons range of the Chinese Kilo and her TEST-71 homing torpedoes.

'Make tubes one and two ready,' Mack ordered. 'But *do not open the outer doors*!' He emphasized that. They were too close, and he didn't want to give the Kilo any chance of detecting their location.

'Make tubes one and two ready but do not open the outer doors, aye, sir.'

Mack had a problem. He had the drop on the Kilo, but he didn't have much maneuvering room. If the Kilo got off a return shot, *Cheyenne* could be in trouble.

And that was the least of his worries. His bigger problem was his lack of intel. Were there other Chinese submarines out there? Naval intelligence said no – but they'd missed one already. Who was to say they hadn't missed more?

This was a problem because he would give away his position as soon as he fired on the Kilo – and even if that submarine didn't fire back, there could be others hiding in the shallow water waiting to pounce.

Captain Mackey ordered *Cheyenne* rigged for ultraquiet. He wanted every effort made to ensure that nothing alerted the Kilo to their location. Word was quickly passed to all compartments over the sound powered phones. Non-vital equipment was quickly secured. The crew whispered when they spoke, wondering what would be next.

On board the Chinese submarine, the captain was growing frustrated. He was assigned to keep watch for American submarines, but he knew that he would never hear them unless they were close enough to fire their Mk 48s. Even under ideal circumstances his passive sonar was never up to par with the American BSY-1 system, but in these shallow waters his Russian passive sonar performance was even worse.

Frustrated, he ordered his sonar room to use their active sonar and ping the area, hoping to even out the playing field and get a better fix on his surroundings. He had no idea that the USS *Cheyenne* was attempting to close in on his position.

'Conn, sonar, the Kilo just went active on its fire-control sonar. He painted the entire area for us.'

Mack knew immediately that this was good news as well as bad. It was bad because the Kilo now knew where *Cheyenne* was and had also received a firing solution. The good news, however, was that the active ping had given the same data to *Cheyenne*. Even more important, that one ping had lit up the murky waters of Discovery Great Reef like a flashlight. Thanks to that ping, Mack now knew that the Chinese Kilo was all alone.

Mack had the upper hand, but he wouldn't have it for long. He had to act fast – and act first.

He initiated the firing point procedures to attack the Kilo, Master 48. 'Open the outer doors on tubes one and two,' ordered Mack.

'Open the outer doors on tubes one and two, aye, sir.'

'Match sonar bearings and shoot tubes one and two.'

'Match sonar bearings and shoot tubes one and two, aye, sir.'

Cheyenne's torpedo tube muzzle doors opened and two

Mk 48 ADCAPs knifed through the murky water toward the enemy submarine.

On board the lone Chinese Kilo, the captain was furious with himself. He had been tasked with waiting quietly for any American target, but he had lost his patience, and it had cost him.

He would have liked to blame it on timing and bad luck – that American submarine showing up just when he decided to take a stroll around the reef was unbelievably bad luck – but he knew he couldn't shrug it off that easily. After all, he had no idea how long the Americans had been out there. No, the simple truth was he'd made a mistake. Now he could only hope that the American captain would make one, too.

That hope died almost immediately. He had barely formed the thought when his sonar room alerted him to their discovery. The American captain had not made a mistake. He'd beaten the Chinese captain to the punch, launching not one but two deadly ADCAP torpedoes before the Kilo had even gotten their tubes ready.

Within minutes the two Mk 48s had acquired the Kilo and their wires were cut. The Mk 48s were on their own as they entered the terminal phase of their 'flight.'

The Chinese submarine launched a series of noise-makers, one after another, and began twisting through the shallow water in an effort to decoy the two torpedoes. It was no use, though. The Kilo had no more room to maneuver than *Cheyenne* did, and no time to run.

The Mk 48s were now using their powerful active seek-ers and they simply ignored the noisemakers. They stayed with the Kilo as it tried to evade.

Within minutes, two nearly simultaneous explosions announced to *Cheyenne*'s crew that their weapons had found their mark. The two Mk 48s had impacted, one next to the other, into the port side of the Kilo.

The explosion caused the Chinese boat to split in half after both sides had filled with water. *Cheyenne* had

128

destroyed another boat – and not just any submarine. This was another Kilo, the pride of the Chinese navy.

'Conn, sonar, I don't hear anything else in the area,' the sonar supervisor reported to the captain after the situation was under control.

'It looks like this area has been "deloused,"' the captain said. 'I don't think that there are any other vessels operating in the area, but just to make sure let's make a quick check around and then head to our second search area.'

Battle stations and the rig for ultraquiet were secured, and the reconnoiter around the reef came up empty. *Cheyenne* turned up no signs that there was a submarine depot operating in this locality. There was also no sonar indication of any other submarines that may have been operating with the Kilo.

Mack was not surprised, but he couldn't help feeling a little relieved. 'Plot a new course for Cuarteron Reef, search area 2, which takes us outside this shallow water,' Captain Mackey said to the navigator.

'Aye, Captain, we've already begun to plot the course,' the navigator replied.

Discovery Great Reef was close to Cuarteron Reef, but the trip itself would take several hours. Mack could have covered it in far less time, but he wanted to remain silent and chose to keep *Cheyenne*'s speed between five and ten knots. Once again, Mack was frustrated with his passive sonar performance in these shallow waters, but he was not going to risk giving away his position, so he kept *Cheyenne* quiet and hoped that if something was out there they would hear it.

As *Cheyenne* approached closer to the abandoned oil rig, Mack got more photographs of the oil platform. Less than three months ago, this area had been crowded with oil workers who were attempting to extract oil from the bottom of the islands. Now, however, there was not a soul on the rig, and the neighboring islands were completely

129

occupied by Chinese troops who would have loved to attack *Cheyenne* if given the chance. But Mack wasn't about to give them that chance. Not if he could help it, anyway.

'Sonar, conn, have you picked up any contacts yet?' Mack asked of the sonar supervisor.

'Conn, sonar, nothing at all, Captain.'

Mack acknowledged the report, but he wasn't sure if this was a good sign or a bad one.

At three knots, *Cheyenne* crept around the entire length of Cuarteron Reef but found no sign of enemy submarine operations in the area. That was definitely a good sign, Mack thought.

'Next stop, Swallow Reef,' Mackey said to the executive officer before turning the conn back over to the waiting OOD.

The captain, satisfied with *Cheyenne*'s search, went back to his stateroom for some rest. He gave specific orders to the executive officer not to have him disturbed unless there was an emergency.

● ● ●

Several hours later the executive officer walked quietly into the captain's stateroom and roused him. As soon as Mack opened his eyes and saw his executive officer standing over him, he knew something was up.

'What happened?' Mack asked. 'Did you run us aground?'

But the executive officer was in no mood for humor. 'We've got numerous contacts near Swallow Reef, Captain,' he said. 'I think we found their submarine depot.'

Mack was on his feet and heading back toward the control room before his executive officer finished speaking.

In the control room, the OOD was examining the plotting tables. Mack glanced over at the OOD, then headed straight for the sonar room and looked at the sonar supervisor. 'What have we got?' he asked.

'Sir, it looks like the abandoned Swallow Reef oil platform is the submarine depot we were sent here to find. So far, we've heard two submarines surface in the area. Both submarines then slowed, heading north. They have since begun to recharge their batteries on all diesels and we can hear lots of activity going on out there.'

'Do you have any classification on those two that surfaced?' Mack asked.

The sonar supervisor nodded. 'We just picked up the contacts three minutes ago, sir. We've positively identified two submarine contacts, both old Romeos. But there might be more of them out there.'

This situation was exactly what Mack had hoped to avoid. He had detected a major submarine operation at Swallow Reef, but he had no permission to attack the targets. He wasn't even sure that his Mk 48s could do a job that was best suited to Tomahawks.

Thinking it over, examining the few possibilities available to him, Mack came up with a plan. It might not have been on the same level of innovation and inspiration as some of his earlier ideas, but it was the only thing that occurred to him.

He knew that *Cheyenne* would eventually be in position to attack both submarines, now designated Masters 49 and 50. He also assumed that there were probably more than two submarines rearming and refueling at this depot. What Mack wanted to do was to attack the depot itself and put it out of commission.

The question was – in addition to whether or not Mack and *Cheyenne* could pull it off – would CTF 74 grant him such leeway? Mack was pretty sure that the answer would be no, but just in case he called his combat systems officer and his communicator in for a meeting in the wardroom.

'Would it be possible,' the captain asked the combat systems officer, 'to destroy that Chinese depot by hitting them with Mk 48s?'

The combat systems officer scratched his head before

looking up at Mack. 'I guess we could do it, sir. The oil platform acts as shelter to the submarines beneath it and we could target those submarines. That would, at the very least, severely disrupt operations at the minibase.' He paused and looked at Mack. 'But, sir,' he went on, 'have we been granted permission to attack the platform and the submarines in it?'

'Not yet,' Mack said, glad that his officers were both involved and aware of what *Cheyenne*'s orders were. Turning to the communicator, he added, 'Which is where you come in. I want you to draft a message to CTF 74, tell him what we've found, and request permission to engage the submarines in the depot and hopefully bring down the entire platform.'

'Yes, sir,' the two officers replied. They were dismissed and both went about their work. The combat systems officer went to the quartermaster to find the best locations from which they could launch their attack. The communicator went straight to the radio room.

'Make preparations to come to periscope depth,' Mack said to the OOD.

'Make preparations to come to periscope depth, aye, sir.'

Minutes later, *Cheyenne* was brought from two hundred feet to periscope depth. Once the safety sweep revealed no surface contacts, the radio communications mast was quickly raised, and the message sent and receipted for. Several minutes later, after an extremely rapid response from CTF 74, the mast was lowered and the captain entered the radio room, one of the most highly classified places on the submarine.

The radio room dealt with encrypting devices and top-secret messages, and the message *Cheyenne* had just received was no exception. As Mack entered, the communicator handed him a computer printout.

Mack glanced at the message, paused, and then read it again. ,

USS INDEPENDENCE UNDER HEAVY CHINESE AIR
ATTACK. AIRCRAFT WILL BE UNABLE TO ASSIST
CHEYENNE IN DESTRUCTION OF OIL PLATFORM/SUB-
MARINE DEPOT. PERMISSION GRANTED TO DESTROY
SWALLOW REEF SUBMARINE DEPOT.

The executive officer came in just as Mack was finishing
reading the message for the second time. The executive
officer had completed a tour of the engineering spaces
with the engineer officer. 'The combat systems officer
told me what's going on,' he said. 'Anything I can help
with?'

Mack showed him the message, and then the two of
them headed for the wardroom to work out the plan for
attacking the Chinese submarine depot. When they had
reached an agreement on the best plan of attack, Mack
instructed the executive officer to provide the appropriate
details to all the areas of the ship which would play a part
in the execution of the operation.

The plan they had come up with was for *Cheyenne* to
head north at a speed of eight knots. Once they were past
Royal Charlotte Reef, and as soon as they came within
35,000 yards west of the depot, they would slow to five
knots and approach the depot quietly at a depth of one
hundred feet. That depth would allow the top of *Cheyenne*'s
sail to clear any of the shallow draft vessels which might
be loitering overhead. They would listen for any signs of
submarine or surface ship activity and then they would
close in for the kill.

Once they were within 30,000 yards of the transformed
oil rig they would launch eight Mk 48s at the vessels being
refitted under the platform. They would then head southeast until they had exited the waters of the Spratly Islands.
Once clear, they would proceed northeast along the one
hundred fathom curve until they were ready to reenter
the islands chain and investigate their fourth search area
– Carnatic Reef.

That was the plan. Now it was up to Mack, his officers, and the crew to execute it.

With battle stations once again manned, *Cheyenne* slowed to five knots as they approached weapons range.

'Conn, sonar, we just detected two Huangfen missile patrol boats,' the sonar supervisor said. 'They sailed underneath the depot platform and pulled in next to the Romeos. I'll bet they're refueling, sir.'

'Sonar, conn, anything else? Any other surface ships in the area?' asked the captain.

'Conn, sonar, it's hard to tell. This shallow water has turned our passive sonar inside out. Sometimes it gives us what we want. Other times it's anyone's guess.'

'Sonar, conn, aye,' Mack said. He thought for a moment, then said, 'Okay, how long until we are in firing position?'

The fire-control coordinator answered him. 'It should be three more minutes, Captain.'

Tubes one and two were readied for firing. Because they had the exact location of the noisy Romeos, and because the Romeos were directly below the platform, they also had the exact location of the platform. They would launch all eight Mk 48s in succession as rapidly as possible, cutting the wires immediately after they had left the tubes. This left the torpedoes to hit their targets without guidance from *Cheyenne*.

Mack had the torpedoes fired two at a time, tubes one and two first, then tubes three and four. He did this twice, and the procedure didn't take long. *Cheyenne* had recently had lots of experience loading and firing torpedoes, and that experience paid off.

'Conn, sonar, we just got another sonar contact,' the sonar supervisor said as the last two Mk 48s were launched. 'A single Huchuan torpedo boat is heading our way. The noise level indicates it's running at full speed.'

Mack had been briefed on the Huchuan hydrofoils and knew that the Chinese had more than seventy of them in service. He also knew that these small ships could reach speeds of more than fifty knots. The Huchuan was designated Master 53.

'What's the range to the Huchuan, Master 53?' asked Mack.

'We can't tell, Captain,' the fire-control coordinator answered. 'The water's too shallow and we can't do an accurate TMA on the boat. Bearings are coming in over a twenty-degree spread.'

'Well, then,' Mack said, 'we have no choice. We have to go active.'

This was one of the rare times Mack could feel right using his BSY-1 sonar system in an active mode. For one thing, the Chinese already knew where they were. Eight torpedoes on essentially the same bearing were a dead giveaway. Besides, he knew that any Chinese vessels with sonar in the area would be concentrating on the eight Mk 48s headed for the naval depot under the abandoned oil rig. With luck, they would be more worried about that and wouldn't care about *Cheyenne*'s rushed getaway.

The Huchuan hydrofoil coming their way was Mack's biggest concern at the moment, but the hydrofoils had no sonar. Without a sonar, they would be unable to determine if *Cheyenne* was active, or even if she launched a torpedo in their direction.

Cheyenne's active sonar pings echoed through the hull. Being foilborne, sonar was actually tracking the wake it generated, not the Huchuan itself. But that was enough for a 'down-the-throat' shot.

When *Cheyenne*'s sonar went active, Mack was able to acquire an accurate firing solution to the Chinese patrol boat. He ordered tube one fired at the Chinese Huchuan. The Mk 48 was set to detonate, at a depth of ten feet, just beneath the foils.

The Huchuan, without a sonar system, was unaware that a torpedo was heading its way and continued on in the direction they expected *Cheyenne* to be. The captain of the hydrofoil had calculated *Cheyenne*'s position correctly

– but that was also the same direction from which the latest Mk 48 was coming. This brought them closer and closer to the oncoming torpedo, closing rapidly at a combined speed of over one hundred knots.

'Conn, sonar, our Mk 48 just detonated beneath the PT boat.'

The Huchuan went airborne, propelled by the force of the water exploding up from beneath it. It rotated in a spiral as it flew, killing those sailors aboard without seat belts as they were thrown around like 'BBs in a boxcar.' Moments later, those who had seat belts – mostly bridge personnel – were killed instantly when the boat finally hit the water, upside down, at fifty knots.

When sonar also reported eight extremely large explosions followed by a dozen smaller ones, Mack went to periscope depth and then broached to get the periscope high enough to visually assess the damage.

Mack was pleased with what he saw. They had blown up two Chinese submarines, Masters 49 and 50, two missile patrol boats, Masters 51 and 52, and a torpedo hydrofoil, Master 53. Most important, though, the Chinese naval depot was no longer usable, with fires raging on the platform as it tilted into the sea.

Cheyenne's captain grinned fiercely, pride in his ship and his crew welling up within him. They'd been given a difficult assignment, and once again they'd carried it out.

He was about to order *Cheyenne* to resume her patrol, heading southeast, out of the islands, when the executive officer walked up to Mack, bringing with him a quiet sense of urgency.

'Captain,' he said, 'we just received an emergency message. Our current mission has been diverted.' He showed the new orders to Mack.

Cheyenne was to deploy directly to the north of the Spratly Islands. A Chinese convoy was forming and would be heading south for the islands. *Cheyenne*'s orders were to sink it. But not just yet.

Cheyenne had expended more than half the Mk 48s she was given. She had enough left on board to complete her current mission, but not enough to take out an entire convoy.

Feeling his earlier sense of pride in his crew turn to frustration at the loadouts he'd been given, Mack ordered *Cheyenne* to return to *McKee*. They'd come back, he knew, and deal with that convoy . . . but not until they'd had the chance to rearm.

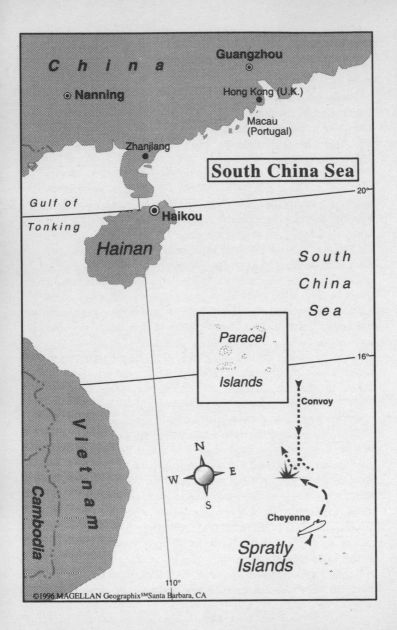

SEVEN

Target: Convoy

Mack was angry. *Cheyenne* had made it through her recent encounters unscathed, and was now safely moored alongside *McKee*, but the fact that Mack and his crew were alive was a tribute to their own superb training, not any reflection on the intelligence they had received. And that was what had Mack so angry. He didn't object to his orders. His job was to take his submarine and his crew into danger – into battle itself, if necessary – but he insisted on giving his men every chance to survive the conflict. That meant proper weaponry, reliable equipment, and accurate information. *Cheyenne* had supplied the first two components, but naval intelligence had dropped the ball on the third.

Mack had been around long enough to know that sometimes lousy intelligence happened. That was why it was called the 'fog of war.' But that didn't make him feel any better. Not when it was his submarine and his crew at risk because of someone else's mistake.

The one good thing that had come out of that mess – besides *Cheyenne*'s performance – was the P4 message he held in his hand. The P4, or 'personal for,' message was an apology from USCINCPAC himself for the lousy intelligence *Cheyenne* had been provided before the last mission. Mack especially liked the part where the admiral had quoted the CNO (Chief of Naval Operations), currently the most senior officer in the Navy, as taking a personal interest in the intelligence fiasco.

He opened the message and read that part one more time. The CNO had directed a 'reevaluation of procedures and decision-making personnel' within the naval intelligence chain of command.

Mack smiled. That meant a lot of people were going to come under fire, and that was good. With luck, the next commanding officer and crew going into battle would be better prepared with accurate intelligence.

Especially since, Mack suspected, he knew who that next commanding officer was going to be. *Cheyenne* was still the best asset the US Navy had in the area, at least for the kinds of missions that were being conducted, and Mack was pretty sure that they would be called upon again soon.

'Excuse me, Captain,' the executive officer said. He had just climbed to the bridge and poked his head through the upper access hatch. 'They're waiting for you on *McKee*. Sounds like something hot.'

'Thank you,' Mack said. 'Any idea what's up?'

'Well, sir, judging from the latest intelligence . . .' The executive officer let the sentence taper off as Mack shot him a hard look.

'Not funny.'

'No, sir, not at all, but snafus do happen. I'm just glad that the crew was ready for the challenge.'

Mack nodded and the executive officer continued, 'From what I can gather from the intelligence officer on board *McKee*, the Chinese merchant convoy that was assembling off the south coast of China has decided to make a fast break for the Spratlys. My guess is somebody figures that we didn't make it out of that last scrap intact and they want to take advantage of that by trying to get some supplies through while there's no one around to stop them.'

Mack nodded. That was a good reading of the situation. Except that the Chinese were wrong. *Cheyenne* had survived, and was, no doubt, about to be assigned to show the Chinese how wrong they were.

Captain Mackey was looking over the side of the bridge as the first Mk-48 was already being hoisted into the air and swung over from *McKee* to *Cheyenne*'s waiting crew.

The job had to be hot if weapons were being transferred even before the mission debriefing.

Mack liked this assignment. He couldn't recall the last time an American submarine went after a real merchant convoy. During World War II, the Japanese had not developed a real convoy system like the United States had with the British. Most of the ships American submarines sank were independents or just ships travelling together. Closely escorted convoys like this one just weren't used.

Which meant that with this mission *Cheyenne* would get to set the standard for how a modern convoy battle occurred. Mack liked that a lot.

Cheyenne had more sophisticated weapons than were available during World War II, weapons that were faster and had a longer range, but so did the escort defenses. It would still be a case of *Cheyenne* getting into position as quietly as possible and then hitting the convoy before they could react.

'So we get to stop that convoy,' Mack said. He nodded and patted the side of the bridge. 'We can do that.'

'Yes, sir,' the executive officer said. Then his eyes focused beyond the captain. 'Looks like they're getting impatient on *McKee*. The combat systems officer and operations officer are already over there.'

Mack glanced over at the submarine tender and nodded. 'I'll be back as soon as I can. Let me know how long until the reload is completed when I get back. I suspect we'll need to be under way again as soon as possible.'

The executive officer gave a quick salute and said, 'Aye, aye, sir,' as Mack scrambled down the ladder to the control room. He then turned and looked out over the vast expanse of the South China Sea and wondered what the next few days would bring and how a modern convoy battle would really shape up.

●　●　●

Far out to sea, the same thoughts were going through the mind of the Chinese escort squadron commander as the convoy was steaming toward the Spratly Islands. The best speed some of the convoy ships could make was ten knots, which was far too slow to attempt a sudden dash to the Spratly Islands. But the South Sea fleet commander had been adamant about taking some of the AK troop transport ships and an ARS repair ship with the convoy.

So now he was in command of a slow convoy with an escort squadron that was too small and underarmed. Only one of his seven ships carried helicopters for ASW prosecution, a mission area that the entire Chinese fleet was sorely inexperienced in. But they did have a lot of ASW ordnance. Years of cooperation with the then Soviet navy had sponsored a reliance on massive firepower. If an American submarine was unfortunate enough to be caught trying to torpedo any of his ships, a tremendous amount of firepower was available to respond. The big problem would be finding the American submarine.

The United States had notoriously quiet submarines. The first indication the Chinese would have that an American was out there would probably be when a ship blew up. But that could not be helped.

The convoy commander tightened his knuckles until white skin showed clearly through the gloom of the closing night. Rapid response and good joss would have to answer for American technology. That *and* a good plan.

He permitted himself a slight smile. Since he could not dissuade the admiral from the convoy mission, he had at least tried his best to guarantee its safe arrival. He knew that the best weapon against a submarine was another submarine. Years of experience had taught him that. It was common sense and a frequently quoted slogan among American submariners, but none of the quiet diesel submarines in the Chinese fleet could keep up for long while underwater and running on its batteries, even with his slow convoy.

But they could be strategically placed in carefully selected locations and thus be in position to listen for, detect, and then kill any American submarine that attempted to attack the convoy.

He had no doubt that an American submarine would find and track the convoy. He had no doubt that an American submarine would attack the convoy. He had no doubt that a few, perhaps even several, of his ships would be sunk by the American submarine. But he also had no doubt that the American captain would never suspect that a string of hidden Chinese submarines would be strewn along the convoy's path like a manned minefield.

The American captain would pay dearly for attacking the convoy.

•   •   •

On board *Cheyenne*, plans for the attack were being made.

'Be seated, gentlemen.' Captain Mackey waved his officers to sit down on the wardroom chairs and bench seat. 'Here's the situation. A Chinese merchant convoy under close escort is headed toward the Spratly Islands with supplies, troops, and a repair ship. As we've already found out, the UN total exclusion zone doesn't mean anything to them. Our job is to intercept the convoy and prevent it from reaching the Spratlys by any means necessary.'

Mack paused to let that information sink in. 'Okay. The operations officer will let you know what we're up against.'

Mack leaned back in his chair and watched his officers as he listened to the briefing. Mack smiled to himself. They were ready. Their last foray had been a crucible to harden them into battle-tested veterans.

As Mack assessed his officers, the operations officer went on with his report. 'The convoy itself is comprised of four military troop transports, one ARS-type repair ship, four merchant container ships, and one merchant tanker. The convoy escort is made up of two Luda class destroyers, four Jianghu class frigates, and one Luhu class destroyer carrying two ASW helos. The convoy should be able to make thirteen knots, but our satellites are tracking it at only ten. We should be able to be in position just after they pass the exclusion zone at dusk in two days. Looks like they want to make the run in darkness to avoid detection for as long as possible.'

Captain Mackey sat upright in his chair after the operations officer sat down. 'Thanks, ops. Any questions?'

There weren't any, so Mack allowed the meeting to break up. 'Okay,' he said. 'You all know what to do. We're under way at 0600. We'll station the maneuvering watch at 0500. Dismissed.'

The executive officer crossed over to the coffeepot, poured two cups, and slowly added sugar to both. 'So how do you intend to play this, Captain?'

Mack leaned forward, interlocking his fingers beneath his chin. 'I'm not sure on this one,' he said. 'It's a different ballgame going after a convoy. There's no one primary target to focus on, planning how to attack it and avoid getting caught. Instead, we're going to have to make an attack, break off to reload as necessary, and then get back into position to re-attack. And keep on doing it until all the ships in the convoy are sunk or turn around.'

'Too bad we don't have a deck gun like the old boats.' The executive officer sipped his coffee as he set the other cup in front of Mack. 'But at least we've got range with both weapons and sensors against these guys. And we're faster, so getting back into position should be fairly easy. It shouldn't be any problem as long as we don't get too cocky.' He looked down at the captain's untouched coffee. 'But you're still not comfortable with it. What's wrong?'

'The escort squadron commander is what's wrong,' Mack said.

The executive officer looked up at his captain. 'Why does he bother you?'

Mack paused as the messenger of the watch entered the wardroom and, standing at attention in front of his captain, reported professionally, 'Captain, the officer of the deck sends his respects and reports the hour of 2000.' He then handed the 2000 report sheet to the captain. When Mack had acknowledged the report, the messenger of the watch left the wardroom as quietly as he had entered.

When the messenger had departed, leaving the two of them alone once again, Mack straightened, took a long drink of coffee, and carefully set the cup back down. Getting to his feet, he moved toward the wardroom door and then paused with his hand on the doorknob. 'Because their commander is reportedly a previous submarine commanding officer, one of their best,' he said. 'Why would a submariner be in command of a surface escort group and baby-sitting the convoy?'

As the captain left the wardroom, the executive officer began to worry, too, and to wonder what would happen when *Cheyenne* located the convoy.

• • •

'Diving officer, make your depth 247 feet,' Mack ordered. *Cheyenne* had met up with the Chinese merchant convoy and had maneuvered into position. 'Fire control, have you got a firing solution on the lead escort?'

'Yes, sir,' the executive officer replied. 'We've got firing solutions on almost all of them, but the best solutions are the lead escort and the front two troop transport ships, Masters 54, 55, and 56, respectively. Should I select a fourth target for torpedo tube four?'

'Negative,' answered Mack. 'I want to keep tube number four standing by for a snap shot in case another submarine shows up like before, or one of those escorts gets too close and damned lucky.'

'Aye, aye, sir.'

'Has anything changed with regards to their defensive posture?'

'No, sir. The escort ships, except for one, are still in a ring around the convoy at an estimated distance of eight to ten thousand yards. All escorts that have an active sonar system are pinging away for all they're worth, but we're still beyond their detection range.'

Mack thought to himself that the Chinese submariner, the escort squadron commander, was wisely shielding himself on board his Jianghu class frigate by steaming in the middle of the convoy.

'Very well,' Mack said. He took a deep breath and slowly turned to survey the entire control room. Everyone was at their battle stations and primed for action. A sense of tense anticipation hung in the air. Not a nervous anticipation, but the kind that came from the pit of the stomach, awakened every nerve, and expanded the senses. The hunter had found his prey and it was time to kill.

'Torpedo room, fire control. Make tubes one, two, and three ready in all respects, including opening the outer doors.'

The standard repeat back came over the sound-powered phones crisp and clear. Captain Mackey himself acknowledged and then crossed to the chart tracking the convoy's route while he waited for the crew in the torpedo room to carry out their duties.

Before long the executive officer reported, 'Tubes one, two, and three are ready in all respects, Captain. Outer doors are open.'

'Very well.' Mack went back to the BSY-1 fire-control and weapons-control consoles in 'Fire Control Alley.' 'Firing point procedures, tube one, Master 54.'

The combat systems officer reported the target's current course, speed, and range from the weapons-control console.

Captain Mackey acknowledged the information and

146

then announced over the open microphone. 'Sonar, conn. Stand by.'

'Conn, sonar. Standing by.'

'Match sonar bearings and shoot, tube one, Master 54.'

'Match sonar bearings and shoot, tube one, Master 54, aye, sir.'

As lights lit up on his console, the combat systems officer reported, 'Captain, tube one fired electrically.'

Moments later the sonar supervisor said, 'Conn, sonar, unit from tube one is running hot, straight and normal.'

'Sonar, conn, aye.' Turning to the fire control party, Mack said, 'I don't want to shoot tubes two and three until after the other escorts, especially the Luhu class destroyer with the ASW helicopters, have settled down a bit. They're bound to chase their tails for a few minutes after their lead escort goes down.'

'Aye, aye, sir,' the fire-control coordinator answered for his operators. In a softer voice, speaking off line so that only Mack would hear, he asked, 'Excuse me, Captain, but why not take the other shots at the two merchants now before they get wind that we're here, or even go after more of the escorts?'

Mack smiled. That was a good question, and he answered it out loud so that everyone could hear him. 'This first torpedo is for effect,' he said. 'I want them scared. Our orders are to prevent them from reaching the Spratlys. I'd rather force them to turn tail and run than have to kill every sailor and soldier on those ships. But until they do turn and run, I intend to focus our weapons on the primary targets – the convoy ships. It's a poor showing for an escort to arrive with minimal damage and no ships left to be escorted. Now, time to acquisition?'

'Thirteen minutes, twelve seconds, sir,' reported the combat systems officer.

When the torpedo closed on its target, it would turn on its active sonar and, after locating the target, would then shift to attack speed. At that range, the lead escort ship would have very little chance to react, and no time at all to escape. The only chance the ship would have was if it detected the initially silent inbound torpedo with its own active sonar pounding through the water.

If that lead escort ship made a rapid course maneuver or a sudden increase in speed, *Cheyenne* would know that the torpedo had been detected. But when the Mk 48 acquired its target, both the convoy and the escorts were still maintaining their course and speed.

'Conn, sonar. We have a detonation on the bearing to Master 54. All escort ships are increasing speed, continuing to ping with active sonar.'

'Sonar, conn, aye. Fire control and sonar, keep a steady track on Masters 55 and 56. I want to shoot as soon as things settle out. Shut the outer door on tube one and reload with an Mk 48.'

Several minutes ticked by slowly while the crew of *Cheyenne* waited for the response of the ships overhead.

'Conn, sonar. Escorts have settled back into their stations. Master 54 had several secondary explosions and it sounds like it's going down.'

'Sonar, conn, aye. Sonar, any indications of assistance or rescue efforts provided to Master 54?'

'Conn, sonar, that's negative, Captain. They all just steamed right past it without slowing.'

'Sonar, conn, aye.' That bothered Mack. The Luda hadn't exploded or sunk suddenly, so there was no reason why one of the convoy ships shouldn't have at least slowed to pick up survivors. Something was wrong, but Mack wasn't sure what.

'Captain, we still have solutions for Masters 55 and 56 being passed to tubes two and three.'

Mack looked over at the executive officer. 'Very well, fire control. Firing point procedures, tube two, Master 55, and tube three, Master 56.'

Once again the deadly drill was carried out and two more torpedoes sped from *Cheyenne* toward their targets.

148

'Conn, sonar. Units from tubes two and three running hot, straight, and normal.'

'Time to acquisition will be sixteen minutes, forty seconds,' reported the combat systems officer.

Again *Cheyenne*'s officers and crew waited. The torpedoes knifed through the water, but this time toward ships that were dependent upon others for protection – a protection those others could not provide.

'Conn, sonar. One of the escort vessels closest to us, the other Luda, Master 57, has started to increase speed and is executing a rapid turn!'

'Sonar, conn, aye. Which way is Master 57 turning?'

'Conn, sonar. It's turning right toward us, Captain. Back along the torpedoes' paths.'

'Sonar, conn, aye. Have the torpedoes acquired yet?'

'Conn, sonar, yes, sir, both torpedoes have gone active.'

'Cut the wires, shut the outer doors, and reload tubes two and three.' Mack looked over toward his executive officer. 'We're going to get out of here. I want to clear this area and be back in a shooting position within the hour.'

'Conn, sonar. Both torpedoes have detonated. Masters 55 and 56 have stopped their screws.'

Mack doubted either ship had been killed. He didn't think that a single Mk 48 each would sink the troop transport ships, but he knew that they must have been crippled.

Mack quickly gave the orders to take *Cheyenne* out of the area, accelerating and diving away from the closing surface ship. Still beyond the detection range of the Chinese sonar, *Cheyenne* increased speed to twenty knots and began a thirty-minute high-speed dash that took her out and away from the convoy and then back along a leading intercept course to wait for the convoy to catch up.

As before, the convoy slowly approached *Cheyenne* while on board the submarine tubes one, two, and three were made ready to shoot once again. Designated as Masters 58, 59, and 60, three ships of the convoy – the two remaining troop transports and the merchant tanker – had been selected as the next targets.

Once again the firing procedures were executed by the numbers against Masters 58 and 59. The torpedoes from tubes one and two ran as expected and soon *Cheyenne* detected two more explosions under the last two troop transports.

The combat systems officer reported to Mack, 'We're ready on Master 60, Captain.'

Master 60 was the merchant tanker, no longer shielded by the troop transports. Mack knew that tanker would be sorely missed by the Chinese.

Mack glanced at the executive officer. 'Very well, fire control. Firing point procedures, tube three, Master 60.' Mack also knew that, with its single hull construction, the tanker would soon be spilling the diesel fuel, lubricating oil, and aviation fuel that the Chinese on the Spratlys really needed.

'Course of Master 60 is 195, speed ten, range fifteen thousand yards.'

'Sonar, conn. Stand by.'

'Conn, sonar. Standing by.'

'Match sonar bearings and shoot, tube three, Master 60.'

'Match sonar bearings and shoot, tube three, Master 60, aye, sir.'

'Tube three fired electrically.'

'Conn, sonar. Unit from tube three running hot, straight, and normal.'

'Sonar, conn, aye. Time to acquisition?'

'Time to acquisition is –' The combat systems officer's report was suddenly cut off.

'Conn, sonar! We have torpedoes in the water off our port bow, SET-53s, bearing 205 and 207!'

Captain Mackey glanced quickly at the executive officer and then turned back to *Cheyenne*'s control station. 'Make your depth five hundred feet, increase speed to flank, *do not* cavitate. Release countermeasures.' Mack then turned to look back at the executive officer. 'Fire control, I need a solution on whoever that bushwacker is, and I need it fast. Cut the wire on tube three, shut the outer door, and reload tube three.'

'Conn, sonar. I think we got it, sir. Must be a diesel boat since it was so quiet. But it's trying to reload and making a racket, bearing 200.'

'Sonar, conn, aye. Snapshot, tube four, bearing 200, Master 61.'

The Mk 48 from tube four was quickly on its way toward the bearing to Master 61. Mack would worry about the classification of Master 61 later.

'Conn, sonar. Both enemy torpedoes have increased speed' – the sonar supervisor paused – 'but they are on intercept course for our decoys,' he added. 'They fell for it.'

But Mack wanted one more piece of news before he was sure that the danger had passed. 'Sonar, conn. What course are those torpedoes on?'

'Conn, sonar. Course is 020. They are headed out and away, sir. No indication of re-attack.'

The immediate threat of the torpedoes had passed, but *Cheyenne* wasn't out of danger yet. The submarine that shot them was still out there.

But not for long. The Mk 48 from tube four acquired the enemy submarine, and minutes later sonar reported an explosion from the bearing of the fleeing diesel. Master 61, which had given itself away as a noisy Romeo as it increased speed, was no longer a threat.

But Mack didn't relax. *Cheyenne* still had a job to do. 'Sonar, conn,' he said. 'What's the surface picture look like?'

'Conn, sonar. The remaining ships of the convoy are still on same course, same speed. Master 60, the tanker, is no longer with the convoy; it's fallen astern of the convoy. Sounds like it's dead in the water, Captain.' The BSY-1 operators confirmed the sonar supervisor's call.

151

'Sonar, conn, aye. What about the escorts?'

'Conn, sonar, the escorts are still on station, but I . . .' The sonar supervisor's voice trailed off.

That was unusual. 'Conn, sonar, go on,' Mack said. 'What is it?'

'Conn, sonar. I could swear that I heard another torpedo and some other explosions in the direction of the convoy. Almost like they were attacking another submarine.'

Mack paused. There were no friendlies in the area, so what could they have been attacking? 'Sonar, conn. Did it sound like they got anything?'

'Conn, sonar, no, sir. But I was kinda preoccupied, Captain.'

Mack smiled to himself. 'Sonar, conn, aye. We're going back after the convoy. Get a clear picture, sonar.'

'Conn, sonar, aye.'

'Captain. What about the cripples?' the combat systems officer asked. 'Are we just going to leave them?'

'That's exactly what we're going to do. Our job is to stop a convoy, not rack up a tonnage score. And your job,' Mack added, 'is to get me firing solutions on three more convoy ships.'

'Aye, aye, sir,' the combat systems officer said.

That diesel submarine bothered Mack. The question that kept coming back to him was how did that diesel know *Cheyenne* was there? A diesel boat couldn't keep up with the convoy while submerged, and the odds of *Cheyenne* running into a diesel like that by coincidence right in the middle of the convoy route were simply astronomical.

The executive officer was thinking about the same thing. Suddenly he smacked a fist into his palm. 'It makes sense, Captain,' he said. 'That's why no one stopped for survivors; why the convoy never changed course when we attacked. They've got to maintain course and speed. The damned Chinese have diesel boats sliding into place just in time to protect the convoy. They just sit and wait while we run up and beg to get hit.'

Mack's eyes narrowed as he thought about what the executive officer had said. 'You're right,' he said. 'And that would explain why they have an ex-submarine commanding officer running the convoy. He's the one who cooked up those little surprises.'

Mack grinned, and it wasn't a friendly grin. The Chinese commander wasn't the only submariner with a trick or two up his sleeve. He looked up at the clock. 'We should be coming up on the next intercept point,' he said. 'We'll start creeping in a little earlier this time.' Mack then ordered *Cheyenne* to slow to five knots and eased her above the layer.

After giving the orders for getting *Cheyenne* into position to make another assault on the convoy, Captain Mackey returned to the fire-control party. 'We may very well run into another diesel boat hiding out here. So let's stay alert and keep in mind that there could be multiple threats.'

No one on board liked the thought of encountering another threat that identified its presence only when it fired a weapon. That was how a Los Angeles class submarine like *Cheyenne* operated, and they had seen for themselves too many times already just how effective that could be.

But there was no time to dwell on profound realizations. There were targets to pick and a convoy to stop.

The three merchant container ships closest to *Cheyenne*'s position became the next targets, designated Masters 62, 63, and 64. 'Let's update the TMA solutions and get it done quickly,' Mack said.

Cheyenne glided quietly into her chosen ambush site. Sonar reported no contacts other than the closing convoy. But the convoy escorts had changed their tactics somewhat. Every one of the escorts was maneuvering erratically though still attempting to stay somewhat on station. Waves of active sonar pulsed through the ocean from the escorts as though the sheer mass of energy used could create a protective wall around the convoy. The remaining five convoy ships maintained a steady course, unable to do anything other than watch and wait and hope that someone else would be the next torpedo's victim.

When the fire-control coordinator was satisfied with the TMA solutions, he informed Captain Mackey. Mack then directed that all tubes be made ready, and opened the outer doors on tubes one and two. This time he would take no chances. Another submarine was out there, waiting. He could feel it.

'Sonar, conn. Keep your ears open after we shoot tube one. You might be able to hear an enemy submarine flooding its tubes and opening the doors. Hopefully we can get off a shot before he does.'

'Conn, sonar, aye.'

'Firing point procedures, tube one, Master 62.'

The range, speed, and course of the target were verified and the torpedo from tube one sped toward the first merchant container ship. The sonar supervisor and his operators all strained to catch the first indication of another submarine reacting to *Cheyenne*'s torpedo launch.

'Conn, sonar. Noise bearing 250. Sounds like . . . yes, sir. It's a submarine flooding his tubes. He's preparing to launch!'

'Sonar, conn. Stand by.' Mack designated the new contact Master 65 and then ordered, 'Match sonar bearing and shoot, tube two, Master 65.'

'Conn, sonar. Standing by.'

'Match sonar bearing and shoot, tube two, Master 65, aye, sir,' the combat systems officer completed the repeat back.

'Conn, sonar. Unit from tube two is running hot, straight, and normal. Target is turning and increasing speed.'

'Sonar, conn. Did he launch?'

'Conn, sonar, negative, sir. Our torpedo has already acquired the target and he is increasing speed. It's another Romeo, Captain.'

In the control room, all hands were silent as the narrative from sonar followed the pursuit of the enemy submarine by *Cheyenne*'s torpedo.

'Conn, sonar. Master 65 has launched countermeasures.'

At the weapons control console, the combat systems officer indicated that he had heard the report and informed Mack that the torpedo was still under positive wireguidance control. The decoys would not work as long as *Cheyenne* could continue to steer the torpedo past the countermeasures.

'Conn, sonar. Impact on Master 65. Multiple explosions. It's gone, sir.'

Before Mack could acknowledge that report the sonar supervisor added, 'Conn, sonar, explosion on the bearing of Master 62. It's breaking up, Captain.'

'Sonar, conn, aye. Good work, everyone. Firing point procedures, tube three, Master 63, and tube four, Master 64. Shut the outer doors on tubes one and two, and reload tubes one and two.'

'Conn, sonar. The escorts have all increased speed and are shifting to cover the forward arc of the convoy. They must have heard their friends get hit.'

'Sonar, conn, aye. Fire control, are we still out of their detection range?'

'Yes, sir. We're well beyond their range.'

'Very well,' Mack replied.

The fire-control coordinator informed the captain that course, speed, and range were verified for targets Masters 63 and 64. Mack prepared to give the shoot order.

'Conn, sonar. The escorts have suddenly changed course toward the northeast. They are all maneuvering to the port quarter of the convoy.'

'Sonar, conn, aye.' Then Mack asked, 'Do the BSY-1 computers show any indication of what's going on?'

'Not yet, Captain,' answered the fire-control coordinator.

'Conn, sonar. Sounds like there's another Romeo out there closing on us at high speed from the direction of the escorts.'

'Conn, sonar. Captain . . . my God, sir! They're shooting at their own submarine! One, two, five torpedoes are in the water. Multiple explosions. Captain, they're dropping all sorts of ordnance in the water!'

'Sonar, conn. Understand.' Mack could have almost expected that. The convoy was on guard against any submarine contact, and they had mistaken the Romeo for *Cheyenne*. 'Any change in the remaining convoy?' he asked.

'Conn, sonar. Negative. Convoy same as before.'

'Sonar, conn, aye. Match sonar bearings and shoot, tube three, Master 63 and tube four, Master 64.'

'Match sonar bearings and shoot, tube three, Master 63, and tube four, Master 64, aye, sir.'

Mack walked to his stool and sat down to wait as the torpedoes raced toward their destination. With the escorts busy attacking one of their own submarines, there would be less warning than ever of the approaching doom. Not that the convoy itself had ever reacted to their ships' being torpedoed.

Mack's attention shifted as a new report came in.

'Conn, sonar. Explosions on the bearings of Masters 63 and 64. They're going down, Captain.'

'Sonar, conn, aye. Any reaction from the escorts?'

'Conn, sonar. Affirmative. They're drawing left, turning north. No, wait, sir. The convoy is changing course. Coming starboard. The convoy is changing course to their right.'

'Captain,' the combat systems officer said, 'the BSY-1 computer shows the convoy is turning to the north as well. Ranges to the contacts indicate the escorts are settling in behind the limping convoy.'

Cheers swept through *Cheyenne* as crew members

congratulated one another. They had done it! The convoy was turning and heading for home.

But when the executive officer suggested standing down from battle stations, Mack shook his head. They would remain at their stations while *Cheyenne* was repositioning to finish that tanker. Mack thought that it might try to get back under way and slip into the Spratlys during the night, if it had not spilled all its tanks' contents.

As *Cheyenne* closed on the wounded tanker, Master 60, Mack's hunch proved correct. The ship was back under way and headed for the Spratly Islands. An Mk 48 from tube one finished the job, however, and soon *Cheyenne* was headed back towards *McKee*. It was time to rearm and resupply, and to take a deep breath before it started all over again.

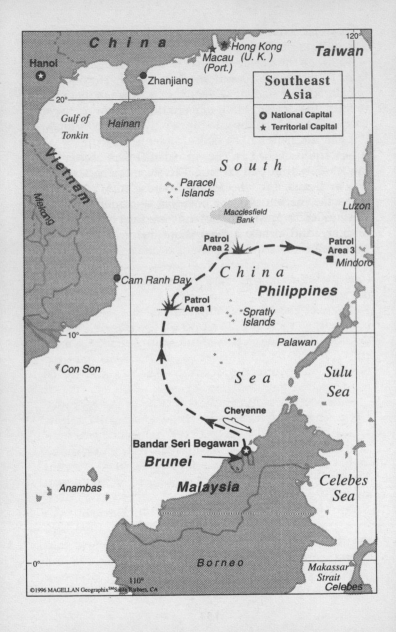

EIGHT

Patrol

It was still dark when *Cheyenne* completed reloading her torpedo tubes and vertical launchers from *McKee*. The submarine tender was still anchored off the coast of Brunei under the protection of the *Independence* carrier air cover.

As in their previous refit, on the final day Captain Mackey, his combat systems and operations officers, navigator and communicator, and sonar officer, proceeded to *McKee*'s war room for their pre-underway briefing, but this time the other officers from *Cheyenne* also would attend the meeting.

Now that *Cheyenne* and *McKee* had established a smooth mini-refit routine, Mack wanted all his officers present. Besides, CTF 74 had requested the remaining officers' presence at this briefing. Partly because of that, Mack expected this upcoming Patrol 3 to be of more significance, if that were possible, than the previous two.

Mack and his group rendezvoused with the executive officer, engineer officer, and the remaining junior officers outside the war room. He knew the younger officers were all excited and beaming with curiosity, but he also knew he could count on them to maintain a professional decorum during the briefing itself. Nodding at them, he led the way into the war room.

CTF 74, the briefing officer, and *McKee*'s captain were already seated. When Mack and his group entered, and after they had all exchanged the normal greetings and taken their seats, the briefing began.

Normally, these briefings were a mix of old information and new orders, but this time there was an added element:

intel that could not be passed to *Cheyenne* via flash traffic. This intel – and this briefing – was based on information that involved the Central Intelligence Agency (CIA).

Operatives in Vladivostok and Beijing had determined that the commander-in-chief of the Chinese navy was personally concerned about losses inflicted by *Cheyenne* on his forces. But that wasn't the only tidbit the Agency had turned up. They had also learned that, somehow, the Chinese had determined that *Cheyenne* was the sole SSN responsible. Their best guess was that the Chinese had probably gotten this information through the loose lips of other SSN sailors in port at Yokosuka, but NCIS (Naval Criminal Investigative Service) was still working on that.

That changed the situation for *Cheyenne*, but it didn't change her orders. *Cheyenne* had another war patrol to undertake before any other US SSNs would be assigned to the same arena as *Cheyenne*.

Mack didn't react to the news, but it didn't really bother him. On the one hand, he was just as happy not to have other US SSNs in the area. It certainly made things simpler, without the need for measures to prevent mutual interference with his fellow commanding officers. Besides, the Chinese had already been gunning for *Cheyenne*. The only thing that had really changed was that until now the Chinese had believed that there were three SSNs operating nearby. Now they knew there was only one – *Cheyenne* – and they would focus their efforts on hunting her.

The only real downside to *Cheyenne* operating solo was that she could use help in tracking down just where and how the seemingly never-ending supply of Russian Kilos and Alfas were getting into the hands of the Chinese. Mack couldn't help thinking that it was almost like the old story that if the Chinese population were to start walking into the sea, the trail of people would be endless, as the reproduction rate far exceeded the destruction rate. Mack grimaced, remembering the story. He knew it was old because for decades the Chinese had been controlling the birth rate, often through inhumane processes.

The briefing officer, continuing on with his report, said that USCINCPAC and CINCPACFLT were not taking the Chinese commander-in-chief's comments lightly, especially since he had found out that the losses inflicted by *Cheyenne* had not, in fact, been the work of three SSNs, but could all be blamed on a single boat. Still, Mack's superiors were more than pleased with *Cheyenne*'s successes, and were not intimidated by the Chinese commander-in-chief.

With that in mind, and with the utmost faith in *Cheyenne*, her officers, and her crew, the Oahu admirals' directives were for *Cheyenne* to proceed back to the north of the Spratly Islands and establish a patrol routine, shifting per the operations order from one area to another. Soon, maybe in a few weeks, *Cheyenne*'s sister 688s, USS *Columbia* and USS *Bremerton*, would arrive on station. Before then, however, they would have to finish their own surveillance assignments in the Sea of Japan and in the northwest Pacific off Petropavlosk, respectively.

The combat systems officer had earlier briefed the captain that the mix of Tomahawks in the vertical-launch tubes had been changed to a mixture of land-attack missiles only, both TLAM-C and TLAM-D. The TASMs had been removed and replaced with the TLAM-Ds. That was Mack's first hint about possible action concerning airfields and runways. The TLAM-D version contained bomblets for creating craters, a real nightmare for aircraft trying to take off.

The briefing officer confirmed Mack's guess. This type of action would be an option once the location of the runways had been confirmed and the imagery processed. Once that happened, *Cheyenne* would be notified via VLF message traffic over the floating wire and directed to periscope depth where targeting data would be down-loaded by satellite directly to *Cheyenne*'s CCS Mk 2 console. This data would come from the theater mission planning center, located at the IPAC intelligence center in the USCINCPAC compound on Red Hill, Oahu.

Mack kept his face impassive, but he didn't like that. He would have preferred to have the information added to *Cheyenne*'s onboard tape library prior to her getting under way, but there simply wasn't time for that.

Once they reached that point in the operation, the Philippine Island of Palawan would again be used for its TERCOM and DSMAC data, but *Cheyenne* would have to establish the initial waypoints for the missile flights to Palawan, which would vary depending on her location at the time. That shouldn't be a problem, however. It was part of the capabilities of the CCS Mk 2 console, a self-contained, onboard mission-planning center.

So far, with the exception of the intel about the Chinese commander-in-chief, the briefing had gone pretty much as Mack had expected, but the briefing officer's next comments caught him off guard. According to the briefing officer, by the time *Cheyenne* completed Patrol 3 and returned for reload, the floating drydock *Arco* would be available as needed.

Mack didn't like hearing that. He didn't like entertaining the notion that *Cheyenne* would suffer sufficient damage to require a floating drydock for repairs. But this was war, he knew, and with the Chinese navy focused on hunting *Cheyenne*, he just might be all too glad of *Arco*'s presence.

He was still thinking about that when the executive officer slipped the captain a note with the letters ASDS on it.

Mack nodded, liking the news of *Arco* even less. He looked over at the briefing officer and asked, 'Are there any intentions for *Arco* to bring the advanced SEAL delivery system, ASDS, out here?'

The CTF 74 admiral answered the question before the briefing officer could speak: 'That option has been discussed, Captain. The concern is that although *Cheyenne* completed the ship alterations for the ASDS and the interface pylon fit checks in San Diego prior to your deployment, the vehicle and your ship have not seen each other.'

Mack nodded. 'So the chances are slim for *Cheyenne* to demonstrate this newest war-fighting capability?' he asked.

'I would say yes,' the admiral replied. 'For the time being.'

'That's a relief, Admiral,' Mack said. 'As you know, operations with that vehicle seem to be extremely intricate – especially the landing on my back. We would need some serious training before any prudent submariner would take that on for the first time in the uncontrolled nature of war.'

'I agree, Captain,' the admiral said. 'And that concern is precisely what I passed to COMSUBPAC.' He paused briefly before adding, 'If the SEALs get involved in this war, and their movements are very tightly secreted by SOCOM (Special Operations Command), we'll probably find out about it after it has happened – unless the intention is to use *Cheyenne*.'

Mack was relieved to hear that. Partially, anyway. Losing control of *Cheyenne* was not part of his destiny – not if he had anything to say about it.

The briefing ended soon after, and when they were back on *Cheyenne* Mack expressed his concern about the floating drydock to the executive officer. The executive officer agreed. He pointed out that it was the only way for *Cheyenne* to get dry for removal of fixed ballast – which would be necessary if the heavy ASDS vehicle were to be installed in its planned location. Installing it over the after escape trunk, which led to the engine room, would put more weight aft than the variable ballast tanks could compensate for.

*   *   *

'Attention on deck and on *McKee*,' the OOD announced over the bullhorn from the bridge. 'Single all lines.' This order was repeated by the bridge phone talker over the sound-powered phones to the phone talkers on deck, one forward and one aft of the sail.

Within minutes, the bow, stern, and spring lines were singled. When the ordered actions had been completed and the reports had been relayed to the OOD by his phone talker, he ordered, 'Cast off the spring lines, lines three and four.'

In peacetime, and under other circumstances, *Cheyenne* would use her own lines. But this was war. During their very first reload alongside *McKee*, Mack had ordered that *Cheyenne*'s line lockers be welded shut. This would prevent any possible noise sources from captive bolts loosening, especially since the chances of encountering torpedo and even depth charge explosions were increasing.

As with the last two war patrols, all lines would be left with *McKee*, where they would be dried and stored with care until *Cheyenne* once again returned from her patrol.

'Check the stern line. Keep the slack out of the bow line,' ordered the OOD. He was concerned about maintaining positive control of *Cheyenne*'s position until the stern was safely clear of the after anchor lines, especially those on *McKee*'s starboard side. He would not back the main engines until she was clear.

In preparation for this next evolution, the OOD had already extended the secondary propulsion motor (SPM), tested it locally in the engineering spaces and from the ship-control console, and trained it to 090 degrees (relative).

'Helm, conn, start the SPM.' That order came from conn on the sound-powered phones.

When the SPM started, *Cheyenne*'s stern swung slowly to starboard. Pivoting around the camel between the two ships, the bow moved slowly toward *McKee*. With the momentum of the 6,900-ton submarine now swinging the stern nicely, the OOD ordered the SPM stopped, trained to 000 degrees, and housed. As the ship continued to swing slowly, the OOD backed the main engines at one-third speed long enough to gain sternway, and just enough to keep the sonar dome from coming too close to *McKee*'s hull.

At his command, the two remaining lines were cast off, snaking through the water as the *McKee* line handlers pulled them on board. With the stern line clear of the stern planes, *Cheyenne* backed safely away from the submarine tender and her after anchors.

Patrol 3 had commenced.

Cheyenne's first patrol area was centered on a line drawn directly between the Spratly Islands and Cam Ranh Bay. Intel suspected that this was the route that Chinese supply ships were using in keeping the Spratly Islands' forces supplied and making the new airfield construction possible. *Cheyenne* was not authorized to attack these supply ships, just to collect intelligence on them. Washington could then use this information against the Vietnamese government for their collaboration with China.

Just to the north of the patrol area, the bottom sloped steadily downward from 1,000 fathoms to over 2,200 fathoms. Mack welcomed this deep water, which would help *Cheyenne* and her Mk 48s. This would allow them to approach a target from deep below the layer without fear of detection by the shallower-running Alfa, which Mack suspected was lurking to the west of Cuarteron Reef.

Although the Alfa's titanium hull would actually allow it to dive deeper than *Cheyenne*, Mack didn't expect it to do so. The Russians did not typically run deep, and he expected the Chinese, who were learning their Alfa handling techniques from the Russians that built her, to follow the same practices.

Mack hoped that he was right. If he was, *Cheyenne* would be able to maintain the tactical advantage as long as possible. If he wasn't . . . well, then things could get very interesting very fast.

• • •

It was nearing midnight. The captain had been relieved of his command duty officer responsibilities by the executive officer. The new section fire control tracking party had just settled in when the TB-23 thin line towed array gained tonal contact. These tonals were the same as those *Cheyenne* had recorded during her earlier encounter with the Chinese Alfa before he was lost in the shallow shoal water.

As towed-array bearing ambiguity was being resolved, more tonals were detected, on different beams, to the east. These tonals were also the same as the Chinese Alfa.

The executive officer knew that there was only one way to interpret the situation: clearly, there were two Alfas. As more data came in, he could tell that the easterly one was closer and was maintaining his distance, but the other Alfa was closing on *Cheyenne*'s position. The fact that neither the conformal nor the spherical arrays had contact as of yet meant that both were easily beyond 60,000 yards away.

The executive officer called the captain to the conn.

Mack, as he always did, made his decisions quickly. In battle, he simply didn't have the luxury of mulling things over for long.

Cheyenne would close on the Alfa to the west. Mack chose that option because he knew the first Alfa might have recorded some of *Cheyenne*'s signature, and by closing on the other Alfa first he would place the easterly Alfa in *Cheyenne*'s baffles. This was, perhaps, not the best place for it to be, but it was the best option available to him. And it had the added benefit of allowing *Cheyenne* to take on the unsuspecting Alfa first.

Battle stations were manned as soon as contact was gained on the conformal array at 40,000 yards.

'Torpedo room, fire control, make tubes one and two

ready in all respects, including opening the outer doors.'
As was Mack's habit, he instructed the executive officer
to order the tubes readied before the range was so close
that the Alfa would hear the evolution.

Acknowledgment, as always, was immediate. 'Make
tubes one and two ready in all respects, including opening
the outer doors, fire control, torpedo room, aye.'

The executive officer, acting in his role as fire-control
officer, passed the acknowledgment on to Mack. 'Captain,
tubes one and two are ready in all respects. Both outer
doors are open.'

'Very well, fire control,' Mack answered.

The Alfa was drawing right now, with contact on all
sonar arrays. When the BSY-1 operator and the fire-
control coordinator were satisfied with the TMA solution
on Master 69, the Chinese Alfa class attack submarine, the
captain ordered, 'Firing point procedures, Master 69.'

His command was acknowledged and the combat
systems officer at the BSY-1 reported the target course,
speed, and range.

'Sonar, conn, stand by.'

'Conn, sonar, standing by.'

'Match sonar bearings and shoot, tubes one and two.'

'Match sonar bearings and shoot, tubes one and two,
aye.'

There was a short delay, and then the combat systems
officer reported, 'Tubes one and two fired electrically.'

'Conn, sonar, units from tubes one and two running
hot, straight, and normal,' said the sonar supervisor as the
two torpedoes executed their wire-clearance maneuvers.
They were running at a slower speed for now. Once they
had acquired they would increase speed and come up from
their deep search depth. When they breached the layer,
the torpedoes would pitch up and complete their acceleration to attack speed.

'Very well, sonar,' Mack replied. 'Time to acquisition?'
he asked the combat systems officer.

'Fifteen minutes, twenty seconds, Captain.'

Hunting two Alfas, with every passing moment increasing the odds that *Cheyenne* would be discovered, fifteen minutes had never seemed so long to Mack. After another eternity had passed, he heard, 'Both units have acquired.'

'Conn, sonar, Master 69 is turning toward and increasing speed, cavitating heavily.'

Mack didn't have a chance to acknowledge the information. Before he could say anything sonar reported noisemakers launched by the Alfa.

Mack nodded and ordered 'steer the weapons.' That would keep them from being tricked into attacking the decoys. He also ordered *Cheyenne*'s course changed to the right by ninety degrees. He wanted accurate targeting information for the torpedoes, and for that he needed the bearings to the incoming Alfa and to the stationary noisemakers to diverge.

It didn't take long to obtain a bearing spread. But Mack didn't have any chance to relax. The combat systems officer had just reported the torpedoes on course for intercept of Master 69, when out of the baffles came sonar contact on the second Alfa.

'Cut the wires, shut the outer doors, and reload tubes one and two,' Mack ordered. 'Make tubes three and four ready in all respects, including opening the outer doors.'

A melee situation was rapidly developing.

'Conn, sonar, we have torpedoes in the water, bearings 285, 290, 110, and 105. Both Alfas have launched weapons at us!'

'Match sonar bearings and shoot, Master 70, as soon as tubes three and four are ready.'

It was time for *Cheyenne* to clear datum. It was also time for their own countermeasures to be launched. As soon as Mack received the report of tubes three and four being fired electrically, he ordered the outer doors shut and the tubes reloaded. The torpedoes they'd just fired would have to do their own thing.

'Steady as she goes, all ahead flank. Do not cavitate. Make your depth one thousand feet.' When those orders had been acknowledged, Mack added, 'Rig ship for depth charge.' It didn't matter that those were torpedoes coming at *Cheyenne*, not depth charges. The phrase had originated in the early days of the Silent Service, and it had stuck.

Mack had done all he could for the moment. His plan now was to let the countermeasures do their own work and to try and slip away from the scene.

Cheyenne reached flank speed, on course 015, and at one thousand feet, as the Chinese-launched, Russian-made torpedoes were entering the baffles. The countermeasures, launched from the dispensers at the stern planes' vertical struts, had worked, decoying the fish and buying time for *Cheyenne*.

That was the good news. The bad news was that sonar couldn't hear *Cheyenne*'s last two torpedoes, and couldn't tell whether they had entered their terminal homing mode at Master 70. With the guidance wires cut, the BSY-1 had no knowledge of it, either.

The next few minutes were tense and silent. Then the sonar supervisor spoke up. 'Conn, sonar, two explosions, one bearing 175 and the other coming from the baffles.'

Sonar didn't have enough bearing information to get both direct path and bottom bounce, so the sonar supervisor couldn't report range. Sonar also couldn't tell exactly what the torpedoes had impacted against. It could have been one or both of the Chinese Alfas, but it could also have been Chinese noisemakers, or even *Cheyenne*'s own countermeasures. To top it off, *Cheyenne* had lost contact on both Alfas in the baffles.

In short, Mack had no idea whether one or both of the Alfas were still there – and he wanted to know. That information was important to *Cheyenne*'s survival, and to the success of her mission.

On his orders, *Cheyenne* slowed and, after proceeding above the layer, cleared her baffles to port. There was no sign of the Alfas, only reverberations from the explosions.

The data did show, however, that there had been three explosions, not two. The one they'd picked up in their baffles had actually been two separate explosions.

Mack didn't have many different ways to read this situation. The Alfas could either have surfaced or have gone to the bottom – and he didn't think they'd gone down. There had been eight separate torpedoes in the area, he knew, four from *Cheyenne* and two each from the Alfas. With only three explosions, it was doubtful that both Chinese submarines had been killed.

But there just wasn't any way to tell from the available data. Not yet, anyway. The sonar tapes would have to be analyzed, a process that would take some time, and then maybe they'd have a better idea.

Cheyenne continued on course toward the second patrol area, at seven hundred feet to keep beneath the layer, while battle stations and the rig for depth charge were secured. The usual all-officer meeting was delayed for at least thirty minutes while the captain and executive officer talked in his stateroom and the melee was reconstructed by the battle stations fire-control party.

It was clear to both the captain and the executive officer that the Chinese commander-in-chief had ordered drastic measures. Both Alfas had continued on course right at *Cheyenne*'s datum without trying to turn away, even with Mk 48s coming their way.

Mack had always hated the Soviet Crazy Ivan maneuvers, but this was even worse. It was more like the Japanese kamikaze, the crazy 'Divine Wind' World War II pilots.

When the officers finally got together in the wardroom, the sonar supervisor and his chief petty officer were there with their tape analysis. They had been able to determine that two of the explosions were Mk 48 ADCAP PBXN-103, one in the baffles and the one bearing 175. The third explosion, originally in the baffles, was from a 53cm torpedo warhead. They were able to determine the difference in kilogram yield based on the duration and decibels of the reverberations.

Their reconstruction of the target courses and torpedo courses proved almost conclusively that the two Alfas had suffered one hit apiece. As for the remaining Chinese torpedoes, in their professional opinion either the 53cm torpedo explosion had destroyed them or they had run themselves to exhaustion while circling *Cheyenne's* countermeasures. The torpedoes, once decoyed, would have waited for the countermeasures to exhibit some doppler – something they had been programmed not to do.

In keeping with his policies, Captain Mackey used the 1MC to inform the entire crew of the reconstructed results of their battle. This time, he told them, the Chinese commander-in-chief's orders had helped *Cheyenne*. The Alfas had been more intent on the kill than on their own survival. But next time . . . well, he didn't want there to be a next time.

From now on, he told them, *Cheyenne* would launch her torpedoes at longer ranges, shooting on towed-array bearing solutions whenever possible. In fact, he added, he was contemplating shooting with the section fire-control tracking parties if need be. Mack had no desire to be rammed by the crazy Chinese COs on a vendetta and who apparently had no respect for their own men's lives. With what he knew of the Chinese, he could only assume that they figured posthumous glory was better than returning to a firing squad.

The crew was silent after the captain finished talking on the 1MC. Each and every man on board *Cheyenne* realized that this could be a long war unless they put more rounds into the Chinese, both above and beneath the surface of the sea, and they couldn't help wondering when *Columbia* and *Bremerton* would be sent to help. Being kept informed was the name of the game on board *Cheyenne*, and the executive officer had passed on the sister ship information at quarters prior to getting under way.

●   ●   ●

Cheyenne's second patrol area was located two hundred nautical miles south-southeast of Macclesfield Bank, a spot which shoaled rapidly from over two thousand fathoms to depths of less than forty feet. The transit there was fast and silent and uneventful.

On arrival near the southwest corner of the area, the captain ordered the OOD to launch an SSXBT. This submarine bathythermograph device was designed to rise to the surface and then drop to the bottom, collecting data on temperature versus depth information through the water column. The SSXBT would send this data back over a thin wire, similar to the torpedo guidance wire, to an onboard recorder in the control room. The information from the SSXBT would be input to the BSY-1 for use by the sonar and fire-control systems. It also would provide layer depth information so that *Cheyenne* could effectively hide beneath the layer, or even a second, deeper layer.

Mack had not had time upon arrival in the first patrol area to obtain the SSXBT information. *Cheyenne* had encountered the two Alfas too quickly. But that wouldn't be the case this time. He was planning the long-range shots now, and the information collected by the SSXBT would be vital to their accuracy. *Cheyenne* would get more SSXBT information at other locations, just in case horizontal gradients were present that could significantly affect the fire-control solution.

Three of the four planned SSXBT 'shots' had been completed when the OOD informed the captain that sonar had gained weak, but slowly closing, Alfa-like tonal contacts to the north, possibly three separate contacts.

Mack acknowledged the information, but he didn't like

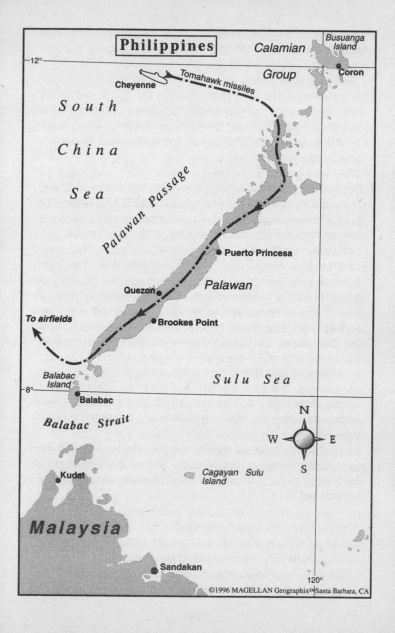

what it meant. These contacts couldn't have been the Alfas from the south, so Russia really was dumping nuclear attack submarines on China.

Minutes later, while he was talking with the executive officer outside the exec's stateroom, the OOD told Mack over the exec's sound-powered phone that he had incoming flash VLF traffic over the floating wire. Mack and the executive officer proceeded to the radio room forward of the control room.

Bad timing, Mack thought as he read the message. As if the inbound Alfas weren't enough, *Cheyenne* had just received orders to prepare to launch their Tomahawks. To do that, they would have to proceed to periscope depth to copy the IPAC Tomahawk targeting data over SSIXS.

Mack didn't like it. Ideally, they would do that quickly, get to periscope depth, copy lengthy SSIXS traffic, and get back down before they lost the long-range shot advantage against the Alfas. Unfortunately, this situation was far from ideal. Launch directives were also coming in over the floating wire, and those launch directives wouldn't allow him that luxury. *Cheyenne* was to remain at periscope depth and launch all twelve missiles as soon as the download was complete and pre-Palawan Island waypoints had been inserted into the CCS Mk 2 console.

Mack didn't like it, but his orders didn't give him any choice. Wasting no time, he ordered the OOD to take *Cheyenne* up to periscope depth.

As soon as *Cheyenne* started copying the targeting data, the captain ordered, 'Man battle stations, missile,' then explained the situation to the crew. *Cheyenne* was to launch the TLAM-Cs to take out aircraft on the ground before they moved from their current revetments. She was also to launch the TLAM-Ds to crater the new runways so additional fighter aircraft, the SU-27 Flankers, could not be so quickly repositioned from the Paracels.

This was a one-shot opportunity. The Chinese would be asleep when the missiles reached their targets – they didn't like to fly at night any more than the ex-Soviet pilots did. And the attack had to take place tonight because the Fleet Numerical Weather Center was projecting rainsqualls for the next two days, starting before daybreak.

The captain also prepared the crew for possible attack by the incoming Alfas. The noise of the VLS launches would not go undetected by them. And in addition, if there were surface ships and aircraft with the submarines, the booster rockets' last-minute illumination of the darkness would provide them with *Cheyenne*'s location, the proverbial 'flaming datum' with *Cheyenne* at the wrong end of the weapon's track.

It was a dangerous mission, no doubt about it. And, if they were unlucky, it would be more than merely dangerous. It could be deadly.

The combat systems officer at the CCS Mk 2 reported that he had completed powering up each missile, downloaded the mission plans and flight profile, and verified proper weapon receipt of the data. He had then powered down the missiles until the Captain was ready to start the automatic launch sequence. All plans and *Cheyenne*'s launch location fit the mission parameters, especially the range of flight to the airfields and the initial waypoint prior to Palawan Island TERCOM and DSMAC updates. Flight time would be just in excess of two hours.

'Firing point procedures, TLAM-C and TLAM-D, VLS tubes five through sixteen,' ordered the captain. The open mike heads-up to sonar and the short delay as the combat systems officer reapplied power to the missiles, inserted the launch key, and pressed the firing button, gave the sonar operators time to prepare their ears for the six to seven minutes of noise that would follow.

Mack wasn't worried about that, though. He was worried that the noise would start those three Alfas cavitating toward *Cheyenne*.

Sonar wouldn't be able to hear that cavitation, but then it wouldn't have to. Mack knew they'd be coming, and they'd be coming fast.

The hatch of VLS tube five opened hydraulically, freeing the interlock to detonate an explosive charge. The first TLAM-C burst upward through the thin plastic membrane of the loading canister which had helped to keep the missile dry until now.

The TLAM-C covered the short trip to the surface, less than thirty feet away, quickly. Just before the missile broached the surface, its booster rocket fired, drying quickly as it cleared the water.

The booster rocket used up the last of its fuel and the missile pitched down closer to the horizontal. Dropping its spent booster, the TLAM-C started its non-illuminating turbojet engine, accelerating to over five hundred knots as it turned toward the first waypoint.

On board *Cheyenne*, tube five backfilled with water to compensate for the loss of the ejected missile's weight and then the hatch shut automatically. That freed the interlock for VLS tube six.

One down, and only eleven more to go, Mack thought. For once he was grateful for the relative slowness of submarines. Even the Alfa's 40 knots were nothing compared to the Tomahawks.

The launch sequence seemed to take forever, but the Alfas were able to close the noisy datum by only four nautical miles. By the time the Chinese submarines had closed an additional two miles, *Cheyenne* had already secured periscope depth operations and had proceeded deep beneath the second layer. There she slowed, tracking the three noisy Alfas, still at battle stations and readying all four torpedo tubes, including opening the outer doors on tubes one and two.

The Chinese submarines had run too fast for too long. When they finally slowed to listen, the sounds of the Tomahawk launches had ceased.

Cheyenne, too, had lost most of her contacts. Due to the range, she had lost all but tonal contact on the towed array when the Chinese slowed. Which was just what Mack had intended. The Alfa class SSN had no towed array, so they

176

couldn't gain tonal contact on the extremely quiet *Cheyenne*.

It was now a waiting game, and Mack knew the game was rigged. The smart thing would have been for the Alfas to slow and attempt to reacquire *Cheyenne*, but they didn't have that choice. Under their new rules of engagement, Mack knew that they would continue to close on *Cheyenne*'s last datum ... which would bring them right into Mk 48 ADCAP range.

The three Alfas were approaching within range, running at fifty meters' depth, abreast of each other and only four thousand yards apart. Mack waited awhile longer. He had six torpedoes planned for them, and he could afford to wait.

Cheyenne fired tubes one and two first, at a range of 25,000 yards, with both torpedoes initially running in slow speed. At 18,000 yards, Mack ordered tubes three and four fired, with the torpedoes initially running in medium speed. At 10,000 yards, *Cheyenne* launched two more torpedoes from the reloaded tubes one and two after cutting the guidance wires to the first two from these tubes, which had still been communicating their search data, on track for intercept. These last torpedoes, the second set from tubes one and two, started their journey at high speed. The result of this salvo was that all six would arrive within their acquisition cone ranges at slightly staggered intervals, and with full depth and azimuthal coverage.

Sonar reported the first two torpedoes increasing speed, signifying acquisition. Minutes later, three of the other four acquired targets, passing the good news over their guidance wires.

Onboard the Alfas, the Chinese were dumbfounded as the ocean in front of them turned from silence into the nerve-racking, high-frequency pinging of attacking torpedoes. Even their prearranged depth excursions and course changes to prevent their own mutual interference were to no avail.

The oncoming torpedoes had passed through both thermal layers and were already locked on, refusing to be fooled by the myriad of noisemakers launched by the fleeing Chinese SSNs. The circuitry of the ADCAP torpedoes allowed them to 'see through' the noisemaker jamming, and to remain locked on their intended targets.

It was over within minutes. All three Alfas had been damaged severely, forcing them to emergency-blow to the surface. Two of them never made it. In those two, seawater leaking through the broken engine room piping caused such an up angle that water filled the steam piping. With the turbine generators damaged by the water from the steam generator, their reactors lost power and shut down.

The two dead Alfas sank stern first to the bottom, more than 12,000 feet below.

Cheyenne returned to periscope depth to report the successful Tomahawk launch and the attack on the Chinese Alfas. Although it seemed like forever, less than two hours had passed since their launch. The missiles were still flying in single file, having completed the final DSMAC updates shortly before, and were now relying on GPS updates during the overwater ingress to the airfields.

Cheyenne and her crew would have to wait for the bomb damage assessment (BDA) to learn the results of the attacks – and they might have to wait a long time. If the rainsqualls precluded the satellite imagery for a number of days, the BDA would not be able to be sent to them via message traffic during the four-day patrol in their third patrol area. If that happened, they would have to wait for their return to alongside *McKee*.

Cheyenne's SSIXS traffic was receipted for, so Captain Mackey directed the ship below the layer for the short transit to the third patrol area. Located to the northeast of the shoal areas and southwest of Subic Bay, this had been a refit site for US and allied non-nuclear submarines until 1992. This patrol was designed to ensure that Chinese submarines would not try to interdict the arrival of the floating drydock, *Arco*.

After its rest stop in Yokosuka following the long open

ocean tow, *Arco* would be towed southward, west of the Philippines, to meet up with *McKee*. Its course would be through the Sulu Sea, away from possible Chinese submarines, which were still swarming in and around the Spratlys.

During the few sane moments aboard *Cheyenne*, afforded by wardroom meals between battle stations, one of the topics of interest among the crew had been the newly instituted political talks between the United States and the Philippines. As one of the original claimants to the contested Spratly Islands, the Philippine government was now showing their appreciation for the submarine war being waged by *Cheyenne*. They had earlier agreed, in a secret Navy summit at CINCPACFLT's headquarters in Makalapa, to the Tomahawk missile flights over Palawan. Not that it would have made any difference, since the missiles would have been programmed to over-fly Palawan anyway. Nevertheless, not having to deal with interfering Philippine aircraft ensured there would not be any international bickering over the flight path.

The crystal-balling by some of the *Cheyenne* junior officers included bets that the Philippines would offer to reopen Subic Bay, at least for the duration of the war against China's submarines and encroaching warships and aircraft. If the price were right – for free – then the United States might even agree.

Mack listened to his officers with interest. He knew that putting *Arco* in Subic Bay would provide a nuclear repair capability closer to *Cheyenne*'s current patrol area. Of course, if they did that, then they would be farther away from *Cheyenne*'s next war patrol assignment and her patrol areas south of the Spratlys.

Mack grinned to himself and shrugged. *Pay now or pay later*, he thought. In the end, though, it didn't really matter. *Arco* or no *Arco*, SEALs or no SEALs, *Cheyenne* would go where she was ordered and carry out the orders she was given.

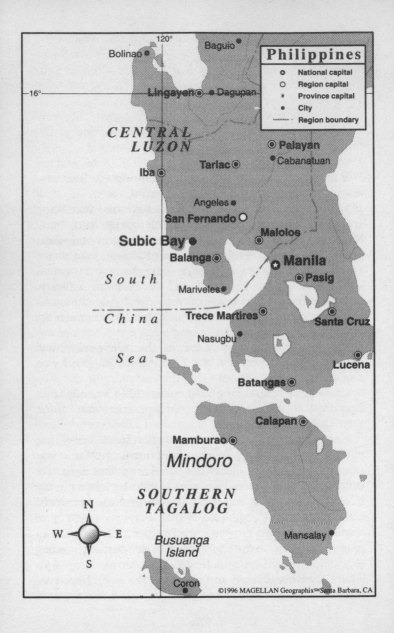

NINE

The Fourth Patrol:
From Russia With Love

The third patrol area was quiet. *Cheyenne* detected no submarines during her short duration patrol.

Which was good, Mack thought. It gave his officers and crew the opportunity to catch up on their paperwork. More important, the respite allowed the newest crew members to finally complete their submarine qualification checkouts with the designated subsystem experts.

Before reaching that stage, each enlisted man had to complete certain at sea and in port watch-stander qualifications required by his department – engineering, weapons, or operations. Qualification boards for the enlisted were held in the 'goat locker,' the chief petty officer (CPO) lounge, mess area, and bunk room, all rolled into one small, but cozy space.

These qualification boards were run by several of *Cheyenne*'s senior personnel. The top two were the chief of the boat (COB), who was also the master chief petty officer of the command, and *Cheyenne*'s qualification officer, the combat systems officer. The qualification officer was responsible to the executive officer, in the executive officer's role as the ship's training officer, for ensuring the timely submarine qualification of each and every enlisted man. The rest of the qualification boards were made up of selected qualification petty officers, the designated subsystem experts, and the individual candidate's leading petty officer and division officer.

Once this board made its recommendation to the executive officer, Mack was always quick to hold a ceremony in the crew's mess. He enjoyed pinning the coveted silver dolphins on each sailor's uniform, conferring the right for the crewman to add 'SS' to his official title.

Officer qualification in submarines included qualification as engineering officer of the watch (EOOW) and officer of the deck, as well as the in port engineering duty officer (EDO) and ship's duty officer responsibilities. These required the captain's certification, as did other senior enlisted watch stations.

Other officer qualifications included candidates for engineer officer of a nuclear-powered ship. Completion of this was generally put on hold during wars because the candidate officer was unable to return to Washington, DC, to be interviewed by the head of Navy Nuclear Propulsion, NAVSEA 08.

For the officers, the same qualification petty officers checked out the candidates, as did the responsible department heads. Once the senior watch officer and the navigator, who was *Cheyenne*'s third senior officer, made their recommendation to the executive officer and captain, a qualification board was held in the wardroom.

The reward for these officer qualifications were the much rarer and even more coveted gold dolphins, which designated the officer as 'submarine warfare qualified.' After *Cheyenne*'s most recent war patrols, Mack felt that all her hands had earned this designation, and he was pleased that they had gotten the chance to catch up on this.

In addition to catching up on paperwork and officer qualifications, the respite also gave Mack the chance to have his junior officers practice their surfacing and diving of the submarine. But Mack didn't let that go too far. This was war, after all, and there was always the chance that some of those pesky Chinese Kilo SSKs were lurking about, so he instructed his junior officers to only simulate blowing the main ballast tanks. That restriction kept *Cheyenne* safe, and it didn't affect the quality of their practice at all.

Mack wasn't worried about their knowledge. He knew

that they had learned, at least on a theoretical level, how to handle the boat. All the officers on *Cheyenne* were nuclear trained – training which had required all officers to complete Nuclear Power School in Orlando, Florida, along with training at one of the reactor prototypes, either in West Milton, New York; Arco, Idaho; or Windsor, Connecticut. This training had taken a year to complete, and it was so intense that they'd had to memorize volumes of information which, when stacked on top of each other, easily reached over six feet high. And it didn't end there. It was followed by a stint at the Naval Submarine School in Groton, Connecticut.

This was all before they ever got to their first submarine. Once on board, they had new reactor and propulsion plant manuals to study, supplemented by ship's information books, weapons manuals, and at least twenty more documents related to operations against what was now the enemy.

After all this, Mack wasn't worried about what they knew, but they needed practice and experience to go with all that book knowledge. It was the procedural steps and the feel of the ship under their feet that the JOODs needed to learn well enough so that they could surface and dive the ship in their sleep. And even more important, they needed to learn how to think on their feet, in case the unusual were to happen, which might not be covered in books.

Cheyenne's junior officers weren't the only ones boning up for qualification boards, either. Her executive officer was shooting for the 'qualified for command' designation – but he didn't know that Mack had recommended him to CTF 74 prior to their last underway. His first hint that he'd better ready himself for the qual-for-command board was a message stating that their commodore, Commander Submarine Squadron Eleven (CSS 11) in San Diego, would be on board *Arco*, the floating repair dock, medium (ARDM-5).

Upon receiving that message, the executive officer initially expected that the board would consist of CTF 74, his CSS 11 commodore, and the captain of *McKee*. That expectation changed, however, when *Cheyenne* received an operations directive routing them to Subic Bay instead of the safe anchorage off Brunei, where they had originally expected *McKee* and *Arco* to be located. Based on the rest of the message traffic, the Executive Officer wasn't sure there would be time for his qual board.

Message traffic indicated that IUSS (Integrated Undersea Surveillance System) had sniffs of a number of the newest operational class of Russian SSNs, the Akula II, heading south from the Sea of Okhotsk area toward the South China Sea – and the numbers did not match naval intelligence's initial expectations. Satellite imagery of Vladivostok showed three submarines missing, and data from Petropavlosk added another missing sub, for a total of four, but IUSS was picking up seven different Akula class SSNs.

New data, however, showed three more missing from the Russian base in the Kola Peninsula. Naval intelligence had been concentrating on the Pacific theater and had missed the departure of the North Fleet Akula II SSNs the week before. These Akulas had completed an under-ice transfer through the Bering Straits before they were detected in the Bering Sea, and had rendezvoused with the PACFLT Akulas east of the Kurile Islands.

According to the message traffic, *Arco* was being diverted to Subic Bay for safety. Had she stuck to her original orders, she would have made a long transit at sea protected only by *Cheyenne*, and the risk of being overwhelmed by the sheer number of Akulas was simply too great.

On a similar note, in order to avoid a repeat of the Chinese Kilo SSK attacks on *McKee* that *Cheyenne* had fought off after returning from the first patrol, the submarine tender was now en route to the safety of Subic Bay via the Philippine Sea. She was scheduled to arrive the day before *Cheyenne*.

Sino-Soviet trade relations were obviously booming, Captain Mackey realized as he read the message traffic. The Russian president, Gennadi Zyuganov, was allowing his navy to supply the Chinese with the Akula IIs. That was bad enough. Worse, though, was the fact that these sales were being consummated so quickly that China could not crew the SSNs, and Russia had wholeheartedly agreed to supply Russian 'observers.' These observers had turned out to be nearly the entire crew. The only real exceptions were some Chinese interpreters for their Chinese message traffic.

The Russian president had, of course, initially denied these sales at all. Then, when the crewing reports surfaced through the CIA, he tried to use the 'observer' gambit. The United States had recognized this for what it was – a feeble attempt for Russia to avoid its own war with the United States – and Mack couldn't help wondering how his own government would respond to this.

But for now, at least, he didn't have to worry about it. All he had to do was to carry out his orders and to execute the missions he was tasked with.

Several days later, as *Cheyenne* 'steamed' past Grande Island inbound to the Subic Bay complex, Mack was saddened at the sight of the once-proud base. The buildings and guest cottages were run down and dilapidated, and even the swimming pool was empty and cracking.

It was clear that nothing had been done to take care of the Grande Island after the departure of the United States five years before. Mack expected that the same would be true of the airfield at what was once the Cubi Point Naval Air Station. That airfield had once been busy bringing in supplies as well as being the launch and recovery field for carrier-based aircraft leaving and returning to Subic Bay.

When *Cheyenne* rounded the point of the airfield and headed for the gaping jaws of the now-flooded-down *Arco*, Mack saw how right his guess had been. At the sight of jungle growth overrunning the Cubi Point Officers' Club, Mack felt a wave of nostalgia and regret wash over him, and he was glad that *Cheyenne* had only two days in the Philippines to reload and resupply.

Since the refit crew was on board *McKee*, which was still in transit to Subic Bay, Mack and the executive officer had informed *Cheyenne*'s crew that they would remain on board, for sleeping and security purposes, until the tender arrived. Seeing the devastation that had occurred since the United States left the Philippines, Mack could see that he had made a wise decision. The CPO and enlisted barracks, as well as the Submarine Sanctuary (where the officers used to partake of rest and recreation), had been looted and destroyed by vandals.

Captain Mackey had also informed the engineer officer and auxiliary division officer – who also was the SUBSAFE (submarine safety) officer – that *Cheyenne* would take the opportunity to complete some of the SUBSAFE maintenance requirement card (MRC) inspections. With the ongoing war against the Chinese, these inspections, which could only be completed while in drydock, were in danger of becoming overdue. Taking care of it now, with the drydock capabilities that *Arco* offered, would ensure that *Cheyenne*'s SUBSAFE certification remained in force and they would have no restrictions in depth during upcoming operations.

Maintaining certification during a war was not just a perfunctory administrative paper drill. It was extremely important. The certification meant that the home which protected the men of *Cheyenne* from the perils of the sea was satisfactory for keeping water out of the 'people locker.'

The SUBSAFE criteria, which began in *Cheyenne*'s new construction period and continued for the life of the ship, included the capability of various important components to withstand underwater explosive shock without endangering the lives of the crew. Integrity of these components was paramount if the crew was to survive the rigors of enemy attacks and reach the surface safely.

Mack planned to avoid that situation, of course, but with the reports of seven Akula II SSNs en route to the South China Sea, he knew *Cheyenne* would have her work cut out for her. And so did her well-informed crew, who set about their inspection duties as soon as the drydock was pumped down.

The late arrival of *McKee* meant that *Cheyenne* would have only one day to reload the vertical-launch tubes with Tomahawk missiles and the torpedo room with Mk 48s. *Arco* had no capability to reload SSN weapons, other than small-arms ammunition. So far, *Cheyenne* had not had to resort to that limited method of warfare, and Mack didn't intend to need them in the near future, either.

Arco, like all the floating drydocks in the fleet, did not have a formal commanding officer. Drydocks. which were not commissioned as United States ships and so did not receive the 'USS' designation, had officers-in-charge instead.

In talking with *Arco*'s officer-in-charge, Mack learned that *Arco* had managed to off-load some Navy Construction Battalion equipment and a small contingent of Seabees at a pleasure boat launch ramp near the Cubi airfields. That would have been very good news if they were on a longer timetable. As it was, repair of the runways would probably be too late for *Cheyenne* to count on any air support in her upcoming missions. Besides, Mack thought, deciding to forget about having to coordinate operations with aircraft, even if the Seabees got the runways repaired, it wouldn't do much good. The supporting infrastructure that had once been at the airfield, as well as the air-traffic controllers and radars, had been spread to other airfields around the world.

Which was fine with Mack. This was a submarine war; it was *Cheyenne*'s submarine war. He did appreciate, however, that *Arco* had brought a replacement screw for *Cheyenne*. She didn't need it yet, but there was always the outside chance that Chinese torpedo shrapnel would get close enough to cause damage to the screw. The 'singing' screw that could develop from that would limit *Cheyenne*'s speed, and that was worse than a SUBSAFE depth restriction to one-half test depth. Singing screws were a condition that could not be tolerated even in peacetime.

Arco also had brought the 'ship's key,' the huge wrench needed to remove and replace the screw's hub nut.

The following morning, *McKee* arrived in Subic Bay under the cover of darkness. She didn't moor at the sea wall, but instead moored outboard of *Arco* at the SRF (ship repair facility) just down the street from the old Naval Forces headquarters building. Mack knew that the captain of *McKee* would consider moving his ship after *Cheyenne*'s departure, and after his men were able to assess the safety of the previously normal berth for large ships like *McKee*. Those berths had been unattended for nearly five years, and he would want to be sure of the sea wall's status, including the mooring bollards, before he felt comfortable enough to moor there for the duration of the war.

There was another good reason for that choice. As Mack knew, the sea wall was located across the relatively narrow channel from the aircraft carrier mooring at Cubi Point, and tending submarines there had never been done before. In the old days, when the United States was maintaining and operating this base, submarine upkeeps always had been conducted within the SRF gates both for security purposes and because it was near the SRF shops and weapons-storage areas.

At daylight, *McKee* slacked its mooring lines to *Arco* for the flooding down of the drydock and the 'dead stick' move of *Cheyenne* to outboard of *McKee*. For safety reasons, the two captains agreed not to load weapons while *Cheyenne* was still inside the drydock.

When the drydock was flooded and seawater systems were once again flooded and vented of any entrapped air, *Cheyenne* received the word 'prepare to snorkel' and passed it along, internally, over the 1MC. With no current to contend with, this move went smoothly and safely. *Cheyenne*'s diesel generator provided power to the emergency propulsion motor (EPM) and to the ship's vital electrical loads, which remained energized during 'rig ship for reduced electrical power.' Had this been done in San Diego, without *Cheyenne*'s reactor power and steam in the engineering spaces, it would have required at least one tug, and maybe two if *Cheyenne* had needed to make the move at other than slack tide.

When *Cheyenne* was positioned properly, the combat systems officer, engineer officer, and their other division officers remained on board *Cheyenne* to take care of the weapons loading and reactor start-up preparations. Captain Mackey, along with his executive officer, operations officer, and navigator, proceeded to *McKee*'s war room for their pre-underway briefing.

There was a new face at this meeting: the CSS 11 commodore was present – which, Mack knew, could mean major changes, or it could mean nothing. Either way, he'd know soon enough.

Once the formalities were out of the way, the briefing officer again took control of the meeting. He informed Mack and the other officers of *Cheyenne* that, with *McKee* no longer requiring air protection from the Carrier Battle Group, CINCPACFLT had decided to move *Independence* and his other surface forces to an area west of the Spratly Islands. USCINCPAC, with JCS approval, had concurred. Which meant that there would be a change in the location of *Cheyenne*'s next patrol.

Mack's earlier orders had been to patrol south of the islands, but those orders were no longer valid. His new orders were for *Cheyenne* to transit to a patrol area located about four hundred nautical miles to the north – deep waters with which *Cheyenne* was now familiar. However, the briefing officer went on, if the inbound Akulas were detected heading for the Paracels, *Cheyenne* was expected to cut them off before the three Akulas from the North Fleet could resupply.

Captain Mackey, his executive officer, and *Cheyenne*'s navigator all knew that this would introduce additional hazards to their mission. At the very least, they would have to contend with the neutral shipping and the oil rigs situated off the northern slopes of the Macclesfield Bank. *Cheyenne* had managed to avoid those problems during the last patrol by staying south of the banks, but that was no longer an option.

After relaying that information, the briefing officer brought up some older intel, emphasizing the information contained in *Cheyenne*'s latest message traffic. In particular, he reminded them that the Akulas were not manned by inexperienced Chinese crews, but had come complete with their normal Russian crews, experienced with their own submarines. And, the briefing officer continued, since the protests from Washington were falling on deaf ears in Russia, *Cheyenne* was being tasked as an instrument of diplomacy: sink the Akulas and Russia would probably stop supplying assets, ships, and men to the Chinese.

Mack spoke up at that. With the dwindling supply of torpedoes aboard *McKee*, the tender was practically rationing them. For this loadout, *Cheyenne* was receiving only twenty Mk 48s, and while he understood the rationale for it, that amount was far short of a full complement, and not enough to go against all seven Akulas.

CTF 74 agreed, but he did not authorize more torpedoes for *Cheyenne*. Instead, he said that if she sank four of the seven Akulas, they would be successful. Losing four new submarines and nearly four hundred of Russia's best submariners, CTF 74 said, might just fulfill Washington's diplomatic needs nicely.

Mack was disappointed. He'd been hoping for a more complete load-out. After all, the Seabees were already at work. Resurfacing the runway at Cubi Point would solve the weapons-reload problem and remove the need for rationing. In the long run, of course, it would do more than that. In the long run, it would solve the whole base resurrection problem.

Before the briefing was terminated, the executive officer asked about 'RuLings' (Russian linguists). The briefing officer replied that the NSG (naval security group) in Yokosuka had provided two RuLings to supplement the 'ChiLings' (Chinese linguists) currently with the NSG detachment aboard *Cheyenne*. They were brought to Subic Bay by *Arco*. With 'hot bunking' the rule for 688s, they were prepared to hot-bunk with their counterparts.

As the briefing came to an end, the executive officer's moment arrived. He was preparing to follow Mack and the other officers back to *Cheyenne* when the CSS 11 commodore stopped him and told him that it was time for his qual for command board.

This was even better than the executive officer hoped. He was prepared, and he felt he was qualified, but he hadn't been looking forward to a long and difficult board. And with *Cheyenne* already stationing the maneuvering watch in preparation for getting under way, there simply wasn't time for an extended board.

The board turned out to be even shorter than he'd dreamed. It consisted of the commodore relaying a message from the chief of naval personnel designating him 'qualified for command.' The executive officer hadn't known it, but *Cheyenne*'s successes and the respect that Washington had for her captain had allowed the chain of command to take a few shortcuts in protocol. The commodore could have placed this on the earlier broadcast, but he hadn't because he had wanted to surprise the executive officer.

This didn't mean that the executive officer was ready to leave *Cheyenne* for a command of his own. They needed to finish this war with China first so that he could start the command schooling route – which was one protocol that would not be circumvented.

*   *   *

Cheyenne got under way in a rainsquall. The weather had little effect on the SSN other than limiting visibility during her surface transit to the dive point west of the eighty-five-degree water of Subic Bay. *Cheyenne*'s navigation radar had been tweaked and peaked by the navigation ETs in order to handle this event – providing that no Chinese warships were around to detect the radar's emissions.

Mindful of the danger, Mack decided to limit the power on the navigation radar, keeping it to only what was needed to detect the nearby landmasses. That meant that *Cheyenne* would have to rely on ESM to detect any incoming surface ship radars. Mack was counting on the fact that Subic Bay had become a ghost town, with almost no traffic in and out.

Subic Bay, it seemed, was about the only place in the area that had little traffic. During dinner that night, as his officers ate quickly, Mack said to them, 'We once again have our work cut out for us. With that many quiet Akulas staring us in the face, we'll need to be innovative in our attacks. We may have to learn how to flush them out. And we won't have much chance to rest before it's time to man battle stations.'

He was right. Sonar had already reported weak tonals from an Akula to the north. As Mack arrived at the conn after dinner, the section fire control tracking party announced that the initial rough range had been established as 75,000 yards. Mack acknowledged the report and ordered the OOD to man battle stations torpedo.

There was still no sign of the rest of the Russian submarines. Just the one set of low frequency tonals, most likely from an Akula – one with sound shorts to its turbine generator.

The captain passed the order for the torpedo room to 'Make tubes one and two ready in all respects, including opening the outer doors.' It was *Cheyenne*'s routine to make the tubes ready as early as possible and as far from the enemy submarine as possible, but it was even more important when facing the quiet Akulas.

The Akula class carried its own towed arrays. Intel had not been able to learn much about its sensor capability, so Mack had to make his own assumptions about it. He had already decided to play it safe and assume that it was equivalent to at least a TB-16 array and a BQQ-5A sonar capability, the first of the US submarine force digital sonar systems.

The acknowledgment of his order came quickly over the sound powered phone. 'Make tubes one and two ready in all respects, including opening the outer doors, fire control, torpedo room, aye.'

Confirmation followed moments later, and the executive officer informed the captain that the ordered evolution with the torpedo tubes had been completed. 'Captain, tubes one and two are ready in all respects. Both outer doors are open.'

'Very well, fire control,' Mack replied.

Cheyenne had faced a number of foes already, and in some of the encounters she'd gotten lucky. This wasn't one of those times.

The Akula was tracking to the west, which put its towed array in a more optimum position for detection than *Cheyenne*, whose array was trained optimumly only when they zigged and zagged while approaching the Akula. *Cheyenne* was closing the range, intending to intercept with a fire-control solution before the Akula could reach the banks, where it would be acoustically shielded. Mack knew that the other Akulas had to be out there as well, but *Cheyenne* could not detect them. They remained silent, deadly holes in the ocean.

The Akula continued drawing left as *Cheyenne* closed. It was still showing up only as sonar tonals, with no contact from the spherical or conformal arrays. But that was enough.

The TB-23 inputs to the three BSY-1 computer consoles,

augmented by *Cheyenne*'s course changes, made the solution possible for the fire-control party. When the BSY-1 operator and the fire-control coordinator were satisfied with the TMA (target-motion analysis) solution on Master 74, the Russian Akula II SSN, the captain ordered, 'Firing point procedures, Master 74.'

The combat systems officer reported the target course as 270, speed eight, and range 22,500 yards.

'Sonar, conn, stand by,' Mack ordered.

'Conn, sonar, standing by.'

'Match sonar bearings and shoot, tubes one and two.'

'Match sonar bearings and shoot, tubes one and two, aye.'

There was a brief pause and then the combat systems officer said, 'Tubes one and two fired electrically.'

'Conn, sonar, units from tubes one and two running hot, straight, and normal,' the sonar supervisor reported as the two torpedoes executed their wire-clearance maneuvers and accelerated to slow speed for the long inbound run.

'Sonar, conn, aye,' Mack replied.

At dinner earlier, he had told his officers they might have to be innovative against the Akulas. He hadn't forgotten. 'Take charge and steer the weapons,' he said. 'Unit one off course thirty degrees to the right and unit two off course thirty degrees to the left.'

The fire-control party immediately knew what Mack had in mind, and they loved it. When the torpedoes were close enough for passive acquisition, they would be steered back in the opposite direction. Upon acquisition, the incoming torpedoes would make it appear that they had come from two separate US submarines, lurking to the west and the east, instead of only *Cheyenne* closing from the south.

'Time to turn the units?' Mack asked.

'Twenty-three minutes, forty-five seconds, Captain,' the combat systems officer replied.

The torpedoes were turned on cue, bearing down on the

Akula. To increase their chances, one torpedo led the target while the other lagged slightly behind.

'Time to acquisition?' Mack asked the combat systems officer.

'Nine minutes, Captain.'

That was his best guess, and it was wrong. Only five minutes had elapsed when the combat systems officer announced, 'Unit two has acquired.' A moment later he added, 'Unit one has acquired, but it's not Master 74.'

That could mean only one thing: the torpedoes had each detected a different Akula – the one they had first targeted and a bonus. Mack didn't have time to celebrate. 'Cut the wires, shut the outer doors, and reload tubes one and two,' he ordered.

The silent ocean didn't stay silent for long. 'Conn, sonar,' the sonar supervisor said with tension in his voice, 'we have two torpedoes in the water, bearings 350 and 010.'

Mack smiled to himself as he heard the bearings. The Russian CO had launched snapshots at the bearings of the incoming torpedoes, but Mack's ploy had worked. The Russian torpedoes were not headed for *Cheyenne*.

'Conn, sonar, the hornets' nest is emptying.' Six new contacts on the spherical array as well as Master 74 indicated that the Akulas were running for it. But they were also turning to the south to avoid the easterly and westerly bearings of the invading Mk 48s. Spherical-array depression-angle changes indicated they were also coming down to *Cheyenne*'s depth zone.

'All ahead flank. Do not cavitate. Make your depth one thousand feet,' Mack ordered.

Cheyenne was already deep beneath the second layer, so it took less than a minute for her to reach flank speed, on course due north, and at one thousand feet. The nearly zero bearing rate she presented to the Russians meant that *Cheyenne* would give them a taste – if they detected her – of the Chinese kamikaze runs weeks earlier. But Mack didn't think they'd detect her, even at flank speed and deep. The range was too great, and the Akulas were running too fast for a TB-16 and BQQ-5-equivalent sensor suited to detect any but the closest targets.

'Conn, sonar, two explosions, bearings 359 and 002, range hard to discern, estimate 18 to 20,000 yards.'

Mack picked up the OOD's JA sound-powered phone and spoke to the officers and men of *Cheyenne* through the compartment phone talkers: 'This is the captain. Gentlemen, *Cheyenne* has won again. Excellent work. We still have a number of Russian SSNs out there, and they aren't too happy.' Hanging up the phone, he turned to the chief of the watch and said, 'Chief of the watch, stand down but do not secure from battle stations.'

Even as he gave the order, though, Mack knew that the stand-down from the tension could easily be short lived, especially if the remaining Akulas continued heading to the south.

'Conn, sonar, we have multiple underwater telephone contacts bearing 355 to 005.' The Akulas had slowed and were conducting range checks with each other. This was exactly why they'd brought the RuLings aboard, to help with range inputs to the BSY-1 by translating the ranges being passed between the remaining five Akulas.

Captain Mackey ordered the towed array housed. They wouldn't need it during the short-range tracking currently in progress.

When that order had been acknowledged and confirmed, he turned his attention on the remaining Akulas. 'Torpedo room, fire control, make tubes three and four ready in all respects, including opening the outer doors.'

'Make tubes three and four ready in all respects, including opening the outer doors, fire control, torpedo room, aye.'

Even in the aftermath of their latest kills, the officers and crew of *Cheyenne* maintained their crisp, efficient, and professional performance.

As soon as the torpedo room reported completing the

ordered evolution with the torpedo tubes, the executive officer relayed the information to Captain Mackey. 'Captain, tubes three and four are ready in all respects. Both outer doors are open.'

'Very well, fire control,' he replied.

Only two of the five Akulas were being tracked, but *Cheyenne* now had contact on all her sonar arrays. When the BSY-1 operator and the fire-control coordinator were satisfied with the TMA solution on Masters 76 and 80, Mack gave the command, 'Firing point procedures, Master 76, tube three and Master 80, tube four.'

As before, the combat systems officer at the BSY-1 reported the course, speed, and range of the two targets.

'Sonar, conn, stand by.'

'Conn, sonar, standing by.'

'Match sonar bearings and shoot, tubes three and four.'

'Match sonar bearings and shoot, tubes three and four, aye.'

'Tubes three and four fired electrically,' reported the combat systems officer.

'Conn, sonar, units from tubes three and four running hot, straight, and normal,' the sonar supervisor reported as the two torpedoes executed their wire-clearance maneuvers.

Unlike the torpedoes *Cheyenne* had fired at the first Akula, these were set to run at slow speed until acquisition. Once they had acquired, they would increase their speed and head up from their deep search depth. When they breached the layer, the torpedoes would pitch up and complete their acceleration to attack speed.

'Sonar, conn, aye,' responded the captain. 'Time to acquisition?'

'Fourteen minutes, fifteen seconds, Captain,' answered the combat systems officer.

By now, Mack had learned that a minute never lasted so long as when you were waiting for torpedoes to acquire the enemy – unless, of course, you were waiting for an enemy torpedo to acquire you.

'Both units have acquired.'

'Conn, sonar, Masters 76 and 80 are increasing speed, cavitating heavily.'

Sonar reported noisemakers launched by the two Akulas. Mack responded by ordering 'steer the weapons.' In order to do this, *Cheyenne* needed to change her course to the left by ninety degrees so that the bearings to the incoming Akula would diverge from the bearings to the stationary noisemakers.

As soon as the course change was completed, sonar detected the other three Akulas. They were to the northwest of the ones being attacked and were heading for the Paracels.

When a bearing spread was obtained, the combat systems officer reported the torpedoes on course for intercept.

'Cut the wires, shut the outer doors, and reload tubes three and four,' ordered the captain. 'Make tubes one and two ready in all respects, including opening the outer doors.'

He didn't expect to need them, but another melee situation was always possible, and it was better to be prepared for an emergency that never happened than to save the effort and regret it.

'Conn, sonar, we have four torpedoes in the water, bearings 358, 359, 006, and 008. Both Akulas have launched.'

'Match sonar bearings and shoot, Masters 76 and 80, as soon as tubes one and two are ready.'

Mack knew it was time for *Cheyenne* to clear datum. It was also time for their own countermeasures to be launched. As soon as he received the report of tubes one and two being fired electrically, he ordered the outer doors shut and the tubes reloaded. That would cut the guidance wires, but there was no help for it, and those torpedoes were outstanding at doing their own thing.

'Steady as she goes,' he said. 'All ahead flank. Do not cavitate. Make your depth one thousand feet.' When those orders had been acknowledged, but before they had been executed, he added, 'Rig ship for depth charge.'

The Akulas were running away. Mack was relying on the countermeasures to hide him from their sonar. That would give *Cheyenne* the chance to slip away – but Mack had no intention of slipping away. He was going after the fleeing Akulas.

Cheyenne reached flank speed, on course 275, and at one thousand feet, as the Russian torpedoes entered the baffles after the countermeasures. Sonar didn't hear *Cheyenne*'s last two torpedoes as they entered their terminal homing modes.

'Conn, sonar, two explosions bearing,' the sonar supervisor began, but he interrupted himself. 'Two more explosions, all to the north. They're lighting up all three sonar consoles, Captain.'

He couldn't provide range information for Mack, however. There was too much reverberation to get both direct path and bottom bounce information. But with the four explosions, sonar was sure the torpedoes found their mark.

Moments later sonar's guess was confirmed. The four explosions were followed by the distinctive sounds of external pressure vessels on the Russian SSNs imploding from their descent to the bottom of the South China Sea. All four Akulas had been killed.

Four of seven, Mack thought. *That's what CTF 74 wanted. But it's not what I want. Cheyenne* would try for the last three, if she could catch them before they entered the territorial waters surrounding the Paracels.

First, though, he had to make sure the Akulas didn't have any support. He ordered *Cheyenne* to proceed above the layer, and then to clear her baffles to starboard. Only the three Akulas fleeing to the Paracels were there.

Satisfied, Mack took *Cheyenne* back beneath the layer. He also took the opportunity to secure from battle stations while they took up hot pursuit toward the shallow waters of the Paracels. At his command, the crew deployed the TB-16 for the time being, at least until they started their approach to shallow water.

Cheyenne continued on course toward the Paracels, at seven hundred feet to keep beneath the layer, while battle stations and the rig for depth charge were secured.

Mack held his all-officer meeting after the battle stations fire-control party had reconstructed the attacks and reported their findings. *Cheyenne* had performed superbly, and the critique was very positive, but one item from the battle was bothering Mack.

It had been clear earlier that the Chinese commander-in-chief had ordered drastic measures. *Cheyenne* had seen that before, and had taken measures to counter it – at least, as much as possible. And Mack could understand it, from the Chinese . . . but not from the Russians. They weren't at war with the United States. They had no reason to sacrifice themselves in battle. But they had.

Just like the Chinese Hans earlier, these Akulas had continued on course right at *Cheyenne*'s datum without trying to turn away, even when Mk 48s were coming their way. And it just didn't make sense. Not with Russian crews aboard those Akulas. And not with Russia not formally involved in this war.

The officers discussed it among themselves, but no one came up with an answer that satisfied Mack. He filed the problem for the time being, but he intended to keep it in mind. Just as he'd shifted his tactics against the Chinese, so, too, would he take this into account the next time he went head-to-head with an Akula.

As *Cheyenne* approached the time for coming shallow, sonar reported numerous merchant ship contacts and also reported contact lost on the three Akulas. Mack wasn't surprised, and at least they were still south of the banks where they didn't have to worry about the oil rigs.

Biologics were also hindering the sonar search, and

increasing the Russians' options. Running beneath and with the merchant ships was an old ploy, and one Mack wasn't about to fall for. He ordered sonar to conduct a careful tonal search on the bearings of the merchants and the biologics. A disturbance of previously undisturbed biologics could mean that a submarine was proceeding in their scattering layer.

The search was painstaking, but it paid off. Sonar gained contact on one Akula as it entered shallow water – and none too soon. *Cheyenne*'s towed array would have to be at least partially retrieved before she could enter the shallows without fear of damaging the array, and Mack couldn't risk that. He expected he would need it for future patrols, especially since neither *Arco* nor *McKee* had replacement arrays for *Cheyenne*. If the runways at Cubi got fixed before the war was over, replacements would come in by airlift. Until then, *Cheyenne* couldn't risk the one she had.

Mack ordered the TB-16 to short stay as *Cheyenne* ventured inside the one hundred fathom curve south of Bombay Reef in the Paracels. There would not be much time before the Akulas were safely in port, which meant that despite the Crazy Ivan or kamikaze Chinese maneuvers, a short-range attack was inevitable.

Battle stations were manned once the range to the Akula closed to inside 15,000 yards. Almost immediately sonar reported transient noises, surfacing submarines bearing 345 and 350. *Cheyenne* was ready with two outer doors already open.

'Snapshots, tubes one and two, bearings 345 and 350 respectively,' Mack ordered. He had no idea what the Master Numbers were from the previous battle in deep water, but it didn't really matter. They would shoot now and reconstruct later.

As with almost all snapshots, the Mk 48s would have to do their own thing in detecting, tracking, and sinking two of the Akulas, but Mack expected them to deliver. This would be just like sinking surface ships. The Russian submarines would increase speed after surfacing and, cavitating heavily, would never hear the torpedoes approaching in their baffles.

No battle plan ever survives contact with the enemy, Mack reminded himself. But there was an answer to that. If the only element of your plan *is* contact with the enemy, there's nothing to survive, and you've got a better chance of success.

He was right. The two torpedoes, which had been set for shallow water, quickly acquired the *Akulas*. They detonated beneath their targets, rupturing the ballast tanks and sending the SSNs to settle to the bottom onto the coral reef.

'Conn, sonar, we have explosions on the bearings of the torpedoes. Also have those same sounds of Christmas balls falling off a tree and breaking.' Two of the Akulas were running aground on purpose after the explosions, hoping to keep their sails high enough out of the water that the crew could escape safely. Mack let them go. He didn't care about the Russian sailors. He cared only that the boats would be useless for the rest of the war.

Cheyenne got to periscope depth in one hundred feet of water in time to see the third Akula passing safely over the horizon. Mack didn't mind the one getting away so much as he minded not being able to get closer to the grounded Akulas. He would have liked to give the crew a special movie that night – periscope videos of Russian submariners jumping ship.

He smiled to himself as he gave the orders to take *Cheyenne* back out into deeper water. They'd have to settle for *The Sound of Music*, which was one of Mack's favorites. Or, he thought, his grin growing wider, maybe he'd give them a real treat and let them watch *From Russia with Love*.

TEN

Rescue

Cheyenne's new orders came through on her floating wire communications antenna. Mack was still thinking about the fact that the Chinese had Akula II class SSNs, and wondering how many other surprises he would have to face before this war was over.

One more, at least, he realized as he read over the new orders. At least one more.

Mack called for a wardroom meeting in half an hour and then headed to his stateroom as he read over the orders again. He could have called the meeting immediately, but he wanted to thoroughly examine the details of these new orders.

Thirty minutes later, the captain was seated at his normal position at the head of the wardroom table when the other officers entered. Mack didn't wait for the normal exchange of greetings and other pleasantries. As soon as the others took their seats he began to speak.

'As you may have guessed from this meeting, we have received new orders.' He nodded at the printout lying on the table before him. 'You all, I'm sure, remember the United Fuels Corporation prospecting ship, *Benthic Adventure*. She was seized by the Chinese back in late July. That seizure, it turns out, is what started this war we are now fighting.'

The officers around the table stirred at that. They knew that Mack wouldn't be bringing this up now unless it impacted on their current mission.

'Thus far,' Mack went on, 'the Chinese had been using the ship for drilling operations around the oil fields in the

Spratly Islands.' He paused for a moment, glancing around at each of his assembled officers. 'The reason I say the Chinese "had" been using the ship for drilling is because at 2300 last night, elements of the US Navy's SEAL Team One were inserted by helicopter from *Independence*, boarded, and recaptured *Benthic Adventure*. Which means, among other things, that we won't have to worry about the ASDS (Advanced Swimmer Delivery System) vehicle. So far, the Chinese have yet to realize that the ship is now back under American control.'

Mack paused again, smiling at the thought of the Chinese's reaction when they learned. Then he sobered and went on, 'The Chinese, of course, will find out soon enough. *Benthic Adventure* is now leaving the Spratly Islands under the protection of two Ticonderoga class cruisers, *Gettysburg* and *Princeton*. We are to join this convoy as soon as they clear the shallow water of the Spratly Islands. I have already directed the navigator to plot the most expedient course for the rendezvous point in order to meet up with the escort group as quickly as possible.'

Several questions were asked of the captain who then dismissed the meeting and headed to the control room to find out from the navigator what timetable they could expect on their voyage to meet the convoy group.

● ● ●

Several hundred miles away, some other members of US Navy SEAL Team One had been inserted into the Spratlys and had begun fortifying their new home. For the next few days, their teammates on board would make every effort to take *Benthic Adventure* out of danger. In the meantime, their job was to deploy Stinger antiaircraft missiles in positions near the probable routes of attack for any enemy aircraft or ships.

These missiles, however, as the SEAL team knew, were more of an emotional security blanket than any real

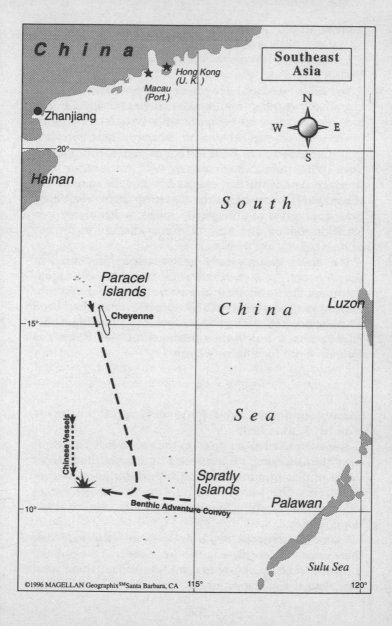

China

Southeast
Asia

★ Hong Kong
(U. K.)

Macau
(Port.)

● Zhanjiang

N
W   E
S

20°

Hainan

South

Paracel
Islands

China   Luzon

15°   Cheyenne

Sea

Chinese Vessels

Spratly
Islands

Palawan

10°   Benthic Adventure Convoy

Sulu Sea

©1996 MAGELLAN Geographix℠Santa Barbara, CA   115°   120°

support. *Benthic Adventure*'s real protection was provided by the two Aegis cruisers, *Princeton* (CG-59) and *Gettysburg* (CG-64), two of the most capable warships in the entire US Navy.

The Aegis warships had been designed to protect American aircraft carriers from massive Soviet air attacks, and these vessels also were equipped with the latest technology in antisubmarine and antisurface warfare. These two warships had sailed from Pearl Harbor as part of the *Independence* CVBG and had been waiting with *Independence* until they received word that the SEALs had recaptured the United Fuels prospecting ship. Once the capture was confirmed, *Princeton* and *Gettysburg* sailed at flank speed to *Benthic*'s position and were now providing an escort out of the shallow Spratly Islands area.

The entire group would be glad once they reached deeper water. Once there, *Cheyenne* would be able to join them and take over their antisubmarine warfare patrols. Each of the warships' two Seahawk helicopters had been working nonstop attempting to track any submarines that might pose a threat to their mission, but they weren't as well equipped for this as *Cheyenne*.

• • •

'What's our time of arrival for rendezvous off the Spratly Islands?' Mack asked.

The navigator looked up from the quartermaster's chart he'd been studying. *Cheyenne* was running at the ordered depth of four hundred feet and twenty-six knots as they approached the islands from the north, having earlier departed the Paracels. 'We should be there within seven hours,' he said.

'Come to periscope depth as soon as we're sure that there are no surface ships in the area,' ordered the captain. 'I want to send a message to *Gettysburg* and tell them what time they should expect us.'

Cheyenne proceeded to periscope depth and transmitted the SSIXS message over her communications mast to the Ticonderoga cruiser escort group. They had been running with their TB-23 thinline array deployed for several hours now, but had not detected any sonar contacts other than biologics, the undersea life of the South China Sea.

As soon as *Cheyenne* arrived in position to work with the escort ships, Captain Mackey would be in charge of ASW operations. *Benthic Adventure* would stay in the center of the group, with *Gettysburg* and *Princeton* to her left and right respectively. In order to cover the group's blind spots to their rear, the cruisers would take turns deploying their SQR-19 towed arrays, and their SH-60B helicopters would provide long-range, over-the-horizon radar coverage, thus giving the group a 360-degree buffer zone protecting the recaptured vessel. *Cheyenne* would run quietly in advance of the group.

Time passed quickly. Five and a half hours later, *Cheyenne*'s sonar supervisor advised the captain that they had detected the Ticonderoga cruisers to their south. Upon hearing this, Mack again went to periscope depth and transmitted their location to the escorts, with an updated ETA and his own tonal map. ·

The sonar operators onboard *Princeton* detected *Cheyenne*'s knuckle soon afterward, and recognized Mack's sonar signature quickly. Mack had realized early on that the top speed of the convoy had never gone above twelve knots. This was, he correctly guessed, *Benthic Adventure*'s top speed.

After making her transmission, *Cheyenne* began receiving updated information on the cruisers' new course, heading 270. The three surface ships were to sail in this direction in order to meet up with the USS *Independence*.

Naval intelligence had reported numerous Chinese surface and submarine groups operating in the area between the Spratlys and USS *Independence*. That didn't bother Mack, though. *Cheyenne* could handle the ASW mission, and the Aegis cruisers would easily deal with any surface or air threats.

As soon as the group left the shallow portion of the waters near the Spratly Islands, *Cheyenne* was once more in her element. Mack ordered the OOD to proceed to four hundred feet and patrol the area in front of their escort group.

Sprinting several thousand yards ahead of the group and then waiting, *Cheyenne* detected her first contact less than an hour later. The TB-23 was receiving tonals on this contact at quite a distance, which indicated that the signal's source was not making any effort to be quiet. Still, it was more than an hour before they were able to provide enough information to the BSY-1 computers to determine range with any reasonable degree of accuracy.

'Conn, sonar, we've got two positive submarine contacts, probable second convergence zone. Both are making turns for thirteen knots, bearing 310. The contacts are coming from the northwest and are closing.'

Cheyenne was currently operating about 14,000 yards in advance of the surface group. Mack did a quick mental calculation and determined that the enemy submarines were roughly sixty miles from *Benthic Adventure*.

Mack didn't have to guess at the orders those two enemy submarines were operating under. They were headed in their direction in an effort to intercept the convoy and destroy as many American ships as possible. The fact that they were coming from the northwest indicated that they were part of the Chinese task group originating at Zhanjiang Naval Base.

Mack couldn't know whether word had reached China yet that *Benthic Adventure* had been liberated, but he was sure that as soon as they learned that fact they would make every effort to destroy it and embarrass the United States.

'Conn, sonar,' the sonar supervisor reported, 'those two sonar contacts have now been positively identified as

Romeo class diesel attack submarines. I estimate that they are ten thousand yards apart. Their speed is constant at thirteen knots based on the blade rate.' Thirteen knots meant that they were in a hurry.

The old Romeos were China's most numerous submarine class, and Mack knew that China had dozens of them. He was also sure that this would probably not be the only attack headed in their direction.

'Captain,' the communicator said, tapping Mack on the shoulder in order to get his attention. '*Gettysburg* just sent us a message. Their radar has picked up three contacts which they think are Chinese missile boats, and they are asking if we have detected them or any other warships in the area.'

Mack analyzed the situation quickly and decided to bring *Cheyenne* back to periscope depth. He wanted to tell the cruisers about the Romeos they had detected, but before he could give the order sonar had another urgent report.

'Conn, sonar, we just picked up five fast attack craft headed in our direction, on nearly the same bearing as the Romeos. They're running at twelve knots, sir, and we can tell that they're operating very close together.'

More information was flowing through the computers, and Mack walked into the sonar room to get the information as soon as it was available.

'Captain, these are definitely Chinese. They sound most like the Hainan class fast attack craft.'

That was enough for Mack. Without waiting for more information, he turned and ran back to the control room. The surface ships in the convoy he was tasked with protecting needed this information, and they needed it fast.

'Come to periscope depth,' he ordered as soon as he reached the control room.

'Come to periscope depth, aye, sir.'

Under normal circumstances, *Cheyenne* would have cleared her baffles at 130 feet, but Mack ordered her to go directly to periscope depth. There simply wasn't time to do everything by the numbers, and he was confident that he had control of the tactical situation and the current contacts.

Once the message was sent, *Cheyenne* proceeded immediately to 247 feet without waiting for an answer. They could receive confirmation via the floating wire. She only needed to be at periscope depth to transmit messages, not to receive them.

Onboard *Gettysburg*, the convoy group commander immediately realized the seriousness of this situation. The submarines he wasn't too worried about – they were *Cheyenne*'s responsibility, and he had absolute confidence in Captain Mackey and his crew. The surface ships were a different matter. They were up to him, but he and his crew had been well trained to deal with situations like this one.

Princeton immediately launched one of her Seahawk helicopters in the direction of the Chinese task group. In order to increase its range, the SH-60 was unarmed for this mission. It would have to loiter for some time and get accurate data on the Chinese ships headed for the Ticonderoga group. The SH-60s from *Gettysburg* would stay ready in case *Cheyenne* needed any help with the two submarine contacts.

Nine hundred feet above the South China Sea, Seahawk 309, assigned to the USS *Princeton*, searched the sea with her powerful radar. It didn't take long to detect their targets. From their vantage point high above sea level, the operators on board could see much farther, both with their eyes and with their instruments.

On board *Cheyenne*, sonar detected the SH-60 launch.

'Conn, sonar, the towed array just detected a helicopter flying overhead,' reported the sonar supervisor.

Mack assumed it was a Seahawk from the Ticonderoga group, heading out to get a better look at those attack craft headed in their direction. Either way, he didn't have time to worry about it. *Cheyenne*'s primary responsibility was those two Romeos, Masters 83 and 84, and Mack set about taking care of them before they could threaten the convoy.

'Increase speed to thirty-two knots,' Mack ordered. At that speed, *Cheyenne* would be within Mk 48 range of the two Romeos within an hour – less if the Chinese submarines continued at their current speed. He also ordered battle stations manned.

Cheyenne picked up speed rapidly. Mack kept his towed array deployed to detect any other sonar contacts that might be in the area, but his first priority was killing the Romeos. He knew very well that the Ticonderoga cruiser group above would be more than a match for the surface boats headed toward the group.

The Chinese missile boats sped forward, confidently. The five Hainan fast attack craft had been scrambled from Zhanjiang Naval Base several hours earlier, just one hour after the Romeo submarines had left. They were part of an all-out effort on the part of the Chinese. As soon as he had received word that the captured American oil vessel had been seized by American SEALs, the Chinese South Sea Fleet commander, Vice Admiral Wang Yongguo, decided to sink it at any cost. He ordered every available ship not already assigned to a prior mission to attack the task force escorting the vessel.

This was more a matter of national pride than of military significance, but it was a decision Vice Admiral Yongguo agreed with. The American-registered prospecting ship had been in Chinese waters – contested waters, perhaps, but Chinese nonetheless – after China had invaded the Spratly Islands. Now the Americans had recaptured the ship and the Chinese military, under direct orders from the Chinese government, wanted the ship destroyed.

The Hainan fast attack craft were generally considered to be ordinary patrol boats. They were usually armed with guns and were often tasked with mining activities. These five boats, however, had their aft 57mm guns replaced – not with the YJ-1 anti-ship missile launchers that were the usual replacement, but with two HY-2 missiles. These missiles had a maximum range of over fifty nautical miles. To take advantage of this, Vice Admiral Yongguo had ordered them to head in the direction of the Americans, hoping that at least some of their craft would get close enough to launch their missiles.

The crew on the Chinese patrol boats had been pleased with their assignment. They had long-range missiles on board. They had help beneath the surface from two diesel attack submarines. And they had a chance to strike a blow for their country.

They remained extremely confident until they heard the whoosh of a helicopter rotor fly near them from the south.

As instructed, the American SH-60 buzzed in for a close look at the five Chinese attack craft. The copilot on board the Seahawk, examining the ship through his binoculars, could tell that each of the ships had what looked like two missile tubes fitted on their aft end. He would have liked to have gotten even closer, but when the pilot tried to move in, the lead Chinese boat opened up on them with a barrage of 25mm gunfire.

The SH-60 pulled back and the pilot radioed *Princeton*. 'Seahawk 309 to *Princeton*, we've just received small-caliber fire from the lead boat. They are fast attack craft and it looked like they are each carrying two big missiles on their aft end.'

'We copy that, 309. Is your current position safe?'

The helicopter had gained altitude and was out of danger. 'Sure is,' the pilot responded. 'You can launch those Harpoons anytime.'

Princeton acknowledged that, and the Seahawk took up station near the five Chinese attack boats. Her job now would be to provide target data on the surface ships, first to *Princeton* and then to the actual missiles in order to ensure that they hit their correct targets.

• • •

212

The Chinese Romeo submarines, like most older Romeo models, carried the standard sonar system given them by the Soviets many years before. Called the Feniks, the Russian word for 'phoenix,' this system dated back to the 1950s. Outdated and obsolete, it was no match for an ultramodern opponent like *Cheyenne* and, unlike its namesake, could not rise again from the ashes of defeat.

'What's the range to our Romeos?' Mack asked. They had been travelling for thirteen minutes at thirty-two knots and had just slowed to get a clear picture of the events going on around them. The Romeos had continued running at twelve knots in their direction, apparently not aware that *Cheyenne* was stalking them.

'BSY-1 convergence zone range to the first Romeo, Master 83, is 68,000 yards, bearing 030,' the fire-control coordinator reported. 'The other Romeo, Master 84, is at 69,000 yards, bearing 320.'

Mack ordered flank speed in pursuit of the closing Romeos, and secured from battle stations until the range was closed.

• • •

On board the USS *Princeton*, five Harpoons exploded out of their missile canisters fitted in the far aft portion of the warship. The missiles streaked fast and low, flying at sea level to avoid radar detection. They had been given the general location of the craft, but because the Chinese boats were moving at a high rate of speed and operating very close together, the missiles would be more accurate when they had direct feedback on their targets via helicopter.

But the Harpoons weren't the only missiles in the air. Shortly after *Princeton* fired off its Harpoons, two smaller, thinner missiles were launched, this time from one of the Chinese fast attack craft. Within seconds, the two SA-14s, hand-held surface-to-air missiles, had reached their top speed and were homing in on the American SH-60.

The American helicopter detected the missiles as soon as they were launched, but that was already far too late. The Seahawk was too close, with no room to maneuver and no time to run. Moments later, they exploded into the bottom of the helicopter, sending it down in a burning fireball.

Princeton knew immediately that something had happened.

'Captain, we just lost contact with the Seahawk. She's no longer showing up on the radar scope.'

There was only one way to interpret that. The captain knew as soon as he heard it that his helicopter had been shot down. His first thought was to get a rescue helicopter out to find any survivors. His second thought was for revenge.

The five Harpoon missiles continued on their way toward the Chinese task group. The plan had been for each missile to strike a different ship, but that plan had depended on the Seahawk to act as a spotter. Without the final data from the SH-60, the Harpoons turned on their active seekers when they neared the programmed area and searched for whatever targets they could find in the water.

The first two Harpoons to hit closed in and slammed into the lead Hainan. They struck directly below the waterline. The entire boat, which displaced less than five hundred tons, was literally picked up out of the water and thrown upside down. Very little was left of the small craft after the two Harpoons exploded.

The third Harpoon homed in on the boat farthest from the pack. The missile streaked in and detonated in the bridge of the ship, killing over half of the seventy-eight sailors on board. The rest died slowly, of smoke inhalation and the fires caused by the burning fuel, ammunition, and aluminum.

Two more Harpoons, as if they were guided by vengeance, crashed into the same ship that had launched the

SA-14s at the helo. One of the missiles hit in the fore section, the other in the aft portion. Between them they tore the thin metal hull apart.

Three ships hit, three ships sunk. In other circumstances, that would have been an excellent record. In this case, however, the important thing was not how many ships had been destroyed. What mattered was the two ships that survived, with their missiles intact, to launch against *Benthic Adventure*.

The remaining Hainan attack craft were in trouble. They lacked good data on the location of the American surface group, but they lacked time as well. They had no idea how long it would be before another salvo of Harpoons appeared on the horizon. Playing it safe, the two commanding officers gave the orders for the two craft to launch their missiles in the overall direction of *Benthic Adventure* and then turn back and head for China. They had lost more than half of their group, but their mission would still be a success if they could destroy an American naval vessel – or, even better, *Benthic Adventure* herself.

●   ●   ●

Mack was notified of the latest developments in his stateroom. The communicator appeared in his doorway, a message printout in his hand.

'Captain,' the communicator said, 'we just received a message from *Gettysburg*. They report that the Chinese task group has shot down their Seahawk. They also report that three of the Chinese craft have been destroyed, but the remaining two have managed to squeeze off four missiles in their direction. They have requested our help, sir. They ask that, if we are within range of the missile craft, we engage them while *Princeton* and *Gettysburg* focus on the incoming antiship missiles. If we are unable to get an exact fix on their location, *Gettysburg* asks us to radio back and they will launch their Tomahawks at the targets.'

The thought of a 1,000-pound Tomahawk missile warhead blowing apart a small Chinese craft brought a momentary smile to Mack's face. Then he thought of the crew on board the Seahawk and suddenly it didn't seem so amusing.

He grabbed a pencil and paper and drafted a quick message.

BASED ON YOUR REPORT, CHINESE FAST ATTACK CRAFT ARE BEARING 279 AND 283 FROM CHEYENNE. RANGE IS NOW 66,000 YARDS. WILL COMMENCE HARPOON LAUNCHING AS SOON AS PRACTICAL.

'Send this to *Gettysburg*,' he said, 'and then have the navigator plot a course to those two Chinese ships.' He didn't say anything else. He didn't have to. *Cheyenne* would worry about the two noisy Romeo submarines later.

Tubes one and two were reloaded with Harpoon missiles and the intercept course to the attack craft was again verified. As soon as *Cheyenne* was in optimum firing position, at one hundred feet beneath the surface, the Harpoons were ejected from *Cheyenne*'s torpedo tubes on the manual fire-control solution, and they headed toward the surface and then toward Masters 85 and 86. Once their engines ignited, there was no stopping them.

The missiles found their targets within minutes. The data provided via *Cheyenne*'s BSY-1 fire-control system was remarkably accurate, and even had the Chinese craft tried to evade, it would have done them no good. As it was, they were confident that with their own HY-2 missiles tracking toward the American surface group and keeping them occupied, they were out of danger.

Their first clue that they were wrong was also their last. The two Harpoons closed quickly, impacting amidships, just below the waterline, one missile per Hainan.

Minutes later, the sea was once again calm as the remains of the two attack craft slipped below the surface.

'Now,' said Mack calmly, 'about those two Chinese submarines . . .'

Tubes one and two were reloaded with Mk 48s.

• • •

On board the American cruisers *Princeton* and *Gettysburg*, an air of tension ran through the control rooms. Their SPY-1B multifunction radars were doing exactly what they were designed to – track the incoming Chinese missiles and calculate optimum intercept locations for the cruisers' SM-2 surface-to-air missiles. The four Chinese missiles were closing in at just under the speed of sound, which left only a few minutes of reaction time.

Less than thirty seconds after the Chinese ships had launched their four HY-2s, the fire-control systems had their data and the two Aegis cruisers began launching their SM-2 SAMs at the incoming missiles. *Gettysburg* was the first to fire, her fore Mk 41, sixty-one-cell launcher shooting off six missiles one after another. Six more SAMs leapt from the deck of *Princeton*, all twelve heading straight for the speeding Chinese HY-2s.

Within seconds, the SPG-62 missile illuminators on board the cruisers began directing the American missiles. These illuminators, four of which were on each ship, switched guidance controls from missile to missile, providing minute flight changes so that the missiles would know exactly where to fly in order to intercept the incoming targets.

Approximately ninety meters above the surface of the sea, thirty miles from *Benthic Adventure* and her escorts, the first SM-2s began to detonate around the incoming Chinese targets.

The first explosions occurred near two of the HY-2s, throwing them off target and then destroying them with shrapnel from the warheads. The remaining two HY-2 missiles were destroyed outright by the American SAMs targeted in their direction.

Three minutes after the launch of the Chinese HY-2 missiles, what was left of all four of them lay scattered on the surface of the sea, floating briefly before slipping beneath the waves.

●   ●   ●

On board *Cheyenne*, Mack had no idea how things were progressing above the surface, and no chance to try and find out. *Cheyenne* out-manned, outgunned, and simply outperformed the two Romeos, but that didn't mean he could afford to treat them lightly.

Mack ordered one Mk 48 targeted at each Romeo. With their antiquated Feniks sonar systems, he doubted that the Romeos would even detect the torpedoes before they had acquired. If one of them were to miss, however, he knew that *Cheyenne* would still be out of range of the Chinese weapons and could re-attack at will.

After establishing firing point procedures, the Mk 48 in tube one was launched at Master 83 and the one in tube two at Master 84. His officers and crew had recently had far too much practice at this, and performed their duties as flawlessly as ever.

The Mk 48s closed the gap and detonated beneath the unaware Romeos, sending both to the bottom, but Mack's pride and pleasure in their performance was short-lived.

Cheyenne had just secured from battle stations and begun to head back to her escort position near *Benthic Adventure* when she received a sonar detection indicating that she had trouble.

'Conn, sonar. We just picked up two possible submarine contacts on the towed array.'

Five minutes later, the sonar supervisor had an updated report for Mack, who had gone to his place in the sonar room.

'Captain, I'm classifying the possible submarine contacts as one Akula II class SSN based on its tonals, and one Kilo class SSK based on his single 6-bladed screw. Both are headed in the direction of the Ticonderoga group. The Kilo just started running at three knots. The Akula's bearing is remaining constant. Captain – I'm pretty sure that they heard us.'

Mack acknowledged the report. He was certain that the sonar supervisor was correct, and that the Chinese submarines had heard them. Launching two Mk 48s, both of which detonated at their intended targets, was bound to attract some attention.

Mack had a hard decision to make. *Cheyenne* could take on the two enemy submarines herself, with a fair chance of surviving – but a fair chance wasn't good enough for Mack. Not when he had a better option.

Cheyenne worked best when she worked alone. The Los Angeles class 688Is were designed to work covertly, without help from any other vessel. *Cheyenne* could work in tandem with other ships, but her biggest strength was her independence.

But that didn't mean that she wouldn't accept assistance when it was offered . . . and when it was needed. And as much as he hated to admit it, Mack believed that *Cheyenne* needed some now.

'Radio *Gettysburg*,' Mack ordered the communicator, 'and give them our best locations of the Kilo and the Akula II. Tell them that we will handle the Akula, ask them to send some SH-60s to help us out with that Kilo. And man battle stations,' he added to the OOD.

'Aye, Captain.'

In order to transmit this information to *Gettysburg*, *Cheyenne* needed to come to periscope depth, which made her much easier to detect by the Chinese submarines. But Mack felt he had to take that chance. Two helicopters and *Cheyenne* were better odds against the two Chinese submarines than *Cheyenne* by herself.

As soon as word reached *Princeton* and *Gettysburg*, two of the SH-60s were launched in the direction of the Kilo. They dropped line after line of sonobuoys, some of them directly on top of the Chinese submarine. Right now, however, Mack could not pay attention to the Seahawks' fight with the Kilo. He needed to concentrate on his silent foe, the Akula II.

The one thing that was bothering Mack was that the Akula hadn't fired yet. He was sure the Chinese captain had a pretty good idea of where *Cheyenne* was, especially after Mack had launched his two Mk 48s and then went to periscope depth to radio for assistance.

With both submarines within torpedo range of each other, Mack could only assume that the Akula captain was waiting for exactly the right moment to strike. What Mack didn't know – and what he couldn't know, especially given *Cheyenne*'s successes in these waters, and the notoriety she had gained from killing so many Chinese submarines – was that the Akula wasn't hunting her at all. The Akula captain was hunting *Benthic Adventure*. He had wanted to avoid *Cheyenne* at all costs.

That little bit of caution was going to cost him his mission, his command, and the lives of himself and his crew.

'Captain,' the fire-control coordinator reported to Mack, 'we've got the firing solution to the Akula II, Master 90.'

Mack immediately ordered firing point procedures. On his command, tubes one and two were immediately readied and fired.

The Akula captain quickly realized that he had been discovered and that his sneak attack had failed. Hearing the American torpedoes enter the water, he did the only thing he could . . . he turned and ran.

The Akula was fast. It turned and increased speed to over thirty-five knots as the Mk 48s closed in on its tail. And its captain was smart. As he fled, he launched several noisemaker decoys in an attempt to throw the Mk 48s off course.

But neither the submarine's speed nor its captain's experience was enough. The first Mk 48 fell for the decoy. The second continued on, until it finished the job.

The incredible explosion tore open the hull of the Akula and sent it to the bottom. The explosion was so loud that it almost masked the two subsequent explosions which soon followed – the sound of two American helicopter-dropped Mk 50s exploding under the hull of the Chinese Kilo submarine.

As soon as the two latest kills were confirmed, *Cheyenne* and *Princeton* exchanged radio messages congratulating each other on yet another successful combat operation.

Once things began to calm down, a helicopter was flown out to the location of the downed SH-60. The remains of the destroyed Seahawk could be seen clearly from the sky. There were no survivors. Wartime losses were to be expected, but they were never without pain and sadness.

With the danger eliminated, *Cheyenne* was free to return to her position, directly west of the Ticonderoga cruiser escort group. Mack gave the order to move out in front once more.

He was beginning to understand why 'May you live in interesting times' was considered a curse in China. Things had been too interesting for too long. With luck, they would be allowed to take things a little bit slower before their next mission.

He knew, though, as the crew of the downed SH-60 had found, that in war luck was a rare and fragile thing.

ELEVEN

Battle Royale

Something was wrong. *Cheyenne* had completed her refit, and once again had as many Mk 48 ADCAPs on board as *McKee* could give her – which was still less than Mack would have liked.

But that wasn't what was bothering him. He was still thinking about their battle with the Chinese Hainan attack boats that, along with the four submarines, had been sent after *Benthic Adventure*.

The thing was, both *Cheyenne* and the surface group had been lucky. Mack knew that, and he'd admit it if he had to. But luck alone didn't account for everything. Since they had destroyed the Chinese surface and submarine group sent to attack *Benthic Adventure*, all aspects of the escort mission were proceeding far better than planned, and that was what was bothering Mack.

Cheyenne, *Princeton*, and *Gettysburg* had not picked up any Chinese submarine or surface contacts for quite a long time now, and while Mack was happy to get the rest, it just wasn't right. The Chinese navy relied almost entirely upon numbers to accomplish their missions, and yet they had sent only five surface ships and four submarines to attack one of their prized targets.

Mack didn't buy it. Something was wrong with that picture. *Cheyenne* should have detected at least several more Chinese surface or submarine contacts probing *Benthic Adventure*'s defenses.

Where, thought Mack, had the Chinese navy gone?

He was about to find out, and he – along with the entire American command – was not going to like the answer.

● ● ●

At Zhanjiang Naval Base in southern China, a massive force of over sixty ships and submarines was being readied. Their mission was simple: destroy the American aircraft carrier *Independence* and her entire Battle Group.

The *Independence* Battle Group consisted of a rather large contingent of ships. This force included three Ticonderoga class Aegis Cruisers, *Bunker Hill* (CG-52), *Mobile Bay* (CG-53), and *Port Royal* (CG-73); two Arleigh Burke Aegis destroyers, *John Paul Jones* (DDG-53) and *Paul Hamilton* (DDG-60); three Spruance ASW destroyers, *Hewitt* (DD-966), *O'Brien* (DD-975), and *Fletcher* (DD-992); and three Perry class frigates, *Rodney M. Davis* (FFG-60), *Thach* (FFG-43), and *McClusky* (FFG-41). Patrolling beneath them was *Columbia* (SSN-771), a Los Angeles class submarine like *Bremerton* and *Cheyenne*.

Within hours of their preparation, American satellites had detected the change in operating tempo at the Chinese naval base. While naval intelligence was not exactly sure what was going on, they did know that it was something major.

As soon as the ships began to leave port, naval intelligence alerted *Independence* of this major movement. A force that size could only have one mission in mind – attack the American carrier group, destroy *Independence*, and sink the remainder of her escorts.

When *Independence* received this message, she immediately went to her highest defensive level. At the same time, the Navy started trying to provide the carrier all the backup available. USS *Cheyenne* was one of the first ships outside the *Independence* Battle Group summoned to assist in her defense.

Cheyenne was running deep, and the only way the Navy could reach her was through the extremely low frequency band of communications. ELF messages took so long to send that they were invariably short – just long enough to alert the submarine to proceed to periscope depth for a longer message.

'Captain,' reported the communicator, 'we just received an emergency message via ELF requesting us to come to periscope depth in order to receive an urgent message.'

'Come to periscope depth,' Mack ordered the OOD immediately.

It took several minutes to make it to periscope depth. As soon as *Cheyenne* was shallow enough she began receiving the important message via SSIXS.

Mack looked at the printout and immediately ordered the communicator to summon a meeting in the wardroom. Mack wanted the combat systems officer, executive officer, navigator, sonar officer, and the communicator there in ten minutes. Mack himself headed straight for the wardroom.

When the officers were assembled, Mack wasted no time. 'We have just received an emergency change of orders,' he said. 'Naval intelligence believes that the USS *Independence* is about to come under a massive attack by the Chinese navy. Several hours ago, over sixty Chinese surface ships and submarines left Zhanjiang Naval Base headed in a southerly direction.'

The room had grown quiet. Mack hadn't been the only one to notice that the Chinese hadn't gone after the recaptured prospecting ship as heavily as expected, and now many officers' suspicions were being confirmed.

'*Independence* is currently sailing in the southwestern portion of the South China Sea,' Mack went on. 'She has been instructed to move slightly east in order to head toward deeper water where her weapons systems and aircraft can be used to the best advantage. We have been ordered to leave the *Benthic Adventure* convoy and head southwest. We are to meet up with the *Independence* Battle Group south of Vietnam. Our orders are to protect *Independence* at all costs.'

Mack paused to let that sink in. The very idea that the

carrier group herself could be in danger took some getting used to.

After a moment he went on, '*Independence* will not be sitting still, waiting for our arrival. She has been ordered to close to within aircraft range of the Chinese task force. Once her aircraft are within range, they will begin a preemptive attack on the Chinese fleet. Our job then will be to assist in the ASW efforts.'

The executive officer spoke up then. 'Will we have other submarine assets in the area?' he asked.

'Yes,' Mack said. 'We will be assisted in our operations by our sister ships USS *Columbia* (SSN 771) and USS *Bremerton* (SSN 698). *Columbia* is currently operating with the *Independence* group. *Bremerton* will be running at flank speed and will be joining us from the Indian Ocean, where she had been sent to check on an unidentified submarine contact reported by the Australians.'

There were no further questions, and Mack dismissed his officers. They all had a lot of work to do before *Cheyenne* arrived on station.

This was not the first time *Independence* had been targeted by the Chinese, but Mack knew that this was by far the most serious threat yet. Several weeks earlier, *Independence* had come under heavy air attack by the Chinese air force. At that time, however, *Independence* had been operating at ranges far in excess of most Chinese tactical aircraft and had escaped unscathed. This time the Chinese would have learned their lessons and would be sending both surface and submarine forces to attack the carrier.

Cheyenne was running deep at flank speed in an attempt to reach *Independence* before the shooting started. Mack knew that the Battle Group commander would not just sit and wait for the Chinese task force to steam closer and closer to them. That was not the American style of fighting. Mack knew that *Independence* would take the initiative and attack as soon as the moment was right. He just hoped that he would be able to get *Cheyenne* there in time.

Hours later, *Cheyenne* proceeded to communications depth to receive the latest intelligence on the Chinese task force. The fleet was heading south in the direction of the Spratly Islands. The latest reports, which came from *Independence* herself, indicated that the Chinese task force was making every effort to close on the *Independence* Battle Group, but they were not very well organized.

As the sixty-odd Chinese surface ships and submarines sped south toward *Independence*, there was as close to zero coordination as a fleet could attain. Each Chinese ship was operating at what their captain felt was the optimum speed for his ship, with no attempt to maintain order or grouping with the other ships in the task force. The fleet consisted of nearly every type of vessel known to be operational with the Chinese navy, from fast attack craft to destroyers, and from reserve Romeo diesel submarines to the newly acquired Akula SSNs.

This battle plan was something of a desperation move on the part of the Chinese. The Americans were accustomed to more orderly warfare, but the Chinese group had not planned on attacking the Americans in an organized fashion. Instead, their orders were for each ship to slowly approach the Spratlys, refuel, and then head for *Independence* without waiting for support. As soon as any given ship was within maximum range of the Battle Group, it would fire its weapons.

Obviously, the Chinese were expecting to take terrific losses. If they failed, they would be facing a major action by the United Nations, who had ruled since the beginning of hostilities that the Chinese were to blame. The United States had begun rallying NATO members in favor of launching an offensive against the Spratly Island chain. If the Chinese failed here, they could face international humiliation if NATO or UN forces captured the islands. But if they succeeded, if they sank *Independence*, the entire operation would be worth any risk.

As Mack had predicted, the Chinese had learned from their previous attack on the carrier. Their last attempt had been a fiasco. They had flown sixty H-6 bombers, Chinese versions of the TU-16 Badger, against *Independence*, but the American F-14s had been able to attack the bombers long before any of them were able to launch their C-601 anti-ship missiles. The Chinese had lost nearly fifty aircraft. The Americans had lost nothing but some AMRAAM and Phoenix missiles.

This time, however, things would be different. Since the failed attack on *Independence*, China had begun basing large quantities of tactical aircraft on several of the larger Spratly Islands. The Americans were unaware of the large numbers of aircraft China had been able to store at these tiny airfields in the Spratlys. While several of the bases had been hit by Tomahawk cruise missiles, several more had stayed intact, and they would now be used to their fullest advantage once the new attack began. And, the Chinese hoped, the Americans would have no idea of the battle they were about to enter into.

Cheyenne was still running at thirty-two knots when Mack asked for the ETA on their rendezvous with *Independence*.

'If we maintain our current speed, Captain, we should be there in six and a half hours,' answered the OOD.

'Very well,' Mack said. 'Maintain flank speed and heading.'

The transit to the South China Sea to meet with *Independence* was filled with tension. All on board *Cheyenne* had been informed of the large attack group heading their way and they were not exactly sure of how their submarine fit into the equation. They knew that they would be playing an essential role in the operation, but they also knew that they would not find out what that role was until their new orders were radioed to them from the surface.

The Americans were not like the Chinese when it came to fleet cooperation. The US Navy put a great emphasis on intership communications. They had learned that through digital data-links and satellite communications, that so-called information warfare could mean the difference between failure and success in a major battle.

'We just picked up *Mobile Bay* on sonar bearing 286,' reported one of the sonar operators to his sonar supervisor. The BSY-1 operators immediately set to work to determine *Cheyenne*'s range to the cruiser.

'Come to periscope depth,' Mack ordered.

'Come to periscope depth, aye, sir.' The repeated order was such a part of Navy life that few even realized that they were saying it.

After four minutes the captain ordered one of the communications masts raised. When that order had been acknowledged and carried out, he instructed radio to transmit a message to *Independence*, indicating that *Cheyenne* had arrived on station and was awaiting their new orders.

It took a few minutes for the new orders to come in, but Mack didn't mind the wait – especially once he got a look at exactly what those new orders were.

Cheyenne was to take up position approximately one hundred miles in front of the Battle Group. This would get her away from the noisy surface ships and allow her to do what she did best: hunt down and destroy any enemy submarines in the area.

When the final message traffic had come in, Mack ordered *Cheyenne* to once again proceed below four hundred feet. His normal routine was to call a meeting in the wardroom, but these orders had been expected and did not require a full meeting. Instead, he then instructed the communicator to type up a summary and distribute it to the appropriate officers.

To: All officers on board USS *Cheyenne*
From: Captain Mackey
RE: Combat operations
    We have just been radioed our new orders. As you

are all aware, the *Independence* Battle Group had been tasked with a preemptive attack on the Chinese task force currently heading for the Spratly Islands.

Cheyenne has been tasked with running out in front of the *Independence* Battle Group on course 090. Once we are in position, west of the Spratlys, we have been ordered to wait for the Chinese submarines to exit the shallow waters near the islands. If we encounter any such contacts, which we invariably will, we have been granted permission to break off from the Battle Group and pursue the contacts.

We have been offered any support which *Independence* can provide. This may come in the form of S-3s, SH-60s, a surface ship, or even a submarine. However, if the battle becomes heavy, and we expect that it will, we may have to operate on our own.

Bremerton and *Columbia* will remain with *Independence*, protecting her port and starboard flanks. Because of the successes we've had in these waters, we have been given a great amount of authority to operate independently from the carrier. So let's stay cautious and keep on our toes.

Mack finished the letter with his plain, recognizable signature and had the communicator run off the appropriate number of copies.

On board *Independence*, flight operations were beginning to take on a tone of tension as well. While all carrier flights involved a fairly high level of risk, combat operations increased this risk. On top of that, within the past hour an ES-3 electronic warfare aircraft flying from the carrier had detected strong Chinese radio activity coming from the direction of the Spratly Islands. Since the invasion of the islands, this had frequently been the case, except that this time the heavy traffic was coming from naval vessels, not ground units.

Currently, two of *Independence*'s E-2Cs were operating

around the carrier, providing radar coverage out to many hundreds of miles. F-14Ds, armed with AMRAAM and Phoenix missiles, were providing air cover around the clock for the Battle Group. This was all happening while two dozen F/A-18s were being armed with two Harpoon antishipping missiles, two underwing fuel tanks, and two Sidewinder missiles each, in an effort to prepare them for the ensuing battle. Twelve F/A-18s also were being kept in reserve in case the air battle got too sticky for the F-14s to handle alone.

On board the carrier's escorts, their crews were preparing as well. The entire group's radars, including the Aegis radars, were shut down. The surface group was relying entirely on the APS-145 radars flying overhead on board the E-2 Hawkeyes. The Battle Group commander wanted to deny the Chinese the opportunity to detect American radar waves via ESM. Without an exact location on the American warships, the Chinese would not be able to launch their missiles until they came within either visual range or their own radar range – and the commander did not intend to allow them to get anywhere near that close.

Beneath the surface, operating twenty miles away from the carrier on either side, were the USS *Bremerton* and the USS *Columbia*. These submarines were playing defense to *Cheyenne*'s ASW offense. They waited just far enough away from the carrier to not be affected by the group's noise while staying close enough to attack incoming threats such as Romeo class submarines armed with shorter-range torpedoes. Both *Bremerton* and *Columbia* were aware that the newer Akulas carried several long-range torpedoes, including the 65cm Type 65 wake homing torpedo, which had a range in excess of fifty nautical miles. These longer-range threats would have to be handled by *Cheyenne* or the S-3 Viking aircraft.

On board *Cheyenne*, Mack was well aware that he would need to take care of the most dangerous ASW threats to *Independence*. The Akula submarines would be hard to detect and had weapons which could attack the carrier from long distances. He would have to take special care to deal with these threats, even if it meant letting the noisier, less dangerous Romeos and Mings slip by, leaving them for *Bremerton* and *Columbia* to handle.

Word passed rapidly throughout the Battle Group that evidence strongly suggested that the Chinese task force had arrived at the Spratly Islands and was now beginning to refuel. That told Mack that the battle was about to begin.

Cheyenne was in perfect position to launch her Tomahawk cruise missiles at the refueling warships and their piers, but Mack agreed with the Battle Group commander's decision not to. Not even *Cheyenne* could have taken out all sixty ships, and launching her Tomahawks would have given away *Cheyenne*'s position. That would have risked exposing her to any Akulas in the area, and hampered her in her ASW mission.

Mack would have liked to go after the Chinese ships while they were still no threat to the *Independence* Battle Group, but he agreed with the decision. He would wait, silently, until the enemy submarines began to show up on his sonar consoles.

●   ●   ●

Cheyenne wasn't the only US asset in the area with Tomahawks on board. The USS *Hewitt*'s entire Mk 41 vertical launch system had been loaded with sixty-one land-attack variants of the Tomahawk cruise missile. And as the Chinese ships steamed into the Spratlys, *Hewitt* received orders to launch her missiles.

Within several minutes, *Hewitt*'s entire arsenal had been fired and the Tomahawk missiles headed, at low altitude, for the Spratly Islands.

By now, USCINCPAC had provided the ships in the area with extremely accurate digital terrain data of the islands. This intelligence, combined with the accuracy of the

Tomahawk's GPS, ensured an unprecedented accuracy when the Tomahawks arrived at their destination.

Forty-six minutes later the Tomahawks arrived at their targets. One by one the missiles impacted, giving the Chinese their first indication that perhaps the attack on the carrier *Independence* was not such a good idea after all.

At the naval bases where the Chinese task force was refueling, many of the piers where the ships were pulling in to be refueled were completely and utterly destroyed.

In all, twenty-three Chinese ships and submarines were destroyed outright. The explosions and fires resulting from the Tomahawks wreaked havoc on the firefighting efforts of the small damage-control contingents at each of the mini-bases.

Ten more fast attack craft and four submarines were soon destroyed in secondary explosions also caused by the Tomahawks.

All in all, following the American Tomahawk attack, the total Chinese task force of sixty-two naval vessels was cut down to twenty-five ships, including eighteen surface ships and seven submarines: three Romeos, two Mings, one Kilo, and a single Akula. Of the eighteen surface ships remaining, not all of them had the fuel to fight the Americans and then return to China – but that didn't matter. The order came down from above that all twenty-five ships would fight – whether they had enough fuel or not.

Win or lose, many of the Chinese sailors would not be coming home from this battle.

●   ●   ●

Cheyenne's sensitive sonars picked up the sounds of destruction as *Hewitt*'s Tomahawks found their marks. These noises were followed almost immediately by the distinctive sounds of the surviving Chinese submarines running out to sea.

Mack ordered *Cheyenne* to proceed to periscope depth. Once there, he radioed *Independence*, alerting her that the

Chinese vessels had started in her direction. When that had been done, Mack manned battle stations and took *Cheyenne* back down to a safer depth.

'Conn, sonar,' the sonar supervisor reported, 'we've got far more than a dozen contacts headed in this direction.'

'Sonar, conn, aye,' Mack said. 'Make tubes one and two ready in all respects, including opening the outer doors.'

As was standard aboard *Cheyenne*, all four of her torpedo tubes were already loaded with Mk 48 ADCAP torpedoes. She was now preparing to use them.

Cheyenne was waiting at a distance of about one hundred miles west of Ladd Reef, one of the westernmost points in the Spratly Island chain. *Independence* was operating two hundred miles west of *Cheyenne*'s position, three hundred miles from Ladd Reef.

The Chinese navy was not rated among the world's finest. As Mack listened to the reports coming in from his sonar supervisor, he could see why.

Active sonar was good for in-close work. Used properly, active sonar could give a competent submariner an effective firing solution, map a minefield, or help navigate an unfamiliar trench. Used poorly, in the hands of incompetent or inexperienced sailors, active sonar was the equivalent of hanging a target on the side of your ship and inviting the enemy to fire.

That's what the Chinese were doing as they sped toward the *Independence* carrier group. Many of the oncoming surface ships were pinging away with their active sonar, obviously searching for American submarines.

Mack was delighted. He could hardly believe it when *Cheyenne*'s TB-23 thin-line array picked up faint signals that matched the variable-depth active sonar fitted to the new Chinese Luhu destroyers. The Chinese ships were too far away to detect *Cheyenne*, but their active sonar was illuminating their own submarines and providing Mack with both range and targeting data on the Chinese.

Nearly thirty minutes passed before the active sonar

source got close enough for the BSY-1 to decipher its range from the bearing rate.

'Captain,' the sonar supervisor reported, 'it's definitely coming from a Luhu destroyer. BSY-1 range is 88,000 yards to the pinging Luhu, bearing 092, but sonar isn't picking up any other signals yet.'

Mack thought to himself that the Luhu, designated Master 98, must have been the first Chinese vessel to leave the Spratly Island chain after the Tomahawk cruise missile attack. He was sure, however, that it wouldn't be the only one.

Mack had to play a delicate balancing game now. As the Luhu drew closer, Mack knew that eventually he would come into active sonar range of the destroyer, and the Luhu would detect *Cheyenne*. Before that happened, Mack would have to take the destroyer out with an Mk 48. But he didn't want to do that too soon. He was relying on the Luhu's sonar to paint a picture of exactly what Chinese ships were headed his way, and he didn't want to alert the other Chinese captains to the mistake they were making.

'Conn, sonar, we just detected another contact, this time a submarine. The active Luhu sonar was reflected off the submarine's hull. We can't tell what class it is yet.' Mack designated the submarine Master 99.

'Conn, sonar, we just got another active ping! This one's coming from a Chinese Luda,' reported the sonar supervisor.

'Range to the new contact is 82,000 yards,' reported a BSY-1 operator as Mack designated the Luda Master 100.

Mack would like to have gone to periscope depth so he could alert *Independence*, but he dared not give away his position. He hoped that on the surface, the Battle Group ships were seeing the same things that *Cheyenne* was hearing.

He needn't have worried. He couldn't tell it on board *Cheyenne*, but even as he was worrying about the ships he was assigned to protect, wave upon wave of F/A-18s were launching off the deck of *Independence*. 14s were waiting in the air to escort them to their targets in case any Chinese aircraft were to take to the sky.

The first raid from *Independence* consisted of twenty F/A-18 Hornets and seven F-14 Tomcats flying cover. These were also escorted by a single EA-6B Prowler intended to jam Chinese radar, which might otherwise be tracking the attacking jets.

As soon as the F/A-18s closed to within one hundred miles of their target, they switched on their APG-73 radars. Prior to this they had been relying on information from the E-2Cs and the F-14s, which carried a new passive infrared search-and-track system, to alert them to any changes in the Chinese operation.

But the Chinese, though reeling from the Tomahawks, weren't finished yet. They had indeed learned from their earlier air assault, and as soon as the EA-6Bs ALQ-99 radar jammer began jamming their ground radar on the Spratly Islands, they launched their secret weapon – air defense fighters. Sixteen SU-27 Flankers and over thirty J-7s, Chinese variants of the MiG-21, lifted off from their tiny bases in the small islands of the Spratlys.

The F-14s' radar detected the swarms of Chinese fighters as soon as they lifted off into the air. Approximately two hundred miles from the carrier *Independence* and just over one hundred fifty miles from the Spratlys, the F/A-18s began picking up speed in order to target their Harpoon missiles at the Chinese fleet before the enemy fighters arrived on the scene.

The F/A-18s formed single-file lines and began launching two Harpoon missiles apiece. After firing, they turned and flew back toward *Independence* to refuel and rearm.

Before the F/A-18s returned, *Independence* launched some of the fighters she normally kept in reserve. Six more F-14s and four F/A-18s began racing from the decks of the carrier in an effort to join in the fight.

The F-14s escorting the strike group attacked the Chinese fighters first. Each of the F-14s was armed with four long-range Phoenix missiles, two medium-range AMRAAMs, and two short-range Sidewinders. The F/A-18s flying in to assist had been fitted with four AMRAAMs and two Sidewinders apiece. As soon as the first SU-27s entered within 120 miles of the F-14s, the first wave of AIM-54C Phoenix missiles were launched at the oncoming Chinese aircraft.

● ● ●

The success of *Independence* and her aircraft was, ironically, making things more difficult for *Cheyenne*. Relying solely on her sonar, she was having a difficult time attempting to grasp what was going on above her. Explosion after explosion from the direction of the Chinese task force told Mack that the American aircraft had begun their attack, but he would have to wait until the noises died down to figure out how many ships were left and which submarines he would target.

Mack had just begun what he thought would be a long wait when sonar reported active sonar from a submarine contact. The continuing loud explosions made it nearly impossible to determine the range. The underwater sonar environment was difficult to interpret using only passive sonar – but Mack refused to use his active suite; he knew it would give away his position.

'Conn, sonar, we just got the classification of that submarine that was active,' the sonar supervisor said. 'It's an Akula!'

That got Mack's attention.

Within minutes, the fire-control coordinator reported, 'Range to the Akula, Master 105, is 33,000 yards; she must have snuck up on us during the air attack.'

He was probably right, but that didn't make Mack feel any better. Letting the Akula get that close was a mistake, and Mack knew he had to make up for it. To do that, he had to maneuver *Cheyenne* closer to the Akula.

Overhead, the barrage of explosions continued, indicating that the immense carrier attack had still not ended.

Slowly *Cheyenne* increased speed to six knots and began proceeding in the direction of the Akula, the quietest non-friendly submarine in the world. The only good thing, from Mack's perspective, was that the Chinese Akula was still pinging away. Their Russian-made passive sonar was worthless in the current underwater environment, and the only way they could detect contacts was to use their active sonar.

'Range to Master 105 is now 28,000 yards,' reported the fire-control coordinator.

'Firing point procedures, tubes one and two, Master 105,' responded Mack.

Both tube outer doors were already opened and ready, and because the Akula was using her active sonar they now had an accurate firing solution on the Chinese submarine.

'Match sonar bearings and shoot, tubes one and two, Master 105,' ordered Mack.

The two Mk 48s were fired in the direction of the Akula and Mack kept the guidance wires attached for as long as possible. He didn't want these torpedoes to miss.

As the Mk 48s left their tubes and closed the distance to the enemy submarine, the sonar room and combat systems officer provided continuous updates on their status. The final updates came after ten minutes.

'Conn, sonar, two explosions in the water, bearing 079. The Mk 48s just detonated.'

Mack acknowledged the report, but he wasn't as elated as he'd have liked. He'd made a mistake, and against a better opponent that mistake could have been deadly.

He wondered how things were going on the surface, and whether any of the other American captains had made similar mistakes.

● ● ●

They hadn't. Not a single shot had gotten through *Independence*'s defenses.

Of the attacking Chinese fleet, not a single surface ship remained undamaged. The few surviving Chinese sailors had been forced to abandon their sinking warships and drifted in lifeboats. Around them, strewn in an unorganized pattern in between many of the small ships, lay the remnants of the Chinese fighters and their air defense effort, which had attempted to stop the American antishipping attack. The Chinese action had failed – miserably.

The Americans attacked the Chinese ships and aircraft so effectively that not one American fighter had been lost. Thirty-four high-performance Chinese aircraft were destroyed in the battle, along with eighteen surface ships. Now the hope of the Chinese navy lay with their six remaining submarines: three Romeos, two Mings, and one Kilo.

●   ●   ●

The explosions had stopped and, with the exception of the occasional Chinese ship sinking beneath the waves, the water was again quiet beneath the South China Sea. As the background noise faded, *Cheyenne* was once again able to use her passive sonar and to begin to build a picture of what they faced.

'Conn, sonar, we've got numerous sonar contacts – probable submarines. We can't tell quite how many at this point, but it's definitely more than two. The contacts sound like they may be operating close together.'

'Sonar, conn, aye.'

Mack had made one mistake based on overconfidence. He wasn't about to do that again.

'Okay,' he said to the communicator, 'let's get some help here. Draft a message to *Bremerton* and the SEC (submarine element coordinator). Ask them if they could give us a hand with these numerous submarine contacts.'

Fifteen minutes later, word was sent to *Bremerton*. *Cheyenne*'s sister submarine, upon receipt of the message over her floating wire and concurrence of the SEC, began running at flank speed in an effort to meet up with Mack and his crew.

The Chinese diesel submarine captains knew that they were in trouble. Once their refueling points were destroyed, they'd lost all hope of striking a significant blow against the Americans. Without the chance to fully fill their diesel fuel tanks at their base in the Spratlys, each of the submarines was running low both on fuel and on battery power.

Communicating with each other as quietly as possible, they all agreed that their best chance now was to simply try to survive. A slow, quiet run for their home waters might get them back to mainland China. If they were lucky. But, as Mack had found out earlier, luck was a fickle, fragile thing, and never to be counted on.

Once *Bremerton* arrived on the scene in her assigned depth zone, she established communications with *Cheyenne* via underwater telephone. That allowed Mack to pass the word that a large Chinese submarine group had been detected some distance away and that the Chinese group had begun to head back in the direction of China, bearing 010.

Bremerton and *Cheyenne* conferred and laid their plans. Then they separated, *Bremerton* on course 300 and *Cheyenne* on course 040. The two American submarines had begun stalking their prey.

One by one, *Cheyenne* and *Bremerton* found the fleeing diesels. The Chinese submarines, however, were so low on battery power that they could put up no fight at all. Mack found it almost like shooting at anchored ships. All the Chinese could do in defense of their lives was to launch a few decoys. The decoys failed, and after they had run out there was nothing left for the Chinese captains to do but just wait, one by one, until they were destroyed by the American submarines.

The last submarine to be attacked by *Cheyenne* was the venerable Kilo, and her captain gave it all he had. In a last-ditch, desperate attempt, he tried to surface after *Cheyenne* had launched her torpedo.

His efforts were noble, but they were doomed. The Mk 48 followed the Kilo, Master 111, all the way up before blowing a hole in the boat's stern and sending it straight back to the bottom.

Mack and his crew on board *Cheyenne* had never had a mission like this. Three submarines had been destroyed by *Bremerton* and four by *Cheyenne* in this one action alone. *Independence* and her Battle Group had, during this battle, destroyed over sixty ships and submarines, more than thirty aircraft, and inflicted irreparable damage on the military installations on the Spratly Islands. The tide in the war against China had now turned completely in America's favor.

But Mack didn't take much satisfaction in that. He knew that glory faded quickly, and tides had a way of turning when you least expected it.

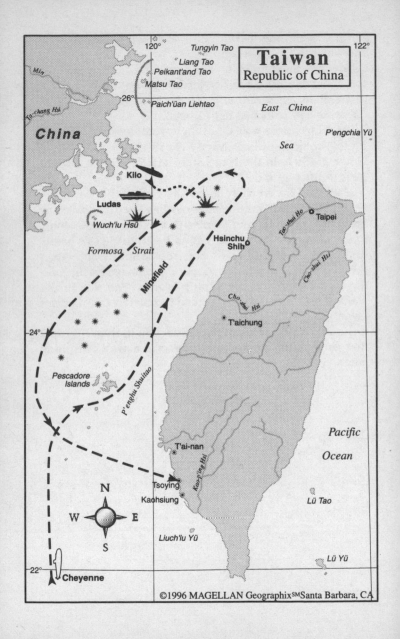

TWELVE

Strait Up

The battle royale was over. Mack still could not believe the losses which *Independence* and her entire group had inflicted upon the Chinese. That battle, he was sure, would go down in history as the single most one-sided battle in naval history.

Cheyenne was currently running at periscope depth, with new information on their latest orders coming in over SSIXS. As soon as the new orders were decoded and printed out, Mack took them and went directly to his stateroom, were he could look at them and analyze the details of his upcoming mission in a quiet surrounding without any distractions.

As soon as Mack finished reading the new orders, he called a meeting in the wardroom with *Cheyenne*'s executive officer, the communicator, the combat systems officer, the navigator, and the sonar officer.

Within minutes, the officers Mack had requested were waiting in the wardroom. As Mack entered, all conversation cut off abruptly.

'Gentlemen,' Mack said, 'I have just received our new orders. We have been tasked to detach from the *Independence* Battle Group and head north. We will have a long transit of over one thousand miles ahead of us. Our destination is the Formosa Strait, in between China and Taiwan.' Mack paused to let that last sentence sink in.

'Let me fill you in on what's been going on in the world around us. Things have been going very well for the United States. Jiang Zemin, the Chinese president who was overthrown in the July coup, has recently surfaced in Taiwan after the USS *Seawolf* smuggled him out of mainland China.'

Mack knew that would come as a surprise to his officers. He gave them a moment to absorb that and then continued, '*Cheyenne* has been asked to "delouse" and reconnoiter the Formosa Strait so that Jiang can be transported back to China when the moment for him to return to power arrives.'

Mack looked around at the officers present, making eye contact with each of them. 'Naval intelligence does not have a firm grasp on what type of enemy warships are in the area. They are expecting large numbers of Luda destroyers and possibly several very dangerous Akula or Kilo submarines. Naval intelligence also reports that large areas of the Formosa Strait are heavily mined, so let's watch our step.'

On that cautionary note, Mack concluded the meeting and the officers went back to their previous duties.

As *Cheyenne* pulled away from the *Independence* Battle Group, Mack thought about the dangers of this new mission. He and his crew had not had much experience with encountering naval mines, but he knew that they presented a great threat to all naval vessels, including submarines. During the 1991 Persian Gulf War, the only naval casualties the US suffered came from two inexpensive and low technology mines. It was an ironic twist on modern warfare, thought Mack, that a mine costing a few thousand dollars could sink a billion-dollar submarine like *Cheyenne* if the mine were to come into contact with her hull.

As soon as the meeting in the wardroom was complete, *Cheyenne* began her long trip north from *Independence*. USS *Bremerton* would be leaving the South China Sea and returning to the Indian Ocean. USS *Columbia* would stay with the *Independence* Battle Group, acting as ASW escort, in the same SSN(DS) role *Cheyenne* had played so many times.

'Make your depth four hundred feet,' Mack said.

'Make my depth four hundred feet, aye, sir,' the OOD said, acknowledging the order.

'Speed twelve knots,' Mack added. This order was also repeated.

There was no emergency rush for *Cheyenne* to get to the Formosa Strait. Safety was Mack's primary concern. He would much rather get to his destination slowly and quietly than to arrive there after having to fight his way up north.

Besides, Mack didn't want to announce his position to the Chinese navy. The strait between China and Taiwan was their home waters, and held the threat of warships coming from all directions. There were four Chinese naval bases within range of Mack's destination. Each of those bases could send submarines, attack craft, or destroyers and aircraft after *Cheyenne* if they knew she was in their waters.

Which meant, Mack knew, that he would have to be sure that they didn't find out *Cheyenne* was there.

●   ●   ●

Mack had expected the entire cruise to take slightly more than four days. At the end of the third day, *Cheyenne* had passed Zhanjiang Naval Base in southern China and was approaching Hong Kong exactly on schedule. So far, she had not detected a single Chinese naval contact, possibly because the Chinese navy was still regrouping after their humiliating loss to the Americans south of the Spratly Islands.

That string ended at the end of the third day.

'Conn, sonar,' the sonar supervisor reported. 'We have a sonar contact bearing 200. Sounds like a surface ship.'

Mack was in the control room when the report came in. He decided that the contact was probably coming from a ship from the naval base directly to their southwest. The normal watch station BSY-1 operators started examining the information to attempt to determine the range to the contact.

'Conn, sonar,' the sonar supervisor said, 'we have active sonars indicating that there are two Hainan fast attack craft – high-frequency sonars.'

With the section fire-control tracking party manned, the BSY-1 computers began to get the information needed to determine *Cheyenne*'s range to the targets.

'Conn, sonar, the active sonars are very far away. This is very probably a convergence-zone contact. According to our calculations, they are pinging from over thirty nautical miles away.'

'Sonar, conn, aye,' responded Mack for the OOD. 'Keep tracking those contacts.'

Mack didn't intend to do anything about the Hainans – not unless he had to. He still wanted to stay silent and undetected, if possible. On the other hand, he couldn't afford to arrive at their destination tailed by a bunch of angry Chinese patrol craft.

Mack needn't have worried – at the moment, anyway. The Chinese patrol craft knew nothing of *Cheyenne*'s transit north. They had gone active to test out their equipment, not because they suspected there was a US SSN in the area. The Chinese craft, built in the early 1960s, had recently been fitted with a new active sonar and their captains often enjoyed using this during training exercises. Their upcoming mission, however, was anything but a training exercise. The two Chinese Hainan class fast attack craft had been fully loaded with twelve mines, and when they reached their assigned location they would begin deploying these naval mines from their mine rails. After they had evaluated their new sonars, the Chinese captains would continue on their assigned mission.

After fifteen minutes of tracking the Hainan attack craft, *Cheyenne*'s sonars lost contact with the two Chinese boats. They reacquired the two patrol craft as *Cheyenne* began to enter the strait.

Mack had gone back to the sonar room. After reporting the contacts to the OOD, the sonar supervisor said, 'Captain, we've just acquired the two Chinese craft again. They must have gone up the eastern coast of China. Bearing is 355.'

Mack went back to the control room. 'Do you have the range to the Chinese active sonars yet?' Mack asked.

'Not yet, Captain, but we should have it ready soon,' the OOD answered. He had worked hard with his section fire-control tracking party, perfecting their technique, and he was proud of them.

Less than a minute later the section fire-control tracking party had an answer to Mack's question.

'Range is 68,000 yards, Captain.'

'Conn, sonar, our Chinese contacts have stopped pinging, sir,' the sonar supervisor said. 'I'll bet that they're laying mines.'

The two Chinese craft were nearly forty miles to the north of *Cheyenne*. One by one their Russian-designed MAG moored contact mines were pushed over and dropped into the water via the mine rails aboard the small craft. These mines were based on technology that was nearly one hundred years old, but they still presented a serious threat to *Cheyenne*.

'Mark that area as a minefield,' Mack said, pointing to the area on the plotting table where they believed the Chinese ships to be operating. 'If at all possible, we want to stay clear of that zone.'

'Aye, Captain,' said the auxiliary electrician forward as he looked up from his plot. He was the plotter for his watch section, and, like all the sailors on board *Cheyenne*, he took pride in his performance and his professionalism.

Mack did not know what types of mines were being laid in the Formosa Strait, but he did know that even the most basic, least expensive underwater pressure-sensitive mines could limit his operation. He hated to think that the Chinese could be laying some of the more advanced bottom-moored influence and acoustic mines such as the type employed by the US Navy.

For now at least, although Mack didn't know it, the Chinese preferred the low-cost mines to the high-tech, expensive ones, and the two Chinese craft were laying only pressure-sensitive types. These were perhaps the lowest-technology and least expensive naval mines a nation could buy. The MAG was a standard Soviet mine that was supplied to the Chinese throughout the early 1960s. One of the benefits of the MAG mine, however, was that it could be laid in water up to about 1,500 feet deep. This made them perfect for attacking submarines such as the American Los Angeles class SSNs.

As *Cheyenne* approached the southern entrance to the Formosa Strait, the communicator came to the control room to deliver a message to Mack.

'Captain, we just received an ELF message from *Nimitz* asking us to come to communications depth to receive a message from them over SSIXS.'

'Very well,' Mack said. 'Come to periscope depth,' he ordered the OOD.

As *Cheyenne* ascended slowly, Mack hoped that the message would contain some good news.

Mack had decided to come to periscope depth in case the incoming message from *Nimitz* required an answer. He couldn't use the floating wire to transmit a message back to the fleet. He also wasn't sure if the message was on the VLF broadcast yet.

With *Cheyenne* at periscope depth, Mack decided to have a quick look around with the Type 2 attack periscope. After raising his periscope, Mack made a quick circular motion in order to get a complete 360-degree picture of the surface, but he didn't see anything out of the ordinary.

As the message was received, it was automatically deciphered by the SSIXS transceiver and brought to Mack. He read it, then handed it to the navigator.

'Take a look at this,' Mack said. 'Several of *Nimitz*'s aircraft, operating from the Pacific, have been monitoring Chinese naval activities in the Formosa Strait for the past week, and they have determined that we are headed straight for a minefield.'

That was good information to have, and Mack appreciated receiving it, but the message didn't end there. *Nimitz* had located two routes which they believed had been designated safe transit zones for Chinese vessels. According to naval intelligence reports they had just received, no mines had been detected floating on the surface in those areas and no Chinese surface ships had been detected laying mines in those zones.

Mack ordered *Cheyenne* back to four hundred feet, and then he and the navigator went over to the quartermaster's table where a large chart of the Formosa Strait was lying flat on the table.

The Formosa Strait was shallow, running from north to south, in between China and Taiwan. The suspected mined area took up a large portion of the strait, running completely through its center. The first mine-safe route was on the western side, along the coast of China. The second route was on the eastern side along the coast of Taiwan. Both officers examined the recommended routes, trying to determine which route was better for *Cheyenne*.

The navigator spoke first. 'Captain, I recommend taking the eastern route, along the western shore of Taiwan. I'm not that comfortable with running along the coast of China. We would probably be faced with who knows what types of Chinese patrol craft, not to mention all the aircraft that we would come into contact with.'

Mack agreed, both with the reasoning and the recommendation. 'The second route it is,' he said. 'Plot a new course just to the starboard side of the Pescadores Islands.'

The navigator remained at the plotting table while Mack headed to the sonar room to find out if any new, interesting contacts had been detected. Then the navigator had the quartermaster of the watch enter *Cheyenne*'s track onto his chart.

● ● ●

Cheyenne headed through the shallow waters of the Formosa Strait at four knots. With their previous experience in shallow waters, Mack ordered the OOD to run at one hundred feet. The strait itself was roughly 350 nautical miles long. At *Cheyenne*'s current speed, Mack would reach the end of his trip north in about three and a half days. His plan was to quietly sail up near Taiwan and listen for enemy vessels. Mack knew that if he detected any they would most likely be maneuvering in the western safe route, on the other side of the minefield from *Cheyenne*'s current location.

But *Cheyenne*'s mission wasn't just to detect enemy vessels. She was tasked with conducting a search-and-destroy mission for any Chinese submarines and major surface combatants. In order to carry out this mission, Mack decided that once *Cheyenne* was completely through the strait he would turn around and search the dangerous area around the Chinese coast, which he was sure would be a 'target-rich' environment.

Cheyenne's sonar operators listened carefully as she made her transit north. As Mack had guessed, there was little to no Chinese naval traffic on the Taiwan side of the strait – but he did gain one key item of importance, however: they now had an exact location on the Chinese minefield and had plotted at least one safe zone around it.

Once again, Mack found himself appreciating the message he'd received from *Nimitz*. Without that, he might have found himself on the wrong end of a mine's contact 'horn.'

Cheyenne crossed north of the twenty-fifth parallel, almost into the East China Sea. Two hours later, Mack ordered *Cheyenne* to periscope depth to have a look around and to check for any incoming SSIXS radio traffic. There were no messages waiting for him and no sign of Chinese surface ships. Mack hoped that this was a good sign.

Once into the East China Sea, Mack ordered the OOD to complete a U-turn, clearing *Cheyenne*'s baffles and also changing course. Moving slowly and silently, he started bringing *Cheyenne* back down to the south, along the Chinese coast.

Ten nautical miles into their return trip in the strait, *Cheyenne* detected their first submerged contact.

'Conn, sonar, we've got a sonar contact bearing 242. I think we've got a Kilo, Captain, running fast on his single six-bladed screw.'

The BSY-1 operators went to work immediately, attempting to determine the range to the Chinese sub-marine contact.

Sometimes that process was excruciatingly slow. Some-times it went very quickly. This was one of the quick ones.

'We've got it,' one of the BSY-1 operators said. 'Range is 39,000 yards. It's running at sixteen knots, course 145.'

'Increase speed to eight knots,' ordered Mack. 'Man battle stations, torpedo.' Mack knew he would cavitate, but that didn't bother him this time. The Kilo was cavitat-ing also, and he didn't believe that the Chinese submarine would run at flank speed for long, not in twenty-four fathoms of water.

As *Cheyenne* got closer, the firing solution on the Kilo submarine got better and better. After closing to within 20,000 yards, Mack ordered tubes one and two made ready, and both torpedo tube outer doors were opened.

The range to the Kilo had been closing slowly, but after Mack opened the torpedo tube doors, sonar reported that the Kilo had slowed down, and the range closed more quickly. The BSY-1 computers showed that the Kilo had turned toward *Cheyenne*. Less than a minute later, sonar had another report for Mack.

'Conn, sonar, the Kilo just went active with its medium-frequency "Shark Teeth" sonar.'

'Shark Teeth' was a NATO nickname for the hull-mounted passive/active sonar carried by the Chinese Kilos.

As soon as the Chinese Kilo went active, Mack had no choice. *Cheyenne* had been discovered. 'Match sonar bearings and shoot, tubes one and two, Master 112,' he ordered.

'Match sonar bearings and shoot, tubes one and two, Master 112, aye, sir.'

Cheyenne had been through this many, many times in the past several weeks, but each new action still carried an edge of tension. The crew performed as well as always, however, and it wasn't long before Mack received the report, 'Tube one fired electrically,' and, seconds later, 'tube two fired electrically.'

Mack acknowledged the report.

'Conn, sonar, both units are running hot, straight, and normal.'

On board the Kilo, the American Mk 48 torpedoes appeared to come out of nowhere. The Kilo had begun using its active sonar in an effort to detect any possible sonar contacts. This close to their home waters, the Kilo's captain had felt safe doing so. He was only now realizing that he had made a grievous error.

'Unit one . . . unit two also, both units have now acquired,' reported the combat systems officer.

'Cut the wires,' Mack ordered. 'I want to be as far away as possible when those torpedoes explode.' The 650-pound warhead, Mack was aware, could damage any submarine, Chinese or not, if it was close when the torpedo detonated. 'Shut the outer doors and reload tubes one and two with Mk 48s.'

When they were far enough away, Mack slowed *Cheyenne* to four knots. They were still close to Chinese home waters and he didn't want to risk detection again. With the loss of the Kilo, they'd probably figure out soon enough that there was an enemy submarine in the area, but Mack felt reasonably comfortable that he could avoid detection by running quietly.

Mack was also confident that the Kilo itself had nowhere to run. On one side was the Chinese coastline; on the other was a large, deadly minefield. Once the Mk 48s had acquired the Kilo, Mack was sure that the Chinese submarine was doomed.

'Conn, sonar,' the sonar supervisor reported, 'the Kilo is drawing left again, heading in the direction of the Chinese minefield. The Mk 48s are still following it.'

Mack was calm as he acknowledged the report, but he had to admit to a certain grudging respect for the Chinese captain. Desperate, knowing that his ship had no chance to survive the torpedoes bearing down on it, he had taken the one gamble left open to him.

'Conn, sonar, explosion in the water, bearing 110.'

Mack tensed, waiting for the end of the report.

'Captain, we just lost unit one. The first Mk 48 hit a mine.'

Mack nodded, his admiration for his opponent growing slightly. The desperate gamble had paid off – so far. But there was still one more Mk 48 out there, and it was locked on to the Kilo.

The twin explosions of the first Mk 48 and the mine it had detonated sent shock waves through the entire minefield. Because the Chinese had, in some locations, laid the mines too close together, the pressure from the first explosions began touching off other explosions, and two more mines exploded within seconds.

Moments later, the sonar room reported a third explosion. The sonar supervisor assumed it was also a Chinese mine because the second Mk 48 was still chasing its prey.

'Conn, sonar, another explosion,' the sonar supervisor said a short time later. 'We've lost contact with unit two. I think it just hit a mine.'

The desperate gamble had paid off. The Kilo had avoided both torpedoes, but it was still in trouble. It was deep in the middle of a minefield, and it knew there was an enemy out there somewhere, stalking it.

Less than one minute after the second Mk 48 hit a mine, sonar detected two more explosions.

'Conn, sonar, two more explosions, bearing 112. I'm hearing breaking-up noises. The Kilo, Master 112, must have run itself into a mine.'

The sound of groaning metal was unmistakable. As the Kilo sank, Mack thought about what had just happened. Desperate times called for desperate measures, he knew, but sometimes they just didn't work.

The irony was that this time it had worked – it just hadn't worked well enough. It wasn't one of the Mk 48s that had killed the Kilo; it was the Chinese's own low-tech mines.

Cheyenne's entire crew had now seen firsthand what damage a Chinese minefield could do to a submarine. The problem, however, was that the narrow path that *Cheyenne* was following could easily turn into a 'killing zone' for her just as it had for the Kilo.

But Mack didn't have much choice. If he was to accomplish his mission, he had to take *Cheyenne* along this route. He just hoped he had better luck than the unfortunate Kilo's captain.

●   ●   ●

Eight hours later, *Cheyenne* was still running at four knots and had her TB-16 towed array deployed to the short stay. Eight sonar contacts had been evaluated as non-threats.

'Conn, sonar, after clearing our baffles, we've got two more contacts bearing 004. Sounds like surface warships, Captain.'

'We're working on range to the contacts right now, Captain,' reported the fire-control coordinator.

Mack immediately began moving *Cheyenne* to a position where they could more easily triangulate the range to the two sonar contacts.

'They're two Luda I destroyers, the kind without the helicopter. The computer just identified their screw characteristics,' one of the sonar operators said to the sonar supervisor.

Since the naval war with China began, *Cheyenne*'s library of sonar contacts, used to identify sonar signals received while on a mission, had grown tremendously. This was due largely to *Cheyenne*'s stellar performance during her undersea operations and her resulting contacts with just about every class of Chinese warship operated by their navy – which allowed *Cheyenne* to record their sound characteristics and correlate to hull type. Without this library, the sonar operators would have little idea what types of targets they were tracking.

Mack ordered the Mk 48s from tubes one and two removed and replaced with Harpoons. This took some time, but it greatly improved his attack options.

Several long minutes passed before the BSY-1 computers were finally able to calculate a range to the two destroyers. 'Range to the closest Luda, Master 121, is 22,000 yards,' the fire-control coordinator reported. 'Range to the second one, Master 122, is 28,000 yards. They are both running at sixteen knots.'

'Very well,' Mack said.

The Harpoon was Mack's weapon of choice for this situation. Not only would it save his multipurpose Mk 48s for future operations, but it also allowed *Cheyenne* more of a chance to escape once they had launched their missiles.

The Mk 48s were seeker-type weapons. After launching them, *Cheyenne* continued to provide them with targeting data until their seeker heads had acquired the target. Only after they had acquired could Mack cut the wires to them and withdraw from the area.

The Harpoons, however, were essentially 'launch and

leave' missiles. Once they were loaded with their flight and target data they didn't need any further assistance. Following their launch, there was nothing for *Cheyenne* to do except get back to deep water and move out of the enemy's way. The Harpoons were also ten times faster than an Mk 48, giving the surface ships less time to react.

Order by order, step by step, Mack readied the Harpoons. When they launched, the noises of combat firings could be heard throughout the submarine.

'Tubes one and two fired electrically, Captain.'

After being ejected from *Cheyenne*'s torpedo tubes, the Harpoon canisters floated toward the surface. As the two buoyant capsules, pointed in a forty-five-degree up angle, reached the surface, they jettisoned their nose caps and aft bodies. The missiles' boosters ignited, sending the missiles out of the water.

The missiles emerged from the water, fast and sleek as they entered their element. Once airborne, their booster rockets continued to burn, as they were designed to, for approximately three more seconds before the Harpoons' main turbojets fired, sending the missiles onward – toward the two unknowing Chinese Ludas.

Mack didn't stick around to admire their flight. As soon as he received word that the missiles had left his submarine, he ordered the OOD to increase speed to ten knots and exited the area, hoping no other submarines were around.

The two UGM-84 missiles made their way quickly toward the two Ludas. As soon as they had closed to within one nautical mile, the Harpoons began their terminal maneuver. Instead of the regular 'pop-up' maneuver, Mack had ordered that these two missiles be programmed to drop from cruising altitude to the sea-skimming height of five feet before sneaking into the two destroyers.

The Harpoons' terminal sea-skimming trajectory worked perfectly and the Chinese Ludas did not even know that the missiles were heading toward them. The missiles were flying so low that the Chinese destroyers' 'Eye Shield' and 'Bean Sticks' radars – the NATO designation for the Russian-derived radars on board – did not even detect the oncoming missiles.

Cheyenne was still relatively close to the two destroyers when the sonar room report came in.

'Conn, sonar, we have two explosions, sixteen seconds apart, bearings 002 and 006 . . .'

Before the sentence was completed, the sonar supervisor revised his report, 'Correction. We just got a third explosion. This one sounds like a secondary explosion, also bearing 002.' He paused, then added, 'Conn, sonar, we've now got breaking-up noises on that same target, bearing 002. It's a goner, sir.'

The Luda destroyer at bearing 002 was a scene of death and destruction. It had a complement of 280 sailors and officers. Within forty-five seconds of the Harpoon's arrival, 180 of them were dead, killed in the fire and melting deluge of metal and fuel that had ignited following the impact. Over forty bodies were scattered around the warship, lifeless and bobbing in the water. Next to these dead sailors were live ones, floating on their backs, trying to adjust to the sudden, ferocious attack and doing anything in their power to stay above the water.

There were only fifty sailors who had managed to abandon the doomed Luda destroyer. The remaining sailors and crew of the sinking warship were trapped inside with no chance to escape. No matter how hard they struggled, they would die, either of smoke inhalation or the burning of the ship around them.

Quietly, and slowly, the Chinese destroyer sank beneath the waters of the Formosa Strait. The crew – those who lived and those who died – never even knew where the incoming missile had come from.

The destruction was not so complete on board the second

257

Chinese Luda, but still the damage was enormous. The Harpoon's 510-pound warhead had detonated at the aft end of the vessel, and the destroyer had lost nearly a quarter of its personnel.

When the Chinese naval commanders received word that both of these powerful Chinese warships had been hit, their immediate assessment was that a lightning strike of F/A-18s had taken part in these ships' destruction. Worried that more American aircraft were operating in the area, the Chinese were afraid to send any aircraft to patrol the seas and, since they had already withdrawn their Akulas, they had no assets in the area capable of detecting *Cheyenne*.

Mack had no way of guessing at the Chinese naval commanders' thinking, but when no enemy vessels showed up hunting *Cheyenne*, Mack secured from battle stations. Traveling at four knots, *Cheyenne* quietly slipped farther away from the area.

Mack and the officers of *Cheyenne* were amazed that here, as close to the Chinese shore as any American warship had ever ventured during this war, there were few operational enemy warships. Mack had had no run-ins with any targets that represented any type of threat to his submarine, and for the first time in a long time, everything was under control and working perfectly.

As *Cheyenne* neared the southern exit of the Formosa Strait, Mack realized that this delousing and reconnaissance operation had revealed the condition the Chinese navy was in. As soon as Mack passed back into the South China Sea, he brought *Cheyenne* to sixty feet and raised the communications mast.

Word was soon passed throughout the Navy that *Cheyenne* had completed her mission of delousing in the 'perilous' strait. Warning also was sent concerning the moored minefield, along with the exact locations of the minefields, and the safe zones. Mack also made a point of sending word that *Cheyenne* and her crew had added three more   ·

kills, one Kilo submarine and two Luda destroyers, to their long list of successes.

As soon as the communications mast was lowered, Mack headed back to his stateroom to get some well-deserved rest. He had returned the conn to the OOD after ordering the navigator to set course for Tsoying Naval Base, Taiwan.

This mission had been very successful, but Mack couldn't count on the next one going so well. He was looking forward to returning to the submarine tender *McKee*. This war was far from over, and he was sure that he was going to need all the weapons he could get.

THIRTEEN

Typhoon Hunt

The combat systems officer and engineer officer and their other division officers remained on board *Cheyenne* to take care of the weapons loading from *McKee* and reactor start-up preparations. Captain Mackey, along with his executive officer, operations officer, and navigator, proceeded to the headquarters of the Tsoying Naval Base for their pre-underway briefing. They weren't sure why the briefing wasn't in *McKee*'s war room where their previous briefings were held. Although the hospitality of the Taiwanese was fantastic, it was still hard to be sure whom they were talking to when the Chinese were just across the strait.

Upon entering the conference room on the second floor, the captain was happy to see that security personnel from the CTF 74 staff were conducting an electronic sweep of the room, hunting for listening devices. This had been standard practice when the foe was the Soviet Union and now it continued as standard practice no matter who the foe was or where the meeting room was.

After *Cheyenne*'s officers arrived, and before they could settle into their places, a couple of heavies preceded what appeared to be a distinguished Chinese gentleman. He *was* Chinese; he turned out to be President Jiang. The heavies were two of his bodyguards.

Mack wasn't too sure about this. A war patrol briefing with the Chinese there?

Noting Mack's concerned expression, President Jiang told him to rest easy. He had only wanted to meet the famous *Cheyenne* captain Bartholomew 'Mack' Mackey, and to thank him for his feats of fortune on behalf of all his people on the mainland. In direct defiance of the renegade Li Peng, songs were being written about *Cheyenne* in nearly every province of his country, children walked to school chanting '*Cheyenne, Cheyenne,*' and Wyoming had become the main subject of United States geography lessons.

After an uncomfortable exchange of pleasantries, Jiang left as quickly as he had arrived. Mack, who had been taken completely by surprise, was pleased to see him go. *Cheyenne*'s commanding officer wasn't much for Chinese politics.

His war was a different story; *Cheyenne* was following orders. It didn't matter much who the enemy was since the Russians were supplying submarines to nearly every Third World country that could afford the bill. Mack and his officers had become intimately familiar with the Romeos, Kilos, Alfas, and Akulas by now.

When President Jiang left, the briefing began. The Chinese had heard of Jiang's surfacing in Taiwan, so they spent some of their dwindling currency on the purchase of a Russian-built Typhoon-class SSBN. Apparently they couldn't trust their own Xia SSBN to be much of an intimidation factor, what with numerous CSS-N-3 ballistic missile test-launch failures, so they took delivery of a North Fleet Typhoon that had already completed its under-ice transit and was nearing the South China Sea. The briefing officer also mentioned that the Typhoon probably had some North Fleet Akula II SSNs 'riding shotgun.'

That's a waste, Mack thought to himself.

The Typhoon had been built with its double-hull construction not just for survival against torpedo attacks, but also to allow it to punch through the polar ice cap and launch its missiles with near impunity. The Mk 48s would have to be accurately placed to damage the SSBN. Screw damage would be assured; but the Typhoon also had dual spinners, in addition to the two main screws, with their

262

90,000 SHP (shaft horsepower), for enhanced slow-speed maneuverability and depth control in and around the ice keels.

The Typhoon's ability to 'ice-pick' – to hover in place under the ice for months at a time – would also make the Typhoon hunt more than a challenge. The lack of IUSS in the South China Sea didn't help much, either. Mack decided he would probably have to use some Mk 48s in the 'swim-out' mode as off-board search sensors in the patrol-area locations where naval intelligence estimated the Typhoon could be located.

Naval intelligence, Mack knew, was basing this on estimates that the Typhoon's SS-N-20 SLBMs (submarine-launched ballistic missiles) were not capable of short-range ballistic trajectories like some of their earlier missile systems – especially on the Yankees – were. The Typhoon could launch at Taiwan from the Arctic Ocean where it would require the United States to detect and track the missile trajectory. By the time it was determined where the missiles were headed, it would be too late.

The captain decided that after today's reactor startup *Cheyenne* would stay critical every time in port so long as there was a threat of ballistic missiles. If the Typhoon launched, there would not be time to conduct pre-critical checks, reactor start-up, and engine room light-off before the missiles detonated in the sky over the Tsoying Naval Base.

Upon returning to the ship, the combat systems officer reported the weapons loading complete, including two Harpoon missiles, just in case. Mack wasn't happy that torpedo space was traded for Harpoons, but at least they weren't loaded in the torpedo tubes.

After departing her mooring alongside *McKee* shortly before dark, *Cheyenne* got under way and headed to the north off Kangshan on the surface. Since the Russian RORSAT satellites had been sweeping the area for the Chinese, the intent was to fool the satellites into believing that *Cheyenne* would be patrolling to the north, when actually she would be doing an end around to the east of Taiwan, where the water was deeper. *Cheyenne* no longer had her running lights energized, nor the submarine ID beacon. She was running 'darkened ship.' But she was not alone in running without any lights to give away her position.

The stillness of the night was broken by the staccato noise of gunshots – smaller caliber in the after port quarter and somewhat larger caliber in the after starboard quarter. These sounds were followed by the distinctive impacts of ricochets off both sides of the sail.

The source of the gunfire maneuvered past *Cheyenne* at high speed, essentially on the same course. There were two attack craft, and their passage could be heard by the bridge watch standers who had ducked down behind the safety of the high-tensile-stress steel.

'Officer of the deck, Captain,' Mack said. 'Rig the bridge for dive and lay below ASAP. I have the conn.'

Never before had the bridge been rigged for dive so quickly. The spray from the opened main ballast tank vents nearly engulfed the men as they made the final closure of the bridge clamshell. *Cheyenne* was already passing forty-five feet when the last man reported being down, bridge hatches secured. Mack had finely timed the dive to ensure that the upper bridge-access hatch was shut before the surface of the sea reached that height.

When the ship stabilized at 90 feet in only 130 feet of water, Captain Mackey used the sound-powered phone to explain to the crew what had happened. A Chinese (Soviet-built) Komar class fast attack craft was in a running gun battle with a Taiwanese fast attack craft. The 25mm (Chinese) and 76mm (Taiwanese) gunfire was what they had heard and what had bounced off the sail.

Cheyenne had needed to submerge quickly before the Komar launched its SS-N-2 surface-to-surface missiles and the Taiwanese craft reciprocated with its Otomat missiles.

The chances of the missiles inadvertently homing in on the 'innocent' *Cheyenne*'s sail had been too great. Similar incidents between the South and North Korean gunboats fighting it out nearly twenty years before had not been lost in the archives of submarine history.

Some of the crew had sustained minor injuries during their rushing to lay below. The OOD, looking at his bleeding fingers and those of his compatriots from the bridge, tried to bring a little levity to the situation. 'Does this mean,' he asked, 'that we're eligible for the Purple Heart?'

The executive officer answered that it would be the first for submariners since World War II, but that it was worth a try. The joking in the crew's mess and the wardroom that night served to ease tensions, as each man from the bridge was presented with large cardboard Purple Hearts attached to their spaghetti bibs. The ship's yeomen had made them up from pictures in the Awards Manual, using the color scanners and printers in the ship's office.

Once *Cheyenne* submerged, Mack reversed her course to the south. He had decided that the squeeze of the shallow water of the Formosa Strait would be too much if they continued to the north submerged. Besides, the RORSAT deception was OBE (overcome by events) by now. If it didn't work, it didn't work. The rest was up to *Cheyenne*'s sonars and their extraordinary operators.

Mack also ordered the ship to periscope depth until they were clear of the shallow water. He would remain in the control room with the navigator and the OOD – who, along with Mack himself, were the officers with the greatest responsibility – to prevent bottoming.

'Conn, sonar, we have that Chinese Komar bearing 355, emerging from our starboard baffles. Designate Master 123.'

'Conn, ESM, the Komar's radar is painting the Type 18, signal strength three.'

Mack ordered the chief of the watch to 'man battle stations, Harpoon.' He followed that with the order to the torpedo room to change the load of torpedo tube one to Harpoon. Torpedo room personnel were already rearranging stows to get one of the Harpoons lined up.

Mack elected not to expend Mk 48s on the Komar. *Cheyenne* would launch the Harpoon on ESM bearings while continuing to the south, an 'over-the-shoulder' launch which Mack had loved practicing in the fire-control trainer.

Five minutes later, the Harpoon was loaded and tube one made ready. After Mack ordered ESM bearings matched and the Harpoon fired, he saw it depart the water ahead of the ship and execute its sweet turn to starboard, racing toward the bearing of the Komar. The Harpoon hardly had time to accelerate to its maximum speed before the seeker found its target, crashing into the bridge of the Komar, tearing it in two as the missile's momentum and its explosive combined to create total destruction. A flash in the night, then nothing, as if the Komar had literally disintegrated.

After a day's quiet transit, *Cheyenne* arrived in the first patrol area. Located two hundred nautical miles east of Macclesfield Bank, Mack had decided this would be the most likely Typhoon patrol area.

On arrival near the northeast corner of the area, Mack ordered the OOD to launch an SSXBT. The information it gathered on temperature versus depth through the water column would be sent by wire to the BSY-1 for use by the sonar and fire-control systems. It also would provide layer-depth information, which Mack wanted. He could use that data to allow *Cheyenne* to effectively hide beneath the layer, or even a second deeper layer.

During dinner in his wardroom – a dinner they all ate quickly – Mack addressed his officers. 'We have our work cut out for us again. With quiet Akulas and the Typhoon staring us in the face, we'll need to be even more innovative in our attacks than we were when we went up against the seven Akulas. We'll have to flush out both the Akulas and the Typhoon.'

Cheyenne had gotten a break earlier. Sonar had reported weak tonals from an Akula to the south, the same tonals as had been detected on the only Akula to have gotten away from her in the Paracels. Apparently, running out of assets, the Chinese had been able to do nothing else but assign that one and the remaining interfleet transfer ones to the Typhoon's protection.

This was fine with Mack. Not only did it give him a second shot at that Akula, but this one was a dead give-away, if the Typhoon were nearby.

The initial range had been established at roughly 80,000 yards in the third convergence zone by the section fire-control tracking party. This time, Mack would wait until he ordered the OOD to man battle stations, torpedo.

There was still nothing from the other Akulas or the Typhoon. Just the lone set of low-frequency tonals. These were coming from the same one with sound shorts to its turbine generator.

Just in case the other Russian submarines were somewhere nearby, Mack passed the order for the torpedo room to 'Make tubes one and two ready in all respects, including opening the outer doors.'

A short while later, the OOD reported to the captain, 'Tubes one and two are ready in all respects. Both outer doors are open.' *Cheyenne* was getting so good that they were taking liberties with the battle stations versus the section fire-control parties.

'Very well, officer of the deck,' answered Mack.

Fortunately, the Akula was not tracking on any particular course. This meant he was loitering in the vicinity of the Typhoon, as Mack had hoped. This also allowed *Cheyenne* to close the range while the Akula did the maneuvering to allow the three BSY-1 computers to compute the fire-control solution before the Akula could detect the launch of *Cheyenne*'s Mk 48s. The other Akulas and the Typhoon remained silent.

Other than the signature obtained earlier, the Akula was quiet. *Cheyenne* was not able to detect it with either her spherical or conformal arrays. The course changes and the TB-23 inputs to the sonar consoles and to the three BSY-1 computer consoles made the solution possible for the section fire-control tracking party. When the BSY-1 operators and the section fire-control coordinator were satisfied with the TMA (target motion analysis) solution, Mack ordered battle stations manned.

As was routine for *Cheyenne*, Captain Mackey ordered, 'Firing point procedures, Master 124.'

The combat systems officer at the weapons control console reported the target course as random, speed three, and range 15,780 yards.

'Sonar, conn, stand by.'

'Conn, sonar, standing by.'

'Match sonar bearings and shoot, tubes one and two.'

'Match sonar bearings and shoot, tubes one and two, aye.'

'Tubes one and two fired electrically,' the combat systems officer reported.

'Conn, sonar, units from tubes one and two running hot, straight, and normal,' came the report from the sonar supervisor as the two torpedoes executed their wire clearance maneuvers and accelerated to medium speed for the inbound run.

'Very well, sonar,' responded Mack.

The next report wasn't long in coming.

'Conn, sonar, the weapons are accelerating.' This was confirmed by the combat systems officer, who reported acquisition by both units. *Cheyenne* had detected a second Akula when it accelerated to flee the situation, but there was still no sign of the Typhoon.

The captain of the Typhoon, a capital ship of the former – and, perhaps, future – Soviet Union, was not about to give up his hovering. He hovered quietly with main engines secured and his two pressurized water reactors at the lowest possible power in order to generate as little steam-flow noise as possible. He had even secured the spinners, allowing his ship to swing with the current. This particular Russian captain intended to make admiral, following in the footsteps of his father.

The two Mk 48s from *Cheyenne* continued on course for their targets, but only the torpedo from tube one had targeted the original, noisy Akula, old Master 74. Mack had retargeted the other Mk 48 at the second Akula as soon as it sped up, allowing *Cheyenne*'s sonars to detect it. Sending the second torpedo toward this Russian submarine was merely Mack's way of welcoming it to PACFLT.

'Conn, sonar, explosions bearing 195 and 178.'

Mack was hoping that the loss of two of his Akula escorts would rattle the Typhoon captain, but he maintained his posture, quiet as a titmouse in a church. Mack knew the Typhoon was out there, but he hadn't flushed it yet.

What Mack didn't know was that there was another Akula out there as well, one whose captain had more experience with the US 688 class than his lost North Fleet fellow captain. The Akula, like the Typhoon, was refusing to be baited.

'Conn, sonar, still nothing from the Typhoon.'

The captain ordered an Mk 48 prepared for 'swim-out' and off-board sensor tactics. This deployment was often extremely useful, especially under-ice, where the torpedo could seek out ice-picking SSBNs and send the information back to *Cheyenne* over the guidance wire. But Mack still wished he had the capability of a slower search speed and a frequency higher than that which could be detected by the Russian acoustic intercept receivers.

There was such a system, FORMIDABOD, but it had not yet reached the fleet for operational use. That system was the brainchild of a previous COMSUBPAC plans officer with a vision, who had noticed that the initial indications were that the 688's original BQS-15 sonar couldn't 'see' mines. Standing for *F*iber-*O*ptic *R*emote *MI*ne *D*etection *A*nd *B*reak *O*ut *D*evice, the remotely operated vehicle could advance the search, out of harm's way from the SSN, and provide acoustic information at over four times the data rate and at six times the frequency of the Russian, or US for that matter, acoustic intercept receivers.

The search for the Typhoon took a while, with the Mk 48 probing the area ahead of *Cheyenne*, but eventually it paid off. The off-board sensor found the Typhoon – and the Typhoon's acoustic intercept receiver found the off-board sensor.

On board the Typhoon, with a true belief in his invincibility, the Russian captain decided to remain in place. His only reactions to the sensor's presence were to operate his spinners to twist his massive ship and to ready his 65cm and 53cm torpedoes for use against the American submarine that had sent the Mk 48 hunting. The Russian captain had no way of knowing who was out there, but he decided it must be *Cheyenne*.

The Typhoon's captain ordered the interlocks broken between the port and starboard tube nests, thereby allowing him to bring all his 53cm torpedo tubes to bear at once. The Soviet Union had developed the equivalent of two torpedo-tube ejection-pump rams, one for port and one for starboard.

At the same time that the Typhoon was making its preparations, Captain Mackey was formulating his own new doctrine. The normal doctrine didn't cover this situation; but that was why he was in command. His choice; his decision; no one could refute it. This situation had never developed before – but it had its parallels, if one had the brains, and the guts, to see it.

'Firing point procedures, Master 126, tubes one and two,' ordered the captain. 'Firing point procedures, Master 126, tubes three and four.'

When the combat systems officer and executive officer looked to the captain with confusion, he elaborated, 'Unit one for the main screws; then, when they spin up on the spinners, units two and three for the spinners. When that happens, we'll be within range behind the Typhoon to light off MIDAS. Then we'll detonate unit four over their missile deck.'

Mack's gutsy plan went off without a hitch. Unit one ran to the Typhoon's screws as intended. When sonar reported the spinners starting up, the next two units were guided to their points of destruction.

With the launch of the last two units, *Cheyenne* increased speed to match that of the torpedoes. The Russian captain finally decided to launch torpedoes at *Cheyenne* and the missiles at Taiwan, but by then it was too late. The fourth torpedo detonated above his missile deck before the first launch tube missile hatch could be opened. The result was the dishing in of all hatches so that they couldn't be opened. In addition, the overpressure wave caused by the last Mk 48's 650 pounds of explosive, coupled with the Typhoon's depth and open torpedo tube muzzle doors, resulted in the Russian torpedo tube breech doors giving way. The torpedo room flooded and the Typhoon started to take on water.

That would have finished just about any other submarine in any navy in the world, but not the Typhoon. With its double hulls still intact, the would-be Russian admiral ordered all internal ballast dumped. Even if the outer ballast tanks were ruptured, the missile-tube water-compensation system would provide some buoyancy.

With the loss of what seemed like an insignificant amount of ballast, the Typhoon accelerated rapidly to the surface, but once there the Russians learned that the emergency escape capsule – which had never been practiced on a real submarine – could not be released.

With the lessons learned from the Mike SSN disaster in the North Sea off Norway, the Typhoon's captain decided to remain where he was to await rescue. Mack knew the Russian captain had lost his cool; he was now in the South China Sea, where no Russian ships could come to his rescue. What's more, *Cheyenne* had finally picked up the last Akula, whose captain had elected to pull off to be able to fight another day and which had managed to distance itself from the fray.

Cheyenne was there as the Typhoon reached the surface. The Russian submarine had been severely damaged, but Mack ordered four more torpedoes into the defenseless Typhoon.

There was seldom mercy in wartime, and *Cheyenne*'s and Mack's orders were clear. If he had allowed the Typhoon to survive, its crew would have cut the missile hatches open with blow torches and completed their launch against Taiwan.

The result of the additional four torpedoes exploding beneath the Typhoon caused major seawater system flooding. The ensuing scene was similar to the devastation experienced by the Yankee class SSBN southeast of the Bermudas years before. Only this time there was no capability to protect and remove the crew.

Life rafts were put over the side, only to be attacked by the South China Sea shark population, so the crew watched helplessly from the huge, flat missile-tube deck. The oversized submarine started settling slowly deeper, the water level rising to within meters of the missile-tube deck, with the crew topside.

The captain – the admiral-to-be – had already sent a message to his North Fleet Headquarters concerning the impending demise of his capital ship and the lack of help from his Akula escorts by name, two of which had been sunk. He had not been given any means to communicate with the Chinese, so he resorted to calling home. After that he went topside to be with his men, sat down, and held hands in a circle as their submarine slid beneath the surface of the sea, sailors to the end, for eternity. The sharks did the rest.

Cheyenne's Type 18 periscope had taped the entire sinking of the Typhoon, but Mack had no intention of showing it to the crew as their evening movie. He had confiscated the tape, ensuring that it would be seen again only in a closed audience as part of his patrol debriefing to a higher authority.

When the Russian North Fleet Headquarters received the message from the Typhoon, the commander-in-chief was astounded, and not just at the loss of one of his strategic assets. He was also furious and astonished at what seemed to be a refusal to follow orders by one of his Akula captains.

The scathing CO-Eyes Only message sent to the remaining Akula was clear. Its meaning was well understood by the Akula's captain, because it made reference to his family – his wife and two daughters – who had been taken into 'protective custody' by the Russian secret service.

•　　•　　•

Mack was nearing the periscope stand when sonar reported low-frequency tonal contact to the north. The tonals were classified by the sonar supervisor as coming from an Akula. They were weak, but closing.

The Akula captain, intimidated by his own chain of command, had decided to take on *Cheyenne*. He'd had no choice. Even without the threat to his family, returning to his homeland without being successful during war, even if it was a Chinese war, was tantamount to certain death.

He made two torpedoes ready for his own snap shots, in case they stumbled upon the quiet *Cheyenne* at close range. The Russian sonar operators were poised, carefully searching for any sign of *Cheyenne* with their towed array. They had all listened to the sounds of the deaths of their comrades on board the Akulas and the Typhoon, and they were eager to defeat *Cheyenne*.

Mack wasn't about to let that happen. He wanted no more close-range encounters for *Cheyenne*. He intended for this battle to be like the earlier long-range attack on one of the earlier Akulas, Master 74.

The Akula was nearing the outer weapon range of both the US and the Russian torpedoes when Mack manned battle stations torpedo. He had already expended eleven torpedoes, including the dead round he'd used as the off-board sensor. Thirteen Mk 48s and one lonely Harpoon remained, and the Harpoon would be of no use unless he could force the Akula to the surface. If it was damaged enough for that, it could be finished as *Cheyenne* had earlier done with the Romeo near Midway Island.

But Mack didn't want it to come to that. The Typhoon's death had been bad enough. Submariners, even the enemy, deserved to die with their ship rather than at the hands of the creatures of the sea.

Once battle stations were manned, Captain Mackey passed the order for the torpedo room to 'make tubes one and two ready in all respects, including opening the outer doors.' In addition to making *Cheyenne*'s tubes ready as early as possible, he intended to launch two Mk 48s in the quiet 'swim-out' mode as he had done with the off-board sensor, but this time they would be armed as weapons.

The remaining Akula, with its own towed array, had shown that he could be a quiet adversary. Naval intelligence still had not learned much about that sensor capability, so Mack decided to play it safe. He elected to follow the same plan he had used successfully earlier, steering the torpedoes off target so they would be attacking from bearings other than *Cheyenne*'s location.

'Make tubes one and two ready in all respects, including opening the outer doors, fire-control, torpedo room, aye.'

After the torpedo room reported completing the ordered evolution with the torpedo tubes, the executive officer informed Mack, 'Captain, tubes one and two are ready in all respects. Both outer doors are open.'

'Very well, fire control,' answered the captain.

The Akula was tracking to the southwest. *Cheyenne* was closing the range, intending to intercept with a fire-control solution before the Akula could reach detection range on *Cheyenne*.

The Akula continued drawing left as *Cheyenne* closed. It, too, was otherwise quiet, with no contact on the spherical or conformal arrays. Because of this, the BSY-1 operators had to rely on the readings from the TB-23, assisted by Mack's course changes, to make the solution possible for the fire-control party. When both they and the fire-control coordinator were satisfied with the TMA (target motion analysis) solution on Master 127, the Russian Akula II SSN, the captain ordered, 'Firing point procedures, Master 127.'

The combat systems officer at the weapons control console reported the target course as 200, speed four, and range 27,250 yards.

'Sonar, conn, stand by.'

'Conn, sonar, standing by.'

'Match sonar bearings and shoot, tubes one and two.'

'Match sonar bearings and shoot, tubes one and two, aye.'

'Tubes one and two fired electrically,' reported the combat systems officer.

'Conn, sonar, units from tubes one and two running hot, straight, and normal,' came the report from the sonar supervisor as the two torpedoes executed their wire clearance maneuvers and accelerated to slow speed for the long inbound run.

'Very well, sonar,' responded the captain. 'Take charge and steer the weapons. Unit one off course ten degrees to the right and unit two off course forty-five degrees to the left.' When the torpedoes were close enough for passive acquisition, they would be steered back in the opposite direction.

'Time to turn the units?' asked the captain.

'Twenty minutes for unit one, captain,' answered the combat systems officer. 'Seventeen minutes for unit two.'

The torpedoes were turned on cue. One was leading the target while the other was slightly lagging.

'Time to acquisition?' Mack asked.

'Ten minutes for unit two, Captain,' the combat systems officer replied. 'Twelve minutes for unit one.'

Exactly on schedule, the combat systems officer reported, 'Unit two has acquired.' Two minutes later he added, 'Unit one has acquired.' This time both torpedoes had acquired their original target. There were no more Russian submarines left out there.

'Cut the wires, shut the outer doors, and reload tubes one and two,' ordered the captain.

'Conn, sonar, we have two torpedoes in the water, bearing 205 and drawing right!' the sonar supervisor called out. The Russian captain had launched his snap shots, but not at the bearings of the incoming torpedoes. He was wilier than the other Akula captains, and had read the report of *Cheyenne*'s earlier tactic, which had been sent by the Akula that got away and made it to the Paracels. Guessing correctly that the captain of *Cheyenne* would try it again, he had launched on a bearing halfway between the oncoming torpedoes.

Mack's ploy hadn't worked. The Russian torpedoes were headed for *Cheyenne*.

'Right full rudder, all ahead flank,' Mack ordered. 'Do not cavitate. Make your depth one thousand feet.' He wasn't sure if the Akula had detected *Cheyenne* on its towed array or if the Russian captain had guessed at Mack's earlier tactic. If the Akula had heard them, it knew *Cheyenne*'s location, but if its captain had just made a lucky guess, then Mack didn't want to reveal *Cheyenne* to its sonar. Not unless the inbound torpedoes acquired *Cheyenne* and he had to. Having been deep beneath the second layer, *Cheyenne* was at flank speed in less than a minute, on course due east, and at one thousand feet. Mack was keeping the torpedoes at the edge of his port baffles so sonar could continue to relay bearing information.

A short while later, the sonar supervisor reported that the torpedoes were speeding up and drawing right faster. At the same time, the WLR-9, *Cheyenne*'s acoustic intercept receiver, started chirping at the frequency of the incoming torpedoes.

'Conn, sonar, explosions coming from our baffles!'

That was the sound of *Cheyenne*'s two torpedoes exploding. Unfortunately, because the explosions occurred in her baffles, the sonar operators could not determine what effect – if any – they'd had on the Akula.

But Mack couldn't worry about that at the moment. The enemy torpedoes were still out there, and closing fast, and they were his top priority. Mack released two gas generators, noisemakers, and brought *Cheyenne* hard right again, circling to the south to open the datum of the gas generators.

Cheyenne's high-speed maneuvers created an additional knuckle that helped draw the attention of the Russian torpedoes, which attacked nothing but the boiling water column. Confused by the noisemakers, they could not acquire *Cheyenne*, but merely headed off into the sea.

When it was time for the Russian torpedo end of run and the torpedoes could no longer be heard, Mack turned to the west and slowed *Cheyenne* to search for the Akula. There was no contact on any of the arrays, and no reverberations from *Cheyenne*'s torpedoes exploding.

The Akula had vanished – though whether it had been destroyed or had merely gone back into hiding could not be determined with any degree of certainty. Mack took *Cheyenne* back toward Taiwan for reload, maneuvering her slowly and cautiously, but he could not gain any more contact on the third Akula.

Following the Navy's standard procedures, Mack's patrol report would list this last Akula as being sunk. Mack only hoped he was right.

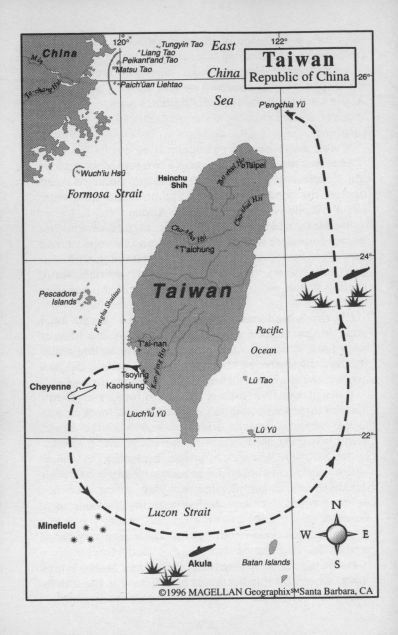

FOURTEEN

Hornets' Nest

Cheyenne arrived safely back at Tsoying Naval Base, once again mooring alongside *McKee*. Before heading over for his next war patrol briefing, Captain Mackey requested a full loadout of Mk 48 ADCAP torpedoes. He ordered *Cheyenne*'s combat systems officer to ensure that the remaining Harpoon was offloaded and its stow refilled with an Mk 48.

Mack's first clue that this briefing, like the last, would have political overtones was when the *McKee* captain notified him that the briefing would once again be held at the naval base headquarters rather than on board *McKee*. Mack didn't mind the politics; he just hoped that this didn't mean he'd have to deal with another Typhoon this time out.

The first thing Mack noticed when he entered the conference room on the second floor was the same CTF 74 staff members who had conducted the electronic security sweep of the room before *Cheyenne*'s last patrol. They had already completed their task and were leaving as Mack and his officers arrived.

There was no sign of the Chinese leader, but the briefing officer said that President Jiang would be along before the end of the briefing. Without waiting for Jiang, the briefing officer launched into the background for *Cheyenne*'s next mission.

As Jiang had pointed out at the last meeting, much of China was enthusiastic in its support and appreciation of *Cheyenne*'s successes – much of China, that is, but not all of it. One group in particular that was unhappy about *Cheyenne*'s effectiveness against the Chinese submarines was the so-called Petroleum Faction. This group of engineers had developed the oil fields in Manchuria, and they had a personal interest in this war. Their leader, General Yu Quili, had taken charge of a squadron of Akula II SSNs and had made it his mission to deal with *Cheyenne*.

'What's a general know about submarines?' Mack asked.

That was the wrong question, though, as the briefing officer was quick to point out. It wasn't what General Yu Quili knew that mattered. The leader of the Petroleum Faction had been a major player in this war from the onset. Not only had he assisted in Premier Li Peng's coup, but his group was also the source of funds for the purchases of Russian submarines and Russian crews.

Besides, Mack realized as he listened to the briefing officer, General Yu wasn't going to be driving any of the submarines. But as a leader since the days of Chairman Mao Tse-tung, he undoubtedly would be effective in motivating and inspiring the officers and the crews.

What Mack really wanted to know about, though, wasn't General Yu and his Petroleum Faction, or even his Akulas. What Mack wanted to know about was what it would take to win this war.

'Back when we went up against those seven Akulas,' he said, 'I was told that killing four of them would stop the Russians from providing more SSNs to China. *Cheyenne* killed six of the seven, and yet Russia continued to provide submarines to China – not only Alfas, Kilos, and Akulas, but that Typhoon as well. Where are they all coming from? When will this end?'

The briefing officer answered frankly, perhaps because CTF 74 was at breakfast with President Jiang. 'You are right, Captain Mackey,' he said. 'To be honest, the intelligence community has not done too well lately. However, the CIA and naval intelligence have determined that the Russian Far East Shipyard, Komsomolsk on the Amur River, really did not go commercial like they had originally thought. Instead, it has been working three shifts a day in building submarines for export to China. Plus, China has been training new submarine crews, actually old Chinese diesel boat personnel, in the Kola Peninsula area.'

That was not good news. Not only did it mean that *Cheyenne* would have more enemy submarines to watch out for, but it also meant that Li Peng was committed to this war. *Cheyenne*'s past successes notwithstanding, it was going to take a tremendous effort to bring this conflict to an end.

Mack didn't have time to mull that over much before the briefing officer started explaining *Cheyenne*'s next assignment. In preparation for eventually moving President Jiang from Taiwan to mainland China, *Cheyenne* would have to ensure that the waters around Taiwan were sanitized of General Yu's SSNs.

That didn't sound so bad, but then the briefing officer went on to the details. Much of China was behind President Jiang – and that included most of its navy. Because of this, Mack's superiors were presuming that Yu's SSNs were the only remaining hostile Chinese submarines in the area, which meant that any other submarines *Cheyenne* detected were off limits for attacks. Unless, of course, *Cheyenne* was attacked first.

Mack didn't like that at all. These attack constraints were like those he had received during his transit from Ballast Point to Pearl Harbor, when *Cheyenne* had encountered the out-of-area Han and had to wait until she was fired upon. But Mack didn't have the chance to object before the CTF 74 admiral arrived with President Jiang and his heavies.

'Good morning, Mack,' the admiral said. 'I presume you are aware of "our" problem, General Yu.'

Mack nodded, but didn't say anything.

'Captain Mackey,' the Chinese president said, 'we do have some good news to offer. Yu and Li Peng have had a falling-out over the general's actions. Li Peng has renounced Yu's authority and has ordered him arrested.

In addition, Li and I are once again communicating with each other – cautiously, I might add – but we are closer to negotiations.'

Mack nodded again, but remained silent.

'You are a hero, Captain,' President Jiang went on, 'but watch your 180. I must leave now, for the roach coach is on the pier with its gedunks.'

Mack blinked at that, caught off guard by Jiang's use of US Navy and submarine lingo. The president laughed, obviously pleased with Mack's reaction, then shook his hand and left the conference room, escorted by his heavies.

Mack wanted to get under way before dark, so once President Jiang had left the CTF 74 admiral told the briefing officer to finish what had not been covered.

According to naval intelligence, General Yu had been supplying the diesel fuel to several of the Romeo, Ming, and Kilo submarine bases – and he'd been supplying it for free. This had naturally won some converts for Yu, which meant that Mack could not discount the possibility of diesel submarines present in the area. Nevertheless, the briefing officer emphasized, CINCPACFLT's orders were that Captain Mackey would have to bide his time, ensuring that any submarine contacts he planned to attack were the Akulas unless fired upon by any other class.

So far, Mack had not been pleased with the nature of this briefing, and he had been even less pleased with the information he had gained. And it was about to get even worse.

In addition to the Akulas and the diesels, the briefing officer said as he neared the end of his presentation, there was a new wrinkle as well. At least one Hainan class attack craft fitted out as a mine layer was active in comms last week, paired with an old Romeo at Zhanjiang Naval Base, the headquarters of the Chinese South Sea Fleet. The old Romeo – which was the Chinese-built version, six feet longer and with eight torpedo tubes – was rumored to be outfitted with twenty-eight mines instead of fourteen torpedoes. To make matters worse, a Pothead radar, probably the Hainan, and a 'Snoop Plate' radar, maybe the Romeo, had been tracking up the coast from Mandarin Bay. They had turned to the east near Hong Kong before being lost two days ago.

Mack was glad when the briefing came to an end. He'd had enough bad news for one day. Unfortunately, there was more to come.

When he got back to *Cheyenne*, Mack learned from the combat systems officer that, against Mack's expressed instructions, *McKee* was still restricting *Cheyenne*'s torpedo loads. It didn't help to learn that *McKee* was doing this for all the right reasons. *Bremerton*, a pre-VLS boat, and *Columbia*, a 688I like *Cheyenne*, also had to be supplied. The arrival of *Portsmouth* and *Pasadena* in two weeks from the Atlantic Fleet would only serve to add to the strain.

Politics again, Mack thought. The shift in the traditional '60–40 split' of submarines, 60 percent for COMSUBLANT and 40 percent for COMSUBPAC, had obviously preceded the equivalent transfer of torpedoes to PACFLT. Now only twenty Mk 48 ADCAP were on board *Cheyenne*, and some might have to be used for long distance off-board minefield sensing before Mack would decide to use MIDAS, the short-range under-ice and mine-detection sonar mounted on the sail.

Although its frequency was nearly twenty times that of the BSY-1 spherical active array, it was still detectable by the enemy. Mack wished even more that he had that FORMIDABOD sensor capability. R and D or not, the United States had shown during Desert Storm that the playing field of war was a better checkout of newly emerging systems than simulated targets and ranges. And its frequency, which was more than five times that of MIDAS, was not detectable by other than its own transducers.

All of which meant that *Cheyenne* would have to contend with quiet diesels and mines while attacking the quiet Akulas, and she'd have to do it with a shortage of torpedoes.

Shaking his head, Mack ordered *Cheyenne* to get under way before anything else could go wrong.

Cheyenne submerged to periscope depth at the fifty fathom curve and then altered her course to the south. In this direction the shallow waters of the Formosa Strait quickly gave way to the depths of the South China Sea. Within a few miles, the ledge would fall off to nearly 1,300 fathoms.

'Captain, officer of the deck. Sonar reports the sound of chains dead ahead of us. I can't see any mooring buoys, but with this sea state three, they could be bobbing up and down, hard to see.'

Mack acknowledged the report and quickly left his stateroom, making a beeline for the sonar room. Putting on his own headset, which he had insisted be available for him whenever he wanted, Mack heard the sounds sonar had reported. But they were not the clunking noise of mooring buoys. They were clinking noises that he had heard once before in the Mediterranean, as the sonar officer during his first submarine assignment on a 637, when Egypt's Romeo submarines had laid mines in the Gulf of Sidra.

'Officer of the deck, come around to the west and get the combat systems officer and executive officer to the conn,' Mack called from the sonar room.

A few minutes later, Mack explained to the officers gathered at the conn that they were up against moored mines. If it had not been for the sea state causing the mines to move up and down and the chain links to rattle against themselves, *Cheyenne* would have been close to being history. He also knew that *Cheyenne* could probably skirt the minefield using MIDAS, but that would not help other sea travelers, including the other 688s on their way to help.

Instead, they would have to try to take out the mines with off-board sensors.

To do this, the warhead grain burn would not be inerted, allowing the torpedo to be command-detonated in the minefield – assuming that the torpedo didn't merely set off the mines with its screw noise. If everything worked as planned, and the torpedo detonated in the proper position, the sympathetic concussions should set off a number of mines.

Mack did not want to expend more than two Mk 48s. That would leave eighteen for *Cheyenne*'s Taiwan-area sanitization duties. To eliminate the minefield with only two torpedoes, *Cheyenne* would have to rely on the high frequency of the torpedo's transducer, nearly twice that of MIDAS, to paint the scene well enough to ensure that the minefield was plotted prior to their attempting the kills.

Cheyenne didn't need to man battle stations for this evolution. The mines couldn't shoot back. Besides, Mack would stay at least five thousand yards away, standing back at a comfortable distance, far beyond the mine detection and destruction capability.

The combat systems officer alerted the TMOW (torpedoman of the watch) of the plan to swim out tube three and then tube four if necessary. At the same time, Mack informed the crew over the 1MC of what would be happening. They would be able to hear the Mk 48 Otto fuel engines spinning up, which one could pick up through the hull while the torpedoes were still close, and Mack didn't want them to be alarmed and wonder what was going on. He also wanted to alert the personnel sleeping in the torpedo room, who would have to get up and move their portable skid bunks so that the tubes could be reloaded.

'Conn, sonar, we have diesel lines bearing 285. No screw blade information yet. But it's not a submarine's diesel. More like two old Chinese twelve-cylinders firing away, out of sync with each other. No bearing drift, either. He's closing.'

Cheyenne had detected the Hainan. Mack was sure of it. Which meant the Romeo might be around.

Mack found himself wondering how accurate his intel was this time. Naval intelligence and the CIA had been wrong a bit too often lately, and it was especially important this time. If he could count on the report that the Romeo had replaced all its torpedoes with mines, he wouldn't have to worry about getting shot at. On the other hand, he couldn't just ignore the Chinese submarine, either. The last thing he wanted was a submerged collision at sea.

Mack decided it was time for some active sonar practice – forward of the beam in sector searches. This would alert the Romeo, but that's what Mack wanted. With luck, the Chinese captain would be smart enough to 'pull up his pants and go home,' as the old saying went. Besides, it was better than two quiet submarines running into each other.

Within minutes of going active, sonar reported contact on a submarine based on the elevation angle of the returning energy. Range 1,850 yards and on the same bearing of the twelve-cylinder diesels' platform, which also was being painted by the BSY-1.

Mack wanted to make tube one ready for a snap shot, but he couldn't. His orders prevented him. He could only fire first at an Akula, not at a Romeo.

Moments later, though, Mack realized that he wasn't going to need to fire. He knew that when sonar reported the submerged contact blowing ballast and increasing speed, two shafts, four blades each, and squawking on his underwater telephone to the Hainan.

The Chinese Romeo's captain had indeed decided to get away from the famous *Cheyenne*, but he had panicked, remembering too late that the Hainan was above him. He ordered the main ballast tank vents opened, but it was too late to stop his ascent. His full rudder turn didn't help either, because the Hainan turned in the same direction.

Moments later, the Romeo's sail sliced through the thin Hainan hull, right at the engine room. The Hainan diesels sputtered and died, their hot engine blocks cracked by the much cooler seawater. Its captain ordered his men to abandon ship as the seawater continued rushing in, helping to put out the fires but causing the tiny craft to sink beneath the waves.

The Romeo was undamaged, but its mission was over. It was going to be busy rescuing the survivors from the diesel fuel-slicked grasp of the sea.

Mack grinned and made another quick decision. He decided to save the torpedoes after all and not use them as off-board sensors. Using their active sonar had given them a pretty good idea where the minefield was, so he ordered a notice-to-mariners message drafted and loaded into an SSIXS buoy. This notice would be transmitted to CTF 74 once the buoy reached the surface and unfurled its tiny satellite antenna. After repeating the transmission four times, the buoy would scuttle itself.

Mack was pleased with his decision. He saved his Mk 48s. He didn't have to go to periscope depth near where the rescue efforts were taking place. And he was able to proceed upon his mission right away.

But there was a downside to his plan, one which Mack hadn't considered. By not being at periscope depth, *Cheyenne*'s WLR-8(V) antenna was not able to detect a radio transmission from the Romeo, a transmission in which the Romeo's captain reported *Cheyenne*'s presence in the area.

This information was picked up and put on the Chinese South Sea Fleet and East Sea Fleet broadcasts. Hours later, with Mack unaware of any of this, General Yu's Akulas and also some Kilos were closing on the datum reported by the Romeo. Three Akulas were closing from the southwest at a comfortable twenty-five knots, while two slower Kilos were making an end around northeast of Taiwan, running on their batteries at eight knots so that they would not have to recharge their batteries before getting on station east of the big island.

By supper time, *Cheyenne* had arrived in her first search area and slowed to one-third speed to launch several SSXBTs, but Mack rescinded the SSXBT order after the OOD reported that sonar had weak tonals from an Akula to the south. These were the same tonals that had been detected on the last Akula that supposedly sank after the Typhoon hunt. Sonar also detected a loud shaft rub, which easily allowed them to determine the Akula's twenty-five knot speed.

Mack realized that they must have only damaged the Akula's shafting. With a word of caution to his officers about their returning adversary, Mack ordered battle stations torpedo manned.

This was a Russian-crewed Akula. Captain Mackey was aware of this, and knew it was dangerous. He also knew that this could be a repeat of a previous hornets' nest, when quieter Akulas popped up out of nowhere. But he didn't expect two hornets' nests.

When the Akula's range closed to 25,000 yards, the shaft rub stopped. The Akula had slowed to determine where his counterparts were. The two other Akulas, manned by Chinese who had only recently completed their training in the North Fleet, lost contact on their leader, so they also slowed.

One lesson the Chinese had learned during their training was not to communicate over underwater telephone. Instead, they had come up with a technique to determine range without using the underwater telephone – a technique that no seasoned submariner would ever employ, but these two Chinese captains were far from seasoned.

The first captain sent a single sonar ping. Upon receipt, the second captain returned the ping. They knew that the time difference in sound reaching each Akula would translate to the range of the pinging Akula, plus they would know the bearing to each other.

The Russian captain was furious at the inexperience and ineptness of his Chinese comrades. He broke his silence, using his underwater telephone to tell them to stop, but he was too late. The second Akula had already returned the ping with his fire-control sonar.

Mack was elated. The bearings and time differences, coupled with tracking of the Russian captain, gave *Cheyenne* the fire-control solution they needed.

All three Akulas were still outside 15,000 yards, so Mack passed the order for the torpedo room to 'Make tubes one and two ready in all respects, including opening the outer doors.'

'Tubes one and two are ready in all respects. Both outer doors are open.'

Captain Mackey ordered, 'Firing point procedures, Master 131, tube one, and Master 132, tube two.' He was going for the two quiet ones first. The noisy one, if it ran, would give away his position by the shaft rub.

The combat systems officer at the weapons-control console reported the target courses, speeds, and ranges.

'Sonar, conn, stand by.'

'Conn, sonar, standing by.'

'Match sonar bearings and shoot, tube one, Master 131, and tube two, Master 132.'

'Match sonar bearings and shoot, tube one, Master 131, and tube two, Master 132, aye, sir.'

'Tubes one and two fired electrically,' reported the combat systems officer.

'Conn, sonar, units from tubes one and two running hot, straight, and normal,' came the report from the sonar supervisor as the two torpedoes executed their wire-clearance maneuvers and accelerated to medium speed for the inbound run.

'Very well, sonar,' Mack replied.

'Conn, sonar, the weapons are accelerating.'

This report was confirmed by the combat systems officer, who announced acquisition by both units.

Mack was right. The two quiet Akulas weren't the only ones increasing speed, but while they were turning away to flee the incoming torpedoes, the noisy Akula wasn't running. Instead, it was heading for *Cheyenne*.

No Russian chicken there, Mack thought as he ordered the wires cut, tubes three and four made ready, and tubes one and two reloaded.

The two Mk 48s from *Cheyenne* continued on course for their targets. The third Akula, Master 130, whose captain was foolish enough to speed up, was within Mack's sights, allowing *Cheyenne*'s sonars to detect it easily and to quickly establish the perfect fire-control solution.

'Conn, sonar, explosions bearing 205 and 198.'

Even with two of his Akulas gone, the Russian captain still maintained his posture, bearing down on *Cheyenne*. He had more experience with the US 688 class, and especially with *Cheyenne*, than his lost Chinese fellow captains, but he was no match for Captain Mackey.

When the Akula captain finally heard the two Mk 48s from *Cheyenne*'s tubes three and four, it was too late. They were both in their terminal phase of homing. They would explode before any countermeasures could be launched – which was questionable at this speed, anyway. The Akula's flank speed combined with that of the Mk 48s, a combined closing rate of over eighty knots.

'Conn, sonar, two explosions, both bearing 250. Lost the Akula, Master 130, in the explosions.'

And when the reverberations died out, the ocean was silent. Too silent, because the two Kilos had slowed to three knots when they heard the first explosion to their south.

Mack cleared the area to the north, not knowing he was closing on the Kilos. That was not a mistake; it was the next phase of Mack's search plan for sanitizing the Taiwan area.

As Mack was approaching communications (periscope) depth to report the attack on the three Akulas, radio reported that they had lost the broadcast on the floating wire. The wire was dead and would have to be changed out.

That was a mistake, for the motor reel noise was detected by the slinking Kilos, even before *Cheyenne*'s radiomen had completed reeling the bad one into the ship past the line wiper.

'Conn, sonar, torpedoes in the water, ET-80s, bearing 355 and 008.'

'Snap shots, tubes one and two, bearings 355 and 008 respectively,' ordered the captain. Mack was not sure if the torpedoes were launched by Akulas or by Kilos. But it didn't matter. If the culprits were Kilos, they shot first.

'Conn, sonar, we have the submarines. They're Kilos, Captain, single six-bladed screws speeding up. The torpedoes are heading right for them.' Mack and all of his officers, as well as all of the sonar men, knew the screw-blade configuration of every adversary. The Akulas had seven-bladed screws which helped in differentiating between the two classes. If foolhardy enough, one could also get close enough to detect steam-flow noises, which the diesels didn't have.

'All ahead flank. Do not cavitate. Make your depth one thousand feet,' ordered the captain.

Cheyenne was already beneath the first layer. In less than three minutes Cheyenne was at flank speed, on course 175, and at one thousand feet, beneath the second layer. There was a deep sound channel present, something Mack would have known if he'd been able to acquire SSXBT information. As it was, he learned of its existence from the sound-velocity profiler.

'Unit three has acquired.' Then, a moment later, 'Unit four has acquired.'

'Cut the wires, shut the outer doors, and reload tubes

three and four,' ordered the captain, but they didn't have to cut the wires. *Cheyenne*'s speed and course away from the torpedoes caused both wires to break right after acquisition.

The torpedo's guidance wires had performed beyond all expectations. They would have to inspect *Cheyenne*'s stern area for any signs of the thin wires being entangled in either the screw, sternplanes, or rudder.

When out of danger from the ET-80 torpedoes, Mack slowed *Cheyenne* and turned to the west to listen.

'Conn, sonar, we have two torpedoes in the water, bearings 275 and 209,' the sonar supervisor reported.

Apparently there were more Akulas out there who had picked up *Cheyenne* as she ran fast and deep. Now that she had slowed, she was able to detect the torpedoes.

'Conn, sonar, two explosions, bearings 359 and 002, estimate range 20,000 yards.'

The Kilos, Masters 133 and 134, had experienced their first and last battle with *Cheyenne*.

Mack once again increased speed to flank, launched two evasion devices, and turned away from the incoming torpedoes. As he did so, he couldn't help wondering how many other hornets' nests there were. He also ordered tubes three and four made ready, so that when he turned back to face the new Akulas, *Cheyenne* would be ready. He kept the muzzle doors shut, though, until he slowed. Once they were open, he would point the direction in which he expected the Akulas to be. Mack actually didn't care if they were Akulas or Sierras. They had shot first.

His orders were acknowledged and executed with *Cheyenne*'s usual thoroughness and professionalism. After the torpedo room reported completing the ordered evolution with the torpedo tubes, the executive officer said to Mack, 'Captain, tubes three and four are ready in all respects. Both outer doors are open.'

'Very well, fire control,' answered the captain.

Cheyenne turned to the southwest and immediately

292

gained contact on two Akulas. The contact was on all sonar arrays, and the tonals allowed the certainty of the classification by the sonar supervisor.

The Akulas had been running at flank toward *Cheyenne*'s last known position. This was simply more stupidity from the new Chinese crews, who were obviously enjoying their high speed submarines – and Mack appreciated it. When the BSY-1 operators and the fire-control coordinator were satisfied with the TMA solution on Masters 135 and 136, he ordered, 'Firing point procedures, Master 135, tube three, and Master 136, tube four.'

The combat systems officer reported the course, speed and range of the two targets.

'Sonar, conn, stand by.'

'Conn, sonar, standing by.'

'Match sonar bearings and shoot, tubes three and four.'

'Match sonar bearings and shoot, tubes three and four, aye, sir.'

'Tubes three and four fired electrically,' reported the combat systems officer.

'Conn, sonar, units from tubes three and four running hot, straight, and normal,' came the report from the sonar supervisor as the two torpedoes executed their wire-clearance maneuvers.

The torpedoes were set to run at medium speed until acquisition, at which time they would increase speed and angle up from their deep search depth beneath the layer. At that point the torpedoes would pitch up and complete their acceleration to attack speed.

'Very well, sonar,' Mack said. 'Time to acquisition?'

'Eight minutes, thirty-five seconds, Captain,' answered the combat systems officer.

A few minutes later Mack heard, 'Both units have acquired.'

'Conn, sonar, Masters 135 and 136 are increasing speed, cavitating heavily.'

Sonar reported noisemakers launched by the two

Akulas. Mack countered that by ordering, 'Steer the weapons.' *Cheyenne*'s course was changed to the right by ninety degrees so the bearings to the incoming Akulas and to their stationary noisemakers would diverge. When a bearing spread was obtained, the combat systems officer reported the torpedoes on course for intercept.

'Cut the wires, shut the outer doors, and reload tubes three and four,' ordered the captain. 'Make tubes one and two ready in all respects, including opening the outer doors.'

He knew a melee was about to occur, and he wanted *Cheyenne* ready.

'Conn, sonar, we have four torpedoes in the water, between bearings 270 and 265. Both Akulas have launched again.'

They're also running nearly side by side, Mack thought. It was time for *Cheyenne* to clear datum. It was also time for more countermeasures to be launched.

'Steady as she goes, all ahead flank. Do not cavitate. Make your depth one thousand feet.' Mack followed this with, 'Rig ship for depth charge.'

His plan was to let the countermeasures do their work while *Cheyenne* quietly ran away from the scene.

Cheyenne reached flank speed, on course 085, and at one thousand feet, as the Russian torpedoes entered the baffles after the countermeasures. Sonar didn't hear *Cheyenne*'s last two torpedoes as they entered their terminal homing modes.

'Conn, sonar, two explosions in our baffles.'

But Mack couldn't slow yet, which meant he couldn't turn and determine the fate of the Akulas. There was also too much reverberation to get both direct path and bottom bounce information, so no range would be available anyway.

A short while later, though, he knew he didn't have to turn. Sonar picked up the familiar implosions as external pressure vessels on the Russian SSNs imploded from their descent to the bottom of the northern Philippine Sea, five thousand fathoms below.

Mack was satisfied. Seven more kills for *Cheyenne*, not counting the Hainan. That's what CTF 74 and CINCPACFLT had wanted: more Akula kills. And they got two Kilo kills to boot.

When they had run far enough that the enemy torpedoes should have run to exhaustion, the captain slowed and cleared *Cheyenne*'s baffles to port after proceeding above the layer. Sonar reported no contact, so Mack secured from battle stations while *Cheyenne* took a course toward the shallow waters of the East China Sea. There *Cheyenne* would search the last sector around Taiwan. The TB-23 would remain deployed for the time being, at least until they started their approach to shallow water. Then the TB-16 would be deployed to the short stay.

The atmosphere aboard *Cheyenne* was one of happiness, but the euphoria of victory was coupled with exhaustion. As the stress level in each man slowly subsided, an unbelievable fatigue set in.

That was the norm of submarining, when warriors returning home could sleep most of a day away. Those who did not have to continue at their watch stations crashed in their narrow bunks. There was time to sleep before they passed by the Ryukyu Islands; then it was back to being ready for anything. Even Mack finally crawled on top of his bunk, curling up to fit on the short bunk.

The following day, as *Cheyenne* approached the time for coming shallow, sonar reported numerous merchant ship contacts, easily identified by their huge, slowly turning propellers. All were cavitating as if they were empty of cargo, riding high in the water.

Mack wasn't about to be careless, however. The Japanese supertankers had drafts of over ninety feet. *Cheyenne* would be cautious on going to periscope depth.

Biologics were once again hindering the sonar search.

During one of his frequent visits to the sonar room, Mack reminded the sonar operators to conduct careful tonal searches on the bearings of the merchants and the biologics. The operators had already been doing this. They remembered the submarine they had found in the biologics of the South China Sea.

The TB-16 towed array, having been earlier deployed in exchange for the TB-23, was ordered to short stay as *Cheyenne* ventured inside the one hundred fathom curve southeast of Taipei. Now at periscope depth, Mack sighted an interesting cluster of smoke over the horizon. There were four different sets of smoke patterns moving north. He ordered *Cheyenne* to track behind them at periscope depth in the shallow water.

Hours later, with the sea bottom once again plummeting to over two thousand fathoms, sonar reported diesel lines on the bearings of the smoke being observed. Mack went deep to catch up for a visual, running at full for the next few hours until the water started to shoal again as they approached the one hundred fathom curve of the East China Sea. He knew the contacts could not be Akulas snorkeling, but if they were Kilos Mack wanted to know what was going on.

Cheyenne got back to periscope depth in one hundred feet of water in time to see the four sources of the now-black smoke. Four Kilos were on the surface, on a course toward the Yellow Sea, the playing grounds of China's North Sea Fleet. Being on the surface, and apparently heading away from the battle zone of the last few days, they were no threat to *Cheyenne*, and Mack decided not to go after them.

Cheyenne had done her part – for now, at least. Mack ordered the floating wire replaced. It had been flaked out in the control room, waiting to be installed.

As the Kilos continued to the north, Mack watched them go, thinking about battles past and those yet to come. When they had steamed over the horizon, he had *Cheyenne* turned to the west, back toward her patrol area, and then on to Tsoying Naval Base and some well-deserved rest and recreation.

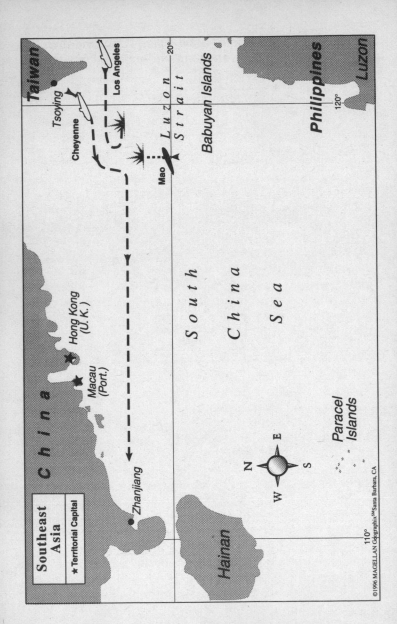

FIFTEEN

Special Delivery

Cheyenne arrived at daybreak, surfacing off Tsoying Naval Base for the slow transit among the seemingly never-ending junks. During his last underway from Tsoying, Mack had remembered the war stories, both from World War II and Vietnam, where the same type of junks were carrying large-caliber machine guns. Mack tried to put that out of his mind. This situation, this entire war, was different, and he didn't believe that any of these Taiwanese junks posed a threat. Still, he was the commanding officer of *Cheyenne*, responsible for the safety of each and every man aboard, and he wouldn't be fully at ease until they were safely away from the western Pacific.

Just in case, however, he also had the M-14s safely hidden away on the bridge while maneuvering on the surface in these waters. This delighted their newest mess specialist, at least. He had been a maximum-security prison guard, a sharpshooter high in a tower adjoining the prison's ramparts, before deciding to join the Navy. When the executive officer had learned this, Mack had granted him the guaranteed, cherished opportunity of being one of the maneuvering watch lookouts on the bridge, even before he was qualified in submarines. Being on the bridge of *Cheyenne* was akin to being back in his tower.

Mack's last briefing had not gone well, but he was looking forward to this one. For one thing, it was a patrol debriefing rather than a pre-mission briefing. Even more, though, he wanted an update on several other situations.

He knew that *Columbia* and *Bremerton* were on station to provide additional ASW protection to the *Independence*

Battle Group. In addition, *Portsmouth* and *Pasadena* had managed to make it safely to an area south of the Formosa Strait, having transited the Indian Ocean and South China Sea without opposition. Mack figured that was because General Yu was throwing everything at *Cheyenne*, east of Taiwan. Unfortunately, both SSNs were blind-sided by an unknown submarine contact before they could surface at the one hundred fathom curve. The hostile submarine tonals that both *Portsmouth* and *Pasadena* detected during the course of the attack did not correlate to any known submarine in the world, and Mack was very anxious to learn more about it.

CTF 74 communications personnel had already re-addressed each submarine's CASREPT (casualty report) to Mack. The unknown assailant had inflicted major damage to each submarine's stern area. Their screws had several blades peened over, and both the TB-23 and TB-16 towed-array housings were damaged.

Mack read these messages with conflicting emotions. On the one hand, he was happy that no *Pasadena* or *Portsmouth* submariners had been hurt. On the other hand, he was saddened by the damage to the two SSNs – and by what that damage meant to him and his own crew. This had been a tough time for *Cheyenne*; only through the grace of God was *Cheyenne* still fully operational.

Upon *Cheyenne*'s arrival in the vicinity of *McKee*, he noted that *Pasadena* and *Portsmouth* had moored to port and star-board, respectively, so they would be close for diver repair services. *McKee*'s cranes were already busy working over both stern areas.

Screw replacement while still waterborne had become an art, since floating drydocks were not always readily available. Plus, neither *Portsmouth* nor *Pasadena* could have made it to Subic Bay. They'd had to be towed into port at Tsoying.

The successful attacks had to have a tremendous emotional impact on the crews of both *Portsmouth* and *Pasadena*, but Mack could see no sign of it. No one appeared demoralized, and they worked as competently and professionally as if nothing had happened. On top of that, both submarines proudly sported their brow covers, telling the world which one was which, ship logos and all. The US submarine force had long supported the policy of not painting hull numbers on the sides of the sail while operating, even in peacetime, so the brow covers provided the public relations gesture.

Cheyenne was directed to moor outboard of *Portsmouth*. These instructions came from the *McKee* CDO over their bridge to bridge radios. When they pulled into position, Mack could see that both *Portsmouth*'s screw and the damaged portion of the TB-16 array housing at the starboard stern plane, the side nearest *Cheyenne*, had already been replaced. These had suffered the least damage of the two sister ships. When final repairs were completed on *Portsmouth*'s TB-23 towed-array housing on the port side, *Cheyenne* would swap places with *Portsmouth* so that the *McKee* cranes could reach her for reloading weapons.

Waiting on *Portsmouth* would delay Mack's next underway for at least an additional two days, but that was all right with Mack. His officers and crew – and Mack himself – needed some time to catch their breath. Besides, he had an indication of what their mission was going to be; if he was right, *Cheyenne* would have to wait a bit anyway while the Chinese political situation caught up to them.

He would have liked to make a speed run up the Taiwan countryside to Taichung. There was a place there, Ruth's Chris Steakhouse, that served the most amazing four-inch-thick steaks. But he couldn't do that – not now, anyway.

A number of *Portsmouth*'s crewmen were exiting the forward escape trunk aft of the sail. Three of them had sound powered phones dangling from their necks. Watching them, Mack could tell that the *Portsmouth* CDO had already passed the word belowdecks, 'All line handlers lay topside. Prepare to take USS *Cheyenne* alongside to starboard.'

Mack waved to the *Portsmouth* CO and CTF 74, who were waiting topside on *Portsmouth* for him, and left the bridge to go on deck himself. Before doing so, he granted the OOD permission to secure the maneuvering watch when he was ready, and to take on shore power and shut down the reactor.

As he had been trained, *Cheyenne*'s OOD took care of *Cheyenne*'s delicate landing alongside *Portsmouth*, gently nudging the camel between the two SSNs. Captain Mackey was completely satisfied with his OODs' abilities to maneuver *Cheyenne* in tight quarters without his having to look over their shoulders; and the maneuvering watch OOD was the best of the best.

When *Cheyenne*'s lines had been doubled, the OOD secured the maneuvering watch, passing the word on the 1MC, then ordered over the 7MC, 'Maneuvering, conn, take on shore power and shut down the reactor.' His last official maneuvering watch duties completed, the OOD laid below to the control room to turn over the officer of the deck duties to the inport duty officer, *Cheyenne*'s CDO for the rest of the day.

Mack had left the ship as soon as the brow was over, and was heading for *McKee* officer country. He expected to meet up with the COs of *Pasadena* and *Portsmouth* and to hear the details of the attacks.

Once aboard, but before reaching officer country, Mack expressed his pleasure to CTF 74 and the *Portsmouth* captain at hearing that all hands were uninjured. That was all he or anyone else said about the attacks until they were within the privacy of the *McKee* captain's stateroom. Mack was a big believer in keeping his crew informed, but that didn't mean he wanted to discuss what could be highly classified information in front of unauthorized personnel.

The chief mess specialist on duty in the *McKee* captain's stateroom departed as soon as Mack and the others arrived. When he had gone, Mack exchanged greetings with the captain of *Pasadena* and again expressed his pleasure at the lack of injury aboard.

Once seated around the table, with cups of fresh coffee at their elbows, the COs of *Pasadena* and *Portsmouth* attempted to explain what had happened, but there simply wasn't much hard information they could provide. The first clue either of them had that they were in trouble was when they found torpedoes in their baffles. In both cases, neither of the torpedoes had gone active until it was too late, and they had detonated at a standoff distance. The skimpy bit of sonar data that had been collected over their towed arrays was only enough to determine that tonals from their attacker could not be correlated to any specifically known submarine.

Mack wasn't surprised at that. The standard tonals that correlated to nearly every Russian, Chinese, and Third World country ships were little help in differentiating submarine classes. Plus there was no screw-blade information.

Mack said, 'Sounds like what saved you was a fire-control placement or detonation planning error. That would fit with *Cheyenne*'s recent experiences: newly built submarines with newly trained Chinese crews sent to attack experienced US submarine crews.'

CTF 74 agreed with Mack's assessment, but he had a further question: If the crews were so inexperienced, how did they detect *Pasadena* and *Portsmouth*? And in an aspect that allowed passive torpedoes to home undetected, for a while at least, on what must have been a reasonably good solution.

'I hate to suggest it, Admiral,' Mack said, 'but maybe someone needs to go back and re-evaluate our position on non-acoustic ASW. Were there any unusual Chinese or Russian aircraft in the area around that time?'

It was a sobering thought for every officer in the room, and the CTF 74 admiral promised to get right on it. He would see what he could learn, and hoped to have an answer before any of his SSNs put to sea.

Mack hoped the admiral could turn something up. He knew that the submarines would not wait for an answer before returning to their patrols. There was a threat out there, and *Cheyenne* and her sister ships would have to deal with it, whether they could put a name to it or not.

While Mack was at his debriefing, discussing *Cheyenne*'s recent patrols and learning what little information was available about this new threat, his officers and crew were overseeing *Cheyenne*'s refit.

The sonar men on *Pasadena* and *Portsmouth* brought their last sonar tapes leading up to and following the torpedo explosions. These tapes were fed to *Cheyenne*'s sonar consoles and her BSY-1 computer consoles, while the sounds were played over both the sonar room and control room speakers. This was not virtual reality. It was *in situ* reality, stark reality of a new foe – a chilling new foe.

Cheyenne's sonar operators and BSY-1 operators put seven different computer consoles, four in sonar and the three in control, to work analyzing the sparse data. They played the tapes over and over again, enhancing them with the computers each time and then starting the cycle again. They were even able to merge the tapes from both SSNs, a feat made possible by the accurate timekeeping systems on US submarines, but they weren't able to learn anything useful.

Then they slowed the tapes, and got their first break. When the tapes were slowed enough to produce sub-harmonics of the main electrical frequency line, the chief sonar man noted a warbling that could not be attributed to slowed tapes, or even merged tapes. The chief sonar man had never heard that particular sound before, but he knew what it was: the sound of a previously unknown submarine. More than that, he knew that it had to be an anomaly of the new submarine's signature, which was masked at higher frequencies, even at the base frequency.

In order to be certain, the chief sonar man, along with *Cheyenne*'s executive officer and the sonar men from

Pasadena and *Portsmouth*, applied this same technique to previous *Cheyenne* recordings of other Chinese and Russian submarines. They found no matches. This anomaly was new, and it was unique. Even better, it was a low, low frequency, something the TB-23 thin line array would thrive on if they let it search that low.

When Mack was informed of the anomaly, he immediately dubbed it, 'a slowly varying constant.' He'd picked up that term in a 'pure math' class, and it seemed more than appropriate for this war with the Chinese.

It was several days before the *McKee* captain notified Mack that the next war patrol briefing would again be at the naval base headquarters. Mack had expected that. He had been alerted earlier that *Cheyenne* had been selected as the obvious choice for this next – and hopefully last – mission: to move President Jiang into Zhanjiang Naval Base.

Prior to the briefing, *Cheyenne* was moved next to *McKee* as planned, except that she didn't actually swap locations with *Portsmouth*. CTF 74 had decided to move *Portsmouth* outboard of *Pasadena* on the other side so that there would be one less move when *Cheyenne* was finally loaded and ready to sail for southern China with President Jiang aboard.

With all *Cheyenne*'s preparations completed prior to this briefing, Mack decided to make it a nearly 'all hands' evolution. All officers definitely needed to be there, and with the promise of information on the new foe lurking out there, somewhere, waiting to take on the famous *Cheyenne*, the entire sonar division also needed to be present. And with President Jiang and his two heavies taking up berthing space, Mack invited the COB to meet the space intruders.

The chief of the boat also needed to figure out how to keep the president and his heavies out of sensitive spaces. Being on good terms with them would be easier than trying to force the cooperation of the heavies, especially since no one aboard *Cheyenne* could match the sheer bulk of Jiang's bodyguards. The COB already had formulated an initial plan: lots of food, desserts, and movies in the 'goat locker.'

Mack had informed the executive officer to take care of the president himself. The executive officer's stateroom had two bunks, and so he would share his space with the Chinese leader. The second bunk had been used by the NSG OIC, but he and his detachment had been off-loaded prior to this last trip, acting as the couriers to Yokosuka with Mack's latest war patrol report under their guard.

It had been difficult for Mack to agree for the detachment to be transferred prior to this patrol. He was concerned about possible non-acoustic ASW aircraft, and had agreed mostly because he knew that if *Cheyenne* remained fully submerged for the entire transit they wouldn't be able to detect ESM contacts anyway. But he did add *Cheyenne*'s ESM operators to the list of briefing attendees, just in case.

The briefing turned out to be one for the books. It started off dramatically when the briefing officer opened the meeting with, 'Captain Mackey, our commander-in-chief sends his greetings.' Then he dimmed the lights and nodded for the video tape recorder to be started.

Mack had half expected the briefing officer to be kidding, or to be referring to someone else, but he wasn't. As Mack and the assembled officers looked on, the face of the President of the United States filled the screen.

'Captain Mackey,' the President said, speaking from the Oval Office, 'the State Department will soon release a report of an impending summit between me, President Jiang Zemin, and Premier Li Peng in Beijing. Premier Li Peng is expected to relinquish his claim to power at that time.' He paused for a moment before going on. 'However,' he said, 'in all fairness to *Cheyenne*, no mention of your involvement in this historic event is authorized, at least not until you have successfully delivered the rightful Chinese president to Zhanjiang Naval Base.' He paused again to allow his words to sink in. 'Captain Mackey, the First Lady and I would like to wish you Godspeed, fair winds, and a following sea. Good luck to you, and to the heroic men of USS *Cheyenne*.'

The briefing officer ordered the monitor turned off and the room lights brightened, but few people noticed. Everyone was talking, with an excitement that was rare even in wartime mission briefings.

The President hadn't really said anything that they didn't know about, but the simple fact of the President talking directly to them added to the importance of *Cheyenne's* mission.

It took several minutes for the room to quiet down. When it did, the briefing officer continued with his presentation. And it didn't take him long to drop another bombshell.

The decommissioning of USS *Los Angeles* (SSN 688) had been canceled, the briefing officer said, and *Los Angeles* was nearly on station south of the Formosa Strait. There had been no traffic addressed to *Cheyenne* concerning *Los Angeles*, but the CTF 74 admiral confirmed her presence. Her mission, pending routing instructions that would prevent mutual interference between *Los Angeles* and *Cheyenne*, was to assist in escorting *Cheyenne* and President Jiang.

That was a serious mistake, Mack thought, but he kept his mouth shut. *Los Angeles* was the first of the 688s. He'd heard that her decommissioning had been postponed due to a lack of funds, but he didn't know that she still had enough crew left to even get under way, much less to fight the Chinese.

On top of that, she had the 'old' fire-control and sonar systems and no TB-23 thin line array, which meant that *Los Angeles* had little chance to detect the new Chinese submarine. Mack was afraid she would be sunk before *Cheyenne* even got under way.

This briefing was turning out even worse than the last one, Mack thought.

The briefing officer informed him that a Chinese North Sea Fleet Alfa class SSN, the *Chung*, would also escort *Cheyenne* and President Jiang. *Chung*'s orders were to stay to the west and eventually to the north of a specially constructed track from the Formosa Strait to Zhanjiang Naval Base, and to proceed at an SOA (speed of advance) of six knots.

Outwardly, Mack didn't react at all, but he couldn't help thinking how quickly that Alfa would disappear at the hands of the hostile submarine. That didn't really matter, of course, he realized, not as long as *Chung* stayed out of *Cheyenne*'s sector as ordered. In fact, it might help to flush out the new foe, whatever it was.

Mack would trade the Alfa for the new enemy submarine with pleasure. But *Los Angeles*, that was a different story. The two 688s could talk to and protect each other, but that would also be difficult at best.

When the room once again quieted, the briefing officer finally got to the subject that Mack and his officers were most interested in: the new threat, and what it might be.

The briefing officer said that, according to the CIA, the unknown submarine was believed to be the culmination of recent Sino-Soviet research and development into a next generation nuclear attack submarine. Deployment of the Mao, as they believed it to be called, had not been expected anytime soon. But now, with the damage inflicted upon *Portsmouth* and *Pasadena* and the evidence of the sonar tapes, it was obvious even to the CIA and naval intelligence that the Mao was out there waiting for *Cheyenne*.

When it looked like the briefing officer had no more to say on the subject, Mack asked the other question he desperately needed answered. 'What about the non-acoustic ASW?'

'Sorry, Captain,' the briefing officer said, obviously prepared for the question. 'CIA still does not believe that an aircraft can use lasers to detect submerged objects and to communicate with their submarines.'

Mack hated that answer. He hated it because the answer wasn't, 'The CIA checked this out and found no evidence.' Instead, the answer was simply, 'The CIA cannot believe this, and so they won't check it out.'

Changing the subject, Mack asked if either the Hainan class mine layer or the mine-laying Romeo which *Cheyenne* sank last patrol could have laid mines near Zhanjiang Naval Base before they proceeded up the coast from Mandarin Bay. The briefing officer answered that Chinese mine-sweepers had scoured the area and found none.

The other COs in the room seemed satisfied with that answer, but Mack wasn't so sure. He would actually have felt better if the minesweeper had found some mines and disposed of them. Either way, though, he knew that there might be mines strewn along the last leg of *Cheyenne*'s route. They would simply have to take appropriate precautions, either with MIDAS or an off-board sensor. If, that is, any Mk 48s remained by the time they entered that last hazard zone, the shallow-water leg en route to the Zhanjiang Naval Base.

The pre-mission briefing came to an end shortly after this, but Mack soon found that there were more unpleasant surprises waiting for him. When he returned to *Cheyenne* he learned from the combat systems officer that *McKee*, on the orders of CTF 74, was still restricting his torpedo loads, even though, to date, *Portsmouth* and *Pasadena* had expended none.

He thought of asking for a few from *Pasadena* and *Portsmouth*, since they wouldn't be putting out to sea anytime soon, but he didn't want to get into interfleet hassles. Once again only twenty Mk 48 ADCAP were on board *Cheyenne*.

Three hours after the briefing was over, President Jiang and his two bodyguards were led belowdecks by the executive officer and the COB. Mack could have allowed them to remain on the bridge, but he didn't. It was too crowded already, and he was still angry over the loadout.

Cheyenne's underway was uneventful, and the M-14s

Mack had on the bridge stayed safely in their racks.

After submerging, Mack ordered the OOD to stream the floating wire. He also ordered the TB-23 towed array deployed far enough to ensure that the 960 feet of hydrophones were clear of their housing. After that, *Cheyenne* headed for the three hundred-fathom curve, which she would follow at the established six-knot SOA until she was due east of the Zhanjiang Naval Base. Then she would have nearly three hundred miles of westerly transit across the widest part of the continental shelf, all in less than one hundred fathoms of water.

The Chinese Alfa, *Chung*, was presumably in board of *Cheyenne*, where it belonged, more than 20,000 yards away according to its sector restrictions. And *Los Angeles* was outboard in the deeper water to the east, where she would remain until the turn to the west. Then *Los Angeles* would watch *Cheyenne*'s 180, as President Jiang had quipped earlier.

Mack's biggest concern was the Mao. The TB-23 was their best bet for detecting it, and if they didn't encounter the unknown submarine before they had to switch to the TB-16 towed array, they could be in trouble.

Cheyenne, *Los Angeles*, and *Chung* heard nothing but fishing fleet and other merchant traffic. All three captains were relying on their contingent to do what and when they were supposed to do.

A day and a half later, as *Cheyenne* was nearing the turning point, sonar reported several conformal-array submarine contacts to the northwest, two at high speed on converging bearings. Mack manned battle stations and launched one of several SSIXS buoys, with pre-arranged reports just in case something like this were to happen. That was the safest way to communicate events to *Los Angeles* – SSIXS to CTF 74 for turnaround to *Los Angeles* for copying on her floating wire.

By the time battle stations were manned, sonar had four sonar contacts to the northwest. Only one was *Chung*, as determined by the Alfa tonals. The other three were Akulas. *Chung* was also communicating by underwater telephone, which was being answered by only one Akula.

Without a Chinese linguist aboard – or a Russian one for that matter – Mack could only guess at what was being said, but he assumed that the *Chung* captain was trying to talk himself out of a bad situation. The Chinese captain's answer came in the form of three torpedoes, one from each of the three Akulas, which were tracking on the bearing of the still-squawking *Chung*.

Mack shook his head. The *Chung* captain had not been inept. He had been ambushed by three of his fellow commanding officers, who were under the command of the still-at-large General Yu Quili, and he had done the best he could against them. His talking with the Akulas on the underwater telephone may have given his position away, but it also gave his Alfa submarine fire control system the ranges and bearings of the Chinese bullies.

He managed to launch two of his ET-80 torpedoes before *Chung* was hit by three 65cm torpedoes.

The *Cheyenne* control room and sonar room were in total silence as they witnessed the carnage. They had seen their share of enemy ships destroyed, but there was something about the spectacle of Chinese submariners killing themselves that made this especially poignant.

Five explosions and four submarines had been involved in the fray, and only one Akula survived it unscathed.

After the explosions, Mack turned to the south to head for the five hundred-fathom curve, where he could fully deploy the TB-23. He hoped that the rapid turnaround promised by the CTF 74 communicators had happened by now. The SSIXS buoy instructions were for moving haven changes to the south for both *Cheyenne* and *Los Angeles*.

Los Angeles had received the instructions and had executed the turn as directed, not knowing that she was heading toward the Mao. The Sino-Russian sub was laying in wait thirty degrees to the left of her track, expecting the attacking Akulas to cause *Cheyenne* to turn away to the south.

The Mao captain did not know that *Los Angeles* was in the area, so when the Mao gained sonar contact he assumed that it was *Cheyenne* and the notorious Captain Mackey. Within minutes, four Mao torpedoes were heading in a depth and azimuth spread at the target.

Los Angeles got off a snap shot. Then she launched countermeasures, turned away toward deep water, and increased speed to flank en route to one thousand feet.

The Mao captain had expected this. He had read the reports from the few surviving commanding officers who had tangled with Mack, and he felt he knew the American's tactics. Even before *Los Angeles* launched countermeasures, the Mao captain was swinging his submarine to starboard. As soon as his ship was in position, he launched four more torpedoes, leading the US SSN perfectly.

He had sprung his trap exactly as he'd hoped, and if the ship he had targeted had, indeed, been *Cheyenne*, Mack's ship would have been destroyed. As it was, the Mao captain's ambush became his own deathtrap.

Cheyenne's sonars had picked up the first set of torpedo launches from the Mao. The noise from the second set finalized the range, bearing and course. Mack launched the two Mk 48s from tubes one and two, and followed them with the two from tubes three and four.

The Mao captain was too busy listening in the direction of his own torpedoes and the frantically racing *Los Angeles* to notice that four Mk 48 ADCAPs were inbound toward his position.

Cheyenne's first two torpedoes acquired the Mao just as the first two Chinese torpedoes struck *Los Angeles*. The Mao never heard Mack's weapons, as the remaining two Mk 48s acquired the hostile submarine at the same time *Los Angeles* was finally destroyed by the last four Mao torpedoes.

The sound of the explosions – two, followed by four,

followed by two, and then by two more – was incredible, and more than the *Cheyenne* sonar men could withstand. They all took off their headsets, turned down the speaker volume, and watched their sonar consoles illuminate.

Mack kept all hands at battle stations and proceeded to take *Cheyenne* to test depth as a salute to their lost shipmates aboard *Los Angeles*. Submariners at sea around the world had done this same thing as soon as they had been informed that *Thresher* and *Scorpion* were lost at sea with all hands aboard.

Mack didn't have to say anything to the crew. They knew. The sound of the explosions through the hull told them at least one submarine had died out there. The down angle as *Cheyenne* headed for test depth told them who it had been.

Only President Jiang and his two bodyguards didn't understand, and Mack was in no mood to tell them.

The ocean was now quiet, except for the occasional 'hull popping' as *Cheyenne* slowly descended, heading south toward the safety of deep water. Only when she had leveled out at test depth did Captain Mackey pick up the 1MC. He'd always thought holding memorial services for a lost crewman was the hardest job he'd ever face, but conducting memorial services for an entire ship was much harder.

Then *Cheyenne* pitched slowly to a gentle up angle and her hull started popping again as Mack came shallower, turning back to the north to look for the last Akula. He wouldn't find it, though. The explosions of the other two Akulas had caused enough overpressure damage that the last Akula captain had been forced to emergency-surface and limp from the area.

As *Cheyenne* approached the time for coming shallow near the shelf, sonar reported numerous merchant ship contacts, but still no submarine contacts. As usual, biologics hindered the search, and they could not gain any contact on an Akula as *Cheyenne* entered shallow water, heading west to deliver her precious cargo. Battle stations were secured and both towed arrays were housed at the one hundred-fathom curve.

Mack had the feeling that *Cheyenne* had faced her last opponent and that they were out of trouble, but he didn't let his guard down. It was only a feeling, and he knew he still needed to be on the look-out for mines.

Finally back at periscope depth, Mack sent his message traffic concerning the battles and the loss of *Los Angeles*. The ESM operator reported communications from a Chinese HF radio to the north. Acting on a previous thought that he had kept to himself, Mack asked if the Chinese president would mind translating something for them. When the tape of the comms was delivered to the wardroom and played for President Jiang, a smile spread quickly over his face.

'Captain Mack, that is the commanding officer of the last of Yu's Akulas. He reported he was damaged and he is heading for Zhanjiang Naval Base on the surface to ask for amnesty from the Jiang Zemin government for himself and his men.'

Since the weather was calm, Mack decided to surface *Cheyenne* and follow the Akula into Zhanjiang Naval Base. This time he allowed President Jiang on the bridge, giving him a hand-held HF radio so that he could act as interpreter for Mack in discussions with the Chinese captain of the Akula. Mack advised the Akula CO that *Cheyenne* would follow him into port from the Akula's stern, but that he had one Mk 48, one Harpoon, and one Tomahawk antiship missile trained directly at him.

Cheyenne steamed safely into the naval base and delivered her cargo, and then made a slow transit back to Tsoying. En route, the news came that China had formally declared a cease-fire.

The war was over. The United States, with the help of *Cheyenne*, had won.

Mack heard the news with a mixture of joy and sadness – joy that his crew was safe once more, with nothing more than the hazards of the deep to worry about, and sadness at the cost. For however long he remained at sea, the memory of those lost would stay with him.

United States Naval Officer Receives Chinese 'Order of Chairman Mao Tse-Tung'

November 9, 1997
Web Posted at 11:00 P.M. EST (1600 GMT)

From Beijing bureau chief Julie Meyer
BEIJING (TCN) – In an unprecedented ceremony at China's South Sea Fleet Headquarters, Zhanjiang Naval Base, Chinese president Jiang Zemin bestowed the coveted 'Order of Chairman Mao Tse-Tung' to the commanding officer of the USS *Cheyenne* (SSN 773) for his valorous efforts in single-handedly devastating the renegade Premier Li Peng's and General Yu Quili's submarines, purchased with funds diverted from the Chinese people. Not to be outdone, the President of the United States recalled the commanding officer to the White House.

President Bestows Medal of Honor on War Hero Submariner

November 10, 1997
Web Posted at 2:00 P.M. EST (1900 GMT)

From Washington chief correspondent Michael Flasetti
WASHINGTON (TCN) – The President today placed the coveted Medal of Honor ribbon with its large medal around the neck of Captain Bartholomew Mackey, commanding officer of USS *Cheyenne* (SSN 773). Captain Mackey's submarine was the single force in Southeast Asia which literally destroyed the Chinese submarine force, accounting for over sixty authenticated kills without sustaining any damage to his own ship. In an unprecedented meeting of

Congress prior to the event, Captain Mackey was selected for promotion to rear admiral, lower half, being read into law by the Senate majority leader. This in itself was an unprecedented move on Congress's part, since the rear admiral selection board, with its congressional confirmation, was months away. And the last officer promotion that Congress had taken out of the hands of the Navy was when they promoted Admiral Hyman G. Rickover, the father of United States Navy Nuclear Propulsion.

And where is Rear Admiral 'Mack' Mackey? A source close to his family, which asked the CIA not to be identified, said that instead of throwing quarters in the lawn to keep the kids out of the house while Mack and his wife renewed their vows, Rear Admiral Mackey and his wife left for the cold and snow of upstate New York, intending on taking part in the Lake Champlain Submarine Team Races, 'Frostbite 97,' followed by two weeks of skiing at their chalet. CIA said the source is deemed reliable, since his family is taking care of the Mackey children. And there you have it, so much for CIA secrecy.

*Interview with Tom Clancy
and Captain Doug Littlejohns*

INTRODUCTION

Captain Doug Littlejohns, CBE, RN (Ret.), is one of the finest naval officers I have ever met, and I am proud to call him my friend. His distinguished career includes three command tours, HMS *Osiris*, HMS *Sceptre*, and HMS *London*, respectively a diesel-powered submarine, a nuclear fast-attack submarine, and a missile-armed frigate. In addition, Doug was operations officer for NATO submarines in the Eastern Atlantic, Assistant Director of Naval Warfare for UK missile submarines, Principal Staff Officer to the Chief of the Defence Staff, Marshal of the Royal Air Force Lord David Craig, during the Persian Gulf War, and commanding officer of the Royal Navy's engineering college, HMS *Thunderer*. He has seen and done it all. If you want to know why the Navy's been around for so long, people like Doug are the reason.

James Adams, who conducted the interview, is also a good friend, and as Washington Bureau Chief of the London *Sunday Times* is one of the finest writers I know. He writes extensively on US domestic and foreign policy and on such issues as nuclear proliferation and international terrorism.

James Adams: Tom, Doug, thank you very much for joining me today. Tom, a hallmark of your work is its reality – it's close to the truth, always on the cutting edge of the political scene. You two have chosen China for *SSN* as the principal antagonist. Do you see China as a threat to the stability of the world today?

Tom Clancy: Well, China is a country that doesn't really know what it wants to be. On the one hand they're trying to develop a free market economy and give their citizens economic freedom. On the other hand we had Tiananmen Square, where they decided that their citizens could have economic freedom, but not political freedom. This is a considerable imbalance. Moreover, in this particular case, we also have the Spratly Islands. There appear to be considerable deposits of oil there. And you'll recall that fourteen years ago that was the reason that Argentina went after the Falkland Islands – the thought that there might be oil there that they could exploit. Even though Argentina is currently self-sufficient in oil.

A war of aggression is really nothing much more than a large-scale armed robbery. Is this scenario plausible? I think it's quite plausible. Because nations are greedy. Particularly Marxist nations.

James Adams: Doug, you served out in the Far East as a submariner. Do you agree with that? Was the potential threat posed by China part of the war game that went on when you were out there?

Captain Doug Littlejohns: I was out there in the mid '60s. That was at the time of the Indonesia confrontation, and we didn't really think much about China in those days.

James Adams: Would you buy the general scenario as seeing China becoming a bigger player on the scene?

Captain Doug Littlejohns: Oh, very much so. And I think this is an extremely good plot.

James Adams: Tom, you talked briefly about the Spratlys. Tell me a bit more about them. We've read a lot about them, and we know that many nations claim them, and

I think that China has landed ships on them. And so have other countries. What exactly is the status of those islands?

Tom Clancy: The Spratly Islands are kind of like a dead grandfather with a heck of a big estate. And everybody wants to claim to be the number-one heir. In fact, I think that China's territorial claim to the Spratlys is fictitious.

James Adams: Tenuous at best.

Tom Clancy: Especially given their location. But they're such inhospitable pieces of real estate that whoever can get there, plant a flag, and defend it is going to own them.

James Adams: And you think that this scenario, where China is an aggressor because of political instability internally, might be a realistic driver in the near future?

Tom Clancy: Well, historically, a nation with internal problems will externalize. And nothing draws a country together like an external threat. Or a *perceived* external threat. It's the classical method historically to unite a country.

James Adams: Doug, you have tremendous experience in submarines. This is a story about submarines. We're in a post-Cold War world now. We devoted a great deal of energy to dealing with the potential threat from the Soviet submarine fleet. But now we're in a different environment. What do you think is the strategic and tactical role of submarines in the post-Cold War world?

Captain Doug Littlejohns: It ranges right across the spectrum, starting obviously with the major strategic use of a submarine – which is to launch intercontinental ballistic missiles. But in this situation, the submarine can be used strategically by taking up a position off an enemy area. Its existence is then made known to the enemy. We had a very good example of that in the '70s when Argentina was making noises about the Falklands. We dispatched an SSN down there, and we told them it was there. And that put off the business for a few years.

James Adams: But in that particular situation, Argentina had no counter force to combat that. They weren't capable really of dealing with the submarines that we had. That's not the case with China, where they have a pretty extensive anti-submarine warfare capability.

Captain Doug Littlejohns: Well, they have an anti-submarine warfare capability. I don't think you can put it in the same league as the anti-submarine capability of NATO nations or, indeed, of the former Soviet Union. So for the game – and for reality – the technical superiority of the US submarine force far outweighs the capability that China, on its own today, could put against them.

James Adams: In other words, the submarines that the Americans can field are quieter and faster than the capability of the Chinese to find with their sonars and other technologies.

Captain Doug Littlejohns: Yes. At this stage. But the world always moves on.

I think that for the scenario that we're looking at here – which isn't cast in today's technological climate – the American submarines would have a pretty good time against their ASW forces.

James Adams: Tom, do you think that the Chinese Navy would have any realistic chance against the United States? They have a lot of numbers but not much capability, and there's a huge technological gap between the two.

Tom Clancy: One of the things you have to remember about combat is that it's not really a technical exercise. It's a human exercise, and a psychological exercise. It's not machine against machine, it's person against person. And we all too often overlook that. The difference between a good navy and a bad navy is the quality in the training of its personnel. You know, better to have good men in bad ships than bad men in good ships. If the Chinese decide to make it a national goal to upgrade their Navy – and, of course, they don't really have a Navy; it's the Naval Branch of the People's Liberation Army – but if they decided to really invest some time and money in it to develop the capabilities they need, they could indeed be quite formidable.

China does have a maritime history that we all too often forget.

James Adams: But they've been trying to upgrade land, sea, and air for some years now. They've invested a lot of money, and a lot of people. But they've not been able to bridge that technological gap between the United States and the NATO forces and what they currently have. They have a lot of things, but can they take that training and that technology and bring them together to make it effective, do you think?

Tom Clancy: The fundamental power base of any country is its economy. China has a very rapidly growing economy. They're making computers. They're making all manner of products, which can be sold worldwide. If they can do that, they can make damn near anything.

James Adams: So do you think that today we treat China with kid gloves that are perhaps inappropriate? Do you see them as a threat, as some people would argue, for the stability of the world?

Tom Clancy: I don't know that I would go quite that far. Probably the country at greatest risk from Chinese aggression would be Russia, the former Soviet Union.

Do we treat China in a way which causes me difficulty? Yes. When Deng Xiaoping stomped on the demonstrators in Tiananmen Square, we should have done something, for two reasons: First of all, America should not do business with countries that do such things to its own citizens. Moreover, and this is something frequently overlooked, that act was deliberately taken in the knowledge that Bernie Shaw and CNN were filming it – or sending it out live at the time – on global television. They were, indeed, therefore telling the world, 'Drop dead. This is the way we do business and if you don't like it, that's too bad.' I question the ethics of doing business as usual with a country that is so grossly repressive as the People's Republic of China.

James Adams: Doug, in *SSN* we have a very realistic portrayal of what it's like to be in command of a submarine. Something that you have done. Can you tell me a bit about what sort of training goes in to make a commander? What is looked for, psychologically and in practical terms, in somebody who can deliver?

Captain Doug Littlejohns: First of all, the game is designed to put the player outside the submarine, if you like, to envisage the tactical situation around him in his mind's eye. And to have a pictorial representation of that. That is where the game is unique. Nothing like this has been done before. As for what makes a good submarine commander, that is really almost impossible to quantify properly.

James Adams: You go on a course in England called the Perisher Course, don't you?

Captain Doug Littlejohns: Oh, yes.

James Adams: What do they make you do in that course?

Captain Doug Littlejohns: First of all, there's a big weeding out process before you ever get to that point. Lots of people want to be submariners, but when they get there they find they don't like the way of life or the hours they have to keep.

James Adams: What about claustrophobia?

Captain Doug Littlejohns: I've only ever seen one member of a submarine who suffered from claustrophobia. In the main, you just don't experience it. Human beings are very adaptable. By the time what we call in the Royal Navy the submarine Perisher comes along, most people are well imbued into submarines. Then it's a question of whether they've got both the stamina and the mental acuity – the particular ability to remember a tactical picture after having glanced at it only very briefly. With the submarine tossing around, maneuvering all over the place, it's very difficult to still be able to know where the various components of that tactical picture are.

That is a particular type of spatial awareness although we didn't have that term when I did the course.

James Adams: That is very similar to the effect in *SSN*, where you're having to simulate essentially what the spatial picture looks like.

Captain Doug Littlejohns: Yes. And the player has got to be able to assimilate the information – which is not coming in as thick and fast as it does on a real submarine, but it's reasonably realistic. If he doesn't assimilate the information, if he can't put things in the right priority order and tackle them in a sensible way, then he will get caught.

James Adams: Tom, Doug is a good friend of yours and has been for a number of years. You also know a number of American equivalents to Doug. What would you say is the difference between a British and an American submarine commander?

Tom Clancy: I've gotten into a lot of trouble on this.

Captain Doug Littlejohns: And you could get in trouble here, now.

Tom Clancy: I've been sufficiently propagandized by Doug and a few of his partners in crime in the Royal Navy that I once published an article suggesting that the Royal Navy trained its submarine skippers better than the US Navy did. Which earned me the undying wrath of a certain senior officer in the United States Navy.

You can argue long and hard about the difference between having a specialist and a generalist. Generally speaking, I think the Royal Navy has a way of developing its officers and identifying its stars. It beats the hell out of them to winnow them out, and then it picks the absolute best of that group to command. It is able to award command at a much younger age than we do in the US Navy.

I think that's a fundamentally healthy thing.

James Adams: So would you say that implies that the British commanders tend to be younger, more aggressive, and have more initiative? Or is it that it merely comes out in a different way?

Tom Clancy: It's well within the range of personal variances – we have good ones, they have good ones, we have bad ones, they have bad ones. Generally speaking, I would say that their method for advancing their prospective commanding officers is somewhat better than ours.

James Adams: Do you agree with that, Doug?

Captain Doug Littlejohns: Yes, I do. I'm not so sure about the 'we have bad ones,' but I'll let Tom get away with that.

To go back to something that Tom said earlier, a lot of the technical capability of the US submarines is of higher quality than ours, but somehow or other we manage to achieve the same sort of results. And the two navies work very closely together. Particularly on the submarine front.

James Adams: And what about the Chinese? What do we know about how they train and perform in their navies? Do we have any sense of that really?

Tom Clancy: Well, it's a Communist country, and the Communists do not reward personal initiative . . . except by execution.

Now, in Communist China, you have the odd situation where they're trying to develop a free market economy without political freedom. And that is ultimately going to fail. Because that doesn't work. But until such time as that happens, we do face a potential adversary, given the fact that they do have the industrial capability to produce just about anything they want, of high enough quality. If they can sell television sets throughout the world, then they can build a nuclear submarine. It's just a matter of quality control. And if they want the oil in the Spratly Islands all that badly, which they probably do, then it's simply a matter of establishing as a national priority to make a Navy which is competitive with the rest of the world. If they decide to do that, they can.

Historically, Kaiser Wilhelm II decided to make a Navy which was quite competitive with the Royal Navy. And they did it in, what? One generation?

Captain Doug Littlejohns: And, of course, the former Soviet Union had to go through the same transformation in the '60s, after the Cuban Missile Crisis. They certainly needed to build up a deep water Navy. And they did that. It took them probably ten, fifteen years – not just to get the equipment, but to be able to use it to a reasonable standard.

James Adams: Yes. And they developed a very effective submarine fleet.

One of the points of this game is that we have Russia passing on some equipment to the Chinese. Do you think that's realistic? Will the Russians sell their soul, so to speak? I mean, their submarine fleet is really the only thing that's left of their Navy that's effective.

Captain Doug Littlejohns: Well, they've sold submarines to other parts of the world.

James Adams: Most of them, though, have been pretty low-grade, old-fashioned things, right? To Iran?

Captain Doug Littlejohns: They've also sold nuclear submarines to India. And whether they're potential adversaries or not, there are clearly still links there. But Tom would know more about that than me.

Tom Clancy: It's a political and economic question. The Russians are so strapped now for hard currency that if you make them the right kind of offer, they'll probably deliver.

James Adams: And the Chinese have enough hard currency by comparison?

Tom Clancy: We've got a trade imbalance in China that would buy half the Soviet Navy.

James Adams: In the same way, the game supposes that a takeover of the Spratly Islands is the beginning of a move on Taiwan. We saw the exercises off Taiwan recently, which looked very intimidating. Do you think that remains a Mainland China ambition?

Tom Clancy: It could be. The Falkland Islands War of 1982 is an interesting historical model. Why did that happen? It happened because the military junta that ruled Argentina at the time was making such a botch of running their nation that they had to find something to distract their people from the screwups they had at home. And they did that by grabbing the Falklands and causing a particularly pointless little war.

In the case of the People's Republic of China, one way to distract their people from their political difficulties at home is to externalize. One target is Hong Kong. They're going to absorb Hong Kong very shortly. And if they can absorb Taiwan, they'll have an enormously powerful economy.

Also, they would put 'paid' on a long-standing bill with Chiang Kai-shek and the Pao Min Tong. And the Chinese are people with long memories.

James Adams: But this would not be without cost. It would be difficult to imagine the United States sitting by and saying, 'Okay, guys, take it over.'

Tom Clancy: This is unknown. It is a fact of US law that America has a particularly schizophrenic policy toward China. On the one hand we acknowledge that there is only one China. And yet, on the other hand, we say this is not true. But if the People's Republic of China attacks Taiwan, we're not going to like it very much.

Now those two statements of policy are incompatible, but that is standing US law.

Captain Doug Littlejohns: I think the world should watch very carefully what the Chinese military does now. When they did their exercises off Taiwan, they had to sort of back down. It will be interesting to see how they respond to that, and whether they feel that they've got to pour more money or focus more money in certain areas to ensure that that never happens again.

Tom Clancy: A further complication: What's the nearest US Navy base? We don't have Subic Bay in the Philippines anymore. We have to stage out of the nearest one we have – which I guess is Japan. And that's a goodly distance.

James Adams: Yes, it is. And would Japan really want that either, if China was rattling sabers?

Tom Clancy: Good question.

Captain Doug Littlejohns: They're not terribly keen on nuclears.

Tom Clancy: No, they're not. The next nearest fleet base is Pearl Harbor, and that's 3,000 miles.

James Adams: Give me a sense of what it's like inside a submarine in a crisis. You're under attack. You don't quite know where the enemy is. You've got to find them, retaliate, and at the same time take evasive action. What's the flavor of that like? What's the smell, the taste of the drama?

Captain Doug Littlejohns: Well, the first thing I'd like to get across to people – and I think the player needs to get that as well – is professionalism. People remain reasonably cool and calm. They have to, to do their job, because everybody is depending on everybody else.

James Adams: It didn't look like that in *Crimson Tide*, of course.

Captain Doug Littlejohns: Well . . . I thought *Crimson Tide* was a great movie until about halfway through it.

James Adams: Until their mutiny started.

Captain Doug Littlejohns: I hope that wasn't made by Paramount.

Having said that, you train for it all the time. And therefore it's almost – well, second nature is probably putting it too far, but if you compare a submarine to a smooth-running engine, then a little perturbation like an attack and so on just notches it up to a different gear. And people respond to that. I've never experienced hysteria or people jumping up and down. They just get on and do the job.

James Adams: What was your worst experience as a submariner?

Captain Doug Littlejohns: I think the worst experience was when I had water coming in when it shouldn't have been coming in when I was pretty close to my maximum diving depth. But that was handled very nicely.

James Adams: What did you do?

Captain Doug Littlejohns: Well, we were in a place where we could surface in a hurry. And actually I was very impressed by the way people responded. They did all the right things in the right order at the right time.

James Adams: Has that always been your experience? There haven't been occasions where people have said or done things that take it outside of the normal performance loop?

Captain Doug Littlejohns: If the submarine is taken outside of the normal performance loop then the Captain will do that – and do it very advisedly, because he knows the risks he's running. But there are tactical scenarios when you will need to do just that. If you're a professional, and you know the capabilities and the limitations, not only of your kit and your crew but of yourself – which is the most important one – then you can do it and get away with it.

James Adams: In one part of the game the commander of the submarine *Cheyenne* is instructed to fire only if fired upon. That seems to me to be a very vulnerable position to be put in, because you're placed not in a proactive position, but in a reactive one. Which is not a happy state to be in.

Tom Clancy: Well, you won't have a Navy commander initiating war between two super powers. That's seventeenth- and eighteenth-century stuff.

James Adams: But do you also want to allow yourself to be in a position where you can get taken out?

Tom Clancy: That's a political decision. In America, the military is controlled by civilians.

Captain Doug Littlejohns: So it is elsewhere. I never served in an SSBN – a boomer – but to answer James's question, when you go to sea in an SSN, you go on semi-war footing. You've got torpedoes loaded, particularly if you're doing some interesting operations. And then you are in the situation you've just described. You could find somebody firing at you at any moment, but you can't go out and initiate things. Because military don't make war, they conduct a war which is made by the politicians.

James Adams: That's a fine distinction. Tom, what about your experiences on submarines?

Tom Clancy: Well, for one thing, they were all tied alongside while I was on board. With one exception.

James Adams: What was the exception?

Tom Clancy: I stepped off a tugboat onto the portside fairwater plane of USS *Hammerhead*, walked across, and climbed up into the sail, so *Newsweek* could take some photographs of me being a fool.

Captain Doug Littlejohns: And you weren't seasick?

Tom Clancy: Not in the least. I was too scared to be seasick. There was only a little bit of water between the pressure hull of the submarine and the tugboat. I figured I was on a real thinning program if I fell off.

James Adams: Getting back to the game, in one of the missions we meet the Akula class submarine for the first time. By then, we've already met the Han class. Describe for me, Tom, the distinctions between the two and their capabilities.

Tom Clancy: It's the difference between a Model T Ford and a current day Ferrari. The Akula is a very formidable platform. Toward the end of the life of the Soviet Union, they actually started to understand what navies were all about.

James Adams: With the help of –?

Tom Clancy: Phillip John Walker. Yes, he was very helpful to them in some ways. Fortunately, one of the other things they found is that it's awfully expensive to do it right.

The Akula is the rough equivalent of an early 688 class, which means that it may be, what? Fifteen years behind current technology. But that's only a few percentage points of performance.

Captain Doug Littlejohns: It's a major step/change/improvement in capability. In my early days in submarines, if one went out to sea in the Atlantic and hung around for a bit, one was bound to find a Russian submarine. And you knew that he wasn't going to be able to find you.

Now the situation is much more mind focusing. Now you can't go out there and just crash around and expect to always have a tremendous sonar advantage over him.

James Adams: But it seems to have been the case, Tom, that since the end of the Cold War the Russians have been organizing a pretty severe change in the way they make up the submarine fleets, getting rid of the old ones, keeping up the new ones, refining the crews so that they're better trained, better organized, and investing in new submarines. Do you think that's right? How does that capability stack up these days?

Tom Clancy: I've yet to figure out exactly what the Russians were thinking about in terms of defense policy. Historically, they're a continental power, not a maritime power, and the biggest national security threat they face is probably China. Now there are people in Moscow who still worry about the Germans, but I guess that's because they've been reading the recent history. They do not face a maritime threat per se, which makes me wonder why the hell they continue to build some ships. Retiring the old ships was just to save money and they had no real tactical utility. Yes, they do seem to be continuing construction on the Akula, the advanced Akula class. But I really don't know why.

Captain Doug Littlejohns: I still think that they're looking to the West. You say they don't have an immediate maritime threat, but the US has got the biggest Navy in the world, and that in being is a threat. Go back to Jutland, a fleet in being is a threat.

James Adams: Why do you think they've been putting the Akulas off the East and West coasts of the United States in the last year or so, successfully I believe – some of them, we think, undetected? That shows first of all an aggressiveness we haven't seen before; second, an ability that we haven't seen before; and third, a worrying potential gap between American capability vis-à-vis Russian capability.

Captain Doug Littlejohns: Well, you've made three points there. The aggression we have seen before. They've always wanted to go into the Atlantic and roam at will and show their capability in so doing, but they couldn't do it. Now they can, to an extent. It's always impossible to say what sort of detection capability the NATO forces or the US special equipment has got because you don't know quite what you're missing in what you have detected.

There is no doubt that they have been doing what you say and getting away with it. And that does a number of things, doesn't it? It gives them a considerable amount of confidence, it worries the Western powers, and it goes back to their political leadership who say, 'Well, we can do something if we want to.' So I think they will continue to do that. Whereas, whether they've got a proper maritime policy since Gorshkov died is another question, and I would agree with Tom that it could do with a re-evaluation.

James Adams: Do you think that's right, Tom? Do you think that that analysis is why this apparent new aggression against the United States is with their submarines?

Tom Clancy: Well, aggression is the wrong word. The sea is free for passage for all and we fought a war over this once. They've got some toys; they probably want to play with them. And, in realistic terms, I don't really think it goes far beyond that. They've got the platforms, they want to see if they work. To me, and from conversations that I've had with people who've talked with the Russian – what they used to call Stavka; I don't know what they call it now, Russian Military High Command – the two big enemies they see in their future are Germany and the People's Republic of China. As for Germany, I think they're just out of their minds, but the Russians have a long history of paranoia. In the case of China, we need to remember that the Chinese have been as far West as Novograd, which is almost in the Baltic. So there is a historical concern there that they have, particularly since China has a growing economy and needs natural resources, and the Soviets in Eastern Siberia have the

336

world's largest unexplored mineralogical treasure house.

James Adams: Later in the game, we meet a new class of submarine called the Mao, which is based on another Russian development, the Severodvinsk class. Can you tell me a bit about that?

Tom Clancy: It's a new boat. As I said earlier, we can anticipate that the Chinese have highly sophisticated industrial capability now. And if they choose to build something that good, they can probably do it. Back in World War I, the Germans built a fleet from scratch, and by 1916 they had ships every bit as good as what the Royal Navy was fielding with hundreds of years of tradition. It's simply a matter of political will and industrial expertise. They have the industrial expertise, and if they develop the political will it's going to happen.

James Adams: In part of the game, we in the *Cheyenne* experience being attacked with sonar buoys extensively. Doug, you must have gone through that yourself. Will you describe for me how that works and what it feels like?

Captain Doug Littlejohns: You don't really get attacked by a sonar buoy.

James Adams: Threatened, then.

Captain Doug Littlejohns: Sonar buoys tend to be dropped from either maritime aircraft or helicopters and they have a limited detection capability. But years and years of research has gone into developing the pattern in which they lay them in the water. And they do have a certain capability to detect. Occasionally in the submarine you can hear a sort of plopping noise as something's

337

dropped into the water, but in the main, you do not know whether there are sonar buoys there or not.

James Adams: So it's passive because it just sits there?

Captain Doug Littlejohns: They are predominantly used passively, but there are active capabilities in these sonar buoys. Now if somebody is active on the sonar buoy close to you, then that probably means either they've seen you because you've been up at periscope depth and they've seen your periscope, or they've got a passive detection on you and they're trying to localize you for a weapon attack. So one wouldn't hang around very long.

Tom Clancy: Or he's trying to spook you.

Captain Doug Littlejohns: Or he's trying to spook you, yes, but then you're getting into the 'Do I/don't I, do I believe it or don't I believe it.'

James Adams: What happens when you hear the ping of an active buoy and you know a weapon's about to go into the water? Or when you feel that's going to happen? What do you do? Do you take immediate evasive action? What shape does that take?

Captain Doug Littlejohns: There is no clear answer to that. If there were a clear answer to what to do in that situation, then people wouldn't try and fire torpedoes because they would never work. You just have to – as you do in the game – sit back and take a global view of the tactical scenario you're in. Sometimes, you would drop countermeasures, speed up, change depth, and basically disappear as quickly as possible. Other times you might lie doggo. Or you might fire a torpedo down a bearing if you think that it's not a sonar buoy but another submarine that's spooking you because you will certainly spook him if you do that. So there is no clear-cut answer. And the captain of the submarine has to have all these thoughts in his mind all the time.

James Adams: What's the environment in the South China Sea like? How does that impact on the sort of decision making you'd have to take in a submarine like the *Cheyenne*? What are the particular aspects of the South China Sea?

Captain Doug Littlejohns: Well, it's certainly shallow in parts, and it would be pretty noisy with a lot of background noise. It's a busy shipping area.

James Adams: Which helps you in?

Tom Clancy: In a lot of ways.

Captain Doug Littlejohns: It helps and it hinders. It helps if you're trying to sneak in and do something. But if you're desperately searching for an elusive target like an Akula, it's not necessarily such a great help.

But there's nothing unique about operations in the South China Sea, really.

Tom Clancy: Keep in mind that this is an odd case of modesty on Doug's part. He knows more about oceanography than some PhD oceanographers. He has to, because a submariner uses the environment as a weapon and with considerable skill. And he's spent fifteen years learning that.

Captain Doug Littlejohns: Well, twenty years.

James Adams: Which leads neatly into the distinctions between reality and fiction. You, Tom, as you said earlier on, have tried to blur the two.

Tom Clancy: The difference between reality and fiction has to make sense. You want to keep that in mind.

James Adams: But how did you find dealing with this game as opposed to writing novels?

Tom Clancy: The point of a game is that you set up a set of circumstances which the user, the game player, defines himself. So, essentially, we're building an intellectual playground and letting somebody else play in it and determine what happens there. Which is sort of the magic of this if you do it right.

James Adams: But aren't a lot of books like a war game? I would think you work it through in a similar kind of a way, although not with a similar result obviously because they're different media. Is that right? I mean, you've got a lot of experience with war gaming, I think.

Tom Clancy: It's kind of like owning a casino and loading the dice. I pretty much determine the way I want the story to turn out. A game in some ways is more intellectually honest because in my books I determine what all the players do. In a game either the artificial intelligence on the CD-ROM or another player determines what the other guy does and in that sense it's much more realistic.

James Adams: How did you deal with that? This is a new medium for you, and you were bringing a lot of the great wealth of your experience to the game to try and create as much reality as possible. Where did reality meet the reality of fiction?

Captain Doug Littlejohns: First, nobody should be under any misconception that this is a sort of submarine attack simulator. It certainly is not that. What it is trying to do is to make a player realize a good percentage of the sort of information and actions one would take when driving an SSN. Take a scenario: if you're homing in on a contact which has been detected by other means, it could take you three days of stealthily going around the ocean. Then you get a sniff of a contact, it goes a bit further, you get another sniff, then get into a firing position. This can. take days, weeks. Clearly, that's not something we could do in the computer game because the player would be asleep. And so the compromise between total reality and the reality of the game player is something that we've debated at length with experts on the marketing side and with those amongst us who enjoy the game for the game's sake. We've reached a compromise which we believe is going to meet expectations.

James Adams: The timing issue, the time compression, was that the most significant compromise? Or were there other areas where you felt, 'Well, okay, in the balance of things, reality has to go here and we'll create this because it'll create the same sort of atmosphere if not the exact thing?'

Captain Doug Littlejohns: Well, timing was by far the biggest, but there are a host of other compromises that have been made as well. They're not particularly big, but if somebody who's done the same sort of job as me plays the game, he should play it in the knowledge that this is a game to entertain rather than to teach.

James Adams: But more accurate entertainment perhaps than *Crimson Tide*.

Captain Doug Littlejohns: Oh, yes, much more so. But it would not enable the game player at the end of fifteen successful missions to go and take command of a Los Angeles class submarine.

James Adams: Well, if it were that easy, I'm sure that many others would have been summoned to the flag.

Tom Clancy: Well, maybe a Los Angeles, but not a Trafalgar, right?

Captain Doug Littlejohns: Well, we're going to get national about this . . .
   If the player gets it wrong, he will be killed, or he will be attacked, anyway. There's a learning process throughout. It starts with a very simple scenario, building up to a crescendo. But by the end of the game, the player will know quite a bit about handling a submarine underwater.

James Adams: Do you agree with that analysis, Tom?

Tom Clancy: On that I have to defer to Doug. I mean, I've never done it for a living, he has. You know, I write about it, but just because I can spell the acronyms doesn't mean I can drive the boats. He spent twenty years learning how to do the things I write about in a few months. So I'm the minstrel in this case and he's the expert.

James Adams: Doug, we see in the game that there is an attack on a carrier battle group, and during this there is infiltration by enemy boats. This creates the danger of friendly fire. How real is that?

Captain Doug Littlejohns: Very.

James Adams: It is?

Captain Doug Littlejohns: One of the more dangerous scenarios – and I hope no submariners will take offense at this – is mixing it up like that. When you've got surface forces, aircraft, and submarines all in the same part of the ocean with enemy submarines infiltrating, there's a temptation to fire at shadows. There are procedures which have been worked on for years to control people in areas which move with the carrier task force, but that requires an awful lot of communications, either underwater communications or satellite type communications. I've done it a few times and never felt entirely comfortable when there's been a known enemy in the vicinity.

James Adams: Those sort of blue on blue instances are all too common on land where people apparently should be able to see each other.

Captain Doug Littlejohns: War's dangerous and that sort of thing does happen.

Tom Clancy: In World War II, we know at least one and possibly as many as three US submarines were killed blue on blue. And in the one known case, the submarine was in a safe travel zone where nobody was supposed to attack anybody.

Captain Doug Littlejohns: My point exactly.

Tom Clancy: Yes, but a tincan skipper said, 'This is it, that's a Japanese submarine.' Boom.

Captain Doug Littlejohns: Yes.

James Adams: We learn in the game that intelligence says, 'There are no enemy around here,' and intelligence, to put it mildly, gets it slightly wrong. What can you rely on? Are you very alone down there? Are you saying it's me against everybody?

Captain Doug Littlejohns: No, I think that would be over-dramatizing it. But there's no doubt that if one puts implicit faith in the intelligence without a questioning mind, then it will end in tears. Intelligence can be reassuring, but as we mentioned earlier, Akula submarines have come out into the Atlantic and not necessarily been detected, or have only been detected infrequently, during which time they could have moved thousands of miles. So intelligence is not the be all and end all, and therefore it is just another part of the brickwork for running your submarine. That's it.

James Adams: You have a jaundiced view of intelligence, Tom, I see.

Tom Clancy: It's imperfect. I've yet to meet a tactical or operational commander who really trusts his intelligence sources.

James Adams: Because they prefer to trust their own judgment on the ground rather than some guy who's somewhere in the rear?

Captain Doug Littlejohns: No, but it is nice to get intelligence, particularly hard intelligence reports, because that can make you frame your thinking for the next several hours. The English language gets very rough treatment in the intelligence service and you go from probable to possible with an awful lot of variations in the middle. And it is possible, after years of reading these things, to know how comfortable they're feeling back at base. But as I said, I would never put total confidence in it.

James Adams: How do you think a player will come out of this game? Will they come out thinking, 'God, who wants to be a skipper of a submarine?' or will they come out thinking, 'This is a gripping, exciting, intellectually challenging task?' What do you think they'll come away with?

Captain Doug Littlejohns: First of all, they'll come out with a sense of achievement, I hope, if they've got through the fifteen scenarios. Secondly, it is not designed to act as a recruiting drive for the US Navy submarine service. But I think what the player will come out with is with a bit of an understanding of what it's like down there, something which nobody really has tried to portray in the past. You mentioned *Crimson Tide*; we've had a few other movies as well, one that was involved with this chap here. But none of those have really been able to pit the player against a few scenarios where he's had to learn, hopefully, by his mistakes – or, if he's bright enough, to operate the submarine intuitively. So I think that, yes, they'll come out of it with a much better understanding of what life on a submarine is about. And that's it.

James Adams: What do you think, Tom?

Tom Clancy: I know people who've done submarine and antisubmarine warfare from the surface, from underneath, and from the air, and they all agree that it's the best game in town, that there is nothing more intellectually challenging than submarine slash anti-submarine warfare. And if the player really pays attention to the game, he'll come out with as realistic a feel for that game as you can get anywhere.

Glossary

Active Sonar: Sonar that provides data by evaluating reflections of its own sound emissions.

ADC Mk 2 Decoy: Electro-acoustic torpedo countermeasure carried by American submarines.

ADCAP: Advanced capability (Mk 48). The most advanced version of the Mk 48 torpedo.

Aegis: Advanced ship-based air defense system designed to protect against massive air and missile saturation attacks. Fitted to Ticonderoga and Arleigh Burke warships.

Akula: The newest and most advanced Russian nuclear attack submarine. There are two variants: Akula I and Akula II. Top speed: 35 knots submerged. Length: 370 feet, 6 inches. Displacement: approximately 10,000 tons submerged. Major weapons: four 65cm tubes and four 53cm torpedo tubes.

Alfa: The Alfa is the first submarine in the world to be constructed of a titanium hull. It is also the fastest and one of the deepest diving. Less than ten units were constructed, however, and the submarine is very noisy and easy to detect. Top speed: 43 knots submerged. Length: 267 feet. Displacement: 3,680 tons submerged. Major weapons: six 53cm torpedo tubes.

ALFS: Airborne low frequency dipping sonar. Joint US-French dipping sonar that will equip future ASW helicopters.

AMRAAM: Advanced medium range air-to-air missile (AIM-120).

Arco (ARDM 5): Medium auxiliary repair dry dock.

Arleigh Burke (DDG-51): Advanced American class of destroyers equipped with the Aegis air defense system. Top speed: 31 knots. Length: 504 feet, 4 inches. Displacement: 9,033 tons full load. Major weapons: Tomahawk, SM-2, and Harpoon missiles.

ASDS: Advanced SEAL delivery system for use on board submarines.

ASW: Anti-submarine warfare.

ASW Mortars/Rockets: Unguided rockets that can be fired from surface ships and are designed to attack submarines.

Baffles: The sonar-blind area to the rear of a ship or submarine. Because of the noise generated by the screw, it is difficult to detect a sonar contact in this area.

BDA: Bomb damage assessment.

Biologics: The name given to the underwater sea-life that shows up as sonar contacts on board US sonar systems.

Blue on Blue Encounters: The US Navy's term for 'friendly fire,' an accidental attack on one's own forces by their own or allied ground, air, or naval forces.

BSY-1: Advanced sonar and fire control system fitted in the 688I class.

CAP: Combat air patrol. Protective air defense cover provided for the aircraft carrier battle group by the carrier's air defense aircraft.

Cavitation: The formation of tiny air bubbles around rapidly revolving propeller blades when the depth is too shallow for the speed. These air bubbles make a popping noise as they collapse, which increases the noise level of a propeller and makes a ship or submarine easier to detect via sonar.

CCS Mk 2: Command and control system carried on Los Angeles class submarines that is used to plan and control missions for the Harpoon and Tomahawk missiles.

CINCPACFLT: Commander-In-Chief, US Pacific Fleet.

CIWS: Close-in weapons system. A last ditch anti-missile system fitted on surface ships.

Cluster Bay and Cluster Gulf mines: Russian manufactured moored rising mines with an acoustic homing warhead.

COB: Chief of the boat. The senior enlisted sailor on board an American submarine.

COD: Carrier on board delivery. Delivery of support items, including mail, to an aircraft carrier while underway. The US Navy's primary COD aircraft is the C-2 Greyhound.

Conn: Control of a ship or submarine's movements.

Convergence Zone: Phenomena whereby, if the water is deep enough, water pressure turns sound waves in the direction of the surface. This occurs at intervals of roughly 30 miles. Multiple convergence zone contacts are possible when the sound bounces off the surface and heads back down, eventually to be turned back upward again by the pressure.

CTF 74: Commander Task Force 74, also known as Commander Submarine Group 7.

Dipping Sonar: Sonar system carried by a helicopter that can be unreeled and dipped into the water to provide variable depth, active or passive sonar detection.

DSMAC: Digital scene-matching area correlation. One of several types of missile guidance used for Tomahawk cruise missiles.

E-2C Hawkeye: Carrier-based airborne early warning aircraft fitted with APS-145 search radar.

EA-6B Prowler: Radar jamming and electronic warfare version of the A-6 Intruder. Carries the ALQ-99 jammer.

ELF: Extremely low frequency radio band.

ELINT: Intelligence collected by electronic means.

ESM: Electronic support measures. A passive receiver system designed to detect radar emissions.

ET-80: 53-cm Russian-manufactured wire-guided, active/passive homing torpedo.

F-14 Tomcat: Long-range fleet air defense fighter carried on board US Navy aircraft carriers.

F/A-18 Hornet: Dual purpose (fighter and attack) carrier- and land-based combat aircraft.

Fathom: Measure of length equal to six feet.

Floating Dry Dock: Movable dock, used to facilitate repairs to the underwater body of ships and submarines.

Floating Wire: Also called trailing wire. Similar to a receiving antenna that can be streamed underwater so that a submarine can remain submerged while it receives messages.

GPS: Global Positioning System. Satellite-based navigation system that can provide extremely accurate location fixes to forces on air, land, and sea. Can also be used in missile guidance systems.

H-5 Harbin: Chinese variant of the Russian Il-28 Beagle attack aircraft.

H-6 Xian: Chinese variant of the Russian Tu-16 Badger bomber.

Hainan: Chinese fast attack craft. Top speed: 30+ knots. Length: 193 feet. Displacement: 392 tons full load. Major weapons: can carry YJ-1 missile, ASW mortar-rocket launcher, depth charges, or mines.

Han: This was Communist China's first nuclear attack submarine. Only five units of this class were built. Top speed: 25 knots submerged. Length: 321 feet. Displacement: 5,500 tons submerged. Major weapons: six 53cm tubes.

Harpoon: Medium range anti-ship missile used by the US Navy and its allies. Air (AGM-84), surface (RGM-84), and submarine torpedo tube (UGM-84) launched variants are all in use.

Huchuan: Chinese torpedo carrying hydrofoil. Top speed: 50 knots foil-borne. Length: 71 feet, 6 inches.

Displacement: 46 tons full load. Major weapons: two 53cm torpedo tubes.

HULTEC: The US Navy's library of ESM information.

HUMINT: Intelligence collected by human operatives.

HY-2: Chinese anti-ship missile with a range of over fifty nautical miles.

Independence (CV-62): The sole surviving active member of the 1950s era Forrestal class aircraft carriers – the first of the American 'supercarriers.' Capable of carrying over seventy aircraft.

IUSS: The US Navy's integrated undersea surveillance system, the combination of SOSUS (sound surveillance systems) and SURTASS (surface towed array surveillance systems) ships.

J-7: Chinese variant of the Russian MiG-21 fighter.

Jianghu: Chinese frigate. Jianghu I, II, III, and IV variants are in service. Jianghu I: Top speed: 26 knots. Length: 338 feet, 6 inches. Displacement: 1,702 tons full load. Major weapons: HY-2 missiles, ASW mortars/rocket launchers, depth charges, and mines.

Kilo: This is the newest class of Russian diesel-electric submarines. Top speed: 17 knots submerged. Length: two hundred twenty-nine feet. Displacement: 3,076 tons submerged. Major weapons: six 53cm torpedo tubes.

Knot: Unit of speed equivalent to one nautical mile per hour.

Komar: 1960s-era Russian missile armed fast attack craft. Top speed: 40 knots. Length: 83.7 feet. Displacement: 80 tons full load. Major weapons: anti-ship missiles and guns.

LAMPS: Light airborne multipurpose system. Multipurpose helicopter carried by many American warships. The latest variant is the SH-60 LAMPS III.

Los Angeles (SSN 688): With the exception of the USS Seawolf class, this is the most advanced nuclear attack submarine class in the world. Built to several major configurations, the 688 class of submarines can be divided into three categories:

- *Flight 1:* SSNs 618–718. Original Los Angeles class
- *Flight 2:* SSNs 719–750. VLS added along with an upgraded reactor core
- *Flight 3:* SSNs 751–773. BSY-1 added, along with bow planes, improving under-ice capability and quieting. This is referred to as the improved Los Angeles class, and received the designation 688I

Top speed: 30+ knots. Length: 360 feet. Displacement: 6,927 tons submerged. Major weapons: four 21-inch torpedo tubes and twelve VLS in later boats.

Luda: Chinese destroyer. There are three variants: Luda I, II, and III. Luda I: Top speed: 32 knots. Length: 433 feet. Displacement: 3,670 tons. Major weapons: HY-2 missiles, ASW mortars-rocket launchers, mines and depth charges. Type II carries two helicopters.

Luhu: New, relatively advanced Chinese destroyer. Top speed: 31 knots. Length: 468 feet. Displacement: 4,200 tons full load. Major weapons: YJ-1 missiles, ASW mortars/rocket launchers. Carries two helicopters.

MAD: Magnetic anomaly detector. A device that can detect a submerged submarine from a low-flying aircraft or helicopter by detecting the distortion of the earth's magnetic field caused by the metal hull of a submarine.

MAG: Russian manufactured moored ASW contact mine.

Master Number: Designation on board US Navy submarines that represents a contact attained by combining one or more signals and/or sensors.

MC: Shipboard announcing system on board US submarines (1MC is the main shipwide announcing system).

MIDAS: Mine detection and avoidance sonar fitted in

improved Los Angeles class submarines. Also used under ice to avoid ice keels.

Mike: This was an advanced Soviet test submarine which was lost at sea in April 1989.

Ming: Chinese diesel attack submarine. Top speed: 18 knots submerged. Length: 249.3 feet. Displacement: 2,113 tons submerged. Major weapons: eight 53cm torpedo tubes.

Mk 41: Vertical launch system used on board several classes of US surface warships.

Mk 46: American lightweight ASW torpedo carried by helicopters, aircraft, and surface ships. The Mk 46 has been widely exported.

Mk 48: Heavy torpedo carried by all American, and some allied, submarines. Can be used for attacks on both surface and submarine targets. The ADCAP is the newest type of Mk 48.

Mk 50: Advanced American lightweight torpedo. Replaces and supplements the Mk 46.

Nautical Mile: 6,076 feet or roughly 1.15 miles, usually rounded off to 2,000 yards.

Nimitz (CVN-68): The first of the nuclear-powered Nimitz class of aircraft carriers, which can carry over eighty-five aircraft.

Noisemaker: nickname for a submarine-launched countermeasure designed to decoy an enemy torpedo away from its target.

Oliver Hazard Perry (FFG-7): Large class of American multipurpose frigates. Top speed: 29 knots. Length: approximately 450 feet. Displacement: 4,100 tons full load. Major weapons: Harpoon, SM-1. Carries two LAMPS helicopters.

OOD: Officer of the deck. The US Navy officer in charge of the ship or submarine. The OOD represents the commanding officer.

P-3 Orion: Long-range land-based maritime patrol and ASW aircraft operated by the US and many of its allies. In Canadian service, the Orion is known as the Aurora.

Passive Sonar: Sonar that passively gathers its data from the noise an object radiates.

PBXN-103: High explosive, 650 pounds of which are found in the Mk 48's warhead.

Phoenix: AIM-54. Long-range air-to-air missile carried by the F-14 Tomcat. Maximum range is more than 100 miles.

RBU-1200: Russian ASW mortar/rocket launcher.

Romeo: Russian designed diesel-electric class of submarines. Construction began in the 1950s. More than sixty are believed to remain in service with Chinese active and reserve forces. Top speed: 13 knots submerged. Length: 252 feet, 7 inches. Displacement: 1,700 tons submerged. Major weapons: eight 53cm torpedo tubes.

RORSAT: Russian radar ocean reconnaissance satellite.

S-3 Viking: Carrier-based long-range ASW aircraft. ES-3 version used for carrier-based Signals Intelligence.

S6G: The pressurized water reactor that provides the main power source for the Los Angeles class of attack submarines.

SAET-60: 53cm Russian-manufactured anti-surface torpedo.

SEALs: Sea air land, US Navy special operations units.

Seawolf (SSN-21): the newest class of nuclear attack submarine to be built for the US Navy. Top speed: 35+ knots submerged. Length: approximately 350 feet. Displacement: 9,150 tons submerged. Major weapons: eight 30-inch torpedo tubes.

SET-53: 53cm Russian-manufactured active/passive ASW homing torpedo.

Seventh Fleet: US Navy Fleet responsible for naval operations in the Western Pacific and Indian Oceans. Headquarters: Yokosuka, Japan.

SH-60 Seahawk: US Navy ASW and multipurpose LAMPS III helicopter.

Sierra: Advanced Russian SSN. Only slightly less capable than the Akulas. Top speed: 35 knots submerged. Length: 351 feet. Displacement: 7,900 tons submerged. Major weapons: four 65cm and two 53cm tubes.

Sierra Number: A designation representing a sonar contact on board a US Navy submarine. Such contacts may be upgraded to Master Numbers if they are deemed possible threats or of other significance.

SLBM: Submarine launched ballistic missile.

SM-1/SM-2: Standard surface-to-air missiles carried on board US and allied warships. SM-2 is the more advanced of the two and is also carried on board Aegis warships.

Snap Shot: Firing a torpedo in an emergency situation. Because no TMA has yet been conducted, the torpedo must be launched in the probable direction of the target.

Snorkel: Device used by a submarine to draw air from the surface while remaining submerged. This allows a diesel submarine to recharge its batteries or all submarines to ventilate while remaining under water.

Sonobuoy: A small, air-dropped sonar device designed to detect submarines and transmit their data back to the aircraft.

Spruance (DD 963): Large class of anti-submarine destroyers operated by the US Navy. Top speed: 33 knots. Length: 563 feet, 2 inches. Displacement: 8,040 tons full load. Major weapons: Harpoon, Tomahawk, and ASROC (anti-submarine rocket). Also carries two LAMPS helicopters.

SQR-19: Tactical towed array sonar carried by several types of US Navy warship.

SSBN: Nuclear-powered ballistic missile submarine.

SSIXS: Submarine satellite information exchange system.

Satellite system through which the US Navy and its submarines can communicate.

SSK: Diesel-electric attack submarine.

SSN: Nuclear-powered attack submarine.

SSXBT: A submarine expendable bathythermograph device used to measure water temperature at varying depths.

Sturgeon (SSN 637): US nuclear attack submarine class. Predates the Los Angeles class. Top speed: 30 knots submerged. Length: 292 feet. Displacement: 4,780 tons submerged. Major weapons: four 21-inch torpedo tubes.

SU-27: Highly advanced Russian air defense fighter. Operated by Russia, China, and other nations.

SUBGRU: Submarine group.

Submarine Tender: A ship designed to provide support to submarines, including logistical support and small repairs.

SUBRON: Submarine squadron.

TB-16: US Navy submarine towed array. The array is 240-feet long and is towed at the end of a 2,600-foot cable. The array is stored in a shroud on the starboard side.

TB-23: US Navy submarine thin line array. The array is four times longer than the TB-16 and housed in the submarine's ballast tank.

TERCOM: Terrain contour matching. One of several missile guidance/navigation systems used in the Tomahawk cruise missile.

TEST-71: Russian 53cm, submarine-launched, active/passive, wire-guided ASW homing torpedo.

Third Fleet: US Navy fleet responsible for operations in the Eastern Pacific Ocean. Headquarters: San Diego, California.

Ticonderoga (CG-47): The most powerful class of cruisers in the world, operated by the US Navy. Fitted with the Aegis air defense system. Top speed: 30+

knots. Length: 567 feet. Displacement: approximately 9,500 tons full load. Major weapons: Harpoon, Tomahawk, and SM-2 missiles. Also carries 2 LAMPS helicopters.

TMA: Target motion analysis. The process of determining a target's course, speed, and range in order to direct a weapon in its direction.

Tomahawk: Family of long-range cruise missiles used by the US Navy. Several variants exist: TASM (antiship variant), TLAM-N (nuclear land attack variant), TLAM-C (conventional land attack version with high explosive warhead), and TLAM-D (conventional land attack with bomblets).

Trafalgar Class: Advanced class of British Royal Naval SSN. Batch 1 is in service, batch 2 is planned for the next century. Data for batch 1 – Top speed: 32 knots submerged. Length: 280.1 feet. Displacement: 5,208 tons submerged. Major weapons: five 21-inch torpedo tubes.

Type 2: Optics only attack periscope carried on board US submarines.

Type 18: Search periscope carried on board US SSNs. Also contains still and video camera systems as well as ESM and communications receivers.

Typhoon: This Russian nuclear ballistic missile submarine is the world's largest. The Typhoon is constructed of titanium with a double hull, making it extremely difficult to kill. Top speed: 25 knots submerged. Length: 560 feet, 11 inches. Displacement: 25,000 tons submerged. Major weapons: six torpedo tubes (65cm and 53cm) and twenty SS-N-20 SLBMs.

UHF: Ultra high frequency radio band.

Underwater Telephone: Device that allows two submarines to communicate verbally with each other while submerged and in close proximity to one another. Also allows submerged submarines to communicate verbally with nearby surface ships.

VHF: Very high frequency radio band.

VLF: Very low frequency radio band.

VLS: Vertical launch system used to launch missiles from warships and submarines.

WAA: Wide aperture array. Advanced sonar system, fitted to the *Seawolf* submarine, employing passive sensors to rapidly determine the location of targets and more accurate target range and tracking data.

WLR-9: Acoustic intercept receiver. This system is used to alert the crew of a submarine if someone is using active sonar against them.

Ying Ji (YJ-1 and YJ-2): Chinese antiship missiles with a range of over twenty (YJ-1) and sixty (YJ-2) nautical miles.

Z-9 Harbin: Chinese version of the French SA-365 Dauphin II helicopter. Used for ASW. Some Z-9s carry the French HS-12 dipping sonar.

Bibliography

Baker III, A. D. *The Naval Institute Guide to Combat Fleets of the World, 1995.* Annapolis, MD: Naval Institute Press, 1995.

Clancy, Tom. *Submarine.* New York: Berkley Books, 1993.

Francillon, Rene J. *The Naval Institute Guide to World Military Aviation 1995.* Annapolis, MD: Naval Institute Press, 1995.

Friedman, Norman. *The Naval Institute Guide to World Naval Weapons Systems 1991/92.* Annapolis, MD: Naval Institute Press, 1991.

Friedman, Norman. *The Naval Institute Guide to World Naval Weapons Systems 1994 Update.* Annapolis, MD: Naval Institute Press, 1994.

Friedman, Norman. *Naval Radar.* Annapolis, MD: Naval Institute Press, 1981.

Friedman, Norman. *US Naval Weapons.* Annapolis, MD: Naval Institute Press, 1988.

Hooten, E. R., ed. *Jane's Naval Weapon Systems.* Surrey, UK: Jane's Information Group, 1996.

Jackson, Paul, ed. *Jane's All the World's Aircraft 1995–96.* Surrey, UK: Jane's Information Group, 1995.

Lennox, Duncan, ed. *Jane's Air Launched Weapons.* Surrey, UK: Jane's Information Group, 1996.

Lennox, Duncan, ed. *Jane's Strategic Weapon Systems.* Surrey, UK: Jane's Information Group, 1996.

Miller, David, and John Jordan. *Modern Submarine Warfare.* New York: Military Press, 1987.

Noel, Jr., John V., and Edward L. Beach. *Naval Terms Dictionary.* Annapolis, MD: Naval Institute Press, 1988.

Polmar, Norman; Mark Warren; and Eric Wertheim. *Dictionary of Military Abbreviations.* Annapolis, MD: Naval Institute Press, 1994.

Polmar, Norman, and Jurrien Noot. *Submarines of the Russian and Soviet Navies 1718–1990.* Annapolis, MD: Naval Institute Press, 1991.

Polmar, Norman. *The Naval Institute Guide to the Ships and Aircraft of the US Fleet, Fifteenth Edition*. Annapolis, MD: Naval Institute Press, 1993.

Polmar, Norman. *The Naval Institute Guide to the Soviet Navy, Fifth Edition*. Annapolis, MD: Naval Institute Press, 1991.

Sharpe, Richard, ed. *Jane's Fighting Ships 1995–96*. Surrey, UK: Jane's Information Group, 1995.

Thomas, Jr., Vincent C., ed. *The Almanac of Seapower 1996*. Arlington, VA: Navy League of the US, 1996.

Vego, Milan. *Soviet Naval Tactics*. Annapolis, MD: Naval Institute Press, 1992.

Watts, Anthony J., ed. *Jane's Underwater Warfare Systems 1995–96*. Surrey, UK: Jane's Information Group, 1995.

JOURNALS

Defense News
Jane's Defence Systems Modernisation
Jane's Defence Weekly
Jane's Intelligence Review
Jane's International Defence Review
Jane's Navy International
Naval Institute Proceedings
Navy Times
Seapower Magazine
The Submarine Review

CD-ROM

Jane's CD-ROM Electronic Library 1995–96

The Hunt for Red October
Tom Clancy

THE RUNAWAY
INTERNATIONAL #1 BESTSELLER

The novel that launched Tom Clancy's phenomenal career and introduced Jack Ryan – the unforgettable story of a spellbinding battle of nerves, above and below the waves, unrivalled in its authenticity and breathtaking suspense.

Silently, beneath the chill Atlantic waters, Russia's ultra-secret missile submarine, the *Red October*, is heading west. The Americans want her. The Russians want her back. With all-out war only seconds away, the superpowers race across the ocean on the most desperate mission of a lifetime. The most incredible chase in history is on . . .

'Absolutely terrific: entertaining, suspenseful and master-fully written . . . superlative.' *Washington Times*

'Offers an extraordinarily detailed glimpse into the secret world of nuclear submarines, and the potentially deadly cat-and-mouse games played by superpowers beneath the oceans.' *Sunday Times*

'A snakily plotted, fast-moving blockbuster . . . terrifying tension to the last page.' *Mail on Sunday*

'Gripping narrative . . . navy buffs and thriller adepts have been mesmerised by the story of Soviet submarine captain Marko Ramius, who seeks to defect to the US, bringing a billion-dollar present with him.' *Time Magazine*

ISBN 0 00 617276 8

Red Storm Rising
Tom Clancy

The superpowers hurtle towards global conflict, in this chillingly authentic vision of modern warfare from the world's #1 thriller writer.

The Muslim terrorists who destroyed the Soviet Union's largest petro-chemical plant thought they were striking a blow for freedom. What they had done, unknowingly, was fire the first shots in World War III.

Desperately short of oil, the Kremlin hawks see only one way of solving their problem: seize supplies in the Persian Gulf. To do that, they must first neutralize NATO's forces and eliminate their response – and so they develop Red Storm, a dazzling master plan of diplomatic subterfuge and intense re-armament. The battle lines are drawn and Armageddon beckons. . .

'Packed with more nerve-shattering tension than anything in print today . . . gripping, audacious, brilliant storytelling at its very best.'   *Washington Times*

'Has the fascination of being on a high-speed train which is about to crash. The description of a submarine patrol racing for the safety of the icepack is as vivid as I ever hope to read.'   *Today*

'Frighteningly realistic, chillingly so . . . I dare you to read one chapter and put it down.'   *Newsday*

'The supreme exponent of the technothriller.'
Sunday Times

ISBN 0 00 617362 4

The Sum of All Fears
Tom Clancy

THE *SUNDAY TIMES* NO. 1 BESTSELLER

As those in power around the globe face up to the challenges of a new world order, in Washington CIA Deputy Director Jack Ryan is putting everything into his own plan, a plan that could finally bring peace to a Middle East still suffering from the ravages of war.

But too many groups have invested too much blood to allow the plan to succeed – the terrorists have one final, desperate card to play. With one terrible act the world is plunged into nuclear crisis.

His dreams of peace shattered, Jack Ryan is confronted with a situation he has never dared to imagine: with the world standing on the brink of war, what do you do if the President of the USA is incompetent to deal with the greatest crisis of all?

'Another classic Clancy . . . accurate and chilling, his most successful book . . . assures his place at the forefront of modern thriller writers.' *Sunday Times*

'Clancy's best book since *The Hunt for Red October*. A treasure trove of geopolitical terrors . . . bulges with technological verisimilitude . . . a whiz-bang page-turner.'
New York Times Book Review

'I was quite entranced . . . Clancy is a brilliant describer of events. I read his lucid exposition with delight.'
PATRICK O'BRIAN, *Washington Post*

ISBN 0 00 647116 1

Tom Clancy's
Op-Centre

Created by
Tom Clancy and Steve Pieczenik

THE INTERNATIONAL BESTSELLER

Situated in Washington, Op-Centre is a beating heart of defence, intelligence and crisis-management technology, run by a crack team of operatives both within its own walls and out in the field. When a job is too dirty, or too dangerous, it is the only place the US government can turn.

But nothing can prepare Director Paul Hood and his Op-Centre crisis-management team for what they are about to uncover – a very real, very frightening power play that could unleash new players in a new world order. . .

A powerful profile of America's defence, intelligence and crisis-management technology, *Tom Clancy's Op-Centre* is the creation of Tom Clancy and Steve Pieczenik – inspiring this novel, as well as the special NBC Television presentation.

ISBN 0 00 649658 X

Tom Clancy's
Op-Centre

Mirror Image

Created by
Tom Clancy and Steve Pieczenik

THE INTERNATIONAL BESTSELLER

The Cold War is over. And chaos is setting in. The new President of Russia is trying to create a new democratic regime. But there are strong elements within the country that are trying to stop him: the ruthless Russian Mafia, the right-wing nationalists and those nefarious forces that will do whatever it takes to return Russia back to the days of the Czar.

Op-Centre, the newly founded but highly successful crisis management team, begins a race against the clock and against the hardliners. Their task is made even more difficult by the discovery of a Russian counterpart . . . but this one's controlled by those same repressive hardliners.

Two rival Op-Centres, virtual mirror images of each other. But if this mirror cracks, it'll be much more than seven years' bad luck.

A powerful profile of America's defence, intelligence and crisis management technology, Tom Clancy's Op-Centre *is the creation of Tom Clancy and Steve Pieczenik – inspiring this and other gripping novels.*

ISBN 0 00 649659 8

Executive Orders
Tom Clancy

THE NO 1 BESTSELLING SEQUEL TO
DEBT OF HONOUR

The US President is dead – and the weight of the world falls on Jack Ryan's shoulders, in Clancy's most extraordinary novel.

At the dramatic climax of *Debt of Honour*, a Jumbo Jet crashes into the Capitol Building in Washington, leaving the President dead, along with most of the Cabinet and Congress. Dazed and confused, the man who only minutes before had been confirmed as the new caretaker Vice-President is told that he is now President of the United States: President John Patrick Ryan.

And that is where *Executive Orders* begins – as Ryan's new responsibilities crush in upon him with stunning force. But how do you run a government without a government? Where do you even begin? He knows that the eyes of the world are on him now – and many of them are unfriendly. In Beijing, in Tehran and even in Washington, there are those eager to take advantage. Soon they will begin to make their moves; soon they will present Jack Ryan with a crisis so great even he could not imagine it.

'Clancy is the supreme exponent of the technothriller . . . excellent, unsurpassed . . . another gripping read.'
Sunday Times

**HIS NEW *SUNDAY TIMES* NO 1 BESTSELLER
AVAILABLE NOW FROM HARPERCOLLINS**